**Lucy Ki** [...] the glamorous and [...] & Boon when she really ought to have been paying attention to her teachers. As she couldn't live in a dream world for ever, she eventually acquired a degree in languages and an eclectic collection of jobs. After a decade in southwest Spain, Lucy now lives with her young family in Wiltshire, England. When not writing, or trying to think up new and innovative things to do with mince, she spends her time reading, failing to finish cryptic crosswords and dreaming of the golden beaches of Andalusia.

**Lela May Wight** grew up with seven brothers and sisters. Yes, it was noisy, and she often found escape in romance books. She still does, but now she gets to write them too! She hopes to offer readers the same escapism when the world is a little too loud. Lela May lives in the UK, with her two sons and her very own hero, who never complains about her book addiction—he buys her more books! Check out what she's up to at lelamaywight.com.

# VIRGIN'S NIGHT WITH THE GREEK

LUCY KING

# BOUND BY A SICILIAN SECRET

LELA MAY WIGHT

MILLS & BOON

All rights reserved including the right of reproduction in whole or in part in any form. This edition is published by arrangement with Harlequin Enterprises ULC.

This is a work of fiction. Names, characters, places, locations and incidents are purely fictional and bear no relationship to any real life individuals, living or dead, or to any actual places, business establishments, locations, events or incidents. Any resemblance is entirely coincidental.

This book is sold subject to the condition that it shall not, by way of trade or otherwise, be lent, resold, hired out or otherwise circulated without the prior consent of the publisher in any form of binding or cover other than that in which it is published and without a similar condition including this condition being imposed on the subsequent purchaser.

® and TM are trademarks owned and used by the trademark owner and/or its licensee. Trademarks marked with ® are registered with the United Kingdom Patent Office and/or the Office for Harmonisation in the Internal Market and in other countries.

First published in Great Britain 2023
by Mills & Boon, an imprint of HarperCollins*Publishers* Ltd,
1 London Bridge Street, London, SE1 9GF

www.harpercollins.co.uk

HarperCollins*Publishers*, Macken House, 39/40 Mayor Street Upper, Dublin 1, D01 C9W8, Ireland

Virgin's Night with the Greek © 2023 Lucy King

Bound by a Sicilian Secret © 2023 Lela May Wight

ISBN: 978-0-263-30673-6

04/23

This book is produced from independently certified FSC™ paper to ensure responsible forest management.
For more information visit: www.harpercollins.co.uk/green.

Printed and Bound in the UK using 100% Renewable Electricity at CPI Group (UK) Ltd, Croydon, CR0 4YY

# VIRGIN'S NIGHT
# WITH THE GREEK

LUCY KING

MILLS & BOON

# PROLOGUE

'SHE'S DOING *WHAT*?'

In response to the bombshell his younger sister had just dropped, Leonidas Stanhope sank into the chair behind his vast glass desk, his stomach tightening and his head already beginning to throb in a horribly familiar way.

'She's having herself painted,' Daphne repeated dully in Greek as she stared out of the window at the view of London that stretched out far below in the late May sunshine. 'In the nude. For Lazlo. As a birthday present, she said. He's turning seventy next week.'

'Seventy?'

'I know,' said Daphne. 'I can only assume he's a fan of Botox. I don't know why she couldn't simply have gift-wrapped a voucher for some more of that.'

'That would have been far too subtle.'

As his sister muttered her agreement, Leo closed his eyes and pinched the bridge of his nose even though he knew perfectly well it would alleviate precisely nothing. He'd been firefighting his mother's scandals for years, ever since he'd become the head of the family following his father's sudden death twelve years ago, when he was nineteen. Some were huge, some were minor, all were exhausting.

Was there to be no end to the drama the woman

caused? She was approaching sixty. At what age would dignity kick in and give him a break? No time soon, by the sound of things.

With a sigh, he fought the urge to grind his teeth, pulled himself together and redirected his attention to this latest incident. 'I thought she and Lazlo had parted ways.'

Daphne turned from the window to take a seat on the other side of the desk. 'That was two months ago,' she said despondently, flopping back against the leather the colour of whisky. 'They've since reconciled. She told me she was missing the sex.'

Leo winced.

'The portrait's to be part of an exhibition by up-and-coming young British artists at the Tate Modern. In a fortnight. Three days before my wedding. Can you believe it?'

'Unfortunately, I can,' he said, stifling a sigh of exasperation. 'All too easily. She's so self-absorbed, I doubt the timing of it would even have crossed her mind. Or the appropriateness.'

'It'll hit the press,' Daphne continued, her voice becoming increasingly tremulous as her dark eyes began to shimmer. 'The tabloids will have a field day. And the photos… God. Everyone at our wedding will be talking about it and gawping at her. As if the outfit she's planning on wearing isn't bad enough. I mean, white. Really? I don't think I can stand it, Leo. I don't know what to do. How do we stop it? Ari has no metaphorical weight to throw around and you know what Mama thinks of him. He begged her to at least hold off for a few more weeks, but she just said she wasn't being dictated to by a waiter and hung up on him.'

'I can imagine,' he muttered, jaw clenched.

'So can *you* do something about it?'

Of course he could. Fixing problems and managing people was a large part of what he did, whether as CEO of the Stanhope Kallis banking and shipping empire or as the protective eldest sibling of a large, much-loved tribe.

But more to the point, he *would* do something because even if he was neither of those individuals, he could never have ignored the rawness in his sister's voice. The tears and pain she was trying to suppress sliced at his chest like a knife, and a white-hot wave of frustrated anger surged through him.

Daphne had overcome so much to get to this point. Eight years ago, at the age of fourteen, she'd been diagnosed with acute myeloid leukaemia. She'd subsequently spent more time in hospital than out of it. She'd had blood transfusions and battled infections. She'd undergone rounds of chemotherapy and radiotherapy and suffered all the grim side effects that went with that. The initial prognosis had not been good, but despite this she'd never lost her optimism. She'd smiled her way through the most gruelling of times.

And so even though she'd eventually beaten the odds and been in remission for three years now, the outlook as positive as it could be, and even though he'd never understand the attraction of romantic love with all the hideous emotion and chaos that seemed to inevitably come with it, Leo would allow absolutely nothing to overshadow a day no one had ever thought they'd see.

'Leave it with me.'

# CHAPTER ONE

BENEATH THE SPARKLING surface of the gorgeously cool water, Willow Jacobs reached the end of the granite-lined pool, executed a lazy tumble turn and emerged with barely a splash to set off on another leisurely length of crawl.

The water slipped over her body like liquid pain relief. The heat of the Greek early summer sun warmed her skin like a balm. With every stroke, the tension in her hands that spread up her arms and into her shoulders and back while she worked eased. With every kick, the twinges and aches that came from sitting in one position for too long dispersed like watercolours in the rain.

She'd been working on and off for nearly a month now, with only one five-day break, which hadn't been much of a break, but she didn't resent the ten-hour days in the slightest. How could she when she was producing the best painting of her life? From the moment she'd put pastel to paper, the lines had come swiftly and the form had taken shape organically, as if her hands and fingers required no conscious input on her part at all.

Willow knew the rare and precious alchemy didn't stem from her environment, luxurious and comfortable though it was. Nor was it attributable to a sudden surge of talent because she already had that in abundance. It came entirely from her subject, who was as charmingly fascinating as she was utterly self-centred.

Not only was the raven-haired, sloe-eyed Selene Stanhope exquisitely beautiful and in possession of a spectacular body that belied her age and the six children she'd borne, she was also a Greek socialite who'd lived an adventurous, glitzy life. When she wasn't grumbling about her eldest son, about how disappointingly staid and repressed he was, about how it was his sole mission in life to pop up and spoil her fun, she liked to reminisce. At length. The stories she regaled made her sparkle and glow, and it was this inner radiance that gave the portrait such unique luminescence and vibrancy.

In that respect, it was a shame the it was nearly finished, Willow reflected as she bumped up against the wall and turned again. She could sit and listen to Selene's exploits for ever. Parties that culminated in literal swinging from the chandeliers. Holidays on private Caribbean islands in the company of glamorous celebrities. The clothes, the extravagance, the men...

The tales were enviably bold, colourful and passionate. Bittersweet, too, since they brought back memories of Willow's own mother, who'd died a decade ago and had been the polar opposite. And while she could see they might prove a challenge to an apparently stiff upperlipped and emotionally barren son, they offered a tantalising glimpse into an exotic aristocratic world that a solidly middle-class, permanently broke Willow would never inhabit.

On the other hand, completion of the painting meant

payment. It meant framing and packaging and shipping the piece to an exhibition that she could never have dreamed of being able to contribute to.

Having her work on such prominent and illustrious display would bridge the gap between struggling artist and success. It would bring in more, perhaps even better commissions, which would establish an exciting career she adored and provide the versatility she needed to be able to manage the endometriosis that had such a massive impact on how she lived her life.

So while her time at the villa in Kifissia was coming to an end, it was a cause for celebration rather than regret. She'd always be grateful to Selene for expressing an interest in her over the canapés at the London event at which she'd been waitressing to supplement her income, and taking a chance on her. Thanks to her current client's openness and connections, Willow's future stretched out before her, brighter and more hopeful than ever before. Barring some catastrophe, it was secure. After years of upheaval, of learning how to manage the monthly agony while trying to break into the tightly knit art world and make a living, everything was finally coming together.

As the significance of this sank in properly for the first time, relief surged through her, so immense that it quickened her pulse and tightened her lungs. Her head spun and her limbs went weak. Dizzy, losing her buoyancy, Willow mistimed her breath and inhaled a lungful of pool water. She spluttered. Coughed. Flailed. She dipped beneath the surface for a moment but was just about pop up again and regain control of the situation when she was suddenly buffeted by a wave, grabbed from behind and hauled against something hard.

Shock and panic slammed into her. Adrenalin flooded her system. Instinctively, she squirmed and lashed out, splashing and struggling, kicking and fighting for breath. But the band of steel clamped around her middle was impossible to shift.

'Let me go,' she gasped, her heart thundering as whoever it was trapping her in a vice began towing her towards the side.

'Keep still,' murmured a deep masculine voice in her ear in faintly accented English. 'I've got you.'

But she hadn't needed getting. She'd been *fine*. 'Release me this instant,' she panted, shivering and breathless and scrabbling frantically to get free.

'Stop struggling. You're making things worse.'

'*I'm* making things worse?'

'I'm trying to save you from drowning.'

'I wasn't drowning.'

'You're lucky I arrived when I did.'

Lucky? Hah! 'Let. Me. Go.'

With a grind of her teeth, Willow pummelled at his forearm, but to her outrage and continued alarm the mule-headed dolt ignored her. He didn't relax his grip on her even an inch, no matter how hard she tried to jab an elbow into his side or kick a heel into his groin. In fact, his arm seemed to *tighten*, ironically stealing the breath from her lungs in a way that inhaling water hadn't.

But perhaps he had a point about the thrashing around. It was achieving nothing other than a sapping of energy that she'd be better off saving for dry land. If she temporarily yielded to his superior physical strength and let him get on with this wholly unnecessary rescue mission of his it would be over infinitely more quickly and that could only be good.

Ceding to logic and giving up the fight for the sake of her strength and her sanity, Willow let herself go limp against him and almost instantly received a growly 'That's better' in response.

But as he carried her along with what felt like broad, confident strokes she wasn't sure that it was. Breathing might be becoming easier, but it was beginning to occur to her that she'd never been this up close and personal to a man before. At least, not moulded to one back to front as she was now.

Obviously she'd been kissed—she was twenty-four, after all—but that was as far she'd ever gone. With her condition, sex could be excruciating she'd read, and quite frankly, she had enough pain in her life without choosing to suffer further. Not only did the thought of it terrify her, she also feared things becoming awkward and having to explain. She dreaded being ridiculed, pitied, called uptight and frigid. And despite the kissing—some of which had been very nice—she'd never met anyone for whom she wanted to make that sacrifice and take that risk.

But were all chests this hard? All forearms this unforgiving? Because he'd altered his hold on her, her bottom was no longer bumping up against him, thank goodness, but now, with her head resting on his shoulder and his breath fanning her face, she was sort of lying on him—a man she didn't know and hadn't even seen—and it was unsettling to say the least.

To her relief, they reached the edge of the pool within moments. The minute the band of steel around her waist loosened, Willow bobbed away and grabbed onto the side. Taking a deep breath to calm herself, she swiped the water from her eyes then turned to face her supposed rescuer, fully prepared to demand to know who he was and what he thought he was doing.

But at the sight of him the words dried up on her tongue. Her pulse skipped a beat and her lungs constricted all over again. He had eyes the colour of raw umber, olive skin that was testament to his Greek heritage and a bone structure that would have made Michelangelo weep. His dark hair was plastered to his head, but she knew from the photos she'd been shown it was lamp-black and ochre streaked. He was very handsome and very stern. Exactly as his mother had described.

And as she recalled Selene's myriad complaints about her eldest son, the tales of control and power he apparently liked to wield over her whenever the opportunity arose and the frequent comments about how much he'd disapprove of the portrait if he knew of its existence, all Willow could think as her heart beat a fraction faster than normal and wariness wound through her, was: What fun was he planning to spoil here?

While an obviously simmering Willow turned to paddle towards the steps, Leo shook the water from his hair then hauled himself out of the pool in one powerful move, still recovering from the events of the past five minutes.

He'd arrived at the villa in one of Athens's most exclusive and expensive suburbs a quarter of an hour ago, burning up with the frustration that came with his failure to date to fulfil his promise to his sister. The moment Daphne had left his office yesterday afternoon he'd swung into action. But the director of the Tate Modern had not responded as he'd expected to his demand the exhibition be cancelled and, unsurprisingly, neither Lazlo nor his mother were taking his calls. Appealing directly to the artist herself had been his only remaining option, which was why he'd commandeered the family jet and flown over from London this morning.

Having located Selene in the drawing room and furnished her with the reason for his visit, he'd ascertained Willow's whereabouts, then stalked the length of the space and out onto the terrace. A flash of movement had had him heading for the pool. En route, he'd clocked a book and a long drink on the table beside the lounger over which a towel lay draped, and had cynically thought that in the month she'd been here allegedly working, his mother's portraitist had made herself extremely comfortable at the luxurious, fully staffed villa.

Briefly, he'd wondered whether the offer he'd put together to get rid of her and the picture would be enough or whether she'd spot an opportunity and force him to double it. But then he'd seen her suddenly stop midlength, thrash about and sink beneath the surface of the water, and the innate instinct to save someone in trouble had overridden any suspicion about what she was and what she might be up to.

Leo didn't regret his actions in the slightest, however much Willow had protested she hadn't needed his help. He might be ruthless in business and intent on neutralising the threat she posed to Daphne's happiness, but he drew the line at letting her drown in order to achieve that goal. And thanks to a swimming gala years ago, during which his youngest sister, Olympia, had fainted in the pool and no one but him had noticed her sink to the bottom, he knew that it was better to be safe than sorry.

What he *did* regret however, was that he was now dripping wet and bereft of the shoes he'd toed off and the jacket he'd stripped from his torso in his haste to dive in to the rescue. With his shirt plastered to his chest and his trousers clinging to his thighs, the image he currently presented was about as far from the cool control and unassailable authority he preferred to exude as it was possible to get.

But at least he had height and breadth in his favour, he thought grimly, as he pulled off his socks and bent to pick up his jacket. Clamped to his chest as he'd carried her to safety, Willow had felt considerably smaller than him. Somehow delicate, despite the kicking. And, once she'd finally relaxed against him, very supple and very soft.

Not that her body was of any interest to him, of course. Her curves, which were barely contained by the tiny black bikini she wore, were generous and her legs were tanned and shapely, but he'd never been distracted by a woman and he wasn't about to be now. He wasn't his mother, after all, ruled by whim, by emotion, by carnality. He wasn't self-centred and thoughtless, scandalous and embarrassing.

Not these days, at least.

As a youth, he'd lived a pretty hedonistic and carefree existence, taking for granted his family's wealth and privilege that meant he could pursue his love of sailing with the best boats and finest kit, and believing himself invincible. But ever since his father's fatal heart attack, which had catapulted him sooner than anyone had anticipated into the role he'd been destined to fill—for which he had not been ready—he'd been a model of strength and restraint. These days, he was focused and driven. With the occasional exception that generally involved obstreperous family members, he was used to being obeyed. He was accustomed to having his demands carried out and he got results.

So he didn't think it a disappointment when Willow towelled herself off and slipped on a silky pink robe that hid her body from view. He easily wiped from his memory the feel of her bottom bumping up against him as he'd towed her to the side and the satiny softness of her skin beneath his fingers. He had no further reason to find himself so close to her that he could make out flecks of amber in the emerald-green depths of her eyes. Her toenails—each painted a different colour—offended his need for order, so he simply wouldn't look at them, and that went for the many earrings and the twinkling nose stud she wore, too.

The only thing that mattered was that he accomplished his mission to ensure his sister's wedding went off without a hitch. And that he would do, right here, right now, whatever it took.

Had Willow not been busy contemplating the reason Leo Stanhope was paying his mother a visit and somehow sensing that it couldn't be good, she'd have thought it a crying shame he donned his jacket and fastened the buttons because his shirt, rendered transparent by his dip in the pool, showcased muscles that really were something else.

However, who or what he looked like was as irrelevant as his impressive size and the raw physicality that had been in such evidence only a moment ago. If by some unfortunate chance he'd found out about the portrait and was here to express his displeasure, she needed to keep her wits about her. If he wasn't, if he'd just happened to catch sight of her flailing about through the window and simply hadn't fancied the paperwork of a hypothetical drowning, then all she needed to do was introduce herself, muster up a grudging 'thank you' and get back to work. Either way—and the latter was infinitely preferable, of course—polite professionalism was the way forward, she was sure.

'Willow Jacobs,' she said, holding out her hand and bestowing upon him her widest smile. 'You must be Leo.'

With a quick frown, he gave her hand a perfunctory shake then strode past her and pulled out one of the six chairs that surrounded the poolside table.

'I know who you are,' he said flatly, pointing at the seat with one long tanned finger. 'Sit down. We need to talk.'

Willow dropped her hand and her stomach sank. Right. So he *was* here for her. 'About?'

'Your portrait of my mother naked.'

As she'd feared.

The set of Leo's expression and the severity of his tone suggested he'd brook no argument, and from what Selene had told her, he was used to ordering about people who immediately rushed to do his bidding, but that was just tough. Willow had no intention of being one of them. Certainly not if he was here to scupper the future she so badly needed. There was simply too much at stake.

And besides, he might be standing there all darkly forbidding and smoulderingly intense, the sun setting behind him giving him a godlike glow, but thanks to Selene and her stories, she knew that that he wasn't as invincible as he obviously liked to make out.

'I prefer to stand,' she said, lifting her chin and folding her arms across her chest to reinforce the message that she was not going to be intimidated.

'Fine.' He stalked towards her and came to a halt a couple of feet in front of her. 'I'll get straight to the point,' he said, close enough for her to be able to feel the simmering tension vibrating off him, close enough to touch.

Willow ignored the instinct to take a step back out of his powerful orbit and stood her ground. 'Please do.'

'This painting of yours will not be going on display.'

*What?* 'That is not your decision to make.'

His jaw tightened. 'It must never see the light of day.'

'It absolutely must,' she said, straightening her spine and lifting her chin a tiny bit higher. 'It's an exceptional piece. My best work yet.'

'That's irrelevant.'

Willow bristled. However handsome and well-constructed he was, his presumption was staggering. 'Not to me.'

'I'll double what my mother's paying you.'

'No.'

'I'll triple it.'

'No.'

'How much do you want?'

'I'm not for bribing,' she said with a bluntness that matched his own.

He arched one sceptical eyebrow. 'I find that hard to believe.'

For a moment, she just stared at him in appalled horror. Was he implying what she thought he was implying? 'And what, exactly, is that supposed to mean?'

'You're hardly a well-known name,' he said, and she inwardly winced because it was undeniably true. 'So how did you come to be painting my mother?'

'Not that it's any of your business,' said Willow icily, 'but we met at the launch of a new art gallery in London. I was waitressing. She admired my hair. We got chatting. She mentioned wanting a portrait done. I sent her some photos of my work and that was it.'

'Does it always take a month?'

'Two to three weeks, usually.' To fit around her menstrual cycle, not that she was going to tell him *that*. 'Hers took longer because she kept disappearing.'

'So you moved in.'

'She invited me to,' she said, annoyed that she was even bothering to give him an explanation when none was needed. 'She was really quite insistent about it. I got the impression she was lonely.'

'Lonely?' he said with a bark of humourless laughter. 'That's ridiculous. She's constantly surrounded by people, some of whom have been known to take advantage of her ridiculous generosity.'

'Yes, well, someone once sang about being alone in a crowded room, and you can think what you like about people taking advantage of your mother, but I'm not one of them.'

Leo's dark eyes narrowed while he considered her words and despite the outrage swirling around inside her, Willow grudgingly supposed she could see where his concern was coming from even if she didn't appreciate his accusations. His family was not only one of the most glamorous in the world, it was also one of the wealthiest. He regularly appeared on various rich lists. He didn't know anything about her, and, possibly understandably, he obviously didn't trust Selene to make sensible decisions.

'What's your objection to the portrait anyway?' she said, choosing to let the matter of her motives go because either he believed her or he didn't, and bringing the conversation back to the point. 'Have you actually seen it?'

Leo visibly shuddered and winced. 'What? No. I can't think of anything worse.'

'You should. It's very tasteful. Your mother is beautiful. She's a woman in love and that shines through.'

'She's always in love. Or thinks she is.'

The disdain evident in his voice piqued her curiosity. 'Do you have a problem with love?'

His jaw tightened. 'I have a problem with a life-size nude picture of my middle-aged mother going on public display.'

'You don't know how lucky you are to have a middle-aged mother to be captured on paper and put on display in the first place,' she said, swallowing down the small tight lump that lodged in her throat. 'Mine died a decade ago, when she was thirty-nine and I was fourteen. I'd give anything to have her back and paint her now, clothed or unclothed, whatever her behaviour.'

Some undefinable emotion flickered across Leo's expression, but thankfully he didn't produce the standard yet meaningless, in this context, *I'm sorry*.

'Tell me what you want, Miss Jacobs,' he said instead, which at least had the benefit of yanking her out of her melancholy and refocusing her thoughts. 'There will be something.'

His arrogance was outrageous, but Willow was not to be deterred. No amount of money—or anything else— was going to sway her. Not when everything she'd ever dreamed of professionally was within touching distance.

'Mr Stanhope,' she said with a tight smile. 'Leo, if I may. It's not about the money. At least, not entirely. It's more about opportunity, and this exhibition is a once-in-a-lifetime one. I want my name to be on everyone's lips in the art world. I want to be the go-to artist for a portrait in pastel. I've waited a long time for this break. So you could offer me the sun, the moon and the stars and it would be in vain. There is absolutely nothing you can say or do that will make me change my mind.'

'No?' he said after a beat. 'Well, how about this? The picture is due to go on show two weeks on Monday, right?'

Wondering where he was going with this, Willow nodded warily. 'That's correct.'

'My sister is getting married the following Thursday.'

'I heard.' Selene had shown her the dress she was planning to wear. Willow had only just about managed to hide her appal and keep to herself her thoughts about the mother of the bride wearing white—and not all that much of it—to her daughter's special day.

'The fact that a wedding is even taking place is a miracle,' said Leo. 'When Daphne was thirteen she was diagnosed with leukaemia. The outlook was not good. She wasn't expected to live more than five years. But she has. She's in remission. And now she's found someone with whom she wants to spend the rest of her hopefully long life. This wedding of hers is a huge event. A celebration of survival as well as their relationship. There will be seven hundred guests in attendance. Family. Friends. Europe's elite and its biggest gossips. I will not have Daphne, or her fiancé, being upstaged by anything or anyone. Least of all a scandalous portrait of our thoughtless, self-centred, hedonistic mother.'

Leo stopped, a muscle pounding in his cheek, his dark eyes blazing, as if this mattered a lot to him, as if it wasn't really about the picture at all. And as Willow processed his words and the tone in which they'd been delivered, which suggested he cared about his sister deeply and wasn't simply out to spoil anyone's fun, she realised she'd been wrong. Because there *was* something that could change her mind, after all.

# CHAPTER TWO

LEO WAITED FOR Willow's response to his last line of defence, his heart beating oddly fast and his head pounding. Persuading her to see the situation his way was proving harder than he'd anticipated. In his experience, the other side always, *always* capitulated. But not the woman standing in front of him with her arms folded across her chest and her chin up. Disconcertingly, she didn't seem remotely fazed by him.

Once he'd realised she wasn't motivated by money, all that had remained was revealing the truth about the situation and appealing to her better nature, but if that didn't work he didn't know what he'd do. Steal the portrait and then destroy it?

He was finding it hard to think straight. His attention kept being drawn to those damn multicoloured toenails. He thought he could make out a faint hint of pink in her still damp hair, which was absurd. The gem in her nostril kept catching the light of the setting sun. And how many piercings did one pair of ears actually need?

Something about this woman was making him feel unhinged. His stomach was roiling in a way that even the choppiest waters he'd encountered while competitively sailing hadn't managed. He had the unpleasant feeling that she could unravel his control with a click of her fingers if he didn't exercise extreme caution, which was a concern because without it, he suspected the many plates he had spinning could well crash to the ground.

But *why* was she having this effect on him? He'd faced down heads of governments. The toughest of business figures. His mother. This bizarre…susceptibility…was as nonsensical as it was unacceptable.

'All right,' she eventually said, snapping him out of his disturbing thoughts and back to the conversation. 'I suggest a compromise.'

He blinked, astonishment jolting through him. 'A compromise?'

'Is that not a word you're familiar with?' she asked dryly.

'No.'

'Then allow me to explain. The portrait is too good and too important to me to be hidden away gathering dust. So it *will* go on display somewhere soon, and that's non-negotiable. But I can understand your concerns with regard to the gossip about your mother overshadowing your sister's big day. So I'm prepared to agree to a delay.'

*A delay?*

'On one condition.'

'Which is?'

'I'd like an invitation to the wedding reception.'

Outwardly, Leo didn't move a muscle. Inwardly, he reeled. That was ballsy of her. But why was he even entertaining this conversation when he could simply ransack the house for the portrait and cart it off with him? Where were his wits? Why were his feet glued to the ground instead of carrying him to the house to do just that?

'The exhibition is a temporary one,' she continued in the same confident tone before he could issue a flat out no. 'By the time the wedding's over it will be, too. I'll miss my best chance of establishing my career. But if your guests are as influential as you claim, then access to them will make up for it. I promise to be subtle. I won't hand out cards or do anything crass like that. You won't even notice I'm there. One more guest among hundreds isn't a huge price to pay to secure your sister's happiness, surely. But it's entirely up to you.'

She stopped, looking as cool as the proverbial cucumber, and he realised with an unsettling jolt that she'd turned the tables on him. He'd set out intending to bribe her into submission if necessary, but she was now the one who had him over a barrel, because he couldn't steal the portrait and destroy it. She—or more likely, his mother—would probably have him arrested for theft and criminal damage, which would create an even greater scandal. If he wasn't feeling so on edge and off balance, he'd have been impressed by Willow's swift thinking and sharp practice.

'So do we have a deal?'

Absolutely not, was the answer Leo instinctively wanted to give. *He* proposed deals. He led the charge. He rarely surrendered control, especially not to beautiful but truculent women with multicoloured toenails, too many piercings and possibly pink hair.

And yet, as he recalled his intention to achieve his goal right here, right now, whatever it took, he had to reassess. 'Whatever it took' was turning out to be remarkably little. He'd been prepared to shell out thousands. All Willow and her better nature wanted was an invitation to a party which, as she'd so astutely pointed out, was going to be attended by hundreds anyway. If he agreed to her demands, he'd actually be getting off exceedingly lightly.

His sister's happiness was more than worth the minor temporary cession of the control he valued so highly. It was worth everything, so he gave a short nod, a tight smile and said, 'We have a deal.'

It had taken Willow twenty-four hours to get over the poolside encounter with Leo. Having sealed the deal with a bone-crushing handshake and a grudging request for her email address, he'd snatched up his shoes and socks and stalked off, leaving her scarcely able to believe she'd had the nerve to do what she'd done.

It could so easily have gone the other way. If he'd refused the invitation point-blank then that would have been that. She was ambitious, sure, but she wasn't so ruthless she'd ride roughshod over another woman's happiness. Especially one who'd suffered so much with her health, which she knew a little about. She'd have delayed the exhibition of the portrait anyway and her career would have been set back by who knew how much, but she'd have found solace in knowing she'd done the right thing.

However, he hadn't refused, thank God. Her gamble had paid off. The question now was, would this one?

The taxi that had picked her up from the hostel she'd moved to after finishing the portrait last week drew up to the kerb some distance from the entrance to Athens's finest hotel. At the sight of the guests making their way up the steps to the front door, the nerves knotting Willow's stomach tightened. Camera flashes were going off left, right and centre, illuminating the dusk and making her blink, and for one brief moment she wondered what on earth she'd been thinking. This was the social event of the year. Celebrities, royalty, the great and the good, and...*her*?

Was she mad?

This wasn't her world. She wasn't wearing a ten-thousand-euro outfit and half a ton of diamonds. Her dress was plain and simple and borrowed, couriered over by a friend back home who owned a shop that rented out evening wear. She wore no jewellery apart from the gold watch she'd inherited from her mother, the tiny diamond in her nose that she'd bought with the money she'd earned from her first-ever commission and a variety of studs and rings that adorned her ears just because she liked them.

But then she rallied. The evening ahead wasn't one to enjoy. It was work. She had a plan, a future to secure and the stakes were high. She was no better or worse than any of the other guests and she could talk to anyone. She hoped. So there'd be no more nerves. No more doubt about her place at this party. Her chin would be up and her shoulders back.

She wasn't remotely bothered about crossing paths with the brother of the bride and host of the reception. Leo, with his wet-shirt-clad chest and his admirable concern for his sister, had occupied far too much of her head space over the last couple of weeks—even when she'd been confined to her hostel for a few days, curled up on the bed in agony and popping painkillers like sweets— but she didn't intend to seek him out. There was no need to do so and it was highly unlikely he'd relish the opportunity to talk to her anyway, given the manner in which she'd wheedled her invitation out of him.

No. She would not be distracted by anyone or anything this evening. She would not dwell on the fact that night after night she'd woken up hot and achy and shaking after dreaming of him, which was baffling when their one and only encounter had been so brief and hostile. She would stop wondering whether he could truly be as devastatingly handsome as she recalled. She would put him entirely from her mind. If their eyes did happen to meet across a crowded room and she discovered that he *was* as gorgeous as she remembered, she'd offer him a cool smile of acknowledgement and that would be it.

She'd created a golden opportunity for herself and her career here, she reminded herself firmly as she took a deep breath, adjusted her dress and opened the door. A chance to generate work and build her reputation like no other. And she was not going to waste it.

'So far, so good.'

In response to the dry comment in Greek that came from his left, Leo swung his gaze away from the guests beginning to amass in the hall below and rested it on his brother, the next one down in age.

Zander was right. So far, things had been very good. Way better than he'd anticipated, in fact. The ceremony that had taken place this morning at the Metropolitan Cathedral of Athens had gone off without a hitch. The dozen or so knee-high bridesmaids had behaved beautifully. The bride had looked radiant as he'd led her down the aisle, and the groom—ridiculously overcome by emotion—had even shed a tear when he'd said his vows. Selene had ditched the white in favour of an unexpectedly age-and occasion-appropriate pale blue skirt and matching jacket and had exhibited far more restraint than Leo could ever have hoped.

Yet he couldn't relax.

The minute he'd woken up this morning his gut had started to churn with apprehension and adrenalin, a leaden weight settling in his chest. Despite the success of the day, none of that had eased. He had to remain alert. He had to keep an eye on his mother because he knew from experience that when it came to her, things could turn on a sixpence.

'The night is young,' he muttered as he resumed his perusal of the throng at the centre of which were his sister and brand-new brother-in-law, looking absurdly happy, as if the car crash of her parents' marriage hadn't given them even the tiniest pause for thought. 'There's still plenty of opportunity for Selene to make a scene.'

'She hasn't yet,' Zander pointed out, 'and I'm assured she won't.'

'Who by?'

'Atticus told Olympia who told Thalia who told me that apparently the woman who was painting her had a word.'

At the eventual reference to Willow, every one of Leo's senses sharpened and his entire body seemed to vibrate, as if he'd suddenly been plugged in and switched on. If someone had asked him to recite the order of siblings through which the information had travelled he'd have failed. 'What sort of a word?'

'A subtle one, apparently.'

'Well, that won't last long,' he muttered. 'We all know subtle doesn't work.'

'Seems to be working so far,' Zander said. 'Who'd have thought? A random artist who's known her for approximately two months succeeds where the rest of us, who've known her for years, fail. She must be quite something.'

She was. Although Leo had no idea quite what.

'You met her, didn't you?'

Met her. Dived into a pool to save her. Argued with her, bargained with her and dreamed about her ever since… 'I did.'

'What was her name?'

'Willow Jacobs.'

Saying the words out loud made his blood heat and his skin prickle, but that reaction was nothing new when it came to her. He'd been driven to distraction by the woman over the last couple of weeks. That their encounter had lasted no more than half an hour and had hardly been scintillating didn't matter. Try as he might, he hadn't been able to get the image of her—arms folded, chin up, green eyes lit with cool fire—out of his head.

In his dreams, she didn't don a robe on exiting the pool. No. That would be far too considerate. Instead, she sidled up to him, all glorious curves and sultry smiles, while he remained rooted to the spot. She pushed aside the lapels of his jacket, put her hands to the buttons of his sodden shirt and huskily said something along the lines of 'Why don't we get out of these wet things?' He, seeing this as an excellent idea rather than a cringe-worthy cliché, then invariably pulled her into his arms and low-

ered her to a lounger before setting about doing as she
suggested.

'What's she like?'

Gorgeous. Annoying. Disturbing. 'I don't know,' he
muttered. 'Our encounter was brief.'

And that was what was so irritating about the bizarrely
intense effect she'd had on him. He didn't know her. He
didn't particularly like her. She had zero respect for his
authority. She challenged the order and control he valued
so highly and ultimately she'd blackmailed him.

Yet he could recall every word of their conversation,
every arch of her eyebrow and every jut of her chin. He
wanted to know what she felt and tasted like. The sounds
she'd make as he ran his hands and mouth over her and
then finally sank into her. What was even more unnerving but equally baffling, he couldn't stop thinking about
the fleeting sadness that had filled her expression when
she'd mentioned her mother and pondering the nature of
their relationship.

Willow—a woman with multiple piercings, a slap-
dash attitude towards nail varnish and possibly pink hair,
whose nanosecond of vulnerability seemed to be permanently etched into his head and who was the complete
opposite of the cool, polished, one-earring-per-ear type
he usually went for—was immensely distracting on a
number of levels, and it was frustrating in the extreme.

'Daph said you invited her tonight.'

Schooling his features so that not a hint of his inner
turmoil showed, Leo shoved his hands in his pockets and
gave a casual shrug. 'All part of the package to keep the
wedding scandal-free.'

'So where is she?'

'No idea.'

Whether she came tonight or not, he didn't care. She wasn't the cause of the adrenalin that had been pounding through him since this morning and he wasn't scanning the guests for her now. He was standing on the balcony simply to get some breathing space after a hectic day. That he had a view of the gathering throng was merely an unintended consequence of that. He wasn't watching the door. He had eyes on his mother and that was where they'd stay.

Yet even before his brother blew out a breath and murmured a low, admiring 'Wow', Leo registered the moment Willow arrived. His entire body tensed. His clothes suddenly felt too tight. His heart rate accelerated and he was aware of it drumming fast and hard everywhere.

'Who's that?'

Despite his every intention not to, he shifted slightly to look in the direction of Zander's gaze, at the woman who was turning to the waiter standing at the door with a tray upon which stood a dozen glasses of champagne. In direct opposition to every effort he made to remain immune, the impact of her hit him like a kick in the chest.

He recognised the wide, stunning smile she gave the waiter as she accepted a glass. He could entirely sympathise with the poor guy, who was blushing and staring at her like a deer in the headlights. That smile had knocked him for six the first time he'd seen it, too.

On the other hand, maybe it was the dress—long, pale yellow, sequinned and just tight enough—that had rendered the waiter speechless. Or her hair. What colour *was* it? Or should that be colours? Because it wasn't just pink, as he assumed when it had been wet from the pool. The wavy predominantly blond tresses that were swept off her face and rippled down her back were also streaked with blue and green. She didn't just paint in pastels…she wore them on her head.

'That's the artist,' he said, running a finger around the inside of his collar and stretching his neck to ease his oddly laboured breathing.

'A unicorn appears to be missing its mane.'

'So it would seem.'

'Want to bet that she's the only one here with beads in her hair?'

'No.'

'She's stunning.'

'If you like that sort of thing.' Which, to his irritation, apparently, he did, despite the offensive nature of pretty much everything about her.

While Zander continued to mutter appreciative inanities about Willow's singular look, in raptures over her striking features and spectacular figure, Leo watched her enter the mêlée and introduce herself to a group of Italian socialites. As she chatted and laughed he thought darkly that it was no wonder she didn't need business cards. She was unforgettable. Anything but subtle. And as for not noticing her, how on earth would *that* ever be possible?

As if aware he was watching her, she suddenly glanced up, her eyes locking with his. For a second she went still, then flashed him another of those incendiary smiles, which momentarily stole the breath from his lungs and fogged his head.

But he recovered swiftly enough. He was well accustomed to stamping out rogue flares of wildness that he'd occasionally experienced over the years when his guard slipped. So he offered her a brief nod—no smile—in return, switched his attention back to his mother, and they were done. His and Willow's paths need never cross again. He had no reason to talk to her. No need to thank her for persuading Selene to see sense for once. He would not surrender to the demands of his body, however clamouring they were, and seek her out simply because he wanted to. He would not be that weak.

'She has quite a smile.'

She did. 'I hadn't noticed.'

'No, well, lucky for me, she's my type, not yours.'

Once again, Zander was right. And that was fine. His brother could make Willow's acquaintance and flirt with her all he liked. He wasn't remotely bothered. It wasn't as if she'd be around for long. The women his brother set his sights on never were. 'Good luck.'

'Thanks. Not that I'll need it. You should try it some time.'

'Try what?'

'Lightening up. You know what they say about all work and no play.'

Leo stiffened. Yes, well, *someone* had to keep the multibillion business he'd inherited from their father afloat. 'You play enough for both of us.'

'Only because you won't let go of the reins and I have a lot of spare time to fill.'

'You're chief commercial officer.'

'Which, thanks to your control issues, I do with one hand tied behind my back.'

Leo didn't have the head space for his brother's familiar grumblings. He'd turned his mind to strategising. Tomorrow he'd have a nice little chat with his mother and make her see the error of her ways in wanting to put the portrait on show. How he'd forgotten that he held her purse strings and therefore all the cards was a mystery. Within twenty-four hours, scandal would be averted. Willow and the havoc she wreaked on him would be gone and the compromise she'd negotiated out of him would be history. Once he'd stopped dreaming about her, he could forget he'd ever met her. Order would be restored and normality would resume.

In the meantime, there was an evening to get through, an unpredictable parent to keep an eye on and seven hundred guests to greet.

'Where are you going?' Zander murmured, not even bothering to take his gaze off the unicorn mermaid siren down below.

'The net worth of this room runs into the hundreds of billions,' said Leo, the irrational and inexplicable irritation he suddenly felt towards his brother as unnecessary as it was perplexing. 'There's business to be done. You and I, therefore, are going to mingle.'

The first thing that had taken Willow's breath away the moment she'd entered the hall was the enormous sparkling chandelier that looked suitable for high jinks of the glamorous socialite kind. The second was the sheer splendour of the space—the lavishly painted ceiling, the old masters on the walls, the marble, the gilt, the silk. Shortly after that, it was Leo.

Fortified by half a glass of bone-dry champagne, she'd been enjoying the conversation she'd been having with two Milanese countesses and one Puglian landowner while discreetly jotting down their names and email addresses in the small notebook she'd stashed in the hidden pocket of her dress.

But then, quite suddenly, she'd tensed. A shiver had raced down her spine and her skin had broken out in goose bumps. She'd glanced up and around and a second later her eyes had locked with Leo's, as if his were a magnet and hers iron filings. She'd managed to muster up a smile in acknowledgement, as planned, but, very much *not* as planned, she'd been so rocked by the immediate impact of his smouldering good looks that she'd lost track of the conversation.

Fortunately for her dignity, Leo had then disappeared from view. Willow had snapped out of her trance and recalled what she was meant to be doing, which was ignoring distractions and working the room.

Dinner had been delicious, her table companions interesting and engaging and, happily, very keen on having themselves committed to paper. Leo's speech, which had switched seamlessly between Greek, English, French, Spanish and Italian had been loudly and enthusiastically applauded. She hadn't understood much more than a quarter of what he said, but that might have been because, despite her best efforts to prevent it, all she could really focus on was his mouth and the way it moved.

Now she'd been persuaded to the dance floor by his

brother, who apparently had been up on the balcony with Leo earlier, not that she'd noticed. He was handsome and charming but in a hard, hollow kind of a way that left her strangely unmoved even though over coffee and chocolates he'd made her laugh until her sides ached.

'How about we take this somewhere more private?' Zander murmured in her ear as he drew her closer and continued to manoeuvre her skilfully around the floor.

At the sensual promise she could hear in his voice, nerves fluttered in her stomach and alarm skittered through her. Flirting was one thing—and she enjoyed that as much as anyone—but she'd never taken anything anywhere and didn't particularly want to now. She was way out of her depth. She had no idea how to handle a man like Zander. He oozed experience and sexuality. All she had was honesty, which would just have to do, so she put her hands on his chest to stop any further advance and said rather abruptly, 'No, thanks.'

In response, Zander jerked back, and his eyebrows shot up in a way that suggested arrogance ran in the family. 'Seriously?'

'Sorry.'

'No need to apologise.'

'Quite right,' said a deep voice behind her, a voice that brought back the memory of being clamped against him as he towed her to the side of the pool, a voice that had murmured not so sweet nothings in her ear in her dreams night after night and now sent shivers down her spine. 'Zander, I heard the Duke of Clervaux is unhappy with his current banking provision and is seeking a change.'

Zander must have felt the tremor that ran through

her for she caught a spark of curiosity in his gaze as he shifted it from her to the man standing behind her and then back again.

'Is he?' he said with a wry arch of an eyebrow.

'Yes.'

'Well, why didn't you say?' he said, releasing her and taking a step back, hands open and up. 'The lovely Willow is all yours.'

'Actually,' said Willow, not really understanding the undercurrents swirling between them but instinctively feeling the need to remind both men of her existence, lovely or not. 'I'm not anyone's.'

'Interesting,' said Zander with a grin, and off he sauntered.

# CHAPTER THREE

WHAT IN THE name of Zeus was he doing? Leo wondered, his blood thrumming like an outboard motor as his brother disappeared from sight and Willow slowly turned to face him. Why was he standing in the middle of a crowded dance floor in front of a woman he'd had no intention of ever talking to again?

Over the course of the evening he'd caught regular glimpses of her, and her name had kept coming up in conversation, but he hadn't responded. He'd merely averted his gaze and changed topic. Sheer willpower had prevented him from reacting to the discovery that her dress was backless and she couldn't therefore be wearing a bra. Years of experience at containing his emotions had kept a lid on the simmering desire that threatened to boil over and consume him. But all that resolve, all that strength of character had evaporated at the sight of Willow in his brother's arms.

So much for not being bothered. One brief glance in her direction, then another when what he was witnessing sank in, and the words *hell no* had flashed through his head in bright green neon. A strange sort of red mist had descended and the urgent need to put a stop to the proceedings had flared into life. Instinct had kicked in and obliterated the cool consideration and calm objectivity with which he usually acted.

He could barely recall excusing himself from the people he'd been talking to. How many apologies had he had to mutter as he'd stalked across the dance floor? How much interest had he attracted? Why did he not care?

Whatever was going on, whatever had driven him to challenge the situation, here he was now. In front of her. Unanchored. Adrift in uncharted waters and standing beneath a giant glitter ball like an idiot with no clue how to proceed. For the first time in his life.

'Did you want something?' Willow asked with admirable composure, although the faint flush on her cheeks and the fluttering pulse at the base of her neck suggested she was anything but composed.

Her. He wanted her. And there was no rhyme or reason to it. Just unfathomable yet clamouring need that he was struggling to subdue and a thrilling rush of adrenalin he hadn't felt since scything through the waves at twenty knots and a forty-five-degree angle over a decade ago. 'Dance with me.'

She looked him, her darkening gaze dipping to his mouth and lingering, as if she'd imagined kissing him as much as he'd imagined kissing her. After a beat, she gave a nod, a faint smile and then, to his unaccountable relief, said a little breathlessly, 'All right.'

Agreeing to dance with Leo had been a mistake.

Willow realised this the instant he wrapped one of his large warm hands around hers and planted the other on her bare back and she nearly went up in flames. Contact with his brother had left her unmoved. Contact with him was electric. Why? She had no idea.

She should have said no to his demand that she dance and walked away. Their one and only encounter had hardly been cordial. No doubt he wanted to discuss the portrait's future with her now the wedding was over and any further delay was unnecessary, and she'd moved on. She shouldn't have succumbed to curiosity. She didn't need to know whether her dreams in any way represented reality. She was here to network and that was all that mattered.

Yet when he pulled her close she did nothing to stop him. On the contrary, she met him more than halfway. She'd never believed that magnetism between people could actually exist but here she was, pressed up against him, one hand on his shoulder, the other clasped in his. They were touching everywhere from chest to hip, and wild horses couldn't have dragged her away.

'How have you been?' he said, his voice low and gravelly as he began to slowly move her around the tight space they occupied, hemmed in by others lured by the hits Europe's number one girl band was banging out.

'Fine,' she replied, strangely husky. 'You?'

'Busy.'

'How was the ceremony?'

'Uneventful.'

'That must have been a relief.'

'You have no idea.'

His gaze roamed over her hair and her face before settling on her mouth, which instantly dried while her pulse raced. He was so close all she'd have to do was lift herself onto her toes, lean forwards an inch while exerting pressure on his shoulder to draw him down and then she'd finally know what it would be like to kiss him.

'Lovely party,' she said, battling back the temptation to do exactly that since it would be wildly inappropriate and no doubt cause a scandal he certainly wouldn't welcome.

'Hmm.'

'Dinner was delicious. Your brother is charming.'

Leo's hand tightened around hers and a quick frown creased his forehead, but only for an instant. 'That's why he's in charge of drumming up new business.'

'I imagine he's very good at it.'

'He is. As are you.'

Willow's heart thudded. Had he been watching her in action? For some reason, the thought of his eyes on her as she worked the room heated her blood. 'I try.'

'Everyone is talking about you.'

'At least I'm not the mother of the bride and naked in a frame.'

'A blessing indeed,' he murmured, but something in his expression made her wish she'd kept her mouth shut because not only did she have the unnerving feeling that he was somehow mentally undressing her, but also all she could think of now was how good he'd looked in a wet shirt and how much better he might look without anything on at all.

Swallowing hard to refocus, Willow reined in her imagination and determinedly sought refuge in manners. 'Thank you for my invitation.'

'I wasn't aware I had much choice in issuing it.'

'That's a fair point,' she had to acknowledge with the hint of a smile. 'I did blackmail you into it.'

'You did. But actually, if anyone's owed a thank-you, it's you.'

'For what?'

'I understand you're the one responsible for my mother's restraint today,' he said. 'And, I'm guessing, both her outfit in church and the dress she has on this evening.'

'You're welcome,' she said, a shiver of pleasure and relief rippling through her. 'Although I did wonder if I was overstepping by intervening.'

'You were.'

'Sorry.'

'Once again, you have no need to apologise. You have my gratitude. And Daphne's.' He leaned back an inch and tilted his head, his hold on her loosening a fraction. 'What's your secret?'

'There's no secret,' she said, relaxing a little now she was on safer conversational ground. 'I like to get to know my clients so I encourage them to talk while I work.'

'What about?'

'Whatever they want. Anything, really. It puts them at ease. Lowers their guard. And from my point of view, it gives me insight into their character, which adds a certain sort of magic to the painting. Some find it hard. Selene's the opposite.'

'That doesn't surprise me.'

'I merely asked her some curated questions and mentioned how much I imagined my own mother would have wanted to be around for my wedding and the sacrifices she'd have made to ensure it was all about me. I suggested that today might be Daphne's chance to shine. I know how difficult that can be sometimes.'

'Do you?'

'Yes.'

'In what way?'

In a constantly-being-thwarted-by-her-condition kind of a way, mainly. How many exams had she failed because she'd been in such agony she hadn't managed to turn up? How many arrangements with friends had she bailed on? How many jobs had she wanted to apply for only to realise she'd never be able to stay the course? Too many to recall.

But she was hardly going to go into all that. It was way too personal and even more inappropriate than kissing her reluctant host in the middle of a crowded dance floor.

'The art world is a hard one to break into,' she said, which both answered his question and was true.

'You've made a good start.'

She thought of the contact details that filled her notebook and felt a surge of pride. 'I hope so.'

'Where's the portrait now?'

'In storage at a gallery here in Athens, where it will stay until the unveiling your mother's planning.'

His jaw twitched and the frown was back. 'The unveiling?'

'That's right.'

'She's utterly shameless.'

Despite the giddy pleasure she felt at being in his embrace, Willow bristled. 'This is my work you're talking about, Leo. There's nothing shameful about any of it. Life drawing is a respected artistic tradition that's been around for millennia. I'm proud of what I do, and if your mother wants to celebrate her sexuality then that's to be applauded, too.'

Leo winced. 'She's nearly sixty.'

'So?'

'I should cut off her allowance.'

She stiffened in his arms and jerked back. 'You'd do that?' she breathed, staring up at him in shock.

'Yes, if necessary. She's a walking scandal and this time she's gone too far.'

'She loves life.'

'She's self-centred and thoughtless.'

'Perhaps, but she's also entertaining and, like you said, generous. She took a risk on me—a complete unknown—and she's the one who arranged the exhibition of the portrait. From my point of view, she's been nothing but supportive.'

Leo muttered something non-committal in response to that and then said, 'What was your mother like?'

'Maternal. Doting. Firm but fair and completely conventional.'

'You said she died when you were fourteen.'

'You have an excellent memory.'

'There's little of that afternoon I *don't* remember,' he said dryly. 'What happened?'

'She went into hospital for a routine surgery and never woke up from the anaesthetic.'

'That must have been devastating.'

In so many ways…

'My father's never really recovered,' she admitted, swallowing down the small lump in her throat that always formed when she thought of the sorrow that still ravaged him. 'He's more or less a recluse.'

'And you?'

Her? Hmm. Where to start? She'd become convinced that the fate that had befallen her mother could well befall her if she ever went under the knife. She'd witnessed first-hand, on a daily basis, the traumatic effect of her mother's death on her father. What if *she* went ahead with the operations she'd been told by doctors would alleviate the pain she suffered month in, month out and one day didn't wake up? He'd have lost a daughter as well as a wife and she couldn't bear to think how he'd cope with that.

From there she'd developed a deep-seated fear of romantic love and falling into it. The idea of history repeating itself had tormented her day and night for months. What would her demise—in whatever form it took—do to someone who loved her, such as a long-term boyfriend or husband of her own? Would *they* withdraw from life, destroyed and hollowed out by grief? Would *she*, if the situation were reversed?

The greater the love, it seemed, the greater the potential devastation and she couldn't—and wouldn't—put herself or anyone else in that position. In the end, she'd figured it was far safer not to let anyone emotionally close in the first place. Far easier to simply keep her heart locked up in a cage, throw away the key and get used to the loneliness. She wished she felt differently; she didn't want to be alone for ever, but it was what it was. At least her way, only one person had to suffer.

But all that was far too intimate to share, so perhaps it would be best to present him with the obvious.

'It took a while,' she said, remembering instead the shock and the sorrow and the many long solitary walks she'd taken to process what had happened. 'It rocked my world. I don't expect the grief will ever go away—or the anger, for that matter—but you learn to live with it.'

'That's true,' he said with a slight nod, never missing a step as he smoothly moved her around the dance floor. 'My father died when I was nineteen. A heart attack. Also sudden.'

'Selene said. He sounded like a formidable man.'

'He was.'

'How did they meet?'

'At an embassy party in Paris. She fell for his British stiff upper lip and dashing looks. By all accounts she was dazzling, but I suspect the real attraction was the Kallis shipping company that he wanted to merge with the Stanhope bank.'

'That's cynical.'

'Or realistic. They married after a whirlwind two-month courtship. The honeymoon didn't last long. They were fundamentally too different. She was temperamental. He was cold. And obviously clueless when it came to handling her. He was perfectly capable of disciplining us, but for some reason he stuck his head in the sand with her. She ran rings around him. Her many affairs are unfortunately well documented. No wonder he had a heart attack.'

'Yes, well, maybe "handling" is the trouble,' she said a little archly. 'Maybe you should try working out and understanding where her behaviour comes from instead.'

His eyebrows lifted. 'Did I ask for your advice?'

'No, but you have it anyway and maybe you should heed it because your current methods aren't exactly working, are they?'

'I live in hope. At least I try to do something about it instead of opting for denial without a care for the effects of her antics on the family.'

'On you?'

'None of us emerged unscathed.'

His cryptic response piqued her curiosity, but the shuttering of his expression indicated it would be pointless to probe. 'Do you know she calls you the fun police?'

'I am aware of that,' he said, the muscles of his shoulders beneath her palms relaxing a fraction, which suggested he appreciated the shift in topic. 'But my youngest sister was only nine when my father died. Someone had to be the adult.'

'And that someone was you.'

'I'm the eldest. I was the head of the family suddenly. It was my duty. And not everyone's definition of fun is the same.'

Despite believing him to be wholly misguided on the subject of his mother, Willow felt a pang of sympathy. Being landed with that *and* inheriting a vast global business at the tender age of nineteen, presumably while still grieving himself, couldn't have been easy. 'She also described you as emotionally repressed and far too serious.'

'So I've heard.'

'Does it bother you?'

'Not in the slightest. If everyone went round behaving like she does, with zero respect for the rules of society, civilisation would collapse.'

That seemed like an overly dramatic assessment of the situation, but what did she know? 'You look like her.'

'There's nothing I can do about that,' he muttered. 'All I *can* do is not act like her.'

'Is that something you struggle with?'

'Absolutely not,' he replied with a sharpness that suggested the opposite, which she found unexpectedly intriguing.

'Shall I tell you what I think?'

'I'd rather you didn't.'

'Whether or not you kill a good time and whether or not you're an ice-cold robot—her words, not mine—I think you're just a man who loves his siblings and would do anything to protect them.'

His eyes bore into hers, a muscle pounding in his cheek. 'You don't know me.'

'I know more than you think.'

'Do you know how many people challenge me?'

'No.'

'None.'

'Well, that's not healthy.'

'Even fewer attempt to negotiate with me the way you did.'

'Maybe they don't have anything to lose.'

He tilted his head and regarded her thoughtfully. 'Are you even *slightly* intimidated by me?'

By the effect he had on her, she was, a bit. But by him? 'No. But I can see why people would be. With your height and breadth and your glowering sternness, you're physically imposing. You're head of a multibillion-euro business. You exude authority and power, even when dripping wet, and you're used to your every instruction being obeyed without question. But here's the thing,' she said, leaning forwards an inch and lowering her voice. 'Remember how I told you that your mother liked to talk?'

Wariness flickered across his handsome face. 'Yes.'

'She told me that as a kid you threw tantrums. You used to have nightmares that made you cry.'

His jaw tightened and a fascinating flush hit his cheekbones. 'I'm surprised she noticed.'

'She heard it from your nanny.'

'Of course she did.'

'She said that as you got older you were reckless and wild and took risks that sometimes landed you in hospital. Apparently, you once deliberately dashed a boat on the rocks.'

'She *is* chatty,' he said, a spark of irritation lighting the dark depths of his eyes.

'You don't like being talked about.'

'I do not,' he said with a minute shake of his head. 'Unlike some, I value my privacy.'

'So is it true? About the boat?'

'Yes.'

'Why would you do a thing like that?'

A fleeting shadow darted across his features, but it was gone in an instant. 'Just one of those wild things teenagers can get up to.'

Hmm. In her world a car was more likely to be taken for a joyride than a yacht. 'So what changed?'

He frowned. 'What do you mean?'

'Well, you don't go around having tantrums and crashing boats now, do you?'

'My father died and I had to grow up. Fast. It was a steep learning curve.'

'How steep?'

'I made a few mistakes,' he admitted with a faint grimace. 'In the beginning.'

'So you might be all-powerful and mighty, but you're human, too.'

'Flesh and blood, bone and sinew.'

All of which she was becoming only too aware, she realised with a skip of her pulse as silence fell. At some point during the conversation the band had stopped and a DJ had taken over. Instead of upbeat and boppy, the music oozing out of the speakers was now sultry and Latin, more suited to an earthy Copacabana club than a swanky Athens hotel.

The lights had dimmed. Sensuality wound around the dance floor, couples moving loosely and sinuously. Willow could feel the beat thudding through her. Leo had slowed the swaying they were doing right down and was holding her impossibly close. Something about the intensity and focus with which he was looking at her made her tremble with anticipation.

What was going on in that head of his? she wondered as strange thrills of excitement began to race through her. Three weeks or so ago they'd parted on very unfriendly terms, yet she wasn't getting unfriendly vibes off him now. Latent heat was simmering in his eyes, adding fuel to the flames flickering along her veins. She could feel the hardening length of him growing and pressing against her and nerves fluttered through her once again.

She really wasn't equipped for this. She'd thought she'd

been out of her depth with his brother, but she'd been paddling in the shallows. Leo was far more dangerous to her than Zander could ever be. Outwardly, he was all steely control but he had an edge that ought to have her running towards the exit because she didn't know any of the rules of the game he was playing. But that didn't seem to matter. As unwise as it undoubtedly was when they, their lives and their experiences were poles apart, she wanted to play anyway.

'Do you know what I've dreamed of recently, Willow?'

The sound of her name in his mouth made her shiver. 'No.'

'You,' he murmured, his gaze hot on hers, this conversation for them alone. 'I've dreamed of you. Every night for the last three weeks. And those dreams have been anything but nightmares.'

Her heart lurched and then began to race while her blood thickened and heated. 'I've dreamed of you, too. They've been wild.'

'I haven't been able to take my eyes off you all night.'

'It's the hair.'

He shook his head. 'It's not the hair. Or the dress.'

'Then what is it?'

'Damned if I know. But my brother was right about one thing. You are lovely.'

'You're the sexiest man I've ever met,' she said a little breathlessly, his unexpected confession loosening her lips as well as her inhibitions. 'I want to draw you.'

'I have something else in mind.'

'What?'

He stared at her mouth and lowered his head, so slowly

the anticipation was almost painful. His lips came down on hers and in that instant everything else—the music, the people, the party—disappeared. All Willow could focus on was the heat and skill of his mouth, his hands sliding to her hips so he could mould her better to him, and clinging on for dear life.

She wound her arms around his neck and tangled her fingers in his hair and the kiss that had started out light and teasing deepened into something darker and wilder.

Leo moved one hand to the back of her head and the other up her side to her breast, and she moaned. Instinctively, she tilted her hips and rubbed them against his in an attempt to relieve the throbbing between her legs, but the low growl that that elicited from him simply stoked her desire.

She'd never experienced need like it. She felt crazed. Drugged. She wanted him naked. She wanted to explore his body by tracing every inch of skin, every muscle he possessed, and then she wanted him on top of her and in her. And it wouldn't be painful. It would be magnificent.

She lowered a hand to the waistband of his trousers and tugged at his shirt. He brushed her nipple with his thumb and she nearly jumped out of her skin. She was trembling with need, mindless with desire, completely ready to sink to the floor with him and take that risk she'd always feared, when suddenly, through the haze of longing, as if it came from far, far away, she heard a dry, amused voice call out, 'Hey. You two. Get a room.'

As if doused by a deluge of icy water, Leo instantly let Willow go and jerked back, shock and horror reeling through him as reality hit with the force of a sledge-hammer.

What was he doing?

What the hell did he think he was *doing*?

He'd danced with her. He'd talked to her and told her things he'd never told another living soul. And then he'd *kissed* her. Right here on the dance floor, in the midst of all these people. Without Zander's timely intervention, he'd have set about stripping her naked and he doubted she'd have stopped him. She'd pulled at his shirt and moaned low in her throat, as if desperate to get her hands on his skin, as if she'd been as oblivious to their sur-roundings as he.

Confusion and appal rushed through him, tightening his chest and coating every inch of his skin in a cold sweat as he thought about what could so easily have hap-pened. The scandal would have surpassed anything his mother had done. It would have shredded his image and destroyed his authority. It would have ruined him. What they *had* done was mortifying enough. Kissing and grop-ing each other in public? He hadn't even engaged in that kind of thing as a permanently horny adolescent.

What on earth was the matter with him? At the start of the evening he'd resolved to ignore her and he rarely changed plan mid-course. But the plan had not only changed, it had blown up in his face. In response to over-whelming desire that he should have nevertheless been able to manage, his rigidly maintained composure had crumbled to dust in an instant.

Well, whatever was going on, whatever madness he'd been afflicted by, it would not happen again, he assured himself grimly as he took a step back and removed himself from Willow's dangerously bewitching orbit. He would not allow himself to be ruled by things over which he had no command. He had no time for emotions with their unpredictability and volatility, the chaos they caused and the pain they could inflict. He might look like his mother, but, as he'd told Willow, he would not act like her. He would not be that weak, that selfish.

Nor would he ever again put himself in a position in which his hard-won control came under threat. He'd never forget the moment he'd learned his father had died and realised that from that moment on he had sole responsibility for his family and the business. He could still recall the onslaught of emotions that had smashed through his weakened defences—the stunning shock, the agonising grief and then the raw, blind panic. The nauseating awareness that he was too young and too unprepared. The crippling knowledge that the shoes he was expected to step into were too big.

For days, bombarded with questions, documents to sign and decisions to make, he'd floundered, terrified that he was going to screw up and let everyone down. A month in and he'd concluded the only way he was going to be able to handle his new role was to bury the wilder side of his nature and the dizzying, unwelcome emotions that had sprung free, and knuckle down.

He'd abandoned his hopes and dreams and given up the yachts. He'd stamped out the bitter, shameful resentment that churned through him like bile because deep down he'd never asked for what he'd been given and didn't want any of it. Ruthless control would carry him through, he'd figured, and he'd spent years honing it into an impenetrable shield of stone and steel, designed to both protect himself and others and handle the immense burden he bore.

Now summoning up every drop of strength he possessed with the ease borne from experience, Leo felt the familiar blanket of ice-cold calm envelop him, which meant he could banish the events of the last quarter of an hour from his head and forget they'd ever happened. As the mad heat disappeared and reason returned, he could look at Willow's swollen mouth, her flushed cheeks and tousled hair and her eyes glazed with lingering desire and not respond at all.

'Enjoy the rest of your evening,' he said with a tight smile and a brief nod, as if she were any other guest rather than one with the potential to upturn his life and decimate everything he valued. 'Good night.'

# CHAPTER FOUR

WILLOW RATHER ENVIED the self-possession and stability
with which Leo spun on his heel and strode off. She'd
never felt less in control of herself in her life. Her head
was swimming. Her heart was pounding. It was a complete miracle that her legs were holding her up.

What a kiss…

It had been a kiss to which every other kiss she'd ever
had paled in comparison. It had been passionate, all-consuming and mind-blowing. She could still feel the pressure of his mouth on hers and the hard muscles beneath
her hands. The hot, heady desire that had taken over her
body and turned it into nothing but sensation.

And she wanted more.

Much more.

Because finally, after all these years of anxiety and
stress, disappointment and regret, she'd met a man with
whom she positively *longed* to lose her virginity. There'd
be no awkwardness or embarrassment or frigidity to
worry about if things progressed and then went wrong
because nothing *would* go wrong.

How could sex with Leo possibly hurt when he had the
ability to melt her bones and turn her body to mush? He
just had to look to her and she burned. His touch set her

alight. And his mouth…well…it was a wicked, wonderful thing. Willow was no expert, obviously, but surely the chemistry they shared had to be off the charts. It would be glorious, fireworks and ecstasy from start to finish.

But it wasn't just the physical aspect of what they'd done and what she wanted to do that so appealed. Spending time with Selene and listening to her tales of adventure and passion had emphasised how staid and small her own life was in comparison. Adventure was hard to come by when work was haphazard and income was irregular. Romantic relationships—even love-free ones—were out of the question with the disruption her endometriosis caused and the possibility of infertility.

However, tonight she'd had a glimpse of both adventure *and* passion—until they'd been interrupted and he'd spooked, which was understandable, given where they'd been, what they'd been doing and his distaste for scandal. It had been sublime and she couldn't help thinking, what if they hadn't been heckled by Zander? Would Leo have manoeuvred her into a dark corner to continue with the kissing in private? Would he have taken things even further and given her the experience she so badly wanted?

She didn't know and quite possibly never would. His parting shot had been definitive and now, with the way he was cutting a determined path through the guests and striding towards the door with only a brief stop for a quick word with the happy couple, it looked as though he planned to leave.

With every purposeful step away from her he took, the hope and excitement whipping through her system withered that little bit more, deflating her by the second.

Would she ever again meet someone like him? Someone who had such an extraordinarily intense effect on her? It didn't seem likely. Men like him didn't grow on trees.

So why was she standing here like a lemon?

Why wasn't she going after him and telling him she wanted more?

What was she *doing*?

She had nothing to lose and everything to gain from pursuing the passion she'd just experienced. Who cared if they were as different as two people could be? She wasn't after a happy-ever-after with him. She wasn't after that with *anyone*. She just wanted one night.

And if he didn't?

Well, she was tough enough to handle rejection, should it come to that. Fighting to establish a career in the notoriously tight-knit art world had strengthened her determination to go for what she wanted, and right now she wanted him and more of the excitement he'd shown her. Her mother's sudden death had proved that life was short, and she'd far rather regret something she had done than something she hadn't.

So, yielding to the instinct that was now drumming so insistently through her and blocking out the voice in her head demanding to know if she'd gone stark, raving mad, Willow galvanised into action. Because if Leo *was* leaving, then he wasn't leaving alone.

The large silver car pulled up outside the hotel just as Leo pushed through the heavy glass door and emerged into the warm Athens night. He stashed the phone he'd used to summon it in the inside pocket of his dinner jacket and jogged down the steps to the pavement. With a brief nod at Stavros, the chauffeur who was now holding open the rear door nearest the kerb, he climbed in, instantly welcoming the peace and seclusion.

The door closed with a soft *thunk*, shutting out the madness and the chaos, and relief flooded his system. He'd had such a lucky escape, he thought grimly, tugging at one end of his bow tie to loosen the knot, then undoing the top two buttons of his dress shirt and feeling as though he could breathe for the first time in hours.

Could he even begin to hope that his moment of complete and utter insanity had been witnessed by no one but his brother? It had been dark. The dance floor had been crowded. On the other hand, in a sea of more muted colours, Willow's yellow dress drew attention and her eye-catching hair—so thick and soft and silky wrapped around his fingers—shone like a beacon.

But no.

He was being idiotic. He had nothing to worry about. Even if anyone had seen him lose his head, they wouldn't risk his displeasure by gossiping about it. Many there tonight had lucrative business dealings with him. The rest sought them. There was no cause for concern. On that front, at least. Walking out on his sister's wedding, however? That would not have gone unnoticed—at least, not by his family—which was yet another thing he'd no doubt have to deal with in the morning.

Leo sat back against the butter-soft leather and rubbed his eyes, a wave of weariness washing over him. He could sleep for a week. But he was flying to New York tomorrow evening to discuss a potential shipping merger that would add billions to the company's bottom line, so that wasn't happening. Once he'd tied things up there, he had a series of board meetings in London to host. And at some point he'd have to put a stop to the unveiling of a portrait that might well make him a global laughing stock if it went on show. Relaxing, taking some time out, was but a distant dream.

As was peace and seclusion clearly, because barely had Stavros taken his place behind the wheel when the other back door of the car suddenly flung open, shattering the silence and jolting him out of his thoughts. A second later, in a blur of colour, movement and sparkle, into the car and onto the seat slid Willow.

Leo jerked upright, his muscles rigid with tension. His heart crashed against his ribs and a powerful combination of shock and alarm pummelled through him.

What the hell?

'Hi,' she said with one of those dazzling smiles that had too often stunned him into speechlessness, but to which now, thanks to the swift reconstruction of his iron-clad control back there on the dance floor, he was immune.

'Get out.'

'That's rude.'

He stared at her, barely able to believe his ears. She had a nerve. 'What's rude is you ambushing me in my car and invading my space.'

'Needs must.'

He clenched his jaw. 'What do you want, Willow?'

'I was hoping you might be able to give me a lift.'

No. Absolutely not. It was out of the question. The back of his car, which he'd always considered airily spacious, suddenly felt unnervingly claustrophobic. When she'd hopped in, the oxygen had whooshed out. Her scent filled his head. Despite the ample width of the seat, he could feel the hot energy she radiated. And something else. Something that had the hairs on the back of his neck quivering and his pulse racing, which he needed like a hole in the head.

Ignoring the entire bloody lot of it, Leo reached into his jacket pocket and extracted his phone. 'I'll call you a cab.'

At that, Willow frowned. 'No, no,' she said, shaking her head, which made the beads in her hair catch the overhead light and twinkle. 'That's no good at all.'

'Too bad.'

'Where are you going?'

'To bed.'

'That will do.'

She settled back and made herself comfortable and he had to dig deep to quell both the furious frustration that surged inside him at her intransigence and the volcano of heat that erupted at the thought of her in his bed. 'Are you going to do as I ask and get out of my car?'

'No.'

Having shoved his phone back in his jacket pocket, Leo leaned forwards, pressed a button on the panel that separated the back from the front and said in English, 'Stavros, please take Miss Jacobs wherever she wishes to go. I'll walk.'

He turned to yank open the door, practically tasting fresh air and freedom, when suddenly her body slammed into his back and her hand landed on his arm. Leo froze.

His senses reeled. Willow was curled around him in the darkness, and he could barely breathe.

'OK, wait,' she said, so close her warm breath tickled his neck while his arm appeared to be on fire. 'Forget the lift. It was just an excuse. I wanted to talk to you.'

He didn't need to know. He didn't *want* to know. There'd been too much talking for one night already. What he wanted was to shake her off and get out of the damn car, even if such a dramatic move did attract the attention of the guests trickling out of the hotel to make their own way home. But her proximity and her touch were pulverising his reason and clawing at his control so instead he heard himself saying, 'What about?'

'About carrying on where we left off. On the dance floor. About doing as your brother suggested and getting a room.'

There was a rushing in his head. A pounding in his chest. And all he could think was *Yes, yes, yes* until into the madness, thank God, plunged a much-needed arrow of cold, hard discipline.

Steeling himself, he removed her hand from his arm and abruptly shifted around to make her scuttle back. 'No.'

'Why not?' she said, to his irritation barely moving at all. 'You seemed pretty into it.' Her gaze dropped to his mouth and her face filled with a dreamy sort of hunger that tightened his chest for a moment. 'That kiss was something else.'

'The kiss was nothing,' he said bluntly, refusing to allow the scorching memory of it into his head and instead offering up heartfelt thanks to whoever had made the decision to tint the car's windows.

'It wasn't. I felt you. Hard. Against me.'

The area in question throbbed and his pulse skipped a beat, but Leo squared his jaw even more and ignored both in favour of a lie. 'It was merely an instinctive response to the environment.' An anathema, in other words. Because, generally speaking, nothing he did was instinctive and he was never affected by an environment. A blip. That was what that moment on the dance floor had been. A momentary lapse after a very stressful day. 'It was nothing out of the ordinary.'

'Don't be so modest.'

The faint smile tugging at her lips fired his mounting irritation at her continued refusal to do as he commanded. 'You're finding this amusing.'

'Not at all,' she said with enviable aplomb. 'I simply know what I want and am intent on getting it.'

'Reverse our roles and this conversation would border on harassment. In fact, it does, even as things stand.'

'Reverse our roles and we'd be naked already because I'd put up no resistance.'

Despite his best efforts, Leo had no defence against the images that cascaded into his head then. They were too many and too vivid. Bodies glued together. Mouths joined, limbs entwined, glorious multicoloured hair spread out on the pillow or swishing down the length of his body. Heat, sweat, breathy moans and soft little cries. In his mind's eye, he could see and hear it all.

'You're playing with fire,' he warned, his voice rough

and thick with the desire that, to his consternation, he was struggling and failing to keep at bay.

A glowing light shimmered and danced in the depths of her emerald eyes. 'Is that a threat or a promise?'

Either. Both. He didn't know. 'A threat.'

'I'm OK with getting burned.'

'Are you?'

'Yes,' she said. 'I am very OK with it. In fact, I positively *yearn* to get burned.'

She might think that, but she had no idea that deep inside him lurked the well-buried traces of the youth he'd once been, the fierce, fearless kid who threw tantrums and took risks and crashed boats. No idea what might result if he relinquished his tightly held grip on his control entirely and those traces broke free of the bonds that shackled them to smash to pieces his veneer of civility and take over. Hell, since it had never happened before, even he had no idea of the raging wildness he could be capable of as an adult and the fallout it could incur unleashed. Burning might be the least of it.

'Forget it.'

'One night, Leo,' she said softly, seductively, stealing his wits and scattering his objections to the wind. 'That's all I want. Truly. I can't imagine I'm your usual type. I doubt I'm nearly chic or sophisticated enough for a worldly yet cynical billionaire like you. Relationships aren't my thing and besides, I have my career to focus on. One night together, I'll leave in the morning and you need never see me again. It's nothing to get worked up about. It's just sex. But if you truly have a problem with that, if you really want me to get out of this car and leave you alone, I will.'

She stopped, waiting breathlessly, the pulse at the base of her neck pounding, and all he could think in the thick thunderingly silent darkness was that he wanted nothing less than to be left alone. He wanted her beyond comprehension, beyond reason, and he couldn't deny it any longer.

There'd been an inevitability to this conversation from the moment she'd invaded his space and shattered his peace. He'd had many opportunities to exit the car and leave her to it yet he'd taken none of them. So what was the point of continuing to fight a battle he'd already lost? And why would he even want to when it had been so long since he'd done something purely for himself?

He'd been overthinking things, that was the trouble. He'd been unsettled by the strength of the desire Willow aroused in him and what that might imply. But it needn't imply anything. He wouldn't lose his head. He never had with a woman before.

And of course he didn't have a problem with a one-night stand, even though for him it would be a first, which was odd, come to think of it, considering he'd got through his fair share of the opposite sex in his younger days. Sure, such behaviour seemed rash and reckless by its very nature and spontaneity hadn't been a word in his vocabulary for years, but he could see the merit in one now. Unaddressed, the relentlessly erotic dreams he'd been having in which she featured so heavily would drive him demented. Addressed, by sunrise, the desire with which he burned could be assuaged and the status quo by which he lived could be restored.

One night spent engaged in the pursuit of ecstasy with a gorgeous, sexy woman who wanted the same...

Maximum pleasure, minimal conversation, no aftermath...

And why, exactly, was he resisting?

'All right,' he growled, all the reasons as to why this was a bad idea wiped out by thoughts of what lay ahead, which accelerated his pulse and hardened his body. 'Fine. Just one night.'

With one last dark, smouldering glance in her direction, Leo hit the button in the panel again and said in Greek something that Willow supposed went along the lines of 'Change of plan—drive us to my house,' and swamped her with relief.

The intended outcome of their conversation had been touch-and-go for a while. Leo had put up quite the opposition, although she had no idea why. She obviously had limited experience, but how many men turned down the offer of no strings attached sex? Not many, she was willing to bet.

But whatever had been going in his head, he'd succumbed in the end. Her instinct, which had told her she hadn't imagined the heat of the kiss and that despite his accusations of harassment he really didn't come across as the sort of man who could be coerced into doing anything he didn't want to do, had been right. Embracing tenacity instead of deliberating for too long and losing one's nerve was definitely the way forward.

Leo was broodingly silent as the sleek car slid smoothly through the dark streets of the city. He stared out of the window, tight of jaw and rigid of body, although whether that was because he was still annoyed at the result of the conversation or simply didn't trust himself to look at her was anyone's guess.

Willow tried to settle into the seat, but she was so aware of him, of every breath he took and every move he made, that it was impossible to relax. Her imagination, even though it had nothing to base anything on, was running riot. If not for the presence of the clearly unflappable Stavros on the other side of the partition she'd have scooted over to Leo's side of the seat and made a start on the night ahead already.

'So where are we going?' she said, partly to cut through the sizzling tension, partly because it was a question she should probably have asked earlier.

'Kolonaki,' he muttered, his gaze fixed on the world of elegant shadowy buildings and bright city lights beyond the window. 'I have an apartment there.'

'Is it far?'

'Ten minutes.'

Willow shivered. A ten-minute build-up and then, pow! She could hardly wait. 'Where's home?' she asked, deciding that time might pass more speedily with conversation than silence, however sticky.

'Santorini.'

'Have you lived there for long?'

'A couple of years. On and off.'

'Selene said the business has offices all over the world.'

'Hundreds of them.'

'As CEO you must travel a lot.'

'I do. Tomorrow evening, I'm flying to New York.'

'Don't worry,' she said, getting the message loud and clear. 'I'll be long gone by then. What are you doing there?'

'Discussing a merger.'

'From one merger to another.'

He slid her a heavy-lidded glance that fired every nerve ending she possessed. The most devastating smile played at his mouth, a glint appeared in his eye, and suddenly her stomach was flipping about all over the place. 'Quite.'

'So,' she said, scolding herself for responding so absurdly to a mere glint and a smile. 'Is there anything you want to know about me?'

'Are you always this nosy?'

She wasn't, but she didn't much care. Conversation was not only passing the time, it was also keeping her nerves under control, which was a bonus. 'Only with men I'm going to sleep with.'

'And is that a common occurrence?'

It wasn't an occurrence at all. Which was something she should probably admit. Leo had to be far more experienced than she was so he was bound to realise at some point that she hadn't a clue what she was doing. Surely it would be better to clarify the situation and neutralise any issue he may have with it now than in the midst of the action.

'No.' She took a deep breath and mentally braced herself for what was no doubt going to be a pretty excruciating conversation. 'In fact, this is a first for me.'

There was a beat of silence. The arch of an eyebrow. And then, 'What do you mean?'

'I've never done this before.'

'Issued an indecent proposition? Or had a one-night stand?'

'Both.'

'That makes two of us.'

Interesting, but possibly irrelevant right now. 'I've never actually slept with anyone before either.'

He stared at her in the shadowy darkness, a flicker of astonishment darting across his face. 'You're a virgin?'

'I am,' she confirmed with a nod. 'It's no big deal, obviously. But I thought you should know. In case I do something wrong. I assume you're not.'

'Not since I was sixteen.'

That came as no surprise. He'd probably been as irresistible then as he was now, at the age of thirty-one. How many women had there been in the intervening fifteen years? Why had he never married any of them? Unimportant questions, both of them. All she cared about was the here and now. 'Does my inexperience put you off?'

'No,' he said, but she caught a glimmer of doubt in his eyes, which suggested otherwise and needed to be speedily addressed.

'I hope you're not going to back out because of some antiquated notion of virginity and its value and force me to find someone else.'

'I should.'

'Why?'

'Do you really want your first time to be a one-night stand?'

Yes. That was exactly what she wanted and all she could ever have with the mountainous emotional baggage she carried. Even if she didn't have a giant stumbling block when it came to love, it wouldn't be fair to expect someone to commit to her when her life revolved around her menstrual cycle, when for approximately five days in every month she had to take to her bed, when staying positive was a battle she didn't always win, when she might not be able to ever have children.

Should she tell Leo about the physical baggage she also came with? Despite her conviction that sex with him would be fabulous, there was the chance it might not be and he perhaps ought to be alerted to that possibility. On the other hand, disclosing her virginity and persuading him it didn't matter was turning out to be risky enough. What if her endometriosis—on top of everything else—proved to be a tipping point and he simply figured that she was too much hassle?

No. She wouldn't do anything to jeopardise the night ahead, and that level of emotional intimacy wasn't necessary or appropriate for a one-night stand anyway. Of course everything would be fine. And if it wasn't, well, really, how bad could it actually be?

'I don't much care how it happens,' she said, clearing her head of these discombobulating thoughts and focusing instead on eradicating any reservations Leo might have. 'I just want fireworks. Our kiss on the dance floor suggested that you can provide them. Not all women get to say that about their first time.'

'You're basing a lot on a kiss.'

'I've had dozens of kisses. None of them like that. Have you ever had any complaints?'

'Not to my knowledge.'

'I didn't think so. I know you'll give me what I want, Leo. I trust you to show me stars.'

One agonisingly long second ticked by, then another.

'Would you really find someone else?' he eventually asked with an assessing tilt of his head.

Of course she wouldn't. She'd never met anyone who affected her the way he did, who transported her to a level of pleasure where pain couldn't possibly exist. She certainly wasn't willing to take a risk on this with just anyone. But she wasn't having him back out now, and the way he'd seen off his brother earlier suggested he had a competitive, possessive and possibly even jealous streak.

'Absolutely,' she lied, mentally crossing her fingers. 'I'm twenty-four. It's beyond a joke.'

He seemed to consider this for a moment, undoubtedly weighing up the pros and cons, then said in a voice that was low, gruff and sent delicious tingles to places she didn't know she had, 'Everyone deserves fireworks.'

Relieved beyond belief, Willow inwardly grinned. Excitement churned through her. Her heart pounded. This was going to be, without question, the most exciting night of her life. 'They do indeed.'

# CHAPTER FIVE

ANY QUALMS LEO might have had about bedding a virgin had vanished the minute Willow mentioned having to find someone else. The thought of it had boiled his blood and once again, the words *hell, no* had flashed through his head. He didn't know why. Possessiveness wasn't his thing. He'd never once warned Zander off anyone, and he didn't get a kick from the thought of being the first man to show Willow what her body was capable of. He wasn't that unreconstructed a male.

Perhaps the strength of his reaction was down to the certainty that he—and only he—could provide the fireworks she wanted. As unlikely a pairing as they were on paper, their chemistry was exceptional and unique. Or maybe it was because the fact that she trusted him made him feel he could take on the world. Either way, it didn't much matter. The deal was sealed.

He couldn't begin to fathom how she was still a virgin when she looked the way she did, oozed such confidence and flirted so adeptly, but it was nothing to be concerned about. In fact, it could turn out to be a blessing. He'd have to proceed with caution and exercise restraint. He wouldn't be able to lose control even if he wanted to, which, as always, he absolutely did not.

While Leo's thoughts turned to the many things he planned to do to Willow once in close proximity to a bed, Stavros swung the car off the road, drove through a pair of gates and down a tunnel that led to the underground car park. The minute the car came to a halt, Leo sprang out of it, heart pounding, body primed, and strode around the back to the other side. He yanked open the door and held out his hand, which Willow immediately took, exiting the car with far more decorum than he had. He muttered a curt *kalinikta* to Stavros and then marched her to the lift. One quick press of his forefinger to the reader and the doors opened with a soft swoosh. He hustled her in and a moment later they closed, shutting out everything but her and him and the night to come.

The air within the confined space seemed to vibrate with taut anticipation, the electricity sizzling between them practically visible. Her scent, even more intense now than in the car, enveloped him and seeped into him, winding around every fibre of his being. She stood so close they were almost touching. He could feel her heat. Sense her urgency. But he wouldn't touch her. Not yet. He could hold on for the ten seconds it would take for the lift to reach his apartment. Of course he could. He wasn't an animal.

At least he wasn't until he made the mistake of casting her a quick sideways glance. One look at the deep flush on her cheeks, the rapid rise and fall of her chest and the scorching haze of desire in the eyes that were gazing into his and all his good intentions evaporated. To know that she wanted him as much as he wanted her pulverised what few wits he'd been clinging on to, and whether he turned to her first or she turned to him, he neither knew nor cared. All that mattered was that one minute they were staring at each other, as if frozen in time, and the next, something snapped and they were plastered against each other, mouths colliding, teeth clashing, hands everywhere.

As the kiss heated and deepened, Leo backed Willow up against the wall of the lift and pinned her in place with his hips. She melted against him and moaned. The wave of lust that rolled over him nearly took out his knees. His heart pounded. His ears popped. His blood rushed round his body like liquid fire.

Becoming dimly aware that the doors had opened—when had that happened?—Leo wrenched his mouth from hers, shifted his hold on her and scooped her up. He didn't allow himself to be derailed by her breathy gasp of surprise that would have had him depositing her on the nearest flat surface, which was the floor. Or by the fact that, having zero time for romance and all the fraught messy emotions that came with it, this was the first time he'd ever held the soft warm weight of a woman in his arms. It didn't occur to him to offer her a drink or something to eat. He simply carried her straight down the wide shadowy hall and into his bedroom at the end of it.

'That was very masterful,' she said breathlessly once he'd reached the bed and reluctantly lowered her to the floor.

'I was going for efficient, but I'll take masterful.'

'What do I do?'

Leo's heart thudded. His mouth dried. He'd never experienced anticipation like it. He was so hard he hurt. So addled with desire he was incapable of issuing instructions. 'Whatever you want.'

Willow tilted her head and bit her lip, as if thinking it through for a moment. Then she put her hands to the buttons of his shirt and started undoing them from the bottom up. Every time her fingers brushed against his skin, his muscles flinched and he hissed out a breath.

'I know I said I wanted to draw you,' she said softly as she pushed his shirt and jacket off his shoulders and down his arms, 'but I think I'd rather sculpt you. You are constructed quite magnificently. You'd look exceptional in marble.'

'Thank you. I think.'

However, with her hands running so lightly and teasingly over his torso it was becoming increasingly impossible to think full stop. Especially when she brushed a thumb over his nipple and then leaned forwards to lick it.

'Are you sure you haven't done this before?' he said, his voice thick and hoarse.

'I'm just doing what I want,' she murmured against his skin. 'It was your idea.'

And a mistake, in hindsight. Because he could feel her touch everywhere, like a brand, and it was undoing him so fast he was a hair's breadth from picking her up again and tossing her onto the bed.

Gritting his teeth and ruthlessly resisting the urge to do exactly that, he batted her hand away and pulled her into his arms instead. He buried one hand in her hair and caressed her satiny smooth bare back with the other and kissed her until she was letting out the soft little moans he'd so easily imagined and pressing against him even more tightly.

In response to the rocketing need to be skin to skin,

Leo slipped his hands beneath the drapey straps of her dress. As he drew them down her arms, the bodice slithered to her waist and then, with a minute wiggle of her hips, to the floor.

'This dress just gets better and better,' he muttered as she stepped out of it and then stood there in nothing more than gold heels and white lace knickers.

'There's less of it than I'd have liked.'

'Why waste fabric?' He felt a tremble ripple through her, stilled for a second, and frowned. 'Are you all right?'

'I'm fighting the urge to cover myself up like the virgin I am.'

'Nervous?'

She swallowed hard and gave a tiny nod. 'A little.'

His heart thumped. 'Are you having second thoughts?'

'Not a chance.'

'You can back out at any time.'

'I won't.'

'*Theos*, you're beautiful.'

'So are you.'

'Get on the bed. Keep the heels.'

Doing as he instructed, for once, Willow sank onto the bed and shifted up it, the moonlight spilling into the room turning her hair to silver and her skin to pearl. Leo kicked off his shoes and stripped off his trousers, shorts and socks with far more haste than elegance, dizzyingly aware she was watching his every move. Her gaze lingered on his erection and she let out a little raspy sort of sigh, which, ridiculously yet inevitably, made it swell and harden even more.

He came down beside her and rolled over her. His

mouth fused to hers, her eyes fluttered shut and with a moan, she lifted her arms to his neck. She ran her hands across his shoulders and over his back and his muscles twitched at the contact. She hitched her knee up and shifted to fit herself better against him.

With desire drumming hot and hard inside him, Leo planted his hand on her leg and ran it up her silky-smooth thigh. He skimmed over the dip of her waist to her breast, and she arched into him. Desperate to taste more of her, he wrenched his mouth from hers and trailed it down her neck and over the gentle slope of her chest. When he closed it over her tight, hard nipple, she gasped and dug her fingers into his hair.

He could feel her trembling. Her ragged little pants stoked his need to unbearable levels. But he couldn't lift himself up and thrust into her as he so badly wanted to. He had to take his time, even if it killed him.

Focusing solely on her and her reactions, Leo slid his hand down her taut abdomen and slipped it beneath the waistband of her pants. Instinctively or not, the knee she'd hitched up fell back, granting him better access to her slick heat, issuing an invitation he could not possibly refuse. He pressed his fingers against the centre of her pleasure and she jerked for a moment before relaxing and breathing, 'Oh, my God.'

She pulled his head up and crushed her mouth to his, kissing him deeply and passionately while her hips began to respond to the movements of his fingers. His head spun as he slipped them inside her. His pulse hammered. She gasped and groaned and within moments she was panting and throwing her head back and crying out his name as she came apart in his arms, faster and harder than he could possibly have envisaged.

'OK?' he said, thinking he'd never seen anything so magnificent as he watched her recover and wondering if he'd ever forget the sight of it.

She gave him a languid smile that tightened his chest in the oddest way. 'I've never felt so good in my life.'

'It gets better.'

'I don't see how it could.'

'Just wait.'

He moved away from her to locate and apply a condom, which took an age since his hands were shaking so badly and required more self-control than he'd ever imagined he possessed. Then he returned to her, his pulse racing at the excitement that glowed in her eyes and the flush on her cheeks. He parted her legs and positioned himself at her entrance and as he captured her mouth in a searing kiss, pushed into her as slowly and carefully as he could, noting her response, hearing her sharp, shuddery gasp, allowing her time to adjust.

Once lodged inside her, he held himself still so she could get used to the unfamiliar feel of him, every muscle he possessed rigid with the effort of restraint. She was so tight, so hot, so wet. He'd never experienced anything like it. His heart pounded. Need roared through him. His control was hanging on by a thread that was fraying by the second, but he clung on to it, because he would not give in, he would not allow his baser instincts to dominate, until she shifted and took him in further and suddenly something inside him snapped.

An overwhelming need to move gripped every cell

in his body. He craved the delicious friction of his flesh sliding against hers with a desperation he couldn't contain. His vision blurred and his head spun. He had to be in her deeper and harder, and as he helplessly succumbed to the drugging desire, she felt so incredible, so unbelievably good, he was losing what was left of his mind.

But then, suddenly, she was twisting her head to the side, pushing at his shoulders, his chest, struggling to dislodge him and kick him off. She was sobbing, 'Stop. Please. Stop,' and everything in him and around him, his body, his heart, the room, *everything,* instantly froze.

In response to the plea that tore from her mouth, Leo jerked as if struck, immediately pulled out of her and reared back. Despite the moonlit shadows, Willow could see that he was as white as the sheets tangled around them. Horror and confusion replaced the wild heat and fierce concentration that had dominated his expression a moment ago, and as she instinctively winced at the acute discomfort of his sharp withdrawal, she wished with all her heart that she hadn't had to call such an abrupt halt to the proceedings.

She'd been having such a good time. The flattering urgency with which he'd yanked her from the car and bundled her into the lift had heated the desire simmering inside her to boiling point. When he'd swept her into his arms and carried her through his apartment to his bedroom, she could have swooned. She'd had a sense of space and air, of high ceilings, thick curtains and ornate decoration, but then he'd removed her dress and his clothes and that had been that for coherent thought. Her nerves had simply melted away. There'd been nothing remotely ice-cold or robotic about him then. She'd never felt so desired.

She'd been right about trusting him to give her what she'd so desperately wanted. The fierce need that had blazed in his eyes as he'd joined her on the bed had set her on fire. The orgasm he'd wrung from her—so much better anything she'd managed herself—had been mind-blowing, and the intense pleasure she'd experienced had gone on and on.

But she'd been wrong about it being enough because when he'd thrust into her, God, it had hurt. She'd felt as if she'd been impaled on a red-hot poker. She'd willed the stabs of needle-sharp pain to lessen, to disappear altogether, hoping against hope that they related to her inexperience, but then he'd started moving and they hadn't. To her distress, they'd worsened, the searing pain spreading a throbbing ache to her abdomen, demolishing the desire and dominating her thoughts, and she simply hadn't been able to bear it.

How naive she'd been to assume that everything would be fine, despite all she knew about her condition. How she wished she'd told him about it back in the car when she'd had the opportunity. She'd been right to be scared all along. Right to avoid sex. She should never have tried to convince herself otherwise. But regret and analysis would have to wait. She had a man in a state of shock to deal with.

'I hurt you,' Leo said gruffly, staring down at her, stunned, clearly appalled, before lifting himself completely off her and jerkily moving away.

Grabbing a sheet and pulling it over herself, Willow rolled onto her side and instinctively curled into the foetal position in an attempt to ease the pain.

'Well, yes,' she admitted, as to her relief the stabbing began to fade. 'But it wasn't—'

'I'm sorry.' He swung round to sit on the edge of the bed, his broad back to her, and shoved hands that looked to be shaking through his hair.

'It's not your fault.'

'I was too rough.'

What? 'No,' she said firmly. 'That's not it at all. Really.'

'I can't believe I missed something,' he said hoarsely.

'You didn't miss anything. Honestly.'

'I should have been more considerate. More patient.'

'You were everything I'd hoped for.'

Even she could hear the sincerity and urgency in her voice, but he obviously wasn't listening to her. It was as if he'd retreated into his own world, a world of misconception and, perhaps, guilt, which she suddenly felt the pressing need to address, whether he heard her or not, because she was not having him thinking he was to blame for this. This was *her* fault.

The pain that had crucified her earlier had dulled to a bearable ache and she uncurled herself, sat up and took a deep breath. 'What just happened is nothing to do with you, Leo,' she said, actually rather glad he had his back to her for the very personal and potentially mortifying explanation she was going to have to give. 'It really isn't. It's me. I have endometriosis. It's a condition where tissue similar to the lining of the womb grows in other places,

like the ovaries and things. A nightmare. Anyway. One of
the many hideous side effects can be painful sex. That's
one of the reasons why I'm—or at least, *was*—a virgin.
I already experience quite a bit of pain every month and
the risk of more never appealed. But then you kissed me
on that dance floor and suddenly none of that seemed rel-
evant. I've never met anyone who turns me on the way
you do. You just have to look at me to make me melt.
You short-circuit my brain with the slightest of touches.
I really had hoped that with you it would be OK. I really
wanted it to be and maybe if I'd had more experience it
would have been. I'm devastated beyond belief it wasn't.'

She stopped to give him the chance to respond. To perhaps accept her apology and thank her for her explanation. He might request more information and assure her
he understood. More likely, he'd renew his offer to call
her a cab and send her on her way, which would also be
acceptable, if disappointing. But he didn't do anything.
He just sat there in the silvery moonlit silence that taut-
ened and thickened with every passing second, and it was
every bit as awful as she'd feared.

What was he thinking? That she was a freak? A tease?
An object of pity? She didn't want to know. In fact, right
now, all she wanted was to go. She was feeling cold and
embarrassed and horribly vulnerable. The loss of her virginity and the stunning orgasm she'd had now counted
for nothing. Fire had turned to ash. Leo was still utterly
frozen, apparently oblivious to her, his head in his hands,
and it was excruciating.

'I realise this isn't what you signed up for,' she said,
swallowing down the lump in her throat with difficulty.

'This wasn't the deal we made. If anyone should apologise, it's me. I didn't think it would be an issue, but I should have at least warned you it could be. I'm really sorry I didn't. I'm really sorry this happened.'

Gutted, disappointed and humiliated at the way the night had ended, but also deeply relieved she'd never have to see him and face this again, Willow eased off the bed and slipped on her dress.

'Have a good trip,' she said, and without looking back, she fled.

Generally speaking, Leo had little time for regret. He wasn't rash. Every decision he made was deliberately and lengthily considered, so he knew beyond doubt that it was the right one to take at the time. Therefore, he rarely looked back to contemplate whether he could or should have done something differently, even on the extremely rare occasion he made the wrong call.

However, over the course of the next few days, whether discussing the merger in New York, sitting through the series of interminable board meetings in London or ignoring Zander's puerile texts about the dance floor kiss and his siblings' interest in his premature exit from the wedding, he came to deeply regret the way the night with Willow had ended.

He had not handled it well. That he'd been so stunned and horrified at the thought he'd hurt her he hadn't been able to even think straight, let alone respond to what she'd told him—most of which had been muffled by the white noise in his head anyway—was no excuse. He should have found a way through the chaos. He should have asked her to repeat what she'd told him and explain it in more detail.

How he could have allowed her to leave like that, to emerge onto the dark city streets and make her way back to wherever she was staying, alone and in pain, he had no idea. That wasn't him. He took care of those around him. He did everything in his power to prevent anguish. Or so he'd always believed.

Whenever he thought of the events of that night—which was pretty much 24-7—he broke out into a cold sweat. He couldn't get the memory of Willow begging him to stop out of his head. The desperation in her voice cut through his thoughts like a knife. How had he not noticed her discomfort? How long had she put up with it before becoming unable to take any more and pushing him off? What madness had driven him to such, well, *madness*? Chemistry? Genetics? What?

From time to time over the years, Leo had wondered what the fallout might be if he ever lost control. He'd assumed that once the spinning plates had smashed on the ground he'd be exposed for the fraud he suspected he was. He'd imagined that as before, the emotions he kept such a tight lid on would burst free and the resentment he still bore deep down would surge up. Mistakes with regard to the business would once again be made and the family's fortunes would flounder. But he'd never imagined that he could be capable of causing someone pain—all his adult life he'd striven to do the opposite—and the resultant guilt at having done so was unbearable.

So if he had any sense at all, he'd track Willow down and apologise properly for both what he'd done and how he'd dealt with it. He'd throw himself on her mercy and beg her for forgiveness, and then he might finally get some peace.

But he didn't.

Because, despite all that, drawing a line under everything and consigning her to history didn't feel right. He still dreamed of her. He still wanted her. The fact that she'd chosen him over anyone else to relieve her of her virginity burned a trail through his brain, along with the revelation that he melted her with a look and frazzled her thoughts with a touch.

He didn't like the notion that a passionate vibrant woman like her was unable to experience the heady delights of great sex. He didn't appreciate the feeling of failure or the fact that the impression she had of him now had to be less than favourable. Their business felt unfinished, the mistakes he'd made clawed at his gut, and all he could think about was reparation.

So he wouldn't be banning the unveiling event that he'd learned from Atticus his mother was planning. In fact, he'd be attending it. It would provide the perfect opportunity to talk to Willow, which he might not get otherwise. And quite frankly, a couple of hours of discomfort at having to come face-to-face with the work that had given him sleepless nights was a small price to pay for the chance to right so many wrongs.

# CHAPTER SIX

FOR THE UNVEILING of her portrait—which, to Willow's surprise and relief, had gone ahead without any intervention—Selene had commandeered the top floor of an exclusive Athens nightclub and rustled up two hundred of her closest friends. Willow had no clue how she'd achieved either with such short notice but presumably those were the perks of being rich and infamous.

Eight days had passed since the disastrous night she'd spent with Leo. It had taken her some time and a concerted effort to be able to think of it without squirming with embarrassment and overheating, but keeping busy had helped. There'd been this evening to prepare for and the contacts she'd made at the party to follow up on.

Going home to her studio in London when there was so much to do here and so little time in which to do it hadn't made sense, but the downsides of staying in Athens in the interim, of course, were the constant reminders of the society wedding of the year. The newsstands were filled with magazines that bore official photos of the bride and groom on the cover. It was only through sheer willpower that Willow had managed to resist the temptation to buy one. She had no desire to see if Leo featured within. She had business and a career to attend to and a night of regret and humiliation to cast into oblivion for good.

Fortunately for that goal, there was no danger of him showing up here tonight and bringing it all back up again. The portrait was huge, spotlit and centre stage. She'd been interviewed and photographed for half a dozen international publications already and one person after another had come up to compliment her on her work. But while she was practically bursting with pride and delight at the response, tonight's unveiling had to be Leo's worst nightmare made real. Which was a shame, really, because no one was gossiping, no one was sniggering, and if only he could get over his issues with it, he'd see that the portrait truly was a—

'So this is it.'

At the sound of the deep, gravelly voice a foot to her right, Willow nearly jumped out of her skin. She whipped round, her heart pounding as if she'd run a hundred metres in ten seconds, to find the man who'd made no bones about his distaste for the portrait, the man she'd assumed would be a million miles away on a night like this, standing beside her and staring straight at it.

One glance at his strong, stern profile and tall muscled body clad in blue jeans and a loose white linen shirt and the memory of the two of them wrapped around each other on his sheets, him blowing her mind before everything went horribly wrong, flew into her head, blurring her vision and crushing the breath from her lungs.

But she forced it out and blinked and breathed and willed her heartbeat to slow. This was a professional event for her. She had to focus on that. She would not dwell on what had happened in his bedroom or allow a return of the mortification she'd worked so hard to eradicate. She didn't need to know what he'd been doing lately or if he'd thought about her at all and in what context. She was all about looking forwards, and not just at the portrait.

'This is it,' she said coolly.

He examined the work from top to bottom and then back up again, his expression inscrutable. 'I didn't know my mother owned a throne.'

'It's not just any old throne,' she said, more than happy to keep the conversation solely on the art. 'It's a replica of Louis the Fourteenth's.'

'Of course it is.'

'She had it made specially. To go with the tiara.'

'The tiara originally belonged to my grandmother.'

'So I understand.'

'She was one hundred and fifty centimetres tall and the same wide,' he said with an assessing tilt of his head. 'I can't imagine her in quite such a pose.'

'Selene drapes—and smoulders—very well.'

'She should. She's had plenty of practice.' He leaned forwards and frowned at the tiny red heart on the inner thigh of his mother's right leg, which was hooked over one gilded arm of the ornate throne. 'Is that a tattoo?'

'It is,' she confirmed. 'She had it done two years ago. A birthday present for a former lover. She thought a portrait might be less painful this time.'

The one eyebrow she could see rose. 'Less painful for whom?'

Willow bit her lip to prevent the smile that developed at Leo's wry observation since he still hadn't said what he thought of the piece and for some reason that was annoying.

'Lazlo likes it,' she said, reminding herself yet again that his opinion was as irrelevant as his approval. Her clients—past, present and future—were the only people who mattered. 'He's going to hang it in his bedroom.'

Leo grimaced. 'I know,' he said. 'I saw him when I arrived a few minutes ago.'

'You missed his speech. It was very impassioned.'

'I dare say I can live with the disappointment.'

'Given your antipathy towards the work, I am rather surprised you didn't try and put a stop to this evening.'

'That was the original plan.'

'What happened?'

'The plan changed.'

'With your need for order and control, that must have been irritating.'

The glimmer of a smile hovered at his sensual mouth. 'You'd think so, wouldn't you?'

'So is it as bad as you feared?' she asked, giving up all pretence of indifference because she might as well admit she badly needed to know one way or another. 'The picture, I mean.'

'Not quite,' he replied after a moment's consideration. 'Obviously, it's not something I'd have on my wall, but you were right. It *is* tasteful. And unexpectedly beautiful. You are exceptionally talented.'

The intense delight that spun through her at his praise nearly took out her knees. She filled with the disturbing urge to throw herself at him and smother him in kisses, which was bizarre. She remained where she was and offered up a small smile instead. 'Thank you.'

'What made you choose portraits?'

'Because I'm better at them than anything else. I feel a stronger connection with animate objects.'

'And why pastels?'

'I like the luscious velvety texture they achieve. The colours are deep and rich and easy to blend. The luminosity they can create is magical. And on a practical level they're easy to cart around, which was useful when I had to bring them to Athens. It'll make the new commissions I've taken on logistically more manageable, too. Shockingly,' she added dryly, 'your friends and acquaintances don't want to come to a tiny studio in London. They expect me to travel to them.'

'That *is* shocking.'

'I know.'

'Have you acquired many new clients?'

'Can you believe I'm booked up for the next twelve months?'

'That doesn't surprise me in the least.'

'Really?'

'Like I said, you're very talented. Although once seen, this particular work of yours can't be unseen,' he mused, shoving his hands in the pockets of his jeans and rocking back on his heels, 'which is something I'll have to get used to.'

'Then why come?'

'I volunteered to take one for the team.'

'The team?'

'My siblings. Daphne's still on honeymoon and strangely enough, the others discovered they had other engagements tonight.'

'That's noble.'

'My motives aren't that altruistic.'

She found that hard to believe. She didn't know him well, but what little she did know suggested he had considered the welfare of those closest to him of paramount importance. 'No?'

'I figured gatecrashing this evening would be a sure-fire way of seeing you. After how I reacted the night of the wedding, I didn't think you'd grant me an audience otherwise.'

Willow took no notice of the faint twinge of discomfort she felt at his referral to the night she'd worked hard to erase from her memory. Instead, she focused on the fact that he was probably right, although his reasoning was wrong. Her mortification, not his reaction, would have been behind her ignoring any calls he might have hypothetically made.

'Why did you want to see me?' she asked, puzzled by that because as far as she was concerned they were done. 'Why did you want an audience?'

'I have a proposition to put to you.'

He turned to look at her and the impact of his darkly brooding good looks stole the breath from her lungs and the wits from her head. She had to blink to snap the sizzling connection and refocus. 'What sort of a proposition?'

'The sort that changed the plan and would be best discussed somewhere more private,' he said, the sudden gleam in his eye sending a shiver racing down her spine. 'Follow me.'

Faintly unnerved by the gleam and the possible nature of this 'proposition', Willow nevertheless did as Leo instructed since apparently she found his innate authority absurdly attractive and impossible to resist.

Somewhere more private turned out to be the terrace, which was strung with festoon lights and featured glossy planting and intimate seating. It had a spectacular panoramic view of the Parthenon, behind which the sun was setting. Bathed in warm evening light, the two-and-a-half-thousand-year-old shrine to Athena was all soaring columns, golden stone and lengthening shadows, but it was Leo who held her attention. He was a man on a mission and by the time they'd sat down in a secluded booth in the corner at one end of the terrace, her curiosity was at fever pitch.

'What's this all about, Leo?' she asked, the intensity with which he was looking at her electrifying her nerve endings and drying her mouth.

'It's occurred to me recently that we have unfinished business.'

Willow's pulse skipped a beat and her entire body flushed with heat. So much for hoping he'd put the details of that night from his mind as she'd tried to. 'We don't,' she said firmly, not wanting to revisit their so-called unfinished business for so many reasons. 'We really don't.'

'I disagree,' he countered, the set of his jaw suggesting he was not to be deterred. 'I owe you an apology. For reacting to the situation badly and letting you walk out.' He paused, frowned, then added, 'Most of all, for hurting you in the first place.'

'That's not your fault,' she assured him with an airy wave of her hand, as if she wasn't curling up with embarrassment inside. 'It's all mine. Like I said at the time, I should have warned you it was a possibility.'

'You weren't to know.'

'I was actually. There's little about my condition I *don't* know. I got carried away, which was stupid and naive, in hindsight. You certainly weren't to know, though. I can't imagine you'd ever hurt someone deliberately.'

'I endeavour not to.'

'But if it's that important to you,' she added, needing this cosy little chat to be over for the sake of her composure, 'I accept your apology.'

'Thank you.'

'Excellent. So. Shall we get back to the party?'

She half got up, more than ready to march back into the throng, only to freeze when his arm shot out and his hand caught her wrist for a moment before instantly letting it go as if he'd been burned. 'I'm not finished.'

Drat.

She resisted the urge to shake the tingles from her arm and reluctantly sat back down. 'Oh?'

'I read up on endometriosis.'

Willow hadn't thought it possible to blush any more, but she'd been wrong. Accusations of frigidity and prick teasing would be infinitely preferable to a conversation about gynaecology with a man who epitomised masculinity. 'Why would you do that?'

He arched one dark eyebrow. 'Why wouldn't I?'

'Because firstly, you didn't need to, and secondly, it's girls' stuff.'

'I have three sisters,' he pointed out dryly. 'I am not remotely fazed by "girls' stuff", as you put it. And I did need to. I dislike ignorance. Knowledge is power. Which brings me on to my next point.'

'And that is?'

'According to my research, which was extensive, sex with endometriosis doesn't have to be painful.'

'Not always, no,' she hedged cautiously, wondering where he was going with this, barely able to believe they were discussing it in the first place when she'd only ever talked about it with medical professionals.

'Position and angle can make a difference.'

Her cheeks burned. 'Apparently.'

'Timing, too.'

'For some.'

He leaned forwards, his burnt umber gaze holding hers so compellingly she couldn't look away even if she wanted to. 'So I suggest we try again.'

At that, Willow's heart gave a great thud against her ribs. Was he nuts? Had he forgotten how awkward it had been? 'Why on earth would you suggest that?'

'Because it doesn't seem fair that you're missing out,' he said. 'Because I'm good at solving problems. Because I've never wanted anyone the way I want you. Because I caused you pain, albeit unintentionally, which is causing *me* guilt and I want to make that right. Take your pick.'

Willow ignored the wave of longing that surged through her in response to the realisation that he still wanted her as much as she still wanted him because it was utterly irrelevant now. 'Well, I pick none of the above,' she said firmly. 'Because I'm never having sex again.'

'Right.'

'I'm serious.'

As the realisation that she meant it dawned, Leo's faint smile faded and a deep frown creased his brow. 'You deliberately choose celibacy?'

She nodded. 'Absolutely,' she said, blotting out the clamouring voice of denial in her head since there was no point wallowing in regret and disappointment. At least alone, she'd be safe, free of emotional intimacy and in absolutely no danger of falling in love and ruining lives. 'It's worked for me so far. It will do so again. Millions of people around the world make that choice. It's a perfectly acceptable one.'

'I agree,' he said with a slow nod. 'But not everything about that night was a disaster.'

The memory of what he'd done to her, of how hard and fast she'd shattered in his arms slammed into her head, and her skin tightened. 'No.'

'Don't you want to know what more there could be?'

'Not if "more" is going to hurt like it did.'

'And that's why I think we should experiment,' he said, clearly not to be deterred. 'See what works for you and what doesn't.'

'Why are you doing this?' she said, baffled by his persistence. 'You could have anyone.'

'I don't want anyone. I want you.'

Her heart soared for a moment before reason intervened and planted her back on earth. 'As a problem to solve,' she said. 'Something broken to fix. A project.'

'I still dream of you,' he said, not denying her accusation, she noticed, although with the way his voice had somehow become a caress, seductive and hypnotic, that didn't seem to matter. 'I still find you irresistible. I want your hands on me. Your mouth on mine. Agree to my proposal and as soon as you're finished here, I'll take you to my estate on Santorini. For the weekend. It's very private. It has its own beach. There'll be no distractions there. Nothing to disturb us. We can take it slowly. Carefully. You will be in control.' His gaze dipped to her mouth and his voice dropped an octave. 'Totally in control.'

Him? Give up control? Really? Hmm. 'I find that hard to believe.'

'I'm willing to make an exception for this.'

'Why?'

'Because our chemistry is unique and I want to know what it will be like between us as much as I think you do. We can experiment until we get it right. And imagine getting it right, Willow. Imagine the fireworks.'

Willow didn't need to imagine them. She was experiencing them now. Tiny explosions were detonating in the pit of her stomach and shooting showers of sparks into every centimetre of her body. His eyes were so dark, so compelling, his voice was so shiveringly spellbinding. She wanted his hands on her and his mouth on hers too, with a desperation that ached.

What if he was right? she couldn't help wondering, her resolve wavering wildly in response to everything he'd said. What if it *was* about position and angle and timing? Maybe it had hurt so badly because of where she'd been in her cycle. Or because he'd been on top of her. Or because, it being her first time, she'd tensed at the unfamiliar intrusion, which was never going to make it good.

Right now, she was roughly in the middle of the month and it would never be her first time again. If he genuinely meant what he said—and she couldn't see why he wouldn't—she could be in charge of the pace and position. She trusted him to stop if she needed him to. He had before.

And while she might never be able to embrace commitment, deep down she didn't want a lifetime of celibacy. She wanted the excitement and pleasure he promised to unlock. She longed to explore her sexuality and discover how *she* could be in control of her body instead of the other way round. Physical intimacy didn't have to mean emotional intimacy and for one weekend, surely, she could be brave?

'All right,' she said, her heart thumping with anticipation and hope, the desire she'd kept at bay rushing through her like a river smashing through a dam wall. 'Why wait? Let's go now.'

Making their escape took longer than Leo had anticipated since frustratingly, people kept coming up to talk to him. But within the hour, having picked up a bag from Willow's hotel, he was pulling into the VIP car park that served the private business aviation terminal at Athens Airport, still congratulating himself on a good plan well executed.

Once he'd devoured all the information on her condition he could find, he'd mentally revisited every encounter and conversation he and Willow had shared and begun to strategise. It hadn't been particularly complicated. He'd known what he wanted, and like her, he'd intended to get it, hence setting aside his issues with the portrait and attending its unveiling.

He hadn't doubted the outcome of the conversation on the terrace for a second. He could be extremely persuasive when he chose and most people came to see things his way eventually. That was why he'd had the jet on standby and the villa restocked. His focus had been wholly on the goal, his decisiveness and self-confidence making a welcome return, and after weeks of feeling utterly at sea when it came to this woman, retaking the helm and steering the ship in the direction *he* wanted had felt good.

What *had* taken him by surprise, however, was the degree of satisfaction and relief he'd experienced when she'd acquiesced. It had nearly floored him. Was the guilt he felt over what had happened the night of the wedding reception really that skewering? Did he want her in his bed that badly? Perhaps her presumably negative image of him bothered him more than he'd assumed. Perhaps altruism *was* his thing, after all.

Ultimately, it didn't matter. The weekend was to be purely physical. An opportunity to right so many wrongs and finally draw a line under the month-long blip in his otherwise rock-steady life. Come Sunday evening, armed with proof that great sex *was* possible for her, Willow would head off to conquer the art world and he'd continue to run the family empire to the best of his abilities and protect his siblings from the capriciousness of his mother. The status quo would be restored and his head would never be turned again.

If Willow had been harbouring any doubts about having made the right decision back there on the terrace—which she wasn't, even though her completely irrational response to the tall, polished brunette who'd accosted them on their way out of the nightclub had made her question whether she was absolutely sure she knew what she was doing— they'd have been swept away by the excitement of travelling by private jet. It certainly beat the no-frills experience she'd had on her journey from London to Athens all those weeks ago. Leo's plane came with a dozen large cream leather seats, a crew of six and a magnum of champagne, a glass of which she accepted from a flight attendant with a smile and an appallingly pronounced *efharistó*.

'So this is very comfortable,' she said, taking a sip of deliciously cool bubbles to control the jumble of nerves and anticipation twisting her stomach into knots, and settling back to enjoy the luxury once they were in the air.

Across the polished walnut table, Leo unfastened his seat belt and shot her the glimmer of a smile. 'It's the only way to travel.'

If you were a billionaire, perhaps. For lesser mortals, a pair of feet or a bicycle did just fine. 'Don't tell that to your shipping shareholders.'

'The shipping we do is commercial,' he said, draining his cup of the coffee he'd opted for since he'd be driving from Santorini Airport to the house. 'The transglobal cargo-in-containers sort.'

'No cruise liners? No corporate yachts?'

'Sadly not.'

'That does seem remiss.'

'Don't feel too sorry for me,' he said wryly. 'The planes more than make up for it.'

Planes, plural? 'How many do you have?'

'The family has this one. The company has another three.'

'Handy for getting around.'

And for whisking women off for a weekend of sex at his secluded island villa, such as the beautiful brunette he'd chatted to at the party? They'd seemed pretty friendly. Not that it was any of her business. She wasn't remotely interested in Leo's romantic past. Just as well she wasn't the jealous type, though. Otherwise the urge she'd had to shove the other woman out of the way would have been down to the desire to scratch her eyes out instead of simple annoyance at the delay.

'So who was the brunette?'

Hmm. Perhaps she was more interested than she cared to admit.

A flicker of bemusement flitted across his face. 'What brunette?'

Willow set her glass down on the table and feigned nonchalance. 'Leggy. Gorgeous. Silky white trouser suit. Very pleased to see you as we made our way out of the nightclub. You gave her a kiss on each cheek, rattled away in Greek for a few moments and then she drifted off with a cool smile.' Not that she'd noticed or anything.

'Ah,' he said with a faint nod. 'That was Sophia.'

'A girlfriend?'

'We dated for a couple of months a year or so ago. I haven't seen her since.'

For some reason, that came as a relief. 'She has excellent hair,' Willow said magnanimously. 'Personally, I've never been able to master the art of the chignon.'

Leo ran his gaze over her head and her face, so leisurely and thoroughly that by the time his eyes met hers, her heart was pounding and her mouth had dried. 'Your hair suits you.'

'I'm not sure whether to take that as a compliment or an insult,' she said, taking another sip of champagne to alleviate her parched throat and willing her raging pulse to slow.

'It's a compliment. It's very unusual.'

'Unusual good or unusual bad?'

'Merely an observation,' he said smoothly, the canny brother of three sisters.

Overly warm, her skin prickling, Willow shifted on her seat to alleviate the sensation, a move which nearly resulted in a wardrobe malfunction. 'Have you had many girlfriends?' she asked, adjusting the asymmetric bodice of her one-shoulder navy dress.

'Many before my father died,' he replied vaguely his gaze lingering on her cleavage before returning to hers, a fraction darker and hotter than it had been a moment ago. 'Only some since then.'

'You never appear in the press with any of them.'

'I take great care not to. My private life is private.'

'Why aren't you married?' she asked, the interest she wasn't supposed to be showing apparently overriding his right to privacy.

'I've yet to meet the right woman.'

That came as no surprise. He'd be a hard man to please. The woman to match his exacting standards probably didn't even exist. 'I got the impression when we first met that you don't have much regard for romantic love.'

'It's not an emotion I'm familiar with.'

'Do you want children?'

'I wouldn't be averse to having a family at some point in the future.'

Which ruled her out. Not that she'd ever ruled herself in, of course. But still, it was good to know where she stood. No point in getting hopes up where regrettably there could never be any.

'And what about you?' he said a little abruptly, breaking into her thoughts before they could drift off into the sorrow and regret she felt whenever she contemplated how different her life could have been if her mother hadn't died. 'What's your issue with relationships?'

Willow pulled herself together and determinedly staunched the flow of dreams of an alternative universe in which she successfully had the operations and, after a string of boyfriends, settled down with a husband to make a dozen adorable babies. 'Who says I have an issue with relationships?'

'You did. In my car. The night of my sister's wedding.'

Ah. He was correct. She had. But she didn't need to give an answer with any great detail. He must have read about the potential fertility issues, the possibility of depression and the general disruption to life associated with endometriosis anyway, and disclosing her complicated feelings towards love and death, which she knew made her sound completely irrational, would necessitate a conversation about her parents' relationship and hers with them that was far too emotionally revealing to have with a man she'd never see again once the weekend was over.

'No time,' she replied with an evasive shrug. 'No opportunity. With everything I've got going on health-wise I am not the world's greatest catch. Although this weekend might change that. Does this plane of yours have a bed?'

'Yes.'

'We could make use of it.'

His dark eyes gleamed. 'We land in fifteen minutes.'

'And?'

'We're going to need hours.'

A bolt of heat speared through her at that and a wave of desire washed over her but somehow she made herself ignore it all. 'Then you'd better tell me about your brothers and sisters instead.'

# CHAPTER SEVEN

IN RESPONSE TO her suggestion, Leo gave Willow a brief potted history of each of his five siblings—focusing on their roles in the business, rather than much in the way of the personal—which did not make for sparkling conversation but did at least keep his mind off the bed in the cabin at the rear of the plane. It was also a vastly preferable topic of conversation than his previous relationships.

He couldn't work out why he'd allowed so many questions to be asked before he'd finally had the presence of mind to shut her down. Insights into their respective feelings about romance—or lack thereof, in his case—had no place in what they were doing here. He'd never shared such personal information with any of the women he slept with, either before or after his father's untimely demise. Yet Willow had moved and her right breast had very nearly come free of her dress and he'd become so preoccupied with not leaping to her side of the table, not putting his hands on her to find out if she was braless, as he suspected, that he'd answered her questions without a second thought.

If he were prone to flights of fancy he'd have assumed she'd cast some sort of spell over him or slipped a drug into his coffee, but he wasn't so he didn't. Instead, as they came in to land, he pulled himself together and reminded himself that this weekend was principally about Willow and her exploring her sexuality.

As he'd informed her earlier, she'd be in charge. It was strange how comfortable he was with that, given his bone-deep need for control, but then the exception he was making for her was a very brief, very minor one. Experience suggested that with her, the results would be stunning. The cost to himself, he was confident, would be zero.

There was no way in hell he was going to repeat the mistakes he'd made before. He was better than the sickeningly self-centred, thoughtless beast he'd briefly turned into the night of his sister's wedding. He'd learned his lesson and he'd use this weekend to prove it to himself and get things back on track. He had a plan, his resolve was rock-solid, and this time, nothing, absolutely *nothing*, was going to go wrong.

As Leo turned off the main road and steered the car down the long windy track to the house, Willow thought that if they didn't arrive at their destination soon she might well explode with need. With every moment that ticked by her imagination grew that little bit wilder, the conversation they'd had on the plane about his family an increasingly distant and blurry memory.

As a result, by the time they passed through a pair of giant gates and travelled up a wide, sweeping drive, desire was bubbling up inside her like a pot on the boil. Her pulse was thundering like a steam train and her ears were buzzing from the pressure.

*This was it*, was the only thought drumming through her head. Her moment for fireworks and glory and vanquishing her fear of sex. The moment she'd never thought she'd be brave enough to seize.

It was only when he brought the car to a smooth stop in front of the large shadowy structure that the nerves unexpectedly kicked in and an insidious voice in her head suddenly started whispering.

*But what if it isn't? What if he's wrong? What if you try and try and it still doesn't work? What would that mean for the future? A lifetime alone? Or what if it does work but it isn't as good as you're anticipating? Has it crossed your mind that chemistry might not be enough, that with your inexperience the sex might be mediocre? And if it is, how humiliating would that be?*

Leo killed the engine and exited the car, leaving Willow to sit there stock still, the questions clattering around her skull obliterating the desire and quickening her pulse. Her lungs were tightening from the crushing pressure she could feel pressing in on her on all sides and she found she was struggling for breath.

Shakily, she got out of the car, leaned back against it and inhaled the warm salty air until her racing heart slowed and she could once again breathe. While Leo popped the boot and extracted their bags, she took a moment to stare up at the vast canopy of stars above, to listen to the soft, soothing rush of the sea, her jangling nerves quieting and her jumbled thoughts clearing.

Only a moment ago all she'd wanted was to head for a bedroom as fast as possible with the man whose confidence and certainty had blasted her objections to smithereens, who'd promised her a weekend of discovery, a weekend to remember.

But now she was wondering if there was any particular need to be quite so hasty. Maybe the frenzied desperation that had characterised their last encounter had been the trouble. Desire had a habit of erupting without warning. Their kisses became blistering within seconds. On the dance floor... In the lift... So perhaps this time, seeing as how they *had* time, they'd be wise to take things slowly, to deal with the heat cautiously as it ebbed and flowed instead of instantly succumbing to it and drowning.

A bag in each hand, Leo strode to the front door and opened it. Willow pushed herself off the car and followed him on in. After dumping the luggage, he shut the door behind them and voice activated the lights, then turned to her and said, 'What would you like to do first?'

She took a deep breath and willed him to understand. 'I think I'd like a tour.'

If he was being brutally honest, a tour of the house was not what Leo had imagined giving Willow on arrival at his estate. But he'd seen her staring up at the infinite sky as she'd leaned against the car, breathing deeply and steadily. He'd sensed her tension as she'd stood there in the hall, looking a little pale, and if a tour would settle her apparent nerves, then that was what he'd do. The last thing he wanted was to dive right in, guns blazing, as they were wont to do, and the night to go wrong again. She'd be out the door in a flash and nothing would have been resolved.

As he showed her around the spacious interlinked rooms of the ground floor, she oohed and aahed her appreciation of the space, while he fought the memories of how she'd made similar noises the night she'd come apart in his arms before it had imploded.

In the sitting room, in response to her questions about the house, he muttered something about the appeal of the bright white walls, the clean lines and sharp angles of the unfussy modern building and the serenity and seclusion of the location, and resisted the urge to pull her down with him onto the soft deep sofa.

By the time he stood aside at the vast glass sliding doors so she could step out of the house and onto the terrace that stretched out high and wide above the sea, his muscles were rigid with the effort of keeping his distance and his head was pounding.

'I bet the views are stunning by day,' she murmured, leaning her elbows on the railing, her body all long lines and soft curves.

'They are.'

'You said you don't get to spend as much time here as you'd like.'

'I don't.'

'That seems a shame.'

What was a shame was that they weren't kissing. But he would not rush. He would not push. He'd promised her control over the proceedings and he would not renege on that. 'The demands made of me are many.'

She straightened and pushed herself off the railing, turning to look at him with an unexpectedly smouldering gaze that made his heart crash against his ribs and nearly took out his knees. 'Can you handle some more?'

'Yes.'

'Then show me upstairs.'

* * *

It was Leo's patience that had given Willow the confidence to rein in her nerves and go for what she was now back to wanting quite desperately. By apparently reading her mind and stepping away, both literally and metaphorically, he'd given her the space and time she needed to get her head around the events to come. It had reassured her that whatever happened between them, whether a spectacular success or another abject failure, everything would be all right.

Correctly interpreting her words once again, Leo took her by the hand and led her back through the rooms and up the sweeping stone staircase, the urgency she could feel vibrating off him tempered with restraint. Keeping up when her limbs were as weak as water and her lungs were short of breath was a challenge, but within moments he'd tugged her down the landing and through an open door. One muttered word and the nightstand lights flicked on, and then, before the doubts she'd vanquished staged an unwelcome resurgence and got the better of her, she closed the distance between them and planted her hands on his chest.

As she slid them up, feeling his heart pounding hard and fast beneath her right palm, and wound them around his neck, his arms encircled her waist. She lifted her head at the same time as he lowered his, and their mouths met in a slow, sensual exploration, as if they had all the time in the world, as if he wanted to prove his intention to keep his promise of slow and careful and continue to give her space.

Melting against him, Willow battled the urge to deepen

and intensify the kiss. Her head swam, the desire surging and the heat inside her rocketing, and when she felt the hard length of him pressing into her, she longed to fall onto the bed in a tangle of limbs and a wild shedding of clothing. But she stayed where she was, locked in an embrace that was the main course, not merely the starter, and which he seemed in no hurry to end.

When they did eventually sink to the bed—limbs weak, breathing ragged—it was in a smooth glide not a frantic tumble, and the kisses continued, scorching yet languid.

'How do you do this to me?' she breathed when he transferred his mouth to her neck and began to lay waste to the sensitive skin beneath her earlobe.

'I should ask you the same thing,' he murmured, his hot breath making her shiver.

'I guess opposites really do attract.'

'So it would seem.'

He rolled onto his back, deftly taking her with him. With one hand, he threaded his fingers through her hair and pulled her head down for another searing kiss. The other, he slid up back of her thigh, ruching her navy dress as it went, until he reached her bottom.

When he pressed her gently but firmly harder against his erection, Willow moaned softly. She was melting from the inside out. She couldn't get close enough. Her head filled with his scent and her body was awash with heat.

She wanted him inside her so badly she ached, but this was where it had gone wrong before. How she'd felt hadn't been enough. He'd been too much. She'd sensed his desperation and the moment his restraint had snapped.

Maybe the depth of his penetration and the power of his thrusts had contributed to her discomfort that night. Maybe there was a way to help with that this time.

Lifting her mouth from his and breathing hard, Willow pushed herself up and shifted until she was sitting astride him. With shaking fingers, she started unbuttoning the buttons of his now badly creased shirt. She pushed the fabric away, set her hands on his warm bronzed skin over which lay a smattering of dark hair and felt a stab of giddy satisfaction when he tensed and hissed out a breath.

She lowered her head and put her mouth to his chest and felt a shudder rip through him. Grappling at the buckle of his belt, she kissed her way down his torso and the rigid muscles of his abs, lingering over the rises and dips of the contours.

'No. Willow,' he muttered, clamping a staying hand over hers when her intentions became obvious.

'How badly do you want me?'

'Can't you tell?'

She could. He was rock-hard beneath her hands. She wanted to feel him, explore and taste him and see if she could make him shatter the way he had her.

'Let me take the edge off it,' she said softly, her heart pounding and her mouth watering at the thought of it. 'You said I'd be in charge and I want to do this. I think it will slow us down. I think it will help. Tell me what you like. Tell me if I'm doing it wrong.'

With a rough groan of defeat, Leo lifted his hips and helped Willow remove his jeans and underwear. He shifted up the bed and fell back against the headboard while she settled between his legs and took him in her hand. Her fingers closed around him and his eyes shut as white-hot darts of pleasure speared through him.

There was nothing she could do wrong. Nothing at all. Every tentative stroke of her fingers, every slow pull of her hand blitzed his brain that little bit more. When he felt her breath on him, his head spun. When her mouth closed over him, his heart nearly leapt out of his chest. He made the mistake of opening his eyes and looking down, and had to grab fistfuls of sheet to stop himself from thrusting his hands in her gorgeous multicoloured hair and guiding her in the way he wanted.

Not that she needed instruction. If he'd been capable of thought, he'd have marvelled at the way she could read his body, despite her lack of experience. He didn't have to tell her what he liked. Somehow, she instinctively knew.

Somewhere in the dusty recesses of his brain he was dimly aware that this should not be happening, that he ought to be focusing on *her* pleasure, but perhaps she was right. Alleviating the intensity of his need so that he could then take care of hers could well be the right call. From his point of view, it was the best call ever.

The wet heat of her mouth and the loose tickling tendrils of her hair maddened him. His breathing was harsh and fast and shallow and was becoming more so with every passing second. The tension coiling inside him was unbearable. He was moments away from losing it and out of habit he tried to pull her head back, but she wasn't having any of it. To his relief, she simply shook him off and carried on, and he couldn't have protested even if he'd wanted to.

When she increased the exquisite pressure and upped

the pace, he lost the ability to think. He was impossibly hot, shuddering uncontrollably, and then, his control history, his hands in her hair, his climax was upon him, ripping through his body with the force of a wrecking ball. With a groan, he threw his head back and exploded, pulsing relentlessly until he had nothing left to give.

'Well, we know *that* works,' said Willow with a throaty lightness that totally belied the thundering of her heart, the hot achy throbbing between her legs and the intense feeling of triumph sweeping through her.

She pushed herself up onto her knees and brushed the hair from her face. The tang of musky saltiness lingered deliciously on her tongue. Her jaw ached but she didn't care. Leo's dazed expression made her feel as if she'd conquered the world.

His eyes were glazed and his voice, once he'd recovered enough to be able to speak, was thick and slurred. 'That was—you are—astonishing.'

'Was there anything I could have done better?'

'I hope not. I doubt I'd survive it.'

'Good to know.'

'You made me lose control.'

'And how do you feel about that?'

'I'm not entirely sure,' he murmured with a faint frown. 'Unsettled? It seems churlish to complain but I'm supposed to be empowering you.'

'You did empower me. I'll prove it.'

She scooted up his body and leaned forwards to kiss him while settling herself on his lap, her knees either side of his hips, his legs stretched out behind her. Her heart thumped at the feel of him against her, still hard—although not as much as earlier—and her nerves fluttered for a second, but she'd read that this position—one in which she could dictate things—was a good one. All he had to do was lie back and think of Greece. And she was hot, wet, as ready and as brave as she'd ever be.

'Condom?' she breathed in his ear.

Eyes dark and glittering, he reached out and rummaged in the drawer of the nightstand. Giving him some space, Willow slipped her knickers off, and then she was there and he was there, and all that remained was to sink down onto him. But she hesitated. She was too tense, and it definitely wasn't going to work if she didn't relax. Yet the more she tried to relax the tenser she became, which would only make things worse, and God, this was *awful*.

As if sensing her doubts and fears, Leo shifted, removing the possibility of penetration, and to her relief the anxiety instantly eased. He kissed her slowly and thoroughly and within moments she was curling into him and practically purring. He ran his hands over her back, found the zip of her dress and tugged it down. She shivered as he pushed the garment up and over her head, then tossed it to the floor.

His smouldering gaze roamed over her. His breathing slowed. He wasn't lying back and he wasn't thinking of Greece. He was looking at her as though he wanted to devour her, which to her delight, suggested that he was as into this as she was despite her no doubt clumsy efforts to pleasure him.

He cupped her full, heavy breasts and rubbed his thumbs over her hard nipples, and she gasped at the strength of her response. Her skin burned when he held her. A thousand volts shot to her core. Instinctively she arched her back, needing his mouth to replace his hands, and when he took up her invitation, she trembled. The faint prickle of his stubble grazing her skin intensified the sensations. She clung on to his shoulders and gripped his hair.

The heat powering through her veins was hotter than before. The desire flooding her body was greater, more insistent than anything she'd ever known. Coherent thought was fast disappearing. She just had to do it, she just had to be strong and fearless and—

Oh.

She stilled.

She'd done it. Somehow her body, her hips, in particular, had moved of their own accord and he was inside her. Not too deep. Not too hard.

And…it was OK.

Thanks to Leo's patience and understanding, his reading of her mind and his willingness to let her do what she needed to do, the sacrifice of his much-vaunted control for her sake and his care and consideration, there was no pain, just a little discomfort that was dissipating by the second.

A hot tight knot lodged in her throat. Emotion swelled within her and her eyes stung and she was now the one feeling shaken and unsettled. But she swallowed down the knot and blinked back the emotion because she was filling with a clamouring urge to move, and she wanted to focus on that. Encouraged, hopeful, she bit her lip and tentatively rolled her hips, and that was wasn't too bad either. It was actually really quite good.

His eyes were on hers, so close she could make out flecks of gold in the warm brown. Her reflection shimmered in his dilated pupils. She had the strangest feeling that if she looked hard enough she'd be able to peer into his soul.

What would she find there? she wondered, feeling him swelling and hardening inside her, although he held himself still. And what would he find in hers? Her deepseated fear of love and heartbreak? The secret, terrible shame of sometimes resenting her mother for dying and destroying her hopes of romance? The agonising conflict of knowing that on the one hand surgery would help physically, but on the other being terrified of going under and also not waking up?

None of that was for his consumption. A meeting of souls was not what this was about. This was about helping her to function in the way she wanted, so she closed her eyes and pressed herself close. She kissed him hard and began to rock.

Leo held her loosely, giving her space to call a halt to the proceedings should she need to, but she was going nowhere. This position was working beautifully. The articles had been right about it putting her in control. Like this, she could adjust and adapt.

The rocking was becoming sensational. Her vision was blurring, her head was spinning and her body was turning into a quivering mass of sensation. Leo's breathing was ragged against her skin. His muscles were taut beneath her fingers. His big body was trembling and his hands were moving over her heated skin increasingly wildly.

The tension gripping her was becoming unbearable,

but just when she thought she could stand it no more, he found her nub and caressed it in the way she so badly needed, and the tingles that had started in her toes swept up her legs, her body, her arms. She could feel a tsunami of something hot and insistent rushing towards her and suddenly, without warning, a volcano of pleasure erupted inside her. It rushed like molten lava through her body, shaking her limbs and jerking her head back.

And as she fought for breath, half gasping, half laughing, the fireworks still exploding behind her eyes, she'd never felt so ecstatic, so relieved, so clever.

'What are you doing?'

Sitting cross-legged on the sofa that stood beneath one of the four windows of the bedroom two mornings later, Willow glanced up from the artist's pad in her lap to find Leo lying on his side, propped up on one elbow. He was watching her with a sleepy yet smouldering gaze that, remarkably, had the power to triple her heart rate and rekindle the desire even though after every delicious thing they'd done together recently she ought to have had enough.

'Sketching you,' she said, heroically resisting the urge to ditch the drawing and return to the bed in which they'd spent much of the past glorious thirty-six hours because her body badly needed a break. 'The light here is incredible. Do you mind?'

'Are you planning to put the end result on show?'

'No. This is solely for me. Something to remind me of the weekend. Not that I'm likely to forget it anytime soon.'

'Then I don't mind.' Leo punched his pillow into shape

and rolled over onto his front. 'Just don't expect me to pose,' he said, his words muffled by the feathers and fabric. 'I'm barely capable of moving.'

'You can stay right where you are.'

Which was sprawled diagonally across the super king-size bed, naked apart from the white sheet that lay bunched over his buttocks and upper thighs, quite the sight for sore eyes.

The morning sun streamed in through the window, giving his bronzed skin and splendid musculature a lovely iridescent glow. There was no inch of him that she hadn't explored. No part of him that she hadn't tasted. Capturing the salty, satiny heat of his skin and the giddying power of his body on paper was an impossible task, but she was giving it her best shot.

'You look very sexy in my shirt,' he murmured, eyes still half-shut.

Willow smudged a line and shivered in awareness as the soft crumpled linen she'd taken a liking to brushed against her body. 'You look very sexy out of it.'

'What time is it?'

'Around ten.'

'I haven't slept so late in years.'

'We've been busy.'

His mouth twitched with the faintest of smiles. 'I haven't been so busy in years either.'

Was the mighty surge of satisfaction and pride his words invoked normal? Willow allowed herself a moment to preen, then got a grip because it didn't mean she was special or anything. It probably just meant that he rarely had a weekend spare to indulge in such things.

'How do you normally spend your Sunday mornings?' she asked, tilting her head and determinedly studying his right foot, which was as absurdly alluring as the rest of him.

'Generally, I'm in Athens preparing for meetings I then fly to.'

'Such as the merger in New York?'

'Yes. Although *that* morning I spent pacing around the apartment in a state of guilty remorse.'

'You've more than made up for it,' she said, vaguely wondering why she found feet so difficult to capture. 'I had no idea experimenting would be so rewarding.'

'How do you feel?'

Now, there was a question.

Giving up on his big toe, Willow tapped her pencil against her chin and tried to formulate an answer. The last thirty-six hours had been incredible. Once her fears had been overcome and her passion unleashed, she'd been insatiable. So many positions. So much pleasure. Not everything they'd tried had worked for her, but on those occasions, it hadn't been awkward at all. Leo had been endlessly patient and her confidence had rocketed, and she'd begun to ponder the pros and cons of carefully timed, short-lived flings in the future.

'Amazing,' she said, wondering how on earth she could sum up the myriad emotions rushing around her system. 'Relieved. Grateful. Optimistic. Very happy I accepted your proposition.'

'I meant physically.'

Ah. She flushed. She'd forgotten that this weekend wasn't as momentous for him as it was for her. 'I ache,' she said, determinedly switching her focus from the intangible to the tangible. 'And I'm sore. But in a good way. I've discovered muscles—and stamina—I didn't know I had.'

'Do you hurt?'

'No.'

'Good.'

'How do *you* feel?' she asked, suddenly needing to know, apropos of the gap in momentousness, whether he found her inexperienced efforts a turn-on or tedious, whether she was just a pity project that appealed to his hero complex and he was simply going through the motions or whether he genuinely found her as irresistible as she found him.

He arched one dark eyebrow. 'Me?'

She nodded.

'Oh, I feel just fine,' he said with a slow seductive smile that, to her relief, suggested he didn't find her remotely tedious and really wasn't just going through the motions. 'In fact, come over here and I'll show you.'

# CHAPTER EIGHT

LEO FELT SO FINE, so utterly content with the situation here, that when Sunday afternoon rolled around and he realised that one weekend wasn't going to be nearly enough, that he needed longer with Willow, it really was no big deal. It was simply that he wanted more of the stunningly inventive sex they'd been having, which was just as incredible as he'd anticipated, possibly even better.

That first time had been it for slow and careful. Having discovered what her body was capable of and newly empowered, Willow had embraced experimentation with an enthusiasm he could never have imagined. The ease and speed with which she picked up new skills was impressive. The brilliant wielding of pastels wasn't her hands' only talent, and the things she could do with her mouth... *Theos.*

She'd made him physically lose control, repeatedly, something he could not recall ever doing before, but despite his initial unease, he'd come to realise that it was no cause for concern. No one had been hurt and as far as he was aware the world had not ended, which why he was so comfortable with the idea of extending the weekend by a day or two.

After all, it wasn't as if he were planning on going AWOL for a month. He'd only be away from the office for forty-eight hours max. He'd been on business trips that lasted longer without any drama. Disaster was unlikely to strike in such a short time and if it did, he was always on end of a telephone. His staff, his clients, the board, *no one* need ever know what he was getting up to when not at his desk answering the occasional email. Assuming Willow was amenable, it was an excellent plan—personally and professionally speaking, the best of both worlds.

'I should go,' sighed the goddess in question, glancing at her watch and peeling herself off him with what encouragingly felt like reluctance.

Before she could get very far, however, Leo rolled her onto her back and pinned her to the bed. 'Do you want to?'

Her shimmering gaze met his, her breath catching, the pulse at the base of her neck fluttering madly. She gave her head a minute shake, the colours of her hair warm in the early evening sun, and he was filled with an absurdly overwhelming relief at the knowledge that she wasn't done with this any more than he was. 'Not right now, no.'

'Then don't.'

Of course Willow was going to agree to stay. She didn't want to give any answer other than *yes, yes, yes.*

The thought of leaving Santorini and Leo had been the only sour note in an otherwise gorgeous weekend. She wasn't nearly ready to go. She was having far too brilliant a time. Not only had she discovered the wonders of great sex, she was also living the adventure and passion Selene had talked about and she'd so envied.

The private jet... The beautiful estate with its shimmering infinity pool and perfect curve of pebbled beach...

The handsome, enigmatic billionaire who burned her clothes off every time he looked at her, who showed her fireworks and patience, whichever was required... Why would she want to give any of that up?

She had nothing pressing to return to. Work on her next commission didn't start for a while. The handful of social engagements she had in the diary were easily cancellable and the neighbour who checked in on her father every other day reported he was fine.

She estimated she had around two weeks before reality struck and her world became one of pain, but she'd be long gone by then. No one had ever witnessed the trauma she went through when on her period and no one ever would. She was at her most vulnerable at such times, weak and a wreck. The thought of the emotional intimacy that having someone with her throughout would engender tightened her throat and curdled her stomach. Leo, with his three sisters, might claim to be unfazed by girls' stuff but even he would probably be thrown by it, and she wanted him to remember her as bright and strong, as a crazy, colourful moment in his otherwise ordered, controlled life.

So a week or so of playing Cinderella and pretending that she was easy-going and carefree, that her life wasn't ruled by endometriosis, was all she could have, but it was infinitely better than the nothing she'd been expecting.

'Tomorrow's Monday,' she said, nevertheless inordinately giddy at the prospect. 'Don't you have to work?'

'I don't need to be in the office to do that. I am certain I can remain here for another day or two without the company imploding.'

A day or two, no more? Hmm. That was a bit disappointing. It wouldn't be nearly enough for her, she suspected. But maybe she could deploy her new-found wiles to persuade him to reassess. He appeared to be in a changing-the-plan kind of a mood, after all, and with the high she was riding at the moment, anything felt possible.

'All right,' she said, smiling up into his dark gleaming eyes, excited at what the next forty-eight hours—hopefully more—might hold.

'Good.'

With the flash of a satisfied smile, Leo leapt off the bed and grabbed his phone. He made a series of calls, all of which were in Greek, none of which she understood. Then he sent for her belongings, which arrived the following morning, and that was the extent of communication with the outside world for a while.

Two days later, mid-morning, Leo's phone rang for what felt like the hundredth time of the day. He set the coffee maker on the lit stove so it could do its thing, then fished the device from the back pocket of his shorts. Zander's name scrolled across the screen. Resisting the temptation to simply cancel the call and get on with preparing breakfast in peace, Leo reminded himself that, however intrusive, he still had responsibilities, and pressed the green button that answered the call.

'So Leo,' drawled his brother, once they'd established that it was indeed a good, if late, morning. 'Where the hell are you and what exactly are you doing?'

'I'm on Santorini,' he drawled right back, reaching for the box that contained four fresh croissants, which he'd just been out to buy, and tipping them onto a plate. 'And I'm working from home.'

'So your assistant said. What I want to know is, why?'

'Why not?'

There was a pause, during which Leo headed to the fridge for the yogurt, and then came a faintly concerned, 'Are you ill?'

'I've never felt better. Why do you ask?'

'Because you haven't worked from home in years. Or ever, come to think of it.'

'As per your instructions,' he said, thinking of Willow still slumbering upstairs and recalling the recommendation Zander had made on the balcony of the hotel at which Daphne's wedding reception had taken place. 'I'm lightening up. While continuing to work. You seem to manage it.'

'Right. What's going on?'

'Nothing's going on,' he said as he tipped the yogurt into a bowl. 'What's going on with you?'

'You sound odd.'

'You sound confused.'

'I am. This isn't like you. When are you back?'

*First thing tomorrow* should have been Leo's answer, given that technically, all remained of his two-days-max weekend extension was this afternoon. Yet he couldn't seem to formulate the words. Because the truth was, he didn't want to have to return to reality just yet. He wanted to prolong his and Willow's Mediterranean island mini break even further, but now not solely to ensure a continuation of the sex.

There were things about her he was increasingly keen to know. Such as how she'd become an artist. Why she'd chosen those colours for her hair and what the multiple earrings and the nose stud were all about. He was interested in finding out about her hopes, her dreams, her fears. To remind himself—in case he should need reminding—of all the reasons why long term she was wrong for him, naturally.

Since they'd arrived on the island and embarked on a sex marathon, conversation had generally been sparse, impersonal and inconsequential. Over a light lunch by the pool yesterday, however, the morning having been taken up with more calls and emails than he'd appreciated, she'd quizzed him on the Stanhope Kallis empire. Somehow they'd ended up talking about his family dynamics, an exchange which had turned out to be anything but trivial.

'Why does it have to be you who does everything?' she'd asked, popping a *dolmades* into her mouth and making distractingly appreciative little sounds as she ate.

'What do you mean?' He'd selected an olive, tossed it in the air and caught it in his mouth, which had earned him a beaming smile and a brief round of applause.

'You have five siblings,' she'd then pointed out. 'You all work for the business in one capacity or another. You're all Selene's children and you're all now adults. You no longer have to be the one with all the responsibility.'

'No,' he'd had to admit, although, oddly, that had never occurred to him before. 'That's true. But it's a role that was always destined to be mine and I've been doing it for years. Giving up control is a hard habit to break.'

'You broke it for sex with me. You could break it for other things if you wanted to.'

Well, yes, he could, in *theory*, he'd supposed, but— 'What I want is irrelevant.'

'I'd give anything to have someone to share the responsibility of a parent with,' she'd said before giving him an irritatingly knowing look and adding, 'I think you're a control freak.'

Leo had agreed. He was. With the suspicion that he shared too many regrettable genes with his mother and the brutal awareness that his success as CEO was down to sheer willpower rather than any innate talent, he had to be. And that was fine by him.

'There are worse things to be,' he'd said, wincing a little on the inside at the defensive note he could hear in his voice.

'There are better things to be, too.'

Not wanting to argue the point, he'd pulled her onto his lap then and that had been that for conversation for an hour. But her observations had nevertheless hit home. The responsibility he bore was crushing, relentless and draining, and he was sick of the endless firefighting.

What if he let his siblings deal with their mother for a change, should the need arise? he thought now while his poor, bewildered brother waited for an answer down the other end of the line. Surely together they could figure it out. He didn't *have* to be the one Daphne and the others always turned to for help. And why couldn't he delegate? Zander, his second in command—albeit hitherto in name only—was always on at him to loosen the reins. He'd be thrilled to take on more of the burden of the business, even temporarily.

In fact, he—Leo—could implement this new strategy this very minute. If he instructed his brother to take the helm for a while, he could remain on the island with Willow, who'd mentioned last night that she had a few weeks before she needed to travel to Italy to start her next commission, without the intrusion of emails and calls. Free from external demands, he could focus one hundred percent on getting to know the woman beneath the surface.

Zander was right. His current behaviour wasn't like him, but the last couple of days had proved that the plates carried on spinning even if he wasn't there to dash between the poles that held them up 24-7, and he hadn't had a break in years. He might never have ditched duty for pleasure before, but he wouldn't be leaving his ship without a captain. It was just that for, say, a few more days, that captain wouldn't be him.

There was no need to feel queasy about it. Zander was extremely competent, and, possibly even more importantly, champing at the bit. He'd be able to handle all the different strands of the business that demanded the CEO's attention. He was tough enough to face Selene down in the event that was required.

And it wasn't as if he himself would somehow find himself in too deep with Willow along the way, even if such an eventuality was on the cards, which it was not. He had no appetite for the level of chaos that emotional commitment wrought, and she was very much not his idea of a life partner. If and when he did marry, it would be to someone like him, someone who wouldn't upend his existence and who wouldn't expect more from him than he was willing to give.

Opposites might attract but they didn't make for happiness. Just look at the example his parents had set. Their marriage had been a volatile train wreck, characterised by fiery yelling on his mother's part and an increasingly cold shoulder on his father's, although since they'd produced six children presumably they hadn't been in opposition all the time.

He wanted none of that. He'd choose an even-keeled union of mutual respect and companionship over passion and ice any day. *His* children weren't going to be subjected to snide comments in the common room. *They* weren't going to repeatedly lose friends through no fault of their own.

But he'd spent over a decade looking out for his family, and actually, now that he thought about it, what he wanted *wasn't* irrelevant. He deserved to think solely about himself for a change and deep down he yearned to kick up his heels and have some contained, harmless fun. Another change of plan was no particular cause for concern. It wasn't a whim. He knew what he wanted. And what he was doing. Everything would be fine.

'Are you still there?' said Zander with a sharpness that jolted him out of his thoughts and returned him to the conversation.

'Yes.'

'So?'

'I'm taking some personal time,' said Leo, switching off the stove beneath the now bubbling coffee pot.

'Some *what*?'

'Some days off. A break.'

'Now?'

'Yes.'

'For how long?'

'Not long. I'll keep you posted. In the meantime, from

this moment on, you're in charge. You know what to do. No need to run anything past me. Just don't let me down.'

Before Zander could start asking more questions he was unable to answer, such as whether he'd completely lost his mind, Leo hung up and tossed the phone on the worktop. He located a tray and began loading it up, only to freeze when his skin started to prickle, an indication, he'd come to realise, that Willow was in the vicinity.

'Who was that?' she said, sidling into the kitchen wearing the black bikini and the pink silky robe that she'd sported the afternoon he'd met her and had caused him so many sleepless nights thereafter.

'That was Zander.'

'Trouble back in Athens?'

If there was trouble anywhere, it wasn't in Athens. It was right here in the seemingly unquenchable desire he had for her that was messing with his behaviour and turning his life upside down. 'Quite the opposite.'

'What do you mean?'

'Do you have anywhere else to be right now?'

She shook her glorious head. 'No.'

'Anything else to be doing?'

'No.'

'Well, as of this moment, for a few more days, at least, neither do I.'

'I don't understand,' she said with a faint frown. 'I thought we were leaving this evening.'

'I've put Zander in charge of the company for a while.'

The frown vanished. Her eyebrows shot up and her jaw dropped. 'Are you serious?'

'Yes.' He handed her the plate of croissants and the bowl of yogurt, which she automatically took.

'Why?'

'Because I,' he said, picking up the tray and heading out onto the patio while vaguely wondering why he wasn't more bothered about both handing over the company keys to Zander and the upheaval to his life Willow was causing, 'need a holiday.'

It took Willow the whole of breakfast to get over her shock at Leo's holiday announcement. She felt the hit of caffeine as it entered her bloodstream—impossible not to with the way he made coffee—but she barely tasted the deliciously buttery and flaky croissant or the soft creamy yogurt sweetened with lightly fragranced honey.

All she could think was, could *she* have been behind his decision to take a break? Had her feminine wiles really worked their magic? Could their conversation over lunch yesterday have somehow made him reassess his relationship with responsibility and his siblings?

Whether they had or not, and realistically she knew that *not* was far more likely, it was ridiculous how pleased she was with this latest development in their affair. She didn't know why. It changed nothing. It proved nothing. Yet her heart was flipping about in her chest and she could hardly contain the smile that kept threatening to spread across her face, which was a concern because she didn't like to think what any of it might mean.

She had to be careful, she told herself sternly as Leo refilled her cup with rocket fuel. She mustn't make the mistake of thinking that what they were doing was anything other than temporary. Longer term with Leo was out of the question. Even if she could change her conflicting feelings about commitment and love—which seemed impossible when they ran so deep—sex aside, she was about as far removed from his usual type as it was possible to be. Lowering her guard and falling for him would be a one-way ticket to disappointment and despair. She had to live in, and make the most of, the present.

'What would you like to do today?' he asked, once again apparently able to read her mind.

Her body wanted to go back to bed with him because amazingly, despite all their efforts to assuage it, desire still burned within her, as hot as ever. But her head was thinking that perhaps it would help to get out of the house. The last few days, although glorious, had been nothing if not intense. It was little wonder she'd lost her sense of perspective. A return to the outside world might give her the dose of reality she needed to stay on track. Besides, with all the drawings of him she'd been producing, she needed to pick up a new sketchbook.

'Seeing as we're on holiday,' she said, confident that a change of scenery was all she required to keep her feet on the ground, 'and I haven't been abroad in a decade, I'd like to see the island.'

That afternoon, as he watched Willow pick her way around the limestone ruins of a settlement that dated back to the eleventh century B.C., Leo reflected that her proposal to explore had been an excellent one. The only reason he hadn't suggested it himself was because for the first time in years he hadn't been thinking with his brain.

In the absence of sex he'd been able to focus more efficiently on his plan to get the answers to the questions about her he had. Among myriad other tiny but oddly fascinating details he'd gleaned en route to the archaeological site of Ancient Thera via a coastal road that required the careful navigation of twenty-two hairpin bends, he'd discovered that she streaked her hair for no other reason than because she liked the colours. She'd bought the tiny diamond nose stud to celebrate her first sale and the earrings because, why not? And she lived and worked in London in a top floor light-filled studio that she'd bought with the money she'd inherited from her mother.

For an hour now they'd been wandering around the deserted remains of temples and houses with mosaic floors. The millennia-old graffiti were fascinating. The sea views were spectacular. His phone hadn't rung once, a novelty about which he wasn't sure he felt pleased or twitchy.

'I wish I'd brought my pastels with me,' said Willow, shading her eyes against the sun as she stood like a queen on a rock that was far too high and close to the edge of the cliff for his liking and gazed around at the rugged scenery from beneath her floppy-brimmed hat. 'The depth and intensity of the colours here could make even the most committed portraitist switch to landscapes.'

'Let me help you down.'

She took the hand he extended and beamed him a smile that was brighter than the sun, which, this being Greece in July, was saying something. 'Thank you.'

'How did you become an artist?' he asked, assuring

himself that the intense relief he experienced at having removed her from potential harm was perfectly normal.

'I didn't have much of a choice. It's the only thing I can do. I left school with just one A level. In art.'

'Why was that?'

'Because of my condition, I missed a lot of classes. The exam timetable was not my friend.'

'Did no one ever notice?'

'My school had two thousand students,' she said dryly, as they retraced their steps down the path that led back to the ruined city and away from lethal four-hundred-metre drops. 'There were three hundred in my year. There wasn't a lot of one-on-one attention. Lots of people slipped through the cracks for a variety of reasons and I was simply one of them.'

Leo tried to imagine such a situation occurring at the top boarding school in England he'd attended from the ages of eight to eighteen and failed. 'Your father?'

'Grief-stricken. But it was fine,' she said with a quick, dismissive wave of her hand that made him wonder if it really had been. 'I was never going to be able to hold down a conventional job with the amount of sick leave I'd have to take, so I didn't need any qualifications anyway.'

'Did you go to art college?'

'No. I've done courses but I'm mostly self-taught. I built up a collection of work—while moonlighting as a waitress—and then basically blagged my way into exhibitions.'

'You're tenacious.'

'I've had to be,' she said with a wry twist of her mouth. 'I wasn't always successful, but luckily, people seem to like what I do. More to the point, *I* like what I do. My work is versatile and varied and fits in with other things and I love it. Not many people can claim that.'

'That's true.'

'Can you?' she said, darting him a quick, unsettlingly probing look as the remnants of the amphitheatre hove into view. 'Do you enjoy your job, Leo?'

*Not particularly* was the answer that broke free of its confines and clamoured to be heard. But he ignored it the way he did every time resentment at his fate reared its ugly, shameful head. There had never been any point in wondering what might have happened if he'd simply refused to leave university mid-course, turned his back on everything he'd been groomed for and pursued his dream of winning the America's Cup. He was CEO of one of the world's largest, most successful privately owned corporations. He had wealth and power. He had no right to envy others for being able to choose their own path. Envy was destructive and it was ridiculous to regret something that had never really been a possibility in the first place.

'I'm extremely good at it,' he said, oddly unable to lie to her outright when usually the words came smoothly.

'That doesn't answer the question.'

'Doesn't it?'

'Perhaps it does,' she said with a tiny nod of understanding. 'Duty is important to you.'

'My destiny was drummed into me at an early age.'

'What would you have done if you'd had the choice?'

'I've have sailed,' he said without a second's hesitation. 'Competitively.'

'Do you own a boat?'

'Not anymore.'

'That's a shame.'

'Why?'

'We could have taken it out tomorrow.'

While Leo stopped to inspect a pile of old stones at the edge of the amphitheatre, Willow sat on a rock and took her brand-new sketchbook out of her bag. After several annoyingly poor attempts to capture the dusty, ruined landscape that stretched out before her, she gave up and slipped on her sunglasses so that instead she could watch the man she was sleeping with, an infinitely more fascinating sight.

She had not missed the evasiveness with which he'd responded to her more probing questions as they'd wandered back along the path. Or the trace of resentment in his voice that she thought she'd caught, not for the first time.

What was the story there?

Because there definitely *was* one.

Since they'd met he'd indicated too many times to count that, for him, duty trumped all else, and if he were comfortable with that then all well and good, but clearly, he wasn't. She had the feeling that he was doing a job he didn't really want. Like her, his life appeared to be limited by circumstances. Maybe, like her, he found the idea of changing those circumstances too great a risk to take.

The question, which was far too personal ever to be broached, of course, the answer to which she absolutely did not need to know, was, why?

# CHAPTER NINE

WHY LEO HAD arranged for a yacht to be brought over to the villa overnight, so that he could take Willow out in the morning, he had no idea. He hadn't sailed for years. When the all-consuming nature of his new job had hit home in the aftermath of his father's death, he'd had to shut down his old life completely in order to be able to concentrate on maintaining the legacy.

But the hint of wistfulness that had woven through Willow's words when she'd asked him if he owned a boat to take out to sea had been answered by an unexpected yearning of his own, which had nagged away at him all the way back to the house until it had eventually occurred to him that one key point of a holiday, surely, was having the opportunity to do the things you didn't usually have time for.

The yacht was moored to a rarely used buoy in the cove. After breakfast, laden with bags and a cool box, he and Willow walked down to the jetty, where the tender was tethered. He stowed the kit and helped her aboard, then fastened her into a life jacket before donning his own.

Itching with the need to get his hands on the sheets and the wheel, to flex his toes against the smooth warm wood beneath his bare feet, Leo fired up the engine. Adrenalin pumped through him at the novel idea of spending all day at sea. His head filled with the memory of how much he'd once loved it, how much he'd relied on being able to get onto the water whenever he'd needed to escape his parents' volatile relationship as an angry teenager burning up with helplessness. And as they sped across the warm south Aegean waters towards the sleek white craft that was bobbing there, calling to him like a siren, the chaos of the last few days dissipated beneath a familiar, welcome blanket of calm.

Leo sailed them into a bay that was perfect for snorkelling and dropped anchor a hundred metres offshore. Willow had never snorkelled before so that was another thing he taught her to do.

Possibly, she didn't pay as much attention to the underwater paradise as she should have done, but then possibly there was no man on earth as compellingly attractive as him. The cool turquoise sea and brightly coloured fish that darted around them and through the rocks were no match for a set of strong shoulders, powerful thighs and a competency on and in water that she found irresistible.

She hadn't been able to take her eyes off him as he'd handled the boat. Apart from the anchor haulage mechanism, there was little other automation. This particular yacht was for working, not for relaxing on with a gin and tonic while computers, or a crew, did the rest.

And Lord, how he'd worked it.

The minute they'd climbed aboard Leo had switched into action. While she'd settled herself on a seat, aware that she'd be of little assistance, he'd leapt from deck to cockpit and back again, familiarising himself with the boat, he'd informed her, and conducting various checks of equipment. Once satisfied everything was in order, off they'd set, and from that moment on, he'd barely stood still, whether at the wheel, scanning the horizon, or responding to the flapping of the sail with an impressively masterful tack.

He might like to come across as icy cold and ruthlessly controlled—although, come to think of it, she hadn't seen that side to him for a while now—but he obviously had a passion for sailing. He'd hardly stopped grinning all morning and he was more relaxed than she'd ever have imagined him capable of being.

She couldn't help but wonder if *this* time, they really were where they were because of something she'd said, and that, as much as the raw physicality and sheer strength which was on display, warmed her in a way that had nothing to do with the sun drying her off as she lay stretched out on the foredeck beside Leo, who was sitting with his elbows resting on his drawn-up knees and staring at the horizon.

'Thank you for arranging this,' she murmured, lethargic after all the snorkelling which had been followed by lunch, her head resting on her folded arms, eyes half-closed.

'You're welcome. It's been good to stand behind the wheel again.'

'I can't imagine a gentle meander along the Santorini coast is quite the same as hurtling across the Atlantic in gale force winds.'

'No,' he agreed, reaching into the cool box for the two remaining ice-cold bottles of beer and popping the caps off. 'But it doesn't matter. The wind in your hair and the spray on your face is exhilarating whatever body of water you're on and whatever the weather. And anywhere there's an unobstructed horizon gives you the freedom of being able to head in any direction you choose.'

Was he aware how wistful he sounded? Was he only talking about sailing? Willow shifted onto her side, partly to take the bottle he handed her but mainly so she could see his expression more clearly. 'It might have been a while, but you seem very at ease on board.'

'I've been sailing ever since I could walk.'

'So why did you give it up?'

'I had to. I had no choice.'

But had he? Really? She got that he'd had to abandon the idea of competition when he took over the company, but couldn't he have continued to do it for fun?

She shouldn't probe. A tiny muscle flickered in his jaw and it was none of her business. And yet the questions had been niggling away at her ever since they'd left Ancient Thera the day before and they had to talk about *something*. Conversation wasn't dangerous. It needn't lead to unwanted intimacy of the emotional kind. She was just curious as to what made him tick, that was all. It wasn't as if she'd be giving any of her own secrets away.

'Why is duty so important to you?'

Leo lifted his bottle and took a mouthful of beer before answering, as if needing the fortification before replying. 'My father wasn't the easiest of men,' he said eventually, with a wry twist of his lips. 'He was weak when it came to my mother, which I didn't realise until I was older, and he could be cold and aloof, but he spent a lot of time with me, discussing the business, when I was a kid. He regularly took me with him to the offices in London and Athens. I remember repeatedly being introduced as the next boss and although it was always said in a joking kind of a way everyone knew he was deadly serious.'

'Did he never consider anyone else?'

He shook his head. 'He came from the sort of family where the eldest son automatically inherits.'

'That must have put you under a lot of pressure.'

'There was never any question or discussion about it,' he said, interestingly neither confirming nor denying her observation. 'It was always presented as a fait accompli.'

'No wonder you're resentful.'

He cast her a quick, sharp glance. 'Resentful?'

'Occasionally it comes through when you're talking about your family,' she said. 'And it's completely understandable. I mean, you were so young. As you once told me, the learning curve was steep. You must have had to make many personal sacrifices along the way.'

'None that I wasn't willing to make,' he said with a shrug that was perhaps a little too sharp to be casual. 'I had to give it everything. I couldn't let him down. In business, he demanded and commanded respect and I had that for him in spades. Within five years of merging the two companies, he doubled the bottom line. He halved staff turnover. Professionally speaking, his shoes were always going to be big ones to fill.'

'But you do fill them, don't you?'

'I do. I more than fill them. But they don't fit very well.'

'Whatever do you mean by that?'

Despite the intensity of the midday sun Leo's blood chilled when he realised he'd just revealed more than he'd meant to. Why had he done that? Had the heat gone to his head? Had too much time under water this morning reduced the oxygen supply to his brain? Was he drunk? Or had he simply been thrown by the discovery that if Willow had noticed his resentment he wasn't as good at keeping a lid on his emotions as he'd always assumed?

Something had to account for the slip, but whatever it was, it wouldn't happen again. The thrill of being back on board and out to sea had obliterated his caution. The blanket of calm had given him a false sense of security. Unwisely, he'd relaxed and then he'd lowered his guard.

But all he had to do to correct the situation was raise it, and that was what he'd do because he could not afford to let the unsettlingly perceptive Willow and the chaos she carried with her get under his skin. This raging affair of theirs was a purely temporary arrangement. It was not in any way even-keeled and cool, so she was not, and never would be, the one for him.

'Nothing in particular,' he said, sliding his gaze from hers back to the horizon and ignoring the shaft of what felt strangely like disappointment that struck him in the chest.

'You're being evasive again.'

'And you're being nosy.'

'I'm just curious about the man I've been sleeping with for five days,' she said with a lightness he sensed was deceptive. 'I've answered all your questions. You have a habit of avoiding mine. It makes me wonder what you have to hide.'

'I have nothing to hide.' Just things he didn't intend to share with someone like her. Or with anyone ever, in fact.

'Prove it.'

'I don't need to prove anything.'

'Then humour me.'

'I don't need to do that either.'

He glanced her way in time to see a triumphant spark light her eyes. 'So you *are* hiding something.'

The only things he was hiding were intense irritation at being tied in knots and a rapidly growing concern about the torrent of words on the subject that were piling up in his head, demanding release. What that was about he hadn't a clue. He had no intention of spilling his guts, which would render him exposed, vulnerable and weak. He had never sought understanding or sympathy, and he didn't want them either, least of all from a potentially destructive force like Willow. He didn't know why he'd started talking about his relationship with his father in this way in the first place. He never had done before, not even with his siblings.

But she was looking at him as if trying to peer into his soul and he couldn't seem to tear his gaze away, no matter how hard he tried. The longer it went on, the greater the trembling of his defences and the less he could remember why he kept his cards close to his chest. Her gaze was shimmering, bottomless and as he lost himself in it, he had the disturbing feeling that his guard wasn't just down; he didn't even know where it was.

'Fine,' he found himself saying, unease drumming through his veins as his protective shield lay shattered about him and the words poured out. 'I might be good at it but the role doesn't come easily to me. I don't thrive under pressure. I don't enjoy zigzagging continents and endlessly crossing time zones. I find the responsibility of employing tens of thousands of staff an unbearable weight and the awareness that if I'm not extremely vigilant everything for which I'm responsible will come crashing down pervades my every waking moment.'

For a moment Willow didn't respond. When she did it was with a slightly stunned, 'Wow.'

'You did ask.'

'That is *not* the image you present.'

Thank God. 'Of course it isn't.'

'Is that why you're so big on control?'

'Yes. It's got me through some tough times.' His father's death… Inheriting the business… His sister's illness… He didn't know how he'd have coped without it.

'I thought it was because you feared you were too like your mother.'

'There's that, too,' he admitted, now that he'd started apparently unable to stop. 'She is wild and self-centred and people can sometimes get hurt by her thoughtlessness. Not only do I share her genes, in my teenage years, I had also had a tendency to behave like that sometimes.'

'The boat you crashed?'

'I'd just discovered in the press that she was having an affair with my then best friend's father.'

'That must have been awful.'

It had been worse than awful. It had unleashed a storm of hurt and embarrassment, frustration and fury that he hadn't know how to handle. 'It wasn't just the once,' he said, ignoring the memories trying to muscle their way into his head. 'I lost count of the number of friends I made and lost. The boat belonged to her. I took it out on my own one morning in the summer holidays and drove onto the rocks. I was sixteen. I was angry. It worked. I'm not angry anymore.'

'Are you sure about that?'

'Absolutely,' he said, with a sharp nod of his head and a mouthful of beer.

It was about the only thing he was certain of at the moment. The crash, unplanned, instinctive, had shaken him up badly. In the aftermath of his rescue, he'd been told by his father—not that he'd needed a lecture, having realised it on his own—that his increasingly reckless behaviour wasn't acceptable. He hadn't been willing to give up sailing just then, so he'd decided to give up emotion. If he allowed nothing to affect him, he wouldn't have the urge to react. There'd be no further loss of control, no more damage. Simple.

'It would be understandable if you were.'

'It would. However, I'm not. I find my mother frustrating and exhausting, but that's it.'

'Right,' she said dryly, with a nod that suggested she knew something he didn't and made him feel as though the deck upon which he was sitting were made of jagged glass shards.

'What?' he muttered eventually, unable to stand the scrutiny and the knowingness any longer.

'You have such a lot going on in that handsome head of yours.'

He did. And he had to keep it all in there. Enough of the soul searching and sharing. It was wholly unnecessary. He hadn't spent years denying his emotions only to let them loose in response to one pertinent question. He would put a stop to this sightseeing nonsense. He and Willow weren't a couple. Bed was where they functioned best and it was ridiculous to have indulged her otherwise. He'd only put her in the driving seat for the first two days they'd been on the island, but somehow she was still in it and it couldn't continue.

'Can you tell what I'm thinking right now?' he said, putting their now empty bottles back in the cool box and closing the lid with a snap.

Her gaze dipped to his mouth and lingered. 'That a siesta in the cabin would be a good idea?'

'No,' he replied, resisting the temptation she presented because to take her down below when he was so on edge, his self-control unnervingly shaky, would be mad, bad and incredibly dangerous. 'What I'm thinking is, it's time to go back.'

Leo wasn't the only one with a lot going on in his head. His confession occupied Willow's thoughts for every one of the nautical miles that sped by.

How on earth had he coped with the stress of doing a job he didn't feel equipped for all these years? The internal struggles he'd had to have faced, the tough decisions he'd had to have made… She couldn't imagine it, although she did now understand his need for control and order and his desire for privacy.

The suppression of his true self to get the job done and protect others, however, didn't sound very healthy at all. But then who was she to judge? She was hardly a model of rational thinking. She was avoiding the operations she'd been told would help alleviate the symptoms of her endometriosis because of a fear that she knew logically was unlikely to materialise. She was as trapped by events of the past as he was.

It was a shame he'd put an end to the day because

she'd been having a fabulous time, but she got it, just as she got why the smiles had vanished and Leo was now tight-jawed and anything but relaxed at the wheel. She'd prodded him into talking when he hadn't wanted to and he wasn't happy about it.

So she'd back off and give him some breathing space, the way he'd done for her when she'd needed it. It would be no bad thing for her either, come to think of it. Because now she'd had a glimpse of the man beneath the facade she wanted to know more. She wanted to know everything, which was not an option, so she could do with some time alone to shore up her defences against the threat to the emotional distance she was determined to maintain.

'What's the plan for tomorrow?' she asked once they'd made it back to the villa, needing to know so she could figure out how to get out of it.

'There isn't one,' came the blunt reply, which meant, she thought with some relief, that she could make her own.

Leo woke up gritty-eyed and grouchy, too unsettled by the events of the day before to have slept well. His dreams had been fractured and disturbing. The one in which he'd stretched out on a couch, his head in Willow's lap, and told her everything while she gently stroked his hair and murmured soothingly at regular intervals had been particularly alarming.

Discovering that he was alone in the bed didn't help his mood at all. Where was she? Had the brooding sullenness into which he'd descended yesterday afternoon driven her away once again? Had she had enough of the monosyllabic grunting that he'd been reduced to, left in the dead of night and gone back home? At the thought of it, something unpleasant slithered into his stomach, until she emerged from the bathroom in a towel and a cloud of rose-scented steam, at which point it slithered right back out again.

'Good morning,' he said, his voice gruff with sleep, although other parts of his anatomy were rapidly waking up.

'Good morning,' she replied absently, reaching for her clothes.

She ditched the towel, which gave him hope, but then she started dressing, which dashed it. Sightseeing might be no longer an option, but he hadn't put a stop to anything else.

'What are you doing?'

'Getting dressed.'

'I can see that.' He frowned. 'But why?'

'Because my taxi will be here any minute.'

Leo sat bolt upright, fully awake now, his pulse pounding and his mind racing. What the hell? She *was* leaving? 'Where are you going?'

'I thought I'd start with the Three Bells of Fira,' she said, fluffing out her glorious hair then pushing her sunglasses into it. 'And see what I felt like doing after that.'

He blinked. Shook his head to clear it. 'What?'

'I'm going sightseeing,' she said. 'I told you I wanted to see more of the island. So that's what I'm going to do.'

'On your own?'

'Yes.'

'I'll join you,' he said, flinging back the sheet and swinging his legs round to surge to his feet.

'There's no need for that,' she countered, alarm flickering across her face as he pulled on his shorts and grabbed a T-shirt. 'We're not joined at the hip.'

There was every need for that. Forget his decision of yesterday to confine them to the villa. He wasn't having her wandering around the place on her own. What if something happened to her? It didn't bear thinking about. She was a guest in his home. She was his responsibility. And that was all there was to it.

While she slipped her feet into flats, he racked his brains for arguments to convince her to see things his way. 'You don't speak the language.'

'I have an app. I'll manage.'

'You don't know where you're going. You could be taken for a ride.'

'That's a risk I'm willing to take.'

'I'd *like* to join you.'

'Well, *I'd* like some space,' she said, picking up her bag and dropping her phone into it, her smile small, the gaze that met his cool. 'So I'll see you later.'

The taxi dropped Willow off at the famous church known for its blue dome, its spectacular views and obviously, its three bells some time later, and she spent an hour exploring first it and then the streets around. Delightful and interesting though the experience was, however, it didn't give her the respite she'd been hoping for.

She'd been looking forward to spending some time alone. To cleansing her head and clarifying her thoughts and ridding herself of the longing to find out more about Leo. She had *not* anticipated missing him. Yet she did.

She kept thinking of things to tell him. Time after time she turned to do so, expecting to find his tall broad frame in the vicinity, and without fail, a stab of disappointment at the realisation it wasn't struck her right through the heart.

It was ridiculous. After all, she was well accustomed to doing things on her own. With a largely absent father, both emotionally and physically, and no boyfriend to snuggle up with on the sofa, she'd been doing so for years. Somehow, though, probably because of the amount of time she'd spent with him, she'd got used to Leo's company. She'd had a glimpse of what it could be like to be part of a couple, and even though she knew it wasn't real, even though she'd be foolish to dwell on such things, secretly she'd found it thrilling.

She finished off the sparkling water she'd ordered at the cafe at which she'd stopped to escape the heat of the sun, her head teeming with exciting, possibly unwise yet unstoppable thoughts. Surely there'd be no harm in letting him tag along on her days out if he wanted to. As long as she remembered that they *weren't* a couple, that this fling of theirs had to come to an end—and soon, because time was marching—she'd keep her head. She was in no danger of falling for him. Nothing had changed in that regard. Her heart was still safely locked away and there it would stay.

'Meet me at the bottom of the Karavolades Stairs in half an hour,' she told him over the phone, blocking out the faint warning voice ringing in her head as she dropped some coins into the saucer that contained the bill and got to her feet, 'and I'll buy you lunch.'

\* \* \*

Leo had spent the morning prowling around the villa, wondering what Willow was doing and whether she was all right. He should have gone after her was the thought that kept zipping through his head. If his common sense hadn't kicked in at the last minute to remind him that he had to respect her request for space, he would have.

He should also have been delighted with the solitude her departure had generated. She wasn't the only one who'd wanted it. Time on his own suited his need to regroup and rebuild his defences perfectly. But the villa felt strangely empty and colourless without her in it. He'd got used to having her, her hair and her jewellery around. To his bafflement, he wasn't grateful she'd gone; he was annoyed.

His phone rang twice, but when he saw that the callers weren't her but firstly Daphne, who must have just returned from honeymoon, and secondly, Zander, he ignored it. Within moments of hanging up on the third call, however, he was out the door and on his way. The Karavolades Stairs, comprising over five hundred steps, were steep and winding and plagued with donkeys. Had Willow taken a hat to protect her from the intense sun? And what shoes had she been wearing? There was no handrail and the stone could be deceptively slippery.

He didn't stop to think about the probing personal questions that might arise during lunch and beyond. He didn't stop to analyse the absurd pleasure and sheer relief he felt at her invitation to join her. He just got in the car and drove.

# CHAPTER TEN

IN THE DAYS that followed, Leo took Willow to the hot springs on the tiny, uninhabited islet of Palea Kameni and the black sands of Kamari Beach. He introduced her to fragrant *souvlaki* and the sweet, creamy, custard-flavoured delights of *galaktoboureko*. One evening at an open-air cinema, they saw a film in Greek, which she didn't understand. He leaned in close to provide a continual translation, but his proximity had such a disastrous effect on her concentration that she didn't follow much of that either.

At no point did Willow regret having invited him to join her for lunch and the sightseeing that came after. Every time she turned to talk to him, there he was, and she felt no stab of disappointment, just a little leap of delight. Thankfully his surliness had gone. In fact, he'd become positively chatty. He'd told her more about his siblings and his relationship with each of his parents. About the sailing competitions he'd participated in as a youth and his job as an adult. By sticking to her modus operandi of getting other people to talk—he wasn't a client she was painting, but the principle was helpful—Willow had actually got away with sharing very little.

Tonight, he'd brought her to a tiny but packed taverna. It sat right over the bay, the wide pergola-covered terrace just a few metres up from the crystal-clear azure shallows. The colour of the painted wooden balustrade around the edge and the tables and chairs matched the cerulean sky. The setting sun radiated off the blinding white walls of the restaurant behind and hot pink bougainvillea trailed down the pergola uprights.

It was rustic and charming. The clientele was laid back, the conversation buzzed and not so long ago she'd have been surprised by the choice. She'd have imagined that a billionaire CEO with control issues and a liking for order might prefer a more formal setting in which to dine. But recently she'd seen less of that man and more of the one she felt he must have been before.

They were shown to a table in the corner, overlooking the sea. It was too small really, and the positioning of the chairs—ideal for maximum appreciation of the view—resulted in a seating arrangement that was far too intimate for two people who were engaged in nothing more than an ultra-short affair. But Leo didn't steer her to another and she certainly wasn't going to object. She'd take all the close contact she could get.

He pulled out a chair for her and she sat down. He took the other and folded his large frame into it. When his knee bumped against hers beneath the table, a thousand volts shot though her. His scent dizzied her head. His proximity made her want to lean in to him and sigh.

Instead, she stayed where she was and picked up the menu. Understanding not a word of it, she put it back down. 'Would you order for me?'

'What would you like?'

She'd like to able to appreciate the romance of the place and the tangerine sunset, to gaze into his eyes and hold his hand. She'd like to burrow into his soul and stay there until she knew everything there was to know about him. She'd like to be able to share with him all her hopes and dreams, her insecurities and her fears, the hallmarks, she felt, of a proper relationship. To be able to overcome the emotional and physical obstacles that littered her life, to be his type and for things *not* to be coming to an end. But unfortunately none of that was on the menu, either in Greek or in English.

'What comes recommended?'

'The calamari is reputed to be excellent.'

'Then I'd like that.'

But unbeknownst to her, Willow had been on borrowed time and the idyll was about to implode. She was lying by the pool the following afternoon when a familiar stabbing sensation suddenly skewered her abdomen. For a moment she lay there, staring up the wisps of cloud streaking the sky like candyfloss, a little confused, a little alarmed, her heart beating a fraction too fast.

No.

This couldn't be happening.

She'd never been very regular, but it was way too soon, surely. It had to be indigestion or something.

What date was it anyway?

With a wince and a sickeningly familiar turn of her stomach, she reached for her phone. She brought up the calendar and responded with a jolt to the details on the screen. The twelfth? She'd been here for ten days already? How had that happened? She was only supposed to have stayed a week.

It wasn't hard to figure out why she'd lost track of time when she'd been so wrapped up in what she and Leo had been doing, but even so she ought to have had a few more days in hand. That was why she'd attributed her bloating to fine food and even finer wine and her extreme fatigue to a simple lack of sleep thanks to their burning the candle at both ends.

But how she'd missed such obvious signals when she'd had over eleven years of this, month in, month out, didn't matter. An analysis of the situation would have to wait. What was important was that she react. Fast. Because she couldn't let Leo see her go through what was about to happen. It would be brutal. Emotional and intimate. She would not appear weak and vulnerable in front of him. And what if he wanted to help? *God.* She'd have not a shred of dignity left.

Willow ignored the hot surge of emotion that suddenly rushed through her system in response to the sodding unfairness of life, and determinedly blinked back the unexpected sting of tears while cursing the hormones behind both. She'd always known their affair had an end date. She'd had a great time while it had lasted. It had been everything he'd promised and everything she'd hoped for, but now it was over. Instead of wallowing in regret and disappointment, she had to focus on getting away from Leo before the lovely bubble they'd created burst and things got very real indeed. So she got up off the sun lounger, gathered together her things and headed inside.

She was throwing her clothes into the suitcase that was lying open on the bed and determinedly ignoring the faint gnawing ache that she knew would soon intensify when Leo eventually found her.

'What on earth are you doing?' he asked, stock still in the doorway, a freshly made margarita in each hand.

The surprise she could hear in his voice bounced right off her. She resisted the temptation to ditch the suitcase and beg him to hold her close and kiss away the pain. She didn't stop for even a second. 'I have to go.'

'Why?'

'This has been fun but it's over.'

Out of the corner of her eye, she saw him set the drinks on top of a chest of drawers, a deep frown creasing his brow. 'What's going on, Willow?'

'Nothing's going on,' she said, plucking the pink silk robe off the armchair with clammy, trembling fingers and adding it to the pile. 'It's just that I need to leave.'

'You're very pale. Something's obviously wrong.'

He headed in her direction, his expression filled with concern she shouldn't—*didn't*—want. She made for the en suite bathroom before he could reach her, take her in his arms and pulverise her resolve. He was too much. Too perceptive. He was also not going to let this lie, she realised as she scooped up her toiletries and dropped them in her wash bag. There was nothing for it but honesty.

'I've started cramping,' she said, avoiding his penetrating gaze as she returned to the room. 'My pelvis aches. My period is imminent.'

'And?'

'It's going to be horrible. I turn into a soggy miserable

wreck. You do not want to see me in that sort of a state. *I* don't want you to see me like that. So I'm going. Now.'

'Where?'

She dropped the wash bag into the suitcase, wishing she were better prepared, never more regretting that she hadn't kept a closer eye on the date. 'I need to get some supplies and then find a hotel.'

'Who will be there to take care of you?'

'No one,' she said, ignoring the brief twist of her heart and shoving everything down hard so it might fit. 'But I'm used to that. I can take care of myself.'

Leo folded his arms across his chest, his jaw set, his brow still furrowed, a stance that unfortunately suggested obstinacy and purpose. 'Who will rub your back and run you a bath?'

'I'll be fine,' she said with some obstinacy and purpose of her own. 'I always am.'

'Stay here and I can do both.'

For a split second, Willow allowed herself to imagine it because it sounded so wonderful. And then she thought of her dignity and the risk to the mile-high walls around her heart, at which point it very much didn't.

She gave her head a sharp shake and stifled the rogue pang of longing. 'No,' she said flatly as she zipped up one half of the case. 'It's too personal. Too embarrassing. I'd probably throw up on you and no one needs that.'

'You don't have to do this on your own,' he said, frustratingly persistent. 'Not this month, at least. Tell me what I can do to help and I will do it. I will make sure you have whatever you need.'

'You still want to solve my problems.'

'I don't like seeing people I care about suffering.'

She went very still, her heart giving a quick lurch, her gaze darting to his. She straightened and stared at him, packing momentarily forgotten. 'You care about me?'

'I'm sleeping with you. I'm sightseeing with you. Of course I do.'

She frowned. 'I see.'

'Is wanting to help you such a bad thing?' he asked with an assessing tilt of his head.

'It's a very bad thing.' The helping, the caring, the knowing that if she had this month she might crave another, and another… None of it was good.

'Why?'

'I don't want a knight in shining armour,' she said as much to remind herself of the fact as inform him of it. 'I never have. If I stay here, you'll see me at my worst. If I let you close enough to rub my back and run me baths, I may forget that this fling of ours was only ever supposed to be temporary, and that simply can't happen.'

'Why not?'

She had to tell him. She had to make him see that she could not and would not indulge his hero complex this time. 'When my mother died, my world fell apart, but I gradually put it back together again. My father didn't. He loved her so much that losing her has virtually destroyed him. He doesn't live. He just exists. He's not there for me. Or anyone. I will not put myself in that position. I will not put anyone else in that position should something happen to me. That's why not.'

'I am not going to fall in love with you.'

Her chest tightened for the briefest of seconds. 'Are you sure about that?'

He nodded. 'Quite sure.'

'Because I'm nothing like the type you usually go for.'

'It's not just that,' he said. 'I've seen how destructive love and the lack of control that goes with it can be and the chaos that can cause. I won't allow it to happen to me. I won't be that weak.'

She wished she had his confidence. 'But I might fall in love with you.'

For a moment he didn't respond. The frown deepened. A muscle hammered in his jaw. 'All right,' he said decisively, clearly having given that unwelcome thought due consideration. 'I won't rub your back or run you baths. I won't come anywhere near you if that's what you want. But give me a list and I will get what you need. I can feed you. Bring you drinks. What I *can't* do is let you walk out of another of my properties alone and in pain. That simply isn't the man I either am or want to be.'

'This isn't about you. It's about me.'

'You don't *really* want to go to a hotel, do you?'

An image floated into her head of her in some small, unfamiliar room, alone, again, robbed of the positivity she fought so hard to maintain, and the ache that throbbed in the pit of her stomach—now more emotional than physical—was so powerful it vaporised her inhibitions. 'No,' she admitted on a sigh.

'So take one of the spare rooms,' he said, unsurprisingly seizing advantage of the vulnerability she'd exposed by her confession. 'Keep the door closed. Message me if and when you need something. You will barely notice I'm here.'

Willow's defences, weakened by the pain, the demoralising knowledge of what was to come and the yearning she was struggling to keep suppressed, were no match for such persuasive arguments. Deep down she didn't want to have to go anywhere. She longed to be looked after, just once, and here Leo was offering her his support.

He was strong enough to handle the days to come, surely. She wouldn't make the mistake of thinking his assistance was anything more than it was. She'd be too preoccupied with managing the pain behind a closed door to think of anything. And when it was over, she would leave and she'd never have to see him again, which was just how it had to be.

'Are you going to counter-argue my every point?' she asked as the last of her resistance crumbled and she gave in to the inevitable.

'Yes,' he said, proving it with the faintest of smiles.

'Fine.'

Five long days later, nursing a large whisky, Leo sat on the terrace and stared out into the dark, warm, quiet night. Lights twinkled in the distance. Waves lapped gently at the beach below. In marked contrast to the peace and tranquillity of his surroundings, his head pounded and his stomach churned.

When he'd offered Willow his services, the thought of her being alone and in pain unbearable, the need to keep her close too fierce to deny, he had not imagined the depth of her suffering. He didn't think he'd ever forget the sight of her doubled up in agony or curled into a ball in the centre of the bed. It had been unexpectedly harrowing. How she dealt with it, month after month, on her own, he had no idea. She was unbelievably tough, but the mental toll had to be immense. He'd experienced a mere five days of it, on and off, as an occasionally useful bystander, and that was bad enough.

He hadn't enjoyed seeing her vibrancy diminished, her light out. Her distress had struck him square in the chest. No one deserved to live with that degree of discomfort and at one point, when she'd been feeling well enough to come downstairs for a couple of hours, he'd asked her if there wasn't anything she could do to alleviate her symptoms.

'The contraceptive pill would make things more manageable,' she'd told him, 'and God, it would be good to have a reliable time frame to work with, but it's possible it contributed to the arterial blood clot that my mother went into hospital to have removed. I just can't bring myself to take it and expose myself to the same sort of risk. It was supposed to be a simple operation, but she had a bad reaction to the anaesthetic and that was it.'

'What about surgery?' he'd asked, completely understanding the influence of the past on the present.

'I've also been told that in my case—which is mild even though the pain is excruciating—that would lessen the symptoms considerably. It would also increase the chances of having a family, which I'd like at some point, so on paper it's a no-brainer. But the thought of an anaesthetic terrifies me. What if I too go to sleep and never wake up? What would that do to my father? Look.'

She'd held out a trembling hand. 'Even the mention of one makes me panic. And it's not just one operation. It could be many.'

Leo had taken her hand in his and held it until it had stopped shaking, itching to research the hell out of anaesthesia and then promise her the best medical treatment money could buy. Was there anything he could do to encourage her to have the surgery? he wondered now, turning his glass in his fingers as he continued to stare out into the distance. Her fears had to run very deep for her to favour the pain.

His phone beeped to indicate the arrival of a message and he knocked back the rest of the whisky before picking the device up. The text was from Zander.

Now I can see why you were so keen to take a holiday.

He frowned, set the glass down, then typed back.

What do you mean?

His brother's reply came in the form of a link, which had apparently been forwarded to him by their sister Thalia and came with the instruction not to shoot the messenger.

Trepidatiously, his heart thudding, Leo clicked on it. It took him to a page that purported to belong to a global magazine with an inclination for celebrity gossip. The subject of that page was him. Or more specifically, him and Willow.

Despite the enveloping warmth of the night, his blood

chilled and his skin tightened as he scrolled down and read the article. The accompanying crystal-clear photos showed the two of them on the yacht the day they'd taken it out, snorkelling, jumping into the sea, talking on the deck, and more from the steep steps, the hot springs and the taverna.

Five stomach-churning minutes later, during which he'd sought and found a dozen similar sites with the same photos and the sort of headlines that came with exclamation marks, his vision was blurring and his chest was tight. How had it happened? was the question ricocheting around his brain as nausea rose up inside him. Why hadn't he noticed the cameras?

Everyone else, however, seemed to want to know, Who was she? Had Europe's most eligible, most elusive bachelor finally found love? If anyone had information about the mystery woman with the colourful hair and multiple piercings, they should click here.

The speculation was hideous. The invasion of his fiercely guarded privacy, and hers, boiled his blood. They were fodder for gossip—his mother's racy past had also been raked up yet again—and it was everything he'd sought to avoid. Only this time, *he* was the one at fault. No one else was to blame. He'd got so used to Willow's striking looks he'd forgotten that they did not fade into the background. He'd lost all sense of perspective. He'd been recklessly careless. He hadn't once considered the fact that he had an image of strength, of control and zero vulnerability to maintain and a business and a family to protect.

How could he have been so weak?

What the hell had he been *doing* all this time?

It wasn't remotely his responsibility to fix her issues but that hadn't stopped him. He *had* got a kick out of showing her sex could be good for her. That first time, here on the island, when she'd laughed with such abandon, such joy, he'd felt like he could rule the world. Ever since then, he'd behaved rashly—asking her to stay, putting Zander in charge of the company and then playing at being a couple as they did the tourist thing. When they'd talked—he, now he thought it, frequently without any filter at all—he'd listened closely to what she said. Her observations had made him question things he'd always accepted as fact. She'd developed unprecedented influence over him and he hadn't even noticed.

As to the reason he'd decided he had to play nurse these last few days, he was at a complete loss. It was yet another example of spontaneous, ill-advised decision-making. He'd been under no obligation to help. As she'd told him, she was used to handling it on her own. He had no business wishing he could take away her pain by absorbing it himself. How she managed her health was none of his concern and the giddy pleasure he'd felt when she'd sent him a message asking him to run her a bath and rub her back, which indicated a level of trust he'd hoped for but never expected, was as unwarranted as it was unwelcome.

Little by little, day by day, he'd been falling further and further under her spell, he realised, a cold sweat breaking out all over his skin. At some point, the nose stud, the earrings and the hair had stopped offending him. Now he couldn't—and didn't want to—imagine her any other way. She was perfect, just as she was, and that was not good, although his heart was thundering in his chest, in his head, in every inch of his body so loudly he couldn't quite remember why.

His phone beeped again, and he snatched it up, his hands shaking, the wariness winding through him intensifying to an almost unbearable degree.

Just as well I was able to rescue the merger, huh?!

Rescue the merger? What merger? Ah. Right. *That* merger. The one he'd flown to New York to arrange. The one that would add billions to the company's bottom line yet had not crossed his mind in days. What the hell had gone wrong with it? And when was the last time he'd even *thought* about the company? he wondered, his lungs constricting so much that breathing was suddenly difficult. When had he stopped worrying about how Zander was doing at the helm? How could he have abandoned his principles, the values with which he'd lived his life for over a decade, so easily?

He was completely out of control. Plates could come crashing down at any minute. It had to stop. All of it. Before his head was turned even further and he found himself entirely in Willow's thrall. Before he became someone he didn't want to be, ruled by emotion and selfishness, a slave to passion and ice and volatility. He had to claw back what was left of the life he knew and needed before it was destroyed for ever. Willow was back on her feet. The holiday was over. They were done.

Contrary to Willow's expectations, she hadn't been in too much pain to notice how magnificent Leo had been.

He'd done exactly what he'd promised. He'd been patience and support personified, a tower of strength, and completely unfazed when she had thrown up on him, as she'd warned.

And now she was out the other side, staring up at the ceiling in the dark, the tumbling thoughts teeming through her head rendering sleep frustratingly elusive, she could see that everything she'd feared could all too easily come to pass. He was complex and intriguing, thoughtful and gorgeous, and her feelings for him were becoming dangerous.

Despite her best efforts to prevent it, she suspected she'd already invested herself emotionally in him. Why would she have caved in and requested the bath and the back rub if she didn't trust him? She wanted to tell him to ditch the job and buy a boat and support him through it. She wanted to take Selene by the shoulders and give her good shake along with an instruction to grow up. She found herself thinking ahead to next month and wishing she could have him by her side.

But that could never be. If she stuck around any longer those unwise feelings could all too easily deepen and she simply couldn't risk it. What if she allowed herself to love him and something happened to him? She'd be destroyed. And what if, despite his certainty that it would not happen, he developed feelings for her? He claimed to care about her. He'd seen her at her worst and hadn't run for the hills. It was possible he wasn't as impervious to love as he believed, and if he succumbed to the emotions he denied then *he* might be destroyed.

She deeply regretted not being stronger and clinging

on to her resistance. She should never have been swayed by his arguments. If she wasn't careful she could be in so much trouble. The potential for heartbreak was immense and unacceptable. But it wasn't too late to rectify the situation. All she had to do was terminate their affair. She'd miss him, their time together and the sex, of course, but it was better to get out now, while she still could.

The security of her emotional well-being depended on the strength of her resolve and, as she finally drifted off into an uneasy sleep, she vowed that no matter how mighty the battle Leo mounted, how ruthlessly he blocked her protests, she would not waver. However hard she had to fight him, and quite possibly herself, in the morning, she absolutely *would* leave.

# CHAPTER ELEVEN

AFTER A RESTLESS NIGHT, Willow woke early, her eyes gritty as if filled with sand, her chest tight as if caught in a vice. She got up and packed her things, which had moved to the spare room with her, ignoring the voice in her head that lamented the way things had to be and the strange aching of her heart. Leaving was the right thing, the only thing, to do, she reminded herself over and over again. She had no choice if she wanted to avoid misery and destruction.

Steeling herself against weakness, armed for battle, she picked up her suitcase and carried it downstairs. She found Leo in the kitchen, sitting at the table, drinking a cup of coffee. He looked exhausted. Tense. Remote. As if recent events had been as tough on him as they had on her.

'Good morning,' he said gruffly.

At the strange lack of expression in his voice, a shiver rippled down her spine and her throat constricted for a second, but she wouldn't question what might be behind it. She could not afford to get sidetracked. She had to focus on the goal. 'Good morning.'

'Coffee?' he asked with a nod in the direction of the stove.

'No, thank you.'

'How are you feeling?'

'Much better.'

'I'm glad to hear it.'

'Thank you for all your support.'

The smile he gave her was brief. Humourless. 'No problem.'

A horribly wintry silence fell, during which all she could hear was the thundering of her heart. Then Leo opened his mouth to speak and Willow immediately focused, needing to get in first, before she lost her nerve. 'So I'd like to go home now,' she blurted, the words exiting her mouth with a rush.

He started, the porcelain of his cup hitting the marble tabletop with a clatter, his eyebrows shooting up. 'What?'

She took a deep breath to calm down, and braced herself. 'This has been a lot of fun,' she began before amending, 'well, not the last few days, of course, but before that. It's been great. However, real life calls. I need to check on my father. I have things to sort things out before starting work on my next commission and roots to touch up.'

'Seriously?'

'Yes.'

He frowned. Then gave a short nod. 'OK.'

And now the surprise was all hers. He agreed? Just like that? Without a fight? 'Really?' she said, totally confused by his acquiescence when not all that long ago he'd resolutely thwarted her attempts to go.

'I should be heading back to work too,' he said, pushing back his chair and getting to his feet. 'I've neglected the business for longer than I intended. Too long, in hindsight.'

At the trace of irritation she could hear in his voice,

Willow flushed with embarrassment and flooded with awkwardness. 'That's my fault,' she said, shifting her weight from one foot to the other, the regret that she hadn't been strong enough to overcome temptation and leave as planned abject. 'I'm sorry.'

He put the cup in the sink. 'Don't be. It's not your fault.'

'You stayed because of me.'

'I gave you little choice.'

'Are you going because of me, too?'

He spun round. His gaze collided with hers, sharp, questioning, and she wished she hadn't said anything because this was not the time to show weakness even if she did, for some reason, badly need to know. 'What do you mean?'

'Do you really have to return to Athens?'

'Yes,' he said. 'Zander messaged me last night. The merger's been causing problems.'

'So it's not because the last few days were a bit too… I don't know…visceral?'

'Absolutely not,' he said, his eyes suddenly blazing with such conviction that she had to believe him. 'Never think that. If anything, know that I am blown away by your strength and resilience.'

'OK, then,' she said, the relief oddly overwhelming.

'When do you want to leave?'

She resisted the urge to tell him she'd changed her mind and she didn't want to leave ever, because she couldn't change her mind. She had to be strong. So she ignored the odd ache in her chest and the tightness of her throat, nodded once, and said, firmly, 'I'm ready to go now.'

* * *

The journey back to Athens could not have been more different to the one out. The tension that filled the car was stony not sizzling, and there was no champagne on the plane. They did not exchange long smouldering looks filled with the promise of passion and adventure. They barely looked at each other.

The minute they boarded, Leo attached himself to his phone while Willow sat back and stared out of the window, stifling the dangerous emotions that were clamouring to be acknowledged. Her heart beat fast and her head buzzed beneath the pressure, but she counted down the minutes and kept her mouth shut.

On landing, they disembarked in silence. On the tarmac, she didn't throw herself into his arms and indulge in one last kiss. She didn't break down and beg him to convince her she was wrong about everything. She simply said a cool goodbye, turned on her heel and walked off in the opposite direction, all the while reminding herself she'd had a very lucky escape indeed.

'So what's up?'

Three weeks after Leo's return to the city, Zander emerged onto the roof terrace of Leo's Athens penthouse apartment and set down two bottles of beer on the table.

'Nothing's up,' Leo muttered, pulling one towards him, wiping his thumb over the condensation and wishing it was as easy to swipe a path through the chaos of his thoughts.

His brother sat down and stretched out his legs. 'You've been like a bear with a sore head ever since you came back from Santorini. Everyone's terrified of you. Especially Maria. She said she's never known you to be like this in all the years she's been your assistant. She even said she preferred me, which means things must be really bad.'

'Tough few weeks,' Leo replied, focusing on the view to avoid his brother's unusually probing gaze. 'It happens.'

'Not to you,' came the dry reply. 'And they haven't been that tough.'

Irritatingly, Zander was right, on both fronts. Generally, when there was an issue at work Leo simply upped his degree of control until it passed, and there'd be far less to catch up on than he'd anticipated, thanks to his brother's eminent capability. He didn't know why he was so on edge and off balance. His usual method of simply burying his concerns and focusing didn't seem to be working.

'So what's this, then?' he asked, indicating the beer with a casual wave of his hand. 'An intervention?'

'Yes. On behalf of all of us. We want to know what's going on.'

His siblings had been discussing him? He didn't much like that either. 'I don't know what you're talking about,' he snapped, opting for denial, hoping against hope his brother would take the hint and leave it.

'Willow Jacobs,' Zander replied, annoyingly doing neither.

At the mention of her name, Leo went still. He clenched his jaw and pushed back the memories that were now trying to barge their way into his head. He would not think of her. Whenever he did, his head spun and his chest tightened. He had no idea why. Yet his brother required some sort of response. 'What about her?'

'Are you in love with her?'

His heart skipped a beat and then began to race, but he drew in a deep breath of warm evening air and forced himself to calm down. 'Don't be ridiculous.'

'I saw the photos,' said Zander. '*Everyone* saw the photos.'

Leo shuddered.

'Olympia said she could see it in your eyes.'

'Olympia is mistaken.'

'You staked a claim on her the night of Daph's wedding,' Zander pointed out unhelpfully. 'I've never known you to do that sort of thing before.'

No, well, he'd lost his mind for a while. But he had it back now. The merger was on track. Lazlo appeared to be keeping their mother under control. The status quo had resumed. Exactly as he'd planned. He hadn't even had to work for it. By announcing her intention to go home that last morning on Santorini, Willow had made it unexpectedly easy for him. It was therefore absurd to feel rejected. At the airport, he'd watched her walk away and he'd been relieved. Not gutted like a fish. *Relieved.* She had the potential to bring out the absolute worst in him. He'd had a very lucky escape.

'It was a blip,' he said flatly. 'A lapse of sanity. It's over.'

'That seems a shame.'

'What would you know about it?'

'Very little, I have to admit. Our parents didn't exactly set a fine example. But look at Daphne and Ari. Where love exists it's a beautiful thing. You did look happy and relaxed with her in those photos.'

No. He hadn't. He hadn't looked anything in those photos, and he was done talking about it.

'I thought you wanted to discuss business,' he said, shifting round and fixing Zander with his iciest glare.

'That's right.'

'Well?'

'Do you genuinely enjoy running the company?' his brother asked, unfortunately not remotely fazed by the glare. 'Because I do. So if you don't, I'd be more than happy to take over permanently.'

Take over? What the hell? That wasn't happening. He would not abdicate the responsibilities his father had given him. He would not fail.

'I'm fine,' Leo said through gritted teeth, a thumping headache beginning to develop at his right temple. 'Everything is absolutely fine.'

A week later however, Leo had to admit it wasn't fine. Something was very wrong indeed. He wasn't sleeping. He wasn't eating. And his behaviour at the office had gone from bad to worse. He was snapping people's heads off and snarling at anyone who got in his way. Zander had ordered him to stay at home before everyone jumped ship, and despite immensely disliking being told what to do, Leo had grudgingly agreed for the sake of the business.

Unfortunately, however, all that meant was that he had time on his hands in which to do nothing by prowl round his apartment, struggling and failing to keep a lid on the bubbling emotions seething away deep inside him and the thoughts generated by the conversation he'd had with his brother on the terrace whirling around his brain on some interminable loop.

He'd never considered stepping down before. He'd never even dared take a break until six weeks or so ago. To not continue his father's legacy—the destiny that had been drummed into him practically from birth—would be a betrayal he could not contemplate.

But as he stalked into the kitchen to make himself the fourth coffee of the day even though it was only nine in the morning, he wondered if perhaps he was too close to be able to see the situation objectively.

What would an outsider think? What would Willow think? She'd had a few pertinent ideas about roles and responsibilities—not that she crossed his mind much. She'd be the first to tell him to stand aside and install Zander as CEO, and she'd be right. Because while Leo merely endured the position, his brother had relished it. He had a knack with people and was insanely driven. He was ruthless and brilliant. He'd always been the better man for the job.

He was also annoyingly perceptive because while Leo liked to tell himself that he rarely thought about Willow, the truth was that she was in his head all the damn time. She ruined his sleep. She disrupted his train of thought. He missed her more than he'd ever thought possible.

Could he have done the unthinkable and fallen in love with her?

In response to the question that flashed through his mind, Leo froze, ground coffee spilling all over the worktop.

No. He couldn't. It was impossible. He'd sworn not to allow it.

And yet, when he ran through all the reasons she was wrong for him, he was suddenly able to counteract every single one of them. Streakless hair and unadorned ears now seemed dull. Far from fearing her influence, he *wanted* to hear her views and seek her input. He wasn't destructive like his mother. He wasn't weak like his father when it came to the personal. He had nothing to fear from emotion. The days he'd spent with Willow on Santorini, he'd felt alive, for the first time in years. Free from burden. Free to be himself. She'd made him feel invincible. The world wouldn't collapse if he wasn't in control of it 24-7. It hadn't when he'd been away. And as for betraying his father's legacy, surely he'd be preserving it by putting the best person in charge.

As the foundations of his existence fell away, so too did the walls around his heart. He did love Willow, he realised with a jolt as unleashed emotions began to batter him on all sides, stealing the breath from his lungs and draining the strength from his limbs so sharply he had to fumble for a chair. He probably had from the moment she'd stood up to him by the pool the afternoon they'd met. Why else would he have pursued her when every fibre of his being had warned him away? He'd dressed it up as guilt, the righting of wrongs, but fundamentally he'd just wanted her.

And he still did.

When he thought of his life without her, bleak, colourless, empty, it chilled him to the bone. When he counted the days and thought of her going through another period alone and in pain, it clawed at his chest. He wanted to protect her, support her, love her until the day he died, which with any luck would be decades from now.

So what was he going to do about it?

And more importantly, given her fears about love, would she ever let him?

Willow had spent the time she'd been back in London principally thanking her lucky stars that she'd escaped Leo's powerful and potentially destructive orbit when she had.

Determined to consign her sojourn on Santorini to history, to wipe him from her head, she filled her diary with visits to her father and arrangements with her friends. She replenished her art materials, had new violet streaks put in her hair and updated her website to include the portrait of Selene and the stunningly positive press that it had generated.

She didn't think about Leo. She didn't wonder what he was doing or how he was and she didn't even contemplate clicking on the links to some apparently gossipy articles that a friend had forwarded. She certainly didn't fish out the sketchbooks stuffed with drawings of him that she'd stashed at the back of a drawer, flick through them and reminisce. Nor, when her period hit again, did she wish someone would give her a backrub and run her a bath. She just got on with things as she always had and always would.

So life was fine. Uneventful, safe, exactly as she wanted it. The sun was shining and London, with its population basking in the fine weather and spilling out of bars and into parks, looked great. She was busy as a bee, preparing to travel to Milan to paint one of the Italian countesses she'd met at that wedding reception all those weeks ago, and excited about getting back to work. She'd dodged a bullet with regards to feelings, and everything was great.

Until one morning a month after she'd returned, when she was rummaging in the drawer for a pencil, she caught sight of a loose sketch of Leo lying sprawled across the bed in Santorini, and it hit her like a blow to the stomach that nothing was great, that everything was, in fact, pretty bloody awful.

Clutching the drawing, pain slicing though her chest like a knife, Willow sank to the sofa and curled up in a ball, the tears she'd managed to keep at bay for weeks breaching the dam and streaming down her cheeks.

Who had she been kidding? Life might be uneventful and safe but it wasn't what she wanted at all. The sun was shining and the city buzzed, but over *her* head was an oppressively thick black cloud that threatened rain. The thought of Milan and getting back to work was the opposite of thrilling.

She missed Leo so much. More than she'd ever thought possible. She missed his smile and the way he'd looked at her as if trying to seek out every one of her hopes and fears. She wanted him badly and not just because he'd shown her pleasure, adventure and taken such good care of her. She'd loved talking to and arguing with him. He was endlessly fascinating and the days they'd lived like a couple had been the best of her life.

So much for keeping her heart safe. It had been at risk

from the moment they'd met. If their relationship really had been purely physical, as she'd so foolishly believed, she wouldn't have wanted things she ought not to want. She wouldn't have done things she'd known were unwise. She'd paid lip service to preventing it, but she'd fallen head over heels in love with him regardless. She loved everything about him.

And it was a disaster. Because Leo did not feel the same way about her. He didn't want her. He cared about her—or he had once upon a time—but he didn't love her. How ironic to have overcome the obstacles that had tormented her for years by falling for someone unavailable.

She hadn't had a lucky escape at all, she thought miserably, a fresh wave of wretchedness washing over her. She should have stayed and fought. For him. For them. She should have persuaded him that she was right for him. Because she was. On paper, yes, they were an unlikely match, but in reality they had a lot in common. They were both ambitious, driven, bound by circumstance. They each had one deceased parent and another not really deserving of the title. She'd never be cool and polished or sophisticated enough to carry off a white trouser suit with any sort of panache, but she believed they understood one another.

If he were by her side she'd have the confidence to overcome her fears and undergo the surgeries. She'd want to do everything in her power to improve her quality of life for herself and for him and to better the possibility of having the children he wanted. She would read the statistics over and over again until she believed them.

She wasn't her father. Leo had been right—she *was*

strong and resilient. And yes, something might happen to her, or to him, but then again, it might not. Surely it would be better to have loved and lost than never to have loved at all. Her parents had adored each other. Maybe his continued grief was a price her father was willing to pay for that love.

So what was she going to do about the situation? Was it too late to try and convince Leo that the patterns of the past didn't have to be repeated? Or would she be fighting a losing battle? If she tracked him down and demanded to talk to him, would he be pleased to see her or appalled?

Willow was so wrapped up in misery and confusion that she almost didn't hear the sound of the buzzer. When she did, she grabbed a pillow and stuck it over her head for no one need see her in this much of a state. But whoever it was wasn't going away, so with a deep ragged sigh she threw aside the pillow, levered herself off the sofa and padded to the door.

'Yes?'

'Willow? It's Leo.'

Her heart stopped, then began to gallop. Was she hallucinating? Had she somehow conjured him up with the strength of her feelings? He'd frequently been able to read her mind, but surely telepathy couldn't cross continents. So why was he here?

With shaking fingers, she buzzed him in and estimated she had one minute to make herself presentable, which wasn't nearly enough, but at least her clothes were clean and her recently touched-up hair was good.

She stood at the open door, her entire body vibrating, her limbs alarmingly weak. His thumps up the stairs matched the thundering of her pulse, and then he was striding towards her, big, broad and so handsome he took her breath away, and God, it was good to see him.

'Leo,' she said, the surge of longing that she'd spent a month trying to deny nearly taking out what remained of her knees. 'What are you doing here? You look dreadful.'

He rubbed his hands over his face, which was haggard and more sharply angled, as if he'd lost weight, then shoved them in the pockets of his jeans. 'Can I come in?'

'Of course.' She stood aside to let him pass then closed the door behind him, her studio immediately filling with a restless sort of energy that put every one of her senses on high alert. 'Would you like something to drink?'

'No, thank you,' he said, heading into the space then turning to face her, the intensity of his gaze pinning her to the spot. 'I'd like to know how you've been.'

Willow swallowed hard, her mind racing. How should she respond? What was he thinking? She couldn't tell. His face gave nothing away. Did she dare use this opportunity to find out? She'd had no time to plan. Yet surely she could be brave. She'd blagged her work into exhibitions. She'd secured an invitation to the wedding of the year then pursued Leo across a dance floor and persuaded him to agree to a one-night stand. When she knew what she wanted she went for it, and she might never get another chance.

'I thought I was doing fine,' she said, her mouth dry, nerves nevertheless tangling in the pit of her stomach. 'But I just realised I'm not. You?'

'The same.'

Her head swam. Her heart thudded. Could she dare to

hope? 'I'm going to Milan next week,' she said. 'I'm not as excited about it as I should be.'

'I resigned.'

She blinked in shock. 'Resigned?'

'Zander is the new CEO of Stanhope Kallis.'

'What? Why?'

'I'm tired of doing things I don't want to do,' he said, his gaze trained on her face as if nothing else but her existed. 'I'm sick of living by rules that don't make me happy.'

'I see,' she said, not seeing at all. In fact, she was actually feeling a bit dizzy. He was taking up too much space, too much air. 'So what are you going to do?'

'I haven't decided yet.'

'That must be a concern.'

'You'd think so, wouldn't you?' he said with the ghost of a smile. 'But oddly enough, it isn't. I feel liberated. As if the weight of the world has been lifted from my shoulders.'

'Then it was the right thing to do.'

'I think so. And do you know what *does* make me happy?'

Right now she knew nothing. She wanted him so much she could barely think straight and this conversation was not proving easy to follow. 'Sailing?'

He shook his head. 'You do.'

She stared at him, reeling. She had to clutch the back of a chair for support. 'What?'

'You make me happy, Willow,' he said, taking his hands out of his pockets as he took a step towards her, his gaze softening. 'When I'm with you there's nowhere else I'd rather be. When I'm not with you, you're all I think about. I'm in love with you. I think I fell for you the moment you challenged me to a compromise by the pool the afternoon I failed to bribe you into not exhibiting your portrait of my mother. Despite what both you and I might have thought, you've turned out to be exactly my type. I've been wrong to fear emotion. I've put too great a value on control. But I am neither of my parents and from now on I intend to forge my own path. I'd like to do it with you.'

He stopped, clearly waiting for a response, but Willow couldn't speak. Her throat was too tight. Her thoughts were spinning too fast. What he'd just said… It was everything she'd hoped for. If she hadn't been able to feel the emotion pouring off him and see it blazing in his eyes, she'd have thought she were dreaming.

'Are you sure?' she managed eventually, her heart crashing against her ribs so hard she feared one might break.

'I've never been more certain of anything.'

'I might not be able to have children.'

'I know that,' he said simply. 'But I just want you. I believe in us, and I badly want the future we could have, whatever shape that takes. I know that love terrifies you and I understand why. I'm here to convince you to reconsider.'

His sincerity swept away the last of her reservations and love and joy rushed through her, hot, fast and free. 'There's no need,' she said shakily, releasing her grip on the chair and closing the distance between them.

He paled. 'Why not?'

She took his hands in hers and held them tight. 'Because love doesn't terrify me anymore,' she said around the small hot lump in her throat. 'Well, it does a bit, but I've recently realised that I've spent too long living in fear of something that will likely never happen. Too long living with pain that could be so much less. I don't want to be shackled to the past any longer, Leo. I want to look to the future and I want you in it.' She took a deep breath. 'Because I love you, too.'

The colour returned to his face. The tension eased from his shoulders and his eyes bore into hers. 'You do?'

'So much,' she said, losing herself in their swirling depths, the heat of his body and moving in closer. 'You're everything I never dared allow myself to dream of. Everything I thought I could never have. I want to laugh with you, argue with you, grow old with you. I want it all.'

'Then you'd better marry me.'

As he drew her into his arms, a small smile playing around his mouth, joy exploded through her, dizzying her with its intensity, swelling her heart with sheer happiness. 'Yes, please,' she said with the brightest of grins and lifted her head for his kiss.

# EPILOGUE

*Three years later*

LEO HAD SPENT quite a bit of time in hospitals over the last couple of years. With immense courage and impressive persistence, Willow had faced and vanquished her demons and had finally elected to have the surgery that the medical professionals believed would help her.

Hating to see her in continued pain, Leo had been keen to get on with the process once the decision had been made. Willow, however, citing professionalism and her reputation, had refused to let the clients she'd already had booked in down and, as she'd pointed out, the new business he'd set up required as much of his focus as he could give because luxury yachts didn't design, build and charter themselves.

The first operation had taken place twelve months after she'd agreed to marry him, two weeks after they'd actually wed in a small ceremony held at the church around the corner from her father's house so that he could attend.

Before, during and after that and each subsequent one, he'd been there for her every step of the way, doing his best to allay the fears that occasionally surged and re-

minding her how much he loved her. Despite the disap-
proval of the surgical team, he'd been at her side both
when she went to sleep and when she woke up every
single time.

It hadn't been an easy ride, by any means, but every
moment of the torment they'd suffered together had been
worth it because while the pain hadn't completely disappeared, Willow was no longer wrenched apart one week
in every four. She could smile and laugh and function,
and the relief and happiness this gave him expanded his
heart until it felt too big for his chest.

This particular wing of the private Athens hospital
and the carpeted corridor along which he was currently
pacing were unfamiliar to him, but the emotions tear-
ing through him weren't. The gut-wrenching terror. The
gnawing impatience. The heart-thumping hope. They
were nothing new, even if the circumstances were.

What was going on in there? he wondered grimly as
he shoved his hands through his hair and glanced at his
watch. It had been hours. Why was it taking so long? If
he didn't get an update soon, heads would roll.

'Mr Stanhope?'

In response to the voice behind him Leo came to an
abrupt halt and whirled round, nearly colliding with the
doctor who was holding open the door. 'Yes?'

'You can go in now.'

He didn't need telling twice. With a muttered thank
you, he barged past the doctor and strode across the lobby.
He pushed opened the door to Willow's room and there
she was, lying in the bed, looking exhausted, frazzled
and lovelier than ever.

'Are you all right?' he asked, his heart turning over as it did every time he saw her.

Her eyes shone. Her smile was wide. His gaze dropped to the bundle in her arms and his throat tightened and his vision swam.

'Come and meet our beautiful baby girl.'

\* \* \* \* \*

# BOUND BY A SICILIAN SECRET

## LELA MAY WIGHT

MILLS & BOON

This book is dedicated to my editor, Charlotte.

Thank you for guiding me to find the true heart of my stories.

# CHAPTER ONE

Her life—her history—had been erased.

Flora Bick stared at the document in her hands. One hundred and twenty-six pages of redacted information. Thick black line after thick black line.

She'd known the risks—the fall-out. The counsellor had prepared her before this, her first visit into the big smoke without her parents. London, a city that had always felt so far away from her life in Devon. But what she hadn't expected was the pain in her chest, nor the tightening of her gut into a clenched fist.

She hadn't expected the...*grief.*

It *was* grief, wasn't it? Something had crashed into her chest, leaving a vast crater. But it wasn't empty. It was full of lots of things she couldn't place—couldn't catch. It was a tightness, a tingle, a breathlessness.

Sitting on the edge of the bed, Flora flipped to the first page of her adoption file with trembling fingers.

It was a chronological account of her life before the farm. Before two strangers had claimed her as their own. As their daughter. But she'd been someone else's daughter, hadn't she? It had taken a broken ankle for her to find that out. To learn that she and her parents were not biologically related.

And it hurt.

The lies.

*Twenty-one years of lies!*

Her instinct was to run. Run hard and run fast. But where would she go? She'd chosen this hotel. Ignored the reservation for the more budget-friendly hotel her parents had booked for her, close to the train station, and walked into this hotel with its golden doors and nodding doormen dressed in white hats and gloves, offering to carry her tatty backpack for her.

Because just for today—for tonight—she wanted to experience a world that was unlike her own. A life she might have had. Who knew?

She hadn't known.

Not until she'd opened this folder.

And she'd wanted to open it in a room like this.

The ceilings were high, with sweeping patterns leading to a chandelier of dangling diamond lights. The dark oak bed almost spanned the width of the room, with layers upon layers of the softest blankets. And when she'd climbed onto it the mattress hadn't given at her weight. It had cushioned her body in a firm but gentle hug. Caressed her skin with the softest touch. And she'd let her head fall against the mountain of pillows and stared at the view.

Her eyes shot now to the floor-to-ceiling windows. She'd pulled back the heavy blue curtains with their intricate gold leaf pattern when she'd arrived, pushed open the French doors which led to nowhere but an iron railing and the view.

The skyline of London—the big city—the home of her birth, of her beginning. The place where she'd discovered the truth about herself when she'd collected her adoption file from the local authority.

She'd had to make a special request for it not to come through the post, because if it had she might never have received it. She didn't doubt for a second that her parents would have intercepted it first.

She'd pushed harder than she'd ever pushed for anything. For her parents to loosen the reins. To trust her to collect her file unaccompanied. To be in this big city with its bright lights and buildings taller than the clouds. So she could be away from the farm, away from them, away from expectation.

She hadn't wanted the people who'd raised her to sugar-coat the impact. All her life they'd been sprinkling sugar over sour apples. Peeling off the tart skin. Removing the core. Presenting perfectly bite-sized pieces for her to consume. Just the way they'd presented life to her. In perfect chunks. Removing the bruises. Sweetening the distasteful...

It made sense now. The over-protectiveness. The never letting her fall from the straight and narrow, never allowing her to make her own choices. They'd never let her make her own choices because she was missing vital information, wasn't she?

The strong pain medication she'd required for her badly broken ankle was something that she should be careful with because of the risks. Risks that may be compounded because of her history. Because of her genes. Her possible addictive personality. Her compulsions...

*Like buying the dress.*

She hadn't been able to resist, had she? Not the dress— not the hotel.

She looked at her bare arms, at her shoulders encased in tight-fitting emerald-green. She'd never worn a fancy frock before. Never had the opportunity. But she'd bought this. Wanted to have it. *Needed* to have it. Whipped it off the charity shop hanger and claimed it as hers.

Because addiction ran in her blood, didn't it? Her mother's blood.

She'd never known her mother. She never would. The file was clear on one thing: her biological mother was dead. The way of life she'd chosen above her own flesh and blood had taken her to an early grave.

What else ran in Flora's blood? A sickness like her mother's? How would she ever know when her life was…*redacted*?

She stood. The file slid from her silk-clad thighs to land at her feet. The symbolism crushed her. Her life, her history, tossed to the ground as if it meant nothing. And it *was* nothing, wasn't it?

This file, these black-and-white-striped papers she'd agonised over for months, had only increased her need to know more. The need to know where and who she came from. It hadn't eased her curiosity, only raised more questions.

*And more doubt.*

She wasn't who she'd thought she was. She was not Flora Bick, daughter of dairy farmers. She was the abandoned child of a drug addict. Father unknown.

Placing a hand to her chest, Flora struggled to drag in a breath. She felt trapped.

She ran then.

Ran fast.

She didn't close the door behind her. She did nothing but make her feet move along the corridor with abstract art on its every wall and past windows offering a different view with every step away from her hotel room to bring her to a spiralling staircase.

Flora fingered the golden banister and hesitated. There would be people if she went down the stairs. No space to move because she'd be shoulder to shoulder with strangers stealing all the air she needed. Just the way her parents stole it at home. Giving her no room. No air. No space to think.

She wasn't in her little village any more, straddling the

border between North Devon and Cornwall. There was no-where to seek sanctuary. No windblown forest to hide in. There were no fields. No cows. No beach to comb. She was in a city. A great big city. With every corner, every street, full of people living, moving, talking. Always talking.

She craned her neck, looking up at the stairs that curved around to another invisible floor. What if she kept going up?

Her chest tight, and panting, she fisted the fabric of her dress at her waist, hiked the too-long skirt above her bare feet and climbed. Seeking another place. Solitude. Sanctuary.

Breathlessly, she reached the top floor. A dead end. With her back to the wall, she leaned against it, catching her breath.

*Click.*

The wall behind her had moved…

Raffaele tugged the buttons loose at his throat, but the stiffness lingered. The tightness in his jaw was becoming an ache.

Every window held a light…every street was ablaze. Even the trees lining the snaking paths far below held little fires in them.

But not the *right* kind.

Not the kind that burnt. Not the kind that raged inside him. Those flickering lights all over London could be turned on and off with a switch. He did not have a switch. His fire always burned. But he kept the oxygen levels low. Never gave it room to breathe. Contained it by will. *His* will.

He pressed a palm to the floor-to-ceiling window and took a sip of the brown spiced drink in his too-tight grip. Its wetness wasn't enough to douse the heat inside him. It roared against it—against the alcohol travelling down his throat and into his gut—challenging it to take him under. Challenging him to take another sip—spill another measure into the tumbler. Knock it back. Find oblivion. Forget for an hour. A minute. A second. Let the rage go.

*For what? Peace will never be yours again.*

The voice mocked him with its truth. Because he would never know peace. He'd never known peace. But sleep…? He craved it. Its blanket of shadows. Its darkness.

But he couldn't sleep.

Every time he closed his eyes he saw his *mamma*. He could not let go because he had no right to. He wasn't allowed to forget or to sleep because he was to blame. Only him.

The inquest had delivered its verdict.

No medical negligence.

He swallowed. Hard. Tried to dislodge the lump in his throat. She'd been too thin. Too frail. She'd left everything she knew, everything that brought her comfort, to live in a facility with people who didn't know her—couldn't protect her the way he could. She'd lost the battle with her depression. Died. Because the one time she'd needed him to hold her hand and pull her back from the edge he hadn't been there.

*Guilty as charged.*

He'd been the one to beg her to go to the facility. L'Essenza del Caso, they'd called it. The Essence of Chance. A haven to explore one's self. To heal in safety with twenty-four-hour therapists available to talk.

His mother hadn't wanted to talk. She'd wanted his father. Still. After thirty years of abandonment…of rejection and lies.

He scrubbed a hand over his mouth but he couldn't wipe away the bitterness lingering on his lips, his tongue.

Raffaele had known his father's death would come as a blow. He'd gone home. Dropped everything to be the first tell his mother that the Count who'd discarded her as if she was nothing—a dirty little secret he'd hidden away from the world in the middle of nowhere in the Sicilian country-side with a wad of cash and a promise of 'soon'—was dead.

'Soon' was never coming.

He thought she'd scream—break things. Cry. Then come full circle to sit mute.

He'd never imagined it would be fatal.

His fingers clenched around the glass. Pain sliced through him. Acute. Searing. He imagined for a moment taking a step back, raising his arm and letting go. *With force.* Shattering the tumbler against the window. Hearing the crack as shards of glass exploded around him to glisten in the deep red carpet at his feet.

Instead, he moved, placing the glass down on a table with noiseless precision.

Control. It was all he had. All he'd ever had. The way he reacted—responded—to the world around him. That judge had sentenced him to a lifetime of regret. He'd reacted without even a flicker of his pulse in the Italian courtroom today. But inside—

His head snapped back to the window and he saw a flash, a movement. What looked like a woman shrouded in green. He watched her pad across the stone terrace. Her eyes, almost black in the darkness, scanned the space. A heart-shaped face shrouded by dark waves that rested on bare shoulders. Her collarbone, pronounced, was taut. The hollow at the base of her throat led down to a perfect V of green silk, drawing his eye to the slope of her small breasts.

The concrete city behind her was ablaze with blues and greens. And The Thames reflected deep violet streaks in the watery depths under the Millennium bridge. She was a shadow against the enveloping city in a too-long ball gown.

Her bare toes peeped out with every step beneath the hem, which dragged along the floor and trailed behind her. Amber lights on the floor guided her with each footfall. She slowed, lingering among the green leaves spiralling from pot plants to trail upwards on trellises in vivid reds and deep blues.

She looked mythical. Out of place.

There were no parties here tonight. No Christmas celebrations. None of the D-class celebrities and influencers who came to this hotel to take pretty pictures of the vintage decor, its iconic status amongst the elite lost.

That would change, in time, when his team gutted it. Put his stamp on it. His brand. *His name.* Not the Nobiltà Italiana name his father had denied him. But *his* name. *Russo.* Then the glitz and glamour of the rich who wore their ball gowns to breakfast would be a daily occurrence, but the previous owner had let standards slip. Everything except the rooms he stood in and the garden terrace outside.

Tonight, he understood the appeal.

This part of the hotel was completely shut off. The previous owner had created a secret world of opulence. A place to hide with every comfort at his disposal. Secret stairs, secret doors, secret passages behind the walls for secret access so staff could enter and leave unseen.

But *she* was not staff. He knew that because he could see her. *Clearly.*

He moved back, his thigh knocking the table, tilting the glass he'd saved from a violent end. He steadied it again by instinct, because he couldn't drag his eyes away from her. This tiny figure invading his privacy.

Raffaele lifted his hand to flick on the floodlights and then hesitated.

She couldn't see him. Outside, where she stood, she would see nothing but a wall. A darkness. Cleverly designed glass let those inside look out, but those beyond wouldn't be aware of their existence.

*His* existence.

But the shadows would disappear in the light.

She'd turned her back to him, was stalking to the iron and brick balcony. Her spine was prominent, and it called to him. The need to trail his fingers along it was instant. To tilt his head. Kiss—

*Kiss?*

She was a trespasser.

A trespasser on his grief.

And trespassers needed to be caught.

Her hair was caught in a wild gust of wind. It danced around her shoulders. She raised her arms high and wide beside her, lifting her face to the night sky and leaning over the edge.

He forgot to breathe.

*Was this a test?*

Was she a messenger, sent to remind him how completely he'd failed his mother? His mother had chosen a roof. His mother had leapt to her fate.

His palm met a square silver panel on the wall. The glass shifted soundlessly to create a door.

She remained still. Standing on the edge. Protected only from falling by a waist-high iron-wrapped wall. Her arms were still outstretched, her face tilted as if she were an offering to the city. To the gods…

*An offering for you? For redemption?*

Raffaele moved towards her, prompted by the tug of his gut. He couldn't see her face. An inappropriate urge stormed through him to see her eyes, to look into them, to be close enough to do that.

He caught her wrist. She turned.

His breath hitched. Big brown eyes met his. His pulse slowed. He searched her gaze, watching the golden flecks in her left eye burn with something primal. Something achingly close to recognition.

But he didn't know her.

He would remember those eyes…

The delicate warmth from her body hit him. It was a caress against his prickling skin. An awareness of her femininity. The male in him responded without his permission. A low heat gathered in his gut, arrowing down to his groin. Mocking him with the ease with which his body was reacting to a familiarity that didn't belong to him.

But the air between them pulsed…throbbed.

He dragged his gaze from hers. Moved it down to where his fingers encased her small wrist. It was her pulse. That throb. It pounded beneath his thumb. And the urge to swipe his thumb against it was so clear, so overwhelming, it consumed him.

So he did it, before he could tell himself not to. He stroked against her skin. Soft. Warm. *Delicate.* But her pulse wasn't. It pounded. Fierce. Strong.

His eyes shot back to her face. The lights of London's skyline flickered around her head like a halo.

'Are you real?'

It was the most delicate of whispers. It tingled across his skin, snapping him out of the haze that had fallen over him since the inquest. Clearing the fog that had travelled with him since his *mamma's* death and plunging him straight into the depths of her eyes.

'Of course I am.' He straightened, wanting to drop her wrist but unable to will his fingers to release her. 'Are you?' she asked.

She blinked up at him, lashes fluttering rapidly. He wanted to count them. Wanted to know exactly how many dark strands it took to create such appealing shadows on her high cheekbones…

He did not ever notice a woman's eyelashes.

He stilled. His jaw hardened.

He was not himself.

'Am I asleep?' he asked, cursing his lack of control over his tongue. This moment was too surreal. Too…*something*…

'Only if I am too,' she said, bringing his attention to a bottom lip so sinful, so plump, his urge was to take it between his teeth and test its fullness.

*What was wrong with him?*

'And are you?' he asked.

He was hoping. But he didn't know what for. He hadn't slept for weeks. A sleep-deprived mind could conjure many things.

A vision.

A mirage of creamy flesh laced in green silk.

A woman with a too-wide mouth. Too delicate. Too soft. Too kissable.

'No,' she replied, with a gentle shake of her head. 'I'm awake.'

Reality tugged at the periphery of his mind and he released her wrist. 'Are you lost?'

'No…' Her eyes moved down his torso to his leather-tipped toes. Brown strands of silk teased forward to caress her cheeks. He clenched his fist, pushing down the urge to push her hair behind her ear. To touch her…*intimately*.

'Who showed you how to get in here?'

'No one.' She craned her neck. Her stare was like a physical caress against his too-hot skin. 'I found it by accident. I just ran…'

'Ran from where?' he asked, his gaze sweeping down

over her slight frame. The dress was too big, and she was too small. 'Do you usually take an evening run in a ball gown?'

'No.'

Her lips lifted into something secretive. *Seductive.*

'I wanted to be alone. London is so busy. Noisy. Everyone's always moving. Always talking.' Her eyes held steady to his. 'But I'm done with running tonight.'

Wasn't that exactly the reason he was here, too? Why he hadn't gone back to the house he'd grown up in. Back to Sicily. He'd run from that Italian courtroom because his head had been too loud with unwanted memories. Too noisy with his own despair. And only now had his mind come to a stop, cushioned by the wide wonder of her brown eyes...

'How did *you* get up here?' she asked.

He wanted to touch the deep lines between her brows. Smooth them.

'I knew the way.'

'You did?'

'I did,' he confirmed.

'And you chose to come here?' Her eyes narrowed. 'Why?'

A rush of words bulged in his throat. Refusing to let him lie or deny this moment of grief. Deny his mother.

'To grieve.'

A smile, small and gentle, moved her lips. 'Me too.'

'And who do you grieve for?' he asked.

Because he truly wanted to know. Curiosity pushed against his consciousness, demanding to understand why on this night the fates had seen fit to throw his grief against hers. To slam their worlds together.

Her slender shoulders dipped. 'Myself...'

He frowned. 'For yourself?'

'Yes,' she said, making small continuous dips of her head.

Her answer pressed against something inside him. Something buried deep.

'Why?' he asked.

'Because—'

She sucked in a breath and he watched. Mesmerised. He itched to find the hardened peaks of her breasts pushing against the fabric of her dress. His hands would bury them— they were so small. He would be able to encase them fully in his palms...

*Stop.*

He rolled his shoulders. The leather jacket was too heavy on his skin. Too tight.

'Why do you grieve for yourself?' he forced himself to ask. Because she was not here for him to bury his grief inside her body. She was here for herself, to find a moment, some quietness, in a city that never slept. To find a place away from the noise. As he was.

'Because tonight,' she replied, 'I realised that the woman I was raised to be is someone else's idea of who I should have become.'

'What does that mean?'

'The woman I might have been wasn't ever given a chance to live.'

'How can you grieve for someone who never lived?'

'I'm allowing myself to grieve for all the things I wasn't allowed to have. I'm grieving for the woman I could have become. For the life I could have had. They denied it to her. *Me.* Withheld information...'

'Who are *"they"*?'

'They're not important. Not tonight.'

She blinked, shutting him out with those obscenely long lashes before piercing him with a penetrating look.

'Who are you grieving for?'

'My mother.'

Her eyes flickered over his face. Each flicker touched him. It was warm. Unnerving. Because it came from the softness inside her. A softness just for him. His abdomen tightened.

She stepped down into his space. Moved into his heat. The fire inside him spat embers into the cool winter night's air and the air between them crackled with it.

'I'm so sorry for your loss,' she said.

And he pushed down the urge to draw her closer. To embrace her grief with his own and offer her the same tenderness shining from the depth of her eyes.

He checked himself.

He did not deserve tenderness.

He was not tender.

He didn't know how to be.

'Tell me of the woman who could have lived,' he said, instead of responding to her sincerity. Because he didn't know how to.

'No,' she refused.

'Why do you not want to tell me?' he asked, his lungs tight, his words hoarse. He wanted to understand it. This idea of grieving for something that had never existed. The idea was raw, because he'd never let himself grieve for the life *he* could have had.

But did he want to grieve for the life he could have had with his father? A liar? A cheat? Because even if his father had claimed him who would have provided for his mother? Protected her?

*She'd needed love too.*

His guilt was loud tonight.

He shut it down. Because what did he know of love? Nothing.

He knew only how to brush his mother's hair. Feed her.

He'd never been taught to love, and he didn't want to learn. Because love was a myth whispered in the act of seduction. *A lie.* His father had seduced his mother—a naïve girl from old Sicilia, who'd left the orphanage behind her and was seeking adventure in Roma, where she'd become a nanny to his three children.

*Raffaele's half-brothers and sister.*

His father had got his mother pregnant, and before his world could come tumbling down he'd hidden her away. Forgotten her and the dirty little secret that would've brought his world crashing around his knees had it been exposed. He'd fobbed her off with words like *soon* and *when the baby is grown.* He'd shut her away, out of sight, and forgotten about her.

Love was a lie.

'I don't need to tell you about her,' said the woman in green, slicing through the rage always ready beneath the surface to explode.

'Why not?'

'Because she's here…standing in front of you,' she said, pulling him out of his head and back into her eyes. 'Do you want to tell me about your mother?' she asked, and her words were…*inviting.*

'No.'

He didn't. He wouldn't deny his grief, but share his memories…? Never.

'I don't want to talk at all,' he finished, his heart thudding too loudly. His throat too dry.

'Neither do I.'

A gust of wind picked up the ends of her hair and threw them into her eyes. He wanted to strip off his jacket and lay it around her shoulders. Warm her.

'Are you cold?' he asked, before he could stop himself. 'Do you want me to protect you from the wind?'

Her lips parted. 'How...?'

A sluggish warmth spilled through his every vein, lodging a heavy heat in his gut. 'With my body.'

She moved into him, so close he could feel the whisper of her body against his. She placed her hand on his chest.

'Like this?'

'Do you think it is safe to play with strangers in the dark?' he asked, his tone laced with amusement and his words accusing. Because he did not like what was happening. This woman's touch was spiralling him into a moment where he couldn't control his responses.

'I'm not playing,' she said.

'What *are* you doing?'

'Choosing.'

'Choosing what?'

'To be present.'

'Present?' he repeated.

'To be present in this moment.'

He felt lightheaded. Suspended in time—in this moment. Locked into the essence of another human being. He could hear every rasp of her breath. Feel the thud of her heart as her chest rose and fell.

He was present in a way he never had been before.

'Who *are* you?' he demanded.

Her lips curved. Not up. Not down. But it was a movement. 'I'm not sure I can answer that.'

Her name didn't matter, he told himself. Hotel security could take her. Rid him of his little interloper. And then he could tighten the leash on whatever this reaction was he was having to her. Remember who he was. Who he'd made himself into.

But he yearned for it.

For her name.

'You don't know your name?' he asked, despite himself.

'I know the name I've been called by all my life. But I don't know if that name—the person who was given that name—is the person who's here in this moment. If it's the person I want to be any more.'

'You can refuse to tell me your name…but you will still be *you*.'

The words spilt from his lips in quick succession. He wasn't sure who he was tonight. But he knew with an unwavering certainty that he was not the man who'd flown by private jet from a courthouse in Italy to arrive in a wet and grey London.

And he wasn't the boy rattling around in a house in desperate need of repair with a woman who cared about nothing but seeing the man she loved again. He was a grown man now, and his house was always in perfect order.

'My name isn't important,' she said, slicing through his grief, his regret. 'It's only a name, isn't it? It doesn't make me *me*.'

'Doesn't it?'

'I don't want it to,' she said.

'Why?' he asked. 'A name can be everything.'

*His* name was everything—because he'd made it so.

'The woman I was before I came up here…the woman with her name —*my* name—is attached to people's assumptions,' she continued, her words coming at him fast and breathless. 'I want to leave all those downstairs.'

'Then who does that leave up here?' he asked. 'With me?'

'Only who I am right now,' she replied. 'A girl who doesn't want to go home,' she confessed. Uncoerced. Unprompted.

The words sitting on her lips were echoed in the flush tingeing her cheeks.

She wanted him.

'Where do you want to go, *piccolina*?'

'Do you have a room here?' she asked.

And then it roared through him. *Understanding.* Understanding of his temptation to smash the glass against the window.

Inhaling deeply, she added, 'I have a room…'

He watched the tendons in her throat constrict. Elongate.

'Would you like to go back to it?' he asked.

She shook her head, and then nodded. He saw the heat rising from her chest to tease at her cheeks.

'Yes. If it's with you.'

A desire to erase all distance between them ripped through him. To press her chest against his. *Without clothes.* To feel the tight peaks of her nipples against him.

'I am a stranger to you,' he said—because he was. But he was strange to himself tonight. Exposed. Raw.

'There's freedom in anonymity, and tonight I want to be free.'

'Free from what?' he asked.

He'd never been free to act on impulse. To follow his desires. His job was to provide. Protect.

'For once—just once—I want to *do* and not think,' she explained huskily. 'Not be told I shouldn't…not to be warned of the consequences. Not to be told how foolish I am for wanting something.'

'And what *do* you want?'

'I want you.'

She placed the palm of her hand on his cheek.

Flames erupted inside him.

Her fingertips flexed against his skin. 'I'm going to kiss you now.'

Her eyes searched his, hesitantly at first, then boldly, as

she recognised his desire, demanded his surrender. She was challenging him to concede. To give it up. His control.

A primal surge of lust pushed against the rage inside him. Coating the anger with something else. Something distinct that he couldn't name. He fought the urge to pull her into him. Into his warmth. He needed her consent—her permission—to lose control.

In his mind, he allowed himself to raise that glass in his too-tight grip. He readied himself to release the tumbler into the night. Because on her cue—if she gave it—he knew the glass would shatter.

'And do you want me to kiss you back?' he asked.

# CHAPTER TWO

'YES,' FLORA CONFIRMED.

She swallowed down the urge to tell him she'd never been kissed, never been touched. Because did it matter? She didn't want it to. Not to her—not to him. Tonight she wanted nothing else to matter but this. Their connection.

A shiver raked through her.

Black brows arched above eyes so bright that it was as if the entire world had crawled inside them and reflected the earth's surface back from space.

'You're cold,' he said, shrugging off his jacket.

He leaned into her, bringing his arms around her back to trail the leather over her shoulders. She clung on to the lapels, pulling the jacket tightly around her. The smell of leather and the heat from his body rose to the cold tip of her nose and infiltrated her lungs.

Her stomach flipped as she found her courage to voice her confession. 'I've never—'

'Never what?'

'Kissed anyone,' she said, expecting to feel vulnerable. Embarrassed. But she didn't. She felt empowered. *Excited.*

She should be horrified. This wasn't how she'd been raised to respond to her feelings. Her wants. But she'd never felt as delicate or as strong as she did now, in her desire for this beautiful stranger.

And he was beautiful.

Her heart stuttered as she took in his broad shoulders, sheathed in a black shirt. He'd flicked the collar up, bringing her attention to the open buttons at his thick bronze neck… the fine black hairs leading down to his chest. A chest she wanted to see. She wanted to pop open those remaining buttons and run her hands over it.

Her eyes lowered to the belt encircling his lean hips, locked in place by a wide silver buckle. Dark tailored trousers clung to the hard muscle of his thighs. The fabric moulded to his muscular calves.

'Would you like me to kiss *you* first?' he asked, and her eyes flicked back to his face.

Her mouth parted. The air tasted of gunpowder and bonfires. The scent of the upcoming season.

She had been acting on impulse before, and she suddenly felt nervous. But still the need to touch and be touched destroyed any doubt that *this* was the way to behave. Even if it was not the way she'd been taught to behave.

'Yes.' Her eyes moved back to his mouth. 'I want you to kiss me first.'

Her core tightened. Deep down inside her. She knew she might never find a connection like this again. A raw, unguarded reaction. A sexual reaction.

'I want you to be my first.'

The blackness swept through the brilliance of his irises to a create a burning edge. Intense rings of smouldering energy. Blue…? Green…? Ethereal.

'Then we will start with your mouth.'

She teased her tongue over her bottom lip. 'Where else would we start?'

'There are many ways to kiss, *piccolina*. Would you like me to show you?'

'Yes,' she said. Because tonight she would say yes to all the things she knew she shouldn't.

She closed her eyes. Anticipation thrummed through her. Quickened her pulse. Her breathing. Every nerve-ending was shredded. Exposed.

She should feel ridiculous, standing here in a charity shop ball gown. But she didn't. She felt...*seen*. Wanted in a way she'd never been wanted. *For herself.* For the woman she was daring to be here, on top of the concrete jungle of London, in this secret oasis of lush green, of such opulence she could almost taste it.

*Taste him.*

His hands slid to the back of her neck, drawing her in closer. She didn't open her eyes. She just let herself *feel*. The pressure of his thumbs on her face. His palms warm against her throat. The heat of his chest against hers. The whisper of his breath against her lips. Sweet. Spiced.

Thunder roared through her, loud and alive, as he captured her mouth with his. His lips were silk against hers. Soft, but firm. Gentle, yet demanding. She opened for him. Let his tongue inside.

A sound burst from her lips. A gasp—a moan. He swiped his tongue inside her mouth as if to taste it. She copied him. Teasing her tongue against his. And the moan she tasted in her mouth this time was his. A guttural noise from deep in his chest.

It tasted...*powerful*.

She kissed him harder. Mimicking him. Pressing her lips to his. She slid her tongue into his mouth. Her hips instinctively pushed against him. She felt him harden.

He tore his mouth from hers and dipped his head to the underside of her ear and whispered, 'Has someone kissed you here?'

His breath tickled at her skin, bringing it to life beneath his words. 'No,' she said huskily. A low heat dragged through her stomach, and it was getting heavier as he lingered on her throat.

His tongue flicked against her skin. 'Would you like to be?'

'Yes, please.'

His hands moved to cup her cheeks, holding her steady as he moved into the crook of her neck, millimetre by millimetre, and blew.

Warm, cold, electrified, she gasped, 'Oh...'

He sucked her skin into his mouth. Harder. Deeper. Her breathing sped up, her heart thumped, but the need for more was overwhelming. The pangs in her stomach told her there was more, and she needed to demand it.

Her hands bit into his shoulders. 'Please...' she murmured.

He dragged his kiss down the length of her throat. 'More?'

*'Please!'* she begged, and she didn't care. She'd worry about it later. Tomorrow.

His hands moved over her body, finding her breasts. He palmed them, cupping their heaviness, and swiped over her tender nipples.

Flora pressed her thighs together to stem the ache. The chaotic need to find release. 'More,' she breathed. *'More!'*

And he didn't deny her. He pulled down the top of her dress, exposing her breasts to the cool night's air, and his head descended. The heat of his mouth was on her, taking her nipple into his mouth—

'Oh, my God!' she cried out, her body pulsing, throbbing, as he sucked harder. Deeper.

He flicked his tongue over her nipple and the ache between her legs intensified. Muted everything but what he was doing to her body. He stopped kissing her breast, moved his mouth slowly over her chest and back up her throat, recaptured her lips. Roughly. *Urgently.*

He slipped his hand inside the slit of her dress that started just below her hipbone and feathered his fingertips along her inner thigh. A moan erupted in her throat. He pulled his hand from between her thighs to grip her hips. He cradled them in the arch of his and walked her backwards. Step by step. Until her back met a wall.

Her bare breasts pushed against the smooth fabric of his shirt, and she rubbed them against him. She felt feral. *Wild.*

He tore his mouth from hers. His breathing as ragged as her own, he said, 'Not here.'

Her fingers clenched around his muscular upper arms. 'But—' Her grip loosened, and she swallowed down the words in her mouth, because the desire to strip naked beneath the stars and push her body against his felt too wanton to say out loud.

'But what?' he pushed, his voice a hoarse rasp.

She looked at him. At the man who'd offered her nothing but gentleness even in his rampant seduction of her senses. The man who was staring at her as if she was the only living thing to exist in the universe. Sharing this moment with a stranger was the closest she'd ever been to really being herself. To reacting honestly. And she didn't want to stop being honest.

'I don't want to stop kissing,' she said, because the vast crater in her chest wasn't for the mother she wouldn't know, but for the parts of herself she'd never been given the opportunity to explore. Her motivations. Her *sexuality.* 'I don't want you to stop kissing *me*,' she corrected.

'Then I won't stop.'

A slow smile spread across his lips and she wanted to know what it felt like to *feel* his smile. But she was frozen.

Entranced by the man who'd kissed her body with the city lights at his back, in the middle of a garden so beautiful it almost didn't seem real.

*This* didn't feel real.

She nodded because she didn't have the right words—*any* words—because all that was inside her mouth was a gasp as he dipped his head. He placed hard kisses on her throat. Between her breasts. On her stomach. And then he was on his knees, spreading the slit in her dress to reveal her white cotton panties.

He didn't look up, but kept his gaze there. Gently, he stroked at the waistband. The heart of her pulsed and clenched tight.

She gripped his shoulders and said the only thing she could. 'Please...'

His mouth sealed to the part of her that ached for him the most. The intensity was só close to the sweetest pain that she couldn't do anything but let her mouth fall open and try to breathe.

'*Ahh...*' She arched her neck. Her back pressed against the hard wall. She closed her eyes and gripped on to the lapels of his jacket.

A firm finger followed the seam of her panties and pulled them across. Exposing the pulsing heart of her. He licked her without the barrier of her panties. Tongued her with masterful stokes along the folds of her opening.

He pushed his tongue inside her.

Everything she'd thought she knew about her body—about the pleasure to be found with the exploration of her fingers—was obliterated, smashed to dust, as he put the pad of his thumb to her core and pulled his tongue out only to thrust it into her again.

She gasped with pleasure, loudly and fiercely.

He was unrelenting in his ministrations as he moved faster, the pace of his tongue increasing. And she let him guide her. Guide her to a place she hadn't known existed. A place where her mind was blank all but for the driving need to be *here*. To feel the building tension in her body, getting tighter and tighter with seemingly no end. And she didn't want it to end. Didn't know how it could end without her shattering into a million pieces.

His mouth suddenly claimed her nub. His thumb moved to her opening…parting her. He slipped a finger inside her.

It was then that Flora's world exploded.

He held her steady against his mouth. Let her body rock against his lips as she screamed in ecstasy into the night sky until she had nothing left to give.

He pulled his mouth from her, easing his grip on her hips. His fingers quick, but gentle, he slid her panties back into place and shifted her dress.

He looked up. Her pulse hammered. *Hard.* Because his eyes echoed what she already knew. This shared intensity under the stars was only the beginning.

He stood, covered her bare breasts. And she let him encase her trembling body in the scent of him. The heat of him. Her throat dry, she swept her eyes over him. This man she'd let touch her body. Claim her mouth in her first kiss. *All her kisses.* She didn't want to wait. Go back to her room. She needed him. *Now.*

'Take me here,' she pleaded. 'Take me now.'

She spread her fingers, moving them over the solid arc of his shoulders, and tried to pull his mouth back to hers. But he dodged her lips and claimed the sensitive spot behind her ear.

'I have a place,' he said, and with a slide of his hand the blackness of the wall behind her turned translucent. Lights shone where none had been before. Like her dad's glasses on a sunny day...

'They're windows?' she said huskily, her eyes widening. 'Glass?'

'Yes,' he said.

'Is that how you saw me?' she asked, as what lay beyond the glass was exposed, watching as the big city revealed it hid more secrets than just the circumstances of her birth.

It hid magic in plain sight.

It was a room. Rooms.

His eyes flashed. 'Do you want to come inside?'

'Yes,' she confirmed, not recognising the huskiness of her voice.

Her stomach tightened. A tight sensation was arrowing between her legs. Making her hotter. Wetter. Her world had caught fire and it was burning around her. Everything she'd known, loved, was in question or gone. She wasn't grieving for the mother she'd never known, and she wasn't grieving for the life she'd had before she'd found out she was adopted. Because she'd been happy. She knew this in her heart. She was grieving for all the moments she might have had if she'd stood up for her own decisions, stood against her parents' fears.

They had moulded her for twenty-one years into the daughter they wanted. *Their miracle baby.* Not allowed to make mistakes, big or small. Not allowed to be anything other than the daughter they wanted.

But what did *she* want?

She wanted this.

She wanted *him*.

Flora stepped over the threshold.

'What is this place?'

It was nothing like the room she had downstairs. These rooms were...*more*. Rich... Vibrant...

'A room for the night,' he answered, his voice a seductive, deep drawl behind her.

'It's beautiful.'

A spacious entry hall with a sparkling speckled marbled floor led to a carpeted lounge scattered with rugs of silk. Heavy-cushioned sofas and high-backed chairs surrounded intimate statues of women of old, cut from black stone, and tall lamps and glided mirrors highlighted the way to more rooms.

'Magical…' she breathed.

For tonight, she belonged here. No alarm for the morning milking. No routines to maintain. Tonight she wasn't a farm hand. She wasn't the abandoned daughter of an addict. She was anonymous. Free to explore the unexplored. To explore the woman never given a voice. Never allowed to use words without trying them out in her head first.

She turned to him. Her confidence roaring, she asked, 'Is there a bedroom here?'

He nodded. His features were drawn. Tight. 'A big bedroom.'

'Will you take me to it?' she asked, praying her confidence wouldn't desert her.

When she went home—back to the farm, to her name— she wanted this night to be hers. Not her parents'. Not a fabricated experience they'd built for her. Something she'd created and experienced all on her own.

'I can…' he told her, and her heart soared. 'But only if you want it. You can leave.' He nodded towards the concealed door she'd entered by on the far side of the terrace. 'Or you can take my hand.'

He turned his hand palm forward and held it out to her like an offering.

*Choice.*

Wasn't that what she'd always wanted? And he'd chosen her, hadn't he? The woman she was right here and now. And she wanted to commit to whatever was happening between them. This shared moment of grief turned to passion.

She slid her fingers through his.

His hold was soft, but strong. He guided her down a long hallway towards a door and pushed open the heavy oak to reveal a room of splendour. And a four-poster bed so big it monopolised *everything*...

Tonight, she'd have no regrets. Tomorrow, she'd go home and remember the doubts—the pain.

Just once, she was going to let her herself act on feelings...

Her grip tightened on his and Flora led the way.

Towards the bed.

It took every shred of control he had left to keep his hold on her hand loose. Not to hurry. To lose himself in her gentle confidence.

Gracefully, she kept on walking towards the bed. His jacket drowned her. Cloaked her in what was his. Protected her from the heat of his gaze on her back. Hid the dip in her spine his fingers had smoothed over as he'd dragged her hips over his mouth.

She'd become his responsibility, hadn't she? It was his responsibility to protect her, to be gentle, to make her first time the best it could be.

He shouldn't be her first.

He was not gentle.

He planted his feet, stopping her from reaching the bed. *'Piccolina...'*

She turned to him. The warning died in his mouth as she released his hand, took a step backwards, and pushed his jacket from her shoulders.

It thumped to the floor. He did not look. Didn't care. Her eyes held his—trapping him, imploring him to forget everything but the desire flaring her pupils into dark discs of desire. Making them glitter. Shine just for him.

He waited.

She reached for the straps hugging the tops of her arms and pushed them down to her wrists, baring her breasts. Her fingers pushed the dress past her waist, her hips, to slide down the creamy whiteness of her thighs and land at her feet with his jacket. Then her panties. She toyed with the waistband and then, in one decisive movement, slid them to her ankles.

Stepping out of the puddle of fabric at her feet, she moved, her gaze never leaving his. The back of her legs met the mattress. The bed. She sat down. Inched her bottom up over the bedspread.

He couldn't breathe…couldn't catch his breath as she presented herself to him…let her knees fall apart. The dark triangle between her legs glistened where his mouth had been. Where he'd tasted her. Torn her apart with his mouth.

'Make love to me.'

The glass shattered.

He gripped his shirt and tore it open, the buttons popping soundlessly to the thick carpet beneath his feet. He pulled it off, along with his trousers and his boxers, kicked them all aside.

'Say it again,' he demanded, ignoring the voice in his head ordering him to tell her it was not love. She did not know what love was. Love burnt. Love hurt. And he would not hurt her. He was going to worship every inch of the body she offered to him.

Her breasts heaved. Her nipples grew taut. Tight. Almost asking for his mouth on them…his tongue. But he waited. Waited for her cue.

Her brown eyes burned black. Wide. Intense.

She was a goddess.

Her neck arched to reveal the slenderness of her throat. Her brown hair trailed back to feather the pillows he wanted to push her into. He wanted to find her mouth and take her. Possess her.

Her fingers pinched at the white bedspread. Grasped it and pulled it. 'Make love to me,' she said again.

And he wanted to be between her legs, desperately, but his last remaining strand of lucidity stopped him from moving. *Protection.*

He knelt and retrieved his wallet from his jacket pocket. He pulled out a foil packet and threw the wallet to join their discarded clothes.

He stood tall. Erect. *Present.*

Her eyes fluttered to the thick length of him.

'You're…'

*He was.*

He held her gaze as he rolled the latex down the length of himself.

'I won't hurt you,' he promised, before he could stop himself. He didn't make promises. But she was ready, and he had no control left. Not over his mouth. Nor his body.

None.

He moved between her legs, gripped her thigh to place her calf on his lower back. Her fingers, delicate, feathered his tight jaw. He stared into her eyes because he couldn't look away. He placed the heat of himself at her entrance.

'Now…' she breathed. 'Love me *now.*'

In one thrust, he was inside her. Had pushed past the barrier that had given little resistance. He stilled. Every muscle in his body was straining—demanding he pull out and then thrust into her again, find his release.

Her grip on his jaw tightened, refusing to let him look away.

'I'm okay,' she said huskily. 'It doesn't hurt. And I need you to move. I need you to—'

He moved. Slowly. Building his thrusts in tempo…in speed. Still, she did not look away. And he couldn't. Mesmerised by her wide eyes. Her gasping mouth. Her innocent awe. And she matched him thrust for thrust, arching her hips to take him deeper.

'Harder!' she gasped, panting her need into existence.

He gripped her hips. Thrust. Hard. *Harder.*

A deep blush bloomed on her neck…her cheeks. He could feel the heat radiating from her. The hotness filled the air between them with humidity, trapping them both inside it. In a bubble of desire.

'I… I…' she murmured between pants for air, whispering across his mouth.

It was a primitive call for release. He felt it too. The pressure.

'Oh. Oh. *Oh!*' she repeated, with every thrust of his body into hers.

He drove into her faster. *Wildly.* Until the pressure had nowhere to go but inside her.

With one last thrust the pressure inside him broke free and he lost himself to her joy, her pure amazement, and to her sighs of satisfaction mingled with his own.

'Thank you for being my first,' she said, and his hands curled possessively over her hips.

The urge to push into her again, to drive out any thoughts of *firsts*, hardened him inside her. Because with firsts came lasts, and— And *what*? He would not be her first and last kiss.

'I didn't know,' she continued, and he stilled. 'That it could be like that…so *instinctual.*'

'Instinctual?' he echoed, but he knew what this virgin

didn't. Instinct did not lead to sex. You had to learn your lover.

'My body knew what it wanted and—' She shook her head, a shy smile creasing her flushed cheeks.

'Nothing else mattered?' he finished for her. Because it hadn't. Not for him. Nothing else but her.

'Exactly,' she whispered, and pressed into him, raising her chin and offering her mouth.

He let their lips meet. Closed his eyes and tasted her.

Her misguided gratitude…it was too much.

He was not nameless. He did not strip his clothes off like an adolescent teen. He didn't make love—and he certainly did not make love to virgins. He had sex. That was all this was.

He dragged his mouth from hers. Pulled himself free from her body and was on his feet, walking away from her. He needed a minute. Just a moment…

He closed the bathroom door and let himself pant. Hard. He shut his eyes and leaned back against the coldness of the door. Let it cool him until he could think, until the heat and the scent of her on his skin was not so strong. So all-consuming.

He opened his eyes and looked down.

*What had he done?*

The condom was torn.

Every vein bulged. Every muscle in his body turned tight. And his brain screamed that history was repeating itself. An innocent. A seduction. A baby.

Before he could stop them, memories that weren't his flashed in his head. The story he'd been told a thousand times. A girl looking for adventure, who'd found love in a place she shouldn't have.

She was exactly like his mother, before she'd had a forbidden love ripped away from her because of the conception of a baby. A child born to be treated with nothing but scorn because the child was to blame. The reason her love had abandoned her. Had been driven away...

He wouldn't cause another woman's unhappiness.

Raffaele disposed of the condom in the bin and opened the door, moved through it. His feet were taking him back to her. He needed to tell her—fix this. Protect her. *Himself.*

He walked back into the bedroom.

Everything stood still. Stopped.

She was gone.

Naked, he moved through the hallway, went back to the lounge, opened every door, flicked every switch, turned on every light. He paused only for a moment to pull on his underwear before jogging out onto the terrace. He moved to the concealed door, yanked it open, took the steps to the floor beneath two at a time.

She was nowhere.

Gone.

He ran to the elevator at the end of the corridor. He jabbed at the buttons. His gut demanded he go and knock on every door. Wake up whoever was inside and demand if they housed her.

But he wouldn't.

The lift arrived. He threw himself inside and hit the buttons. All of them. He dragged his fingers through his hair. If she had a room...if she was still in the hotel...he would find her. He had to tell her.

With each stop of the elevator he stepped outside, searched the quiet halls on every floor with his eyes. The emptiness was so loud his ears ached.

The lift doors pinged for the last time and opened to an empty reception area. His chest heaved. He strode forward. Stood still in the centre of the grand foyer. Raised his head

to the chandelier and stained-glass ceiling and took in the
hotel's hugeness.

*His hotel.*

Twenty floors. Four hundred and thirty-seven rooms. Fifteen more hidden rooms adjoining secret stairs and hidden
exits. Possibly hundreds of occupants in the entire hotel…
thousands of names…

He wanted to roar. Demand her presence. But he did not
know her name, this anonymous woman who might have a
piece of him growing inside her.

The image of a boy no more than five flashed in his mind.
Alone. Kicked out of his house by his mother, screaming for
him to get out. Telling him that she didn't want him. That she
never had. Lonely and afraid, the little boy had left. Because
he didn't know how to make his mother happy. How to keep
the fridge full. How to make her *want* him.

His child would never be unwanted.

It would always be aware of who it was and where it came
from.

His child would not only survive—it would thrive. With
*his* name and the empire he'd built around it. His child would
know it had a place in this world. His child would be protected.

*If she was pregnant.*

Whatever it took—*however long it took*—he would find
her…

# CHAPTER THREE

*Six weeks later...*

RAFFAELE GRIPPED THE CONTROLS. The view before him was a patchwork quilt of dull green, with black shadows of gnarly trees dotting the hills and dips of the English countryside. Ancient woodlands, shaped and bent by the coastal winds at his back, bowed to him as he flew past. His helicopter sliced through the lavender streaks of a determined sun, turning the grey mist lingering in the air into a display of contrasts.

For six weeks she'd lived in his head.

Finding her had been more difficult than he'd expected because she hadn't used her real name to book into the hotel.

She'd used her birth name.

Flora Campbell. Abandoned into the care system at four-teen weeks old. Remained in the foster system until two farmers adopted her and whisked her away to a dairy farm straddling the borders of two villages housing only a few thousand people.

He'd grown up in a village, too—of sorts. An untouched wilderness in the eastern hills of Sicily. Too far away from the coastal towns to attract tourists, too wild for the civilised.

It had been a small community who'd often noticed a young boy out alone at night. Who'd whispered among themselves that if that boy whose mother lived in the house on top of the hill, who told stories of a count who lived in castles and who was coming back to claim her as soon as he'd left his wife, was wandering lost and alone you sent him back home with some food.

Because that boy lived with a woman so deep in her depression that the villagers knew his whereabouts before his mother did.

Without them he—

Raffaele thrust the memories aside. He'd survived largely on his own. Strangers' generosity had filled his belly when the money hidden under the bed had run out, but he'd always been an outcast. On the periphery. Having to rely on himself. And he'd made it on his own.

He'd scrimped and he'd saved to buy his first renovation project. An abandoned house in the village. He'd pulled it apart and put it back together. Brick by brick. And then he'd posted it online, imploring tourists to flock to it and take pretty pictures of his renovations. Then he'd sold it. And then he'd done it again. Until a one-man band had become a crew. A business. An international multi-billion-dollar company.

But there was no time to think about that now. Because every time he'd closed his eyes since that night it had not been his mother's face he'd seen. It had been *hers*. Flora Campbell. Flora Bick.

Raffaele pulled the helicopter to a hovering halt above a snow-speckled field. Anticipation feathered over his skin. His team had delivered more than her adopted name. He had an address. Details of her routines—the farm's routines. Knew the fields they used for wildflowers to encourage nature. And which were the kale fields…the fields full of turnips for the livestock to graze, or something or other. He didn't care. Only wanted to know that it was safe to land—and it was.

He circled the fields in a three-hundred-and-sixty-degree

turn, found the field marked with an X in his mind's eye, and descended. It was the only destination he'd thought of for six entire weeks.

He was making his way back to *her*.

And if she was pregnant there was only one choice to be made.

She wouldn't run again. He'd tether them together for the sake of his child.

They'd be bound by law and marriage.

Flora was tired. The fatigue running through her mind and body was so intense it was bone-deep. She'd fallen back into the farm's routine as if her night alone in London hadn't happened and her life had resumed as normal.

But her body hadn't forgotten.

It remembered...

For one night there had been no alarm set for morning milking. No routine to maintain. With him, she hadn't been a farm hand, nor the abandoned daughter of an addict. She'd been a woman. Free to explore herself when she'd never been given a voice. Never been allowed to use her words without checking them first in her head for fear of hurting those who loved her.

He hadn't known her. He hadn't even known her name. Her actions on that one occasion wouldn't give strength to her parents' worries for their adopted child. Her compulsive nature couldn't hurt *him*. So the rules hadn't applied. There had been no rigid expectations.

But going off the script, allowing the intensity of her feelings to take root, had overwhelmed her.

So she'd run. Back to her life. To what she knew. Because she wasn't *that* woman. Not in real life. Not now the haze of pleasure had faded. She didn't know how to be *her*. The possibility of staying longer in his bed and letting herself explore that woman in his arms had terrified her.

But he'd awoken her body in London, and her body couldn't forget the change he'd brought about in her. She felt restless. She felt...*restricted.*

A heavy, dull sound reverberated in her ears. She knew all the sounds on the farm. And the times they occurred. The low hum of the milking parlour, the deep trumpeting sound of the cows, the tick of the tractors. Most of all, she knew the stillness. The quiet. But there was no longer silence.

The air hummed with something unknown.

Something imminent.

And it was getting louder.

Closer.

Flora slipped off her yellow rubber gloves, placed them on the draining board, and followed the noise outside.

Everything looked the same as it always did.

She'd stood in this exact spot many times. With the gravel beneath her feet, the farmhouse to her back, the stone drive in front of her leading to more fields and to roads that hadn't made it on to a map.

Only this time there was a shadow amongst the snowy fields. A mountainous man in a black suit.

*Him.*

Flora tugged her bottom lip between her teeth and pressed down, stemming the roar of something deep inside her...the part of her that recognised him.

And all six feet plus of masculine energy was charging towards her.

He crossed the field in the sun he'd brought with him. It pierced through the broken clouds, highlighting the black curls kissing his earlobes.

Goosebumps prickled to life on Flora's arms, beneath her

woollen jumper. She swallowed. He was as out of place as a city high-rise in the middle of a field. With a helicopter at his back. He didn't belong here. But excitement sang to life inside her. Her pulse became a frantic beat.

He'd tracked her down...

*Why?*

He stopped before her, filling the air with the scent of him. Something deeply male. Uniquely him. Masculine. But it seemed different. *He* seemed different. Restrained inside his suit...

*'Piccolina...'*

That word. A word she didn't know the meaning of, but he'd given it to her. An unknown name for a temporary woman.

But she wasn't that woman now.

She was Flora Bick, daughter of farmers. An adoptee. A miracle baby saved from the hands of her maternal mother.

'How did you find me?' she whispered. The sound of her voice was foreign. Husky.

'Did you not want to be found?'

The seams of his jacket tightened on his shoulders, bulging under the strain of his muscles as they moved. And she wanted to touch them.

She curled her hands into tight fists to stop herself from reaching out.

'We said no names,' she reminded him as flashes of the woman she'd been with him entered her consciousness. Her slipping off the straps of her dress, presenting herself to him...

*No.* That wasn't the woman she'd been trained to be. She wasn't spontaneous. She didn't push against the invisible walls around her. She stood exactly where she was told to stand. To sit. To eat. To stay.

When they'd shared that night together she'd been someone else.

And those two women did not align.

They could not co-exist.

'We said many things,' he said, interrupting her racing
justification of who she was…who she'd allowed herself to
be with him. 'And things changed.'

'Changed…?' Her eyes travelled over the taut lines of his
clean-shaven cheeks to the pulse that pounded there. '*Nothing* has changed,' she said.

Because it hadn't for her. Their time together lived in the
shadows of her mind, not in the broad light of day.

'Has it not?' His eyes blazed, a colour she still couldn't
name. Burned into her with every caress of his gaze along
her skin. And he didn't rush. He took in every detail.

She shook her head, her heart racing. 'No. Nothing has
changed,' she repeated—because it hadn't. Not for her. She'd
gone back to her life. Back to her risk-free existence.

There were no choices now. She could be only one woman
here. The person her parents needed her to be. The only person she truly knew how to be.

His eyes flicked back to her face. 'Nothing?'

An unwavering confidence exuded from his every pore,
and Flora couldn't help feeling that he knew something she
didn't. His gaze pulled at something inside her. Something
she'd buried deep.

Her breath hitched, stuttering in the chilly morning air
and burning away into dew on the heat of her parted lips.

Because something had changed.

In a world where she wasn't allowed to keep her own secrets, she had one.

Her night with him had been a forbidden erotic salute to
her DNA. To the part of herself that she couldn't allow. And

she didn't want to give it any more freedom than one night, those few hours. Otherwise satisfying her own needs, her own desire, might consume her.

The way it had consumed her mother.

'How did you find me?' she asked, ignoring the desire ripping through her to ask *why* he'd found her.

She'd left no traces of Flora Bick. She'd checked in to the hotel under her birth name and she'd left Flora Campbell behind in London.

And yet here he was.

The presence of him filled the stillness. The quiet. And it was loud, demanding her attention. She couldn't stop looking at him and remembering the choices she had made with him.

She suppressed the shiver threatening to crawl across her skin and clenched her fists tighter. Afraid that she'd reach out and touch him. Test the reality of him in the light of day.

'The way I find anything,' he answered, slicing through her thoughts and dragging her gaze back to his.

He stepped towards her, shortening the space between them, stealing the air she was trying to inhale and replacing it with something visceral. Something new, something *possessive*, that reached across the distance between them.

'I hunt.'

A helpless sound left her lips. 'I'm not an animal,' she said, because it terrified her. *Excited* her. His words hit her stomach in rush of need. Ignited an instant hunger inside her to be claimed. *Found.* 'You can't hunt human beings.'

'And yet here I am,' he corrected her. 'Having hunted *you*.'

He'd been a ghost in her life...reminding her of her past, that she was an addict's daughter. Reminding her of how easily she'd given in to her compulsions. And here he was now. Reminding her of the kissing, the touching, the *free-*

*dom* she'd felt in his arms. How she'd acted no better than an animal driven by need.

But she was not her biological mother. She might be susceptible to addiction, but she could resist, couldn't she? She had to. She wouldn't give in to her body's demands again. She would control her impulses. This instant and all-consuming pull to touch him could and would be held at bay.

'I should go back inside,' she said.

He placed a hand on her hip. Gently. But she was rooted to the spot by the heat radiating from his palm, infiltrating the layers of clothes covering her skin.

He swallowed thickly, the taut lines in his throat stretching. 'Do not run from me again.'

It was a command, but a pleading note punctuated it.

Flora couldn't do anything but plant her feet to the ground. The danger was standing right in front of her, touching her, but she couldn't shrug off his hold on her body because his fingers on her jean-clad hip weren't what was holding her in place. It was the intensity in his eyes.

'I didn't run the first time,' she lied, because she couldn't confess the truth. 'I walked straight out through the front door of the hotel.'

He pulled his hand away. 'Without saying goodbye?'

Shame gripped her. Quietly, she'd slipped from his room and gone back to her own. She'd collected the folder containing the redacted version of her life and then she'd run all the way home. From bus to train. City to country. From field to farm. Ready to fall back into line. Obey the rules. Forget everything she'd learnt in London.

She'd locked her time in London away…justified her reckless actions as being just one night. One slip from grace.

She wouldn't slip again.

'Why would I say goodbye when we didn't say hello?'

'We shared—'

'A night. A moment,' she interrupted. 'And you're not following the rules.'

'Rules?'

'Of one-night stands.'

He raised a dark brow sardonically. 'You'd know because you've had so many?'

She clamped down on her bottom lip. He was scribbling outside the lines on purpose. While she was trying to stay within them with painstaking determination.

But it clawed through her. The realisation that she wanted to break the rules, too. She wanted to stem the itch on her palm by placing it on his cheek, to see how smooth his skin was without the stubble he'd had all those weeks ago. She wanted to run her fingers along his jaw, to stare into his eyes and demand he kiss her. *Everywhere.* She didn't want to be this woman who lived to make others happy. She wanted to be free.

One more time.

Flora shut those thoughts down and looked at him. Tried to concentrate on the black suit sheathing his muscles and the leather shoes cushioning his feet. On anything but how he made her feel. Chaotic. Unsteady. When her life had always been so balanced and so sheltered.

'You have no right to be here,' she said, stamping down on the idea that he might have found her again because he wanted to extend their night. To claim her again.

'I have every right,' he contradicted her.

She shook her head and the messy bun piled on top of her head wobbled, strands of hair falling around her face.

He raised his long fingers to her cheek, and she held her breath as he caught a tendril between his thumb and forefinger and tucked it behind her ear. 'You are coming undone, *piccolina*.'

'Undone?' she echoed.

'Unravelling,' he confirmed, his voice a sultry caress to the heavy weight in her chest.

Throatily, she repeated her earlier question. 'Why are you here?' She shouldn't care. But she did. She wanted and she needed to know.

Softly, his fingers wrapped around her wrist. 'Can you not guess?'

Heat penetrated her skin. Not a trickle, not a seeping warmth, but a shot of hotness directly into her veins.

'No...' She swallowed thickly. Her throat was too dry.

'Guess,' he urged her, his eyes fixed on her face. 'Why would a man you spent the night with seek you out? *Hunt* you?'

His words were gentle. Inviting. Coaxing her to tell him a secret she didn't have access to. She felt trapped. He was a hunter moving in on his prey, ready to pounce.

'Don't play with me,' she said. 'Why are you here?'

'Because I need to know.'

'Know *what*?' She breathed the words, low and long.

'Are you or are you not?' he asked.

'Am I or am I not what?'

'Pregnant.'

*'Pregnant?'*

In that moment, everything stilled. Went blank. Before it all collided. Every memory of her safe and predictable life and her night with him. 'What?'

'Are you or are you not pregnant,' he confirmed, his voice a low husk of possession.

Her gaze turned fuzzy around the edges. A huge shadow

wobbled before her eyes. *Him.* The mountain of a man she'd chosen to give herself to.

*What had she done?*

The air, hot and pulsing, from her lips swirled together and pushed out a question. 'You're talking about a baby?'

He gave a single nod.

And Flora fainted.

# CHAPTER FOUR

'HAVE YOU EATEN?'

Flora ignored the voice, somewhere distant but somehow close almost in her ear. She wasn't hungry. She was warm. *Toasty.* She snuggled closer to the source, pressing her nose against something soft and hard at the same time.

There was a touch. Something gentle stroking at her forehead. Lulling her into awareness…into consciousness.

Her eyes flew open and there was the world looking back at her. Swirls of green and blue and vivid streaks of grey.

Her gut clenched. Reality was trying to push at her senses too rapidly for her to catch anything coherent.

She was cocooned in the embrace of his body, sitting in his lap. In his arms. Her neck was resting in the crook of his elbow as he stared down at her—

*Pregnant.*

She scrambled out of his arms and into the seat beside him. She looked over the field to her house and then back at him.

'Did you carry me across the field?'

'I don't know who's inside.' His broad shoulder dipped. 'I didn't want to shock them.'

'It must be handy, having a portable spaceship to haul damsels in distress to safety.'

The smile she'd intended to put on her lips never appeared, because her joke wasn't funny. None of this was funny.

'It's the easiest form of transport,' he said, not acknowledging her attempt at…at what? Humour?

'I suppose so…'

She straightened, pressing her back against the hard leather. The helicopter doors were open. The cab was big and there were two rows of seating behind the flight deck. But he filled them. Long legs outstretched, his body was turned towards her, his knees a millimetre from touching hers.

'Have you eaten?' he repeated.

'No.' She pulled her knees together, placed her sweaty palms down on her thighs, refused to drag them over her jeans to remove the sweat. 'I'm sorry I fainted. I don't faint. Have never fainted before.'

'It was a shock? Finding out that you might be pregnant?' She heard it, the dip in his voice making his response a question.

She nodded, and she forget to exhale, because he seemed to get bigger. His shoulders widened as he leaned into the inhalation of breath.

His eyes skirted to the left briefly and then shot back to hers. 'What do you usually eat for breakfast?'

'Porridge,' she answered absently.

'You need to eat.'

'Why are you talking about food?' Her nose pinched as a wave of nausea crawled up her throat. 'You don't have to feed me up. I'm not pregnant,' she declared. 'I can't be.' But her bottom lip wobbled.

'You know this as a certainty?' His gaze burned into her. Diving inside her. Seeking secrets. Seeking answers. Answers she didn't have.

'We used protection…'

As rapidly as a fire spreading after receiving a gust of oxygen he was on his phone, blasting out a long stream of words that were foreign to her. But there was no doubting that it was a series of commands that he spoke into the mouthpiece, while never taking his eyes off her.

Slipping the phone back into his inside pocket, he shook his head. 'You *could* be pregnant,' he corrected.

His voice was a low husk of possession, and it reached across the distance between them. This was surreal... *Impossible!* Her life was scripted. Planned. Her days followed a routine down to the minute.

After London—after collecting the file and discovering the truth of her adoption—she'd returned to her life because it was safe And predictable. But she'd been unable to hide from all the questions in her head, from the intensity of what she'd felt.

The night she'd met him she hadn't had to think. She'd operated on autopilot, supressing her emotions, never allowing them to overwhelm her. She hadn't needed to be anything other than the woman she knew she could be. She'd managed to lock everything away.

Only now it all threatened to spill out, to escape. And she wasn't ready for that. She had to be able to think clearly.

'I'm *not* pregnant.' She swallowed convulsively. 'We— *you*—used protection. I saw—'

Her body tightened deep down inside as the memory of the pleasure of feeling him pushing inside her flooded her brain. Her senses.

'The condom tore,' he told her, his tone matter-of-fact. Unemotional. Toneless.

Rapid and shallow, her breathing picked up pace. 'Tore...?'

He moved then. Slid himself along the seat until there was no more than an inch between them. Their knees knocked, and it took all of her concentration not to inhale the scent of soap and clean cotton. Of *him*. The scent was something so familiar and yet so unknown that it was as terrifying as it was exciting.

'If you hadn't run,' he said, 'I would have told you that night.'

It was like a punch to the gut. Flora closed her eyes. Breathed in through her nose and out through her mouth. 'I... I was afraid,' she confessed, opening her eyes to meet his unwavering steady gaze.

'Of me?' he asked, his voice deep. Gravelly.

She shook her head and swallowed thickly. 'Couldn't you feel it?' she whispered.

A deep furrow appeared between his eyebrows. 'Feel what?'

A blush crawled up her throat. What was the point of lying? He was here, and her decision to run had affected them both. Pulled them out of their dreamlike encounter into reality. Into her real life. Why shouldn't she ask all the questions that had plagued her for weeks? About her reaction to him? About her body's response to his touch.

She pressed her palms to her thighs and told him the truth. 'The temptation to do it all over again.'

The vein in his throat became more pronounced as he asked, 'This frightened you?' His eyes narrowed. 'Because I hurt you?'

'No, the pain was minimal. But the pleasure was...' She hesitated. 'It was all-consuming. It was too intense, too frantic, and I... I was afraid that what you'd awoken inside me would never go back to sleep if I stayed for a second longer in your bed.'

His fingers flexed at his sides. 'You ran because you were afraid of who you were with me?'

'Yes.' She blew out a shaky breath between pursed lips. Eyes narrowed, he nodded.

'Is it always like that?' she asked, because a part of her re-

ally wanted to know. 'Sex?' she clarified. 'Is it always so…
intoxicating?'

The idea that he might have tracked her down simply because he wanted her was distant. Was she naïve to think a
man would seek her out because the sex had been *that* good?

But she *was* naïve, wasn't she? Had been sheltered from
life on purpose. Wrapped in cotton wool so she didn't ac-
cidentally discover that her biological mother had a disease
that might live inside her too, deep in her genetic make-up.

His eyes darkened. 'No.'

'Was it like that for you too?'

*Did it matter?*

She didn't know. Only that she wanted the answer. 'With
me?' she asked.

'I…' He faltered. The pulse in his cheek hammered. 'That
is not important. Not right now. What is important is that it
has been six weeks,' he said. 'Time enough for your body to
tell you if there have been consequences of the pleasure you
were so afraid of, *piccolina*.' He paused before continuing.
'Has your period arrived?' he asked,

But the question wasn't filled with recrimination or accusation. He wanted the facts. Facts she was still trying to put
in order. It didn't make sense. None of it.

Heat crept into her cheeks. Maybe she hadn't been listening to her body. Maybe she had been too busy trying to slip
back into her life to listen.

Her hands moved to rest on her flat stomach. 'I don't *feel*
pregnant,' she said, more to herself than to him.

She looked down at her hands, at the makeshift cradle
she'd created around her stomach. Her body still felt like
hers. Not a host to a new life.

'We will take a test,' he said.

Flora snapped her gaze back to his. 'You have brought a pregnancy test with you?'

'Unfortunately I don't keep pregnancy tests in my breast pocket,' he said.

Her breath shuddered in her chest. Was this his attempt at humour?

'But I've purchased one.'

'Where is it?' she asked.

'It will be waiting for us at my home.'

'Us?' she repeated. She'd never been part of an *us*.

'I can't do it without you,' he said, closing his mouth and watching her watch him.

'No, I suppose you can't,' she agreed. 'But why is someone taking a test to your house when you're here, in my home? With me?'

'It was the easier choice,' he dismissed, without further explanation.

'But we're *here*…' she pressed.

'And soon we will be *there*,' he countered, matter-of-factly.

'How did you find me?' she asked, brows knitted. He hadn't answered her before. 'Did you hire a private investigator?'

'A team of them,' he replied, without so much as a blush.

She pointed a trembling finger at his chest. 'You read all the files on me?'

'How else was I to find you?'

'You weren't *supposed* to find me.'

She dropped her hand into her lap and raised her gaze to the ceiling. It felt like a betrayal. He'd so easily summoned information on her when she'd had to wait twenty-one years to learn about Flora Campbell.

She looked at him. 'I didn't want to remember.'

His eyes flashed, his pupils growing larger. 'There's no forgetting now.'

Flora looked at him—at this man who'd given her a taste of life outside the farm—and she recognised that some part of her had wanted that night, and him, to stay separate from her real life. Her farm life. Something to remind her that there was magic in plain sight if she pushed to look for it.

'I might *not* be pregnant,' she reminded him. And herself.

'But if you are I insist our child will know its roots. Its beginnings. Its biological parents. I will not leave it to think it is unwanted. That there is no one to protect it. Because I will claim it. I will want it.'

'How dare you use what you've read about me to bring me on side?'

His eyes narrowed. 'Why do you assume it is *your* past that guides me? I am not trying to manipulate you. I have come to you, I have found you, and I have offered you facts. We will discover if there are consequences together. Now you must trust me.'

Her head spun. 'Trust you…?'

'Trust me to navigate the next steps.'

'The next steps…?'

Flora closed her eyes briefly. What was she? A parrot? If she *was* pregnant, where would that leave her? Single? But tied to a man she'd given her virginity to for the rest of her life simply because a condom had split?

'What choice do you have, *piccolina*?' His features did not move. Not even a flicker. 'We will leave here now and do a test together.'

'What if I am pregnant—?'

'First,' he interrupted, 'we will find out if you are.'

'And if I am?' she pushed. Because this was her life, and she was tired of facts being withheld from her. Of finding out after everyone else.

'We'll get married, of course.'

'Married?' she repeated, because so easily had the word fallen from his mouth. As easily as the news that she might be carrying his child. She wasn't finding any of those words easy. 'Why?'

'If you are pregnant with my child, the child also belongs to me. I protect what is mine.'

'A baby's not a possession. You can't claim ownership. Pass it around like an unwanted pet—'

'Would you have preferred that I left you to discover this on your own? That I left you to struggle with single motherhood?'

'I *am* single,' she reminded him.

His lips compressed. 'Not any more.'

'You can't claim me just because you will it,' she said, dismissing his possessive claim with a wave of her unsteady hand.

'If you are pregnant,' he said, 'our baby deserves to know where it comes from. *Who* it comes from. It has a right to its father's name. *My* name.'

There was something in his tone—something raw. As though he'd revealed too much.

'Are those your own words?'

She bit hard on her lower lip. Words were swimming in her head. *Pregnant. A baby. Failure. A mistake. Discovered and abandoned. Unwanted.*

'Or words you've taken and recycled from my file? Did you read that my biological father is unknown to me?'

'I did.' His eyes darkened. 'And I too understand—*intimately*—the weight of being denied your true origins.'

'You were adopted too?' she asked, her brain jumping quickly to that conclusion.

'No. But I lived only with my mother, who told me stories of my father being a count. Italian nobility.'

His tone was flat and sober as he told her this, giving nothing away.

'He'd hidden her away for the shame of having his illegitimate son.'

'You're the illegitimate son?'

'I am,' he confirmed.

'Did it hurt?'

'Which bit?'

'The stories?' she asked.

She'd never know who her biological father was, and that would always leave a hole inside her. But at least she hadn't been soothed by stories of a father who might be aristocracy to lessen the blow.

'Until I reached twenty-one my parents told me stories too,' she said. 'Not as wild as having nobility for parents. But never the facts. Never the truth.'

'What kind of stories?'

'Stories to hide the reasons why I was home-schooled. The reasons I shouldn't follow my instincts but plan and execute carefully designed routines, so I didn't ever become consumed by my passions.'

'Why would they do that?'

'I have an addictive personality. I focus on things...' she shrugged, tugging her bottom lip between her teeth '...and I fixate.'

'What things do you focus on?'

'Fixing things, usually...' She paused, feeling a tightness that was making it difficult to form a placating smile. Making it difficult to swallow.

He shrugged. 'Focusing—*prioritising*—in a world full of noise is a skill, not a fault.'

'Maybe...' she conceded.

'Is that why you think you don't know yourself? Because you were never told your truth? Your story?' he asked, and with that he catapulted her six weeks into the past.

'You remember?'

'I remember everything.'

And so did she. Every caress of his fingers. Every touch of his—

She pushed them down. The memories. And she ignored the heavy drag in her stomach.

'I'm their miracle baby,' she said, as if that would explain everything. And to her it did.

'I was an unwanted bastard,' he answered. 'And you were a miracle. Two opposite ends of the spectrum. No child of mine will never be a mistake. My child will never be a bastard. Never unwanted or illegitimate,' he bit out between tight lips. 'If you are pregnant, our baby will always know where it belongs. That it is protected. Safe.'

His eyes held hers with an intensity so strong she could feel the pulse of it in her chest.

'With me,' he said.

'You weren't safe?' she asked, feeling a stab of something visceral to her solar plexus. 'When you were growing up?'

'I grew up in the eastern hills of Sicily. It's…' he frowned '…beautiful. Untouched and out of the way of things. If we'd lived closer to the coastal towns, to people who might have seen my mother's illness—'

'Your mother was ill?'

'Mentally ill. To the point where she couldn't function.'

She watched his Adam's apple drag up and down his taut throat.

'Or care for a little boy who was hungry more often than not.'

'You don't want the same for you child?' she said. 'That's why you're here? Because—?'

'Exactly.' His gaze locked on her stomach. 'My child will not be hungry. My child will never be cold.'

Connection surged between them. Not like the night they'd met. Something deeper. Something she couldn't name or place. But she recognised it was happening.

'Did your mother tell you stories of Italian nobility because she didn't know who your father was? Or did she tell you them because she didn't want to tell you the truth?'

'Some of my mother's stories were true...some false,' he answered. 'I only found out which when I was much older, and then it didn't matter to me any more what was fiction or fact. I'd grown up without a father...without his name. All I knew was that we were hungry and that my mother had been abandoned by a man who didn't want to claim either her or me. He paid her off with a wad of cash that lived under the bed in a jar until it was all gone. He left us in a village where they called my mother—'

He looked away, at the floor, and she felt the rawness of his vulnerability.

He raised his head, his face an emotionless mask of beauty. 'But she knew who my father was.'

'So it's true?' she asked, eyes wide. 'Your father's an Italian count?'

'He is—*was*,' he corrected. 'My father is dead.'

'When did he die?'

'Six months ago.'

'And your mum?'

'Three months ago.'

'Oh...so much death...'

Her throat constricted. And yet they might have made life in all the grief.

She swallowed. Shook herself. 'I'm so sorry.'

'I didn't know my father.' He blinked slowly. 'I didn't grieve for him. I didn't *need* my father, or his name. But I deserved it. And you deserve to know *my* name, Flora.'

Her name on his lips was too real. It brought their night together, their future, to the real world of names and consequences. Actions and reactions. Negatives and positives.

'I am Ra—'

'No!' she pleaded, palms forward. 'I'm not ready. Please, don't tell me your name.'

Nostrils flaring, he asked, 'Why not?'

'If—' Her tongue grappled with words, refusing to organise them inside her mouth. 'If you tell me your name you become real,' she said, trying to explain. '*This* becomes real,' she concluded, her hands splayed in front of her chest.

'This *is* real.' His eyes probed her face but he didn't move. Not a muscle. '*I'm* real.'

And that was the problem, wasn't it? He was being honest about his life and so was she—for the first time. There she sat in a helicopter, in the middle of a field, with a man she'd never been supposed to see again.

But none of it would matter if she wasn't pregnant. This intensity, this sense of being overwhelmed, this influx of emotion that so terrified her would be temporary.

She opened her eyes. 'I'll come with you,' she said, deciding to be honest. Because why not after all he'd shared with her about his mother? His illegitimacy? 'Under one condition.'

'What is it?'

'That you don't tell me your name unless I'm pregnant. Because if I'm not pregnant, none of this will matter.'

He nodded. 'I will remain a stranger to you until we become something else,' he promised, the pulse flickering wildly in his cheek.

'*If,*' she corrected. 'If we become something else.'

His eyes flashed and her stomach flipped, and the *'we'* lingered in the air.

And then, just as he had that night, he offered her his hand.

A rush of excitement—or was it fear, perhaps?—pulsed through her veins in waves.

Tentatively she slid her fingers between his and he claimed her hand, lifting her out of the helicopter to pull her into step beside him. He opened the door to the flight deck, nodded towards the co-pilot's seat.

Flora climbed inside. His hands were on her waist, guiding her. He buckled her in and then climbed in himself, buckled himself into the pilot's seat.

He flicked a switch on the dashboard, handed her a headset. She mimicked him as he put his own on, sliding it on her head and pulling down the mouthpiece even though she knew they were out of words. There was nothing left to say.

The helicopter blades spun furiously and pulled them up into the air. Away from the farm. Away from everything she'd ever known.

Flora realised that she wasn't leaving as Flora Campbell, the abandoned daughter of an addict. But neither was she Flora Bick, a miracle baby adopted by farmers. She was leaving as a potential mother...and maybe someone's soon-to-be wife.

*His* wife.

She'd have to learn a whole new script—a brand-new list of rules for a completely different life where she'd decide how she lived it. Who she wanted to be.

And if the time came to make a choice, who would she choose?

# CHAPTER FIVE

THE HELICOPTER SWOOPED between the coastal cliffs and out over the open sea straight towards a white and blue vessel. A boat—a *yacht*—of magnificent proportions.

Flora's skin prickled. She turned her head, looking back towards the beach. She *knew* that beach. Combed it regularly for shells, or driftwood, for signs of life outside the farm. But she'd dragged nothing back to the farm as large as *him*.

She turned back to him…the man who was piloting the helicopter. Was it *his* helicopter?

Her temples pounded with the realisation of that. Surely if they were having a baby together that was information she should know? But she didn't. She'd been too swept up in the other revelations of the last hour. His return. The failed contraception. The potential pregnancy. A baby…

Suddenly a barrage of images slammed against her brain. *The helicopter. The suit. The roof. The opulent rooms at the hotel!* Her eyes snapped to the view in front of them, focusing on the yacht…a water palace. She'd been blinded by emotion, by passion. She hadn't seen what was right in front of her.

He lowered the helicopter onto the tail-end of the yacht, onto a helipad. Flora held her breath during the descent. He was a man of means, wasn't he? A man who'd been able to find her when she'd barely been able to find out any information about herself for herself. He'd hired a team of private investigators…

'The hotel…'

She hesitated as he flicked some switches. Turned off a blinking light and removed his headset. The whir of the helicopter propellers slowed to a gentle buzz.

Did she truly want to know more about the man who could be the father of her child? Did she want to make this real before they confirmed the consequences? Did she need to?

Before Flora could swallow he was getting out, walking around the front of the helicopter to appear on her side. He pulled open her door and stood there expectantly. The sea stretched out behind him, calm, and a new world of opulence surrounded the helicopter. Gleaming glass and polished silver rails were stacked in rows, on top of one another, which she could only assume signified more decks, more rooms…

'I'm not getting out.'

He cocked a brow. 'You're not?'

She shook her head so violently that she dislodged her headset. She caught it. 'No, I'm not.'

How could she when she didn't know what kind of world she was stepping into. She'd hadn't considered it before. She'd been too focused on finding out if she was pregnant, never stopping to question where he'd be taking her. Where his home was.

He took the headset from her hands, his fingers brushing the tips of hers.

No. She wouldn't look at his hands. She wouldn't recognise the jolt in her stomach for what it was. Because desire was intoxicating. *Consuming.* She needed facts—not emotion. She must not let herself be swayed by these addictive feelings.

She needed not to recognise the sensations in her stomach, and lower, that the single caress of his hand against hers had caused. Because it was ludicrous how badly she wanted him when she still didn't know who he was. This stranger—this man—the potential father of her potential baby...

He threw the headset onto the dashboard. 'Why not?' Amusement laced his voice.

Flora inhaled deeply through her nostrils and squared her shoulders, steeling herself. She'd let her emotions overrule logic. With him, she'd ignored every lesson ingrained by her parents to call for rational thinking before impulse. Now she needed information. She needed to be able to think clearly.

'Tell me who you are?' she demanded tightly.

He narrowed his eyes. 'Why is it important now?'

'Because I don't think your world is anything like mine. I think—*I thought* the man on that rooftop was staying in the hotel, like me. He just had a better room with a better view. But you *own* that view, don't you?'

'What do you mean?'

'I need to know who you are,' she repeated. 'I need to know the facts. *Now.*'

'I have no problem telling you who I am. You were the one who wished not to know my name—'

'I was wrong,' she admitted. 'The truth is that this is real—whether or not I want to acknowledge it. I can't hide from it because here we are...'

She raised her hands and gesticulated to the view. To the sea surrounding them at every turn.

'I want to find out if I'm pregnant knowing all the facts. *Real* facts. I want to rip off the blindfold that's been obscuring the view my whole life and go into this with my eyes wide open. I owe it to any potential child to know who I might've made it with.' She sucked in a breath. 'And don't we owe it to ourselves?'

'Of course,' he agreed. 'We deserve to have each other's names.'

'Then tell me yours.'

'I am Raffaele Russo. CEO of Russo Renovations. Sicilian born and bred. Multi-billionaire.'

He closed the distance even between them and, his mouth a whisper's breadth from her own, said, 'I am the father of the potential baby who potentially grows inside you.'

Desire pulsed between them even now, throwing her the absurd image of herself leaning in and pressing her mouth to his.

She shook it off.

'Billionaire?' she repeated, and pulled back enough so that she couldn't taste the warmth of his breath on her lips.

'*Multi*-billionaire,' he corrected.

'But you said you grew up in the middle of nowhere. That your mother couldn't afford heating. How did you make so much money?'

Eyes hooded, he asked, 'Does it matter?'

'Of course it does. Why didn't you tell me you were rich?'

'You never asked.'

Of course she hadn't. How could she ever have imagined herself to exist in the same world as a billionaire? To be desired by a billionaire? How could she ever have imagined that a billionaire wanted her? A woman who had no idea where she really came from...

'And you never thought to say?' she asked,

What did this mean? For her? For her potential child?

Raffaele shrugged. 'I'm comfortable with the man I am. There is no need to flaunt my existence.'

There was more to it—she could tell by the casual way he threw the comment out into the world. There was no time to dwell on that. But was Flora comfortable with it?

'Tell me how you became a billionaire?' she asked.

'I won't romanticise the past. It was hard. Scarlata is small.'

'Scarlata?'

'My village. Only a hundred people. It didn't have access to many things, but it had access to the outside world. A connection to the internet. For the posting of the kind of pretty pictures people like to post on social media.'

'What do pretty pictures on social media have to do with anything?'

'Pretty pictures make money.'

Her brain couldn't connect the dots. 'I don't understand...'

He smiled, but his eyes didn't. Shadows played inside them and she couldn't make out their shape.

'You don't like pretty pictures, *piccolina*?'

'Why?' She smiled tentatively. 'Are you a photographer?'

'I'm a builder,' he said. 'I build things. Fix things. But back then I found an old digital camera on a farm on the outskirts of the village.'

'There was a farm?'

'They made cheese there for three generations and sold it to the big cities. Tourists didn't visit my village, but they visited the farm online, to watch, and I watched them.'

'You lived on a farm?' she asked, her heart absurdly lifting at the idea that he'd grown up in a place exactly like her.

He shook his head. 'I helped there sometimes, because they gave me cheese and bread enough to feed my *mamma*. To feed myself. But tourists need more than bread dipped in cheese. More than pasta and tomatoes. Tourists need a place to go. They've seen the pretty pictures online. They need a place to sleep.'

'You gave them a bed?'

'No. I built them one.'

'You built them a place to sleep?'

'Where do *you* sleep, Flora?'

'In a bed…'

'Where did the bed come from?'

'A shop.'

'Where did the shop get the bed?'

She frowned. 'From a bed-maker…?'

'Exactly.' He applauded without sound, pressing his palms together. 'Well done.'

'No need to patronise me.'

'I'm not,' he placated. 'Where I'm from, there weren't the commodities you have in your village. If I needed something the only option was to travel to one of the major towns or big cities to get it, or to build it myself. I didn't have the means to travel, so I built things. And I traded for them. I traded my physical strength for a meal. The work of my hands…'

He held them out in front of him and her eyes snapped to them. To the calluses on his palms that would never heal. She remembered their slight roughness against her hips as he'd held her in place and devoured—

'These hands,' he continued, 'wrapped parcels of cheese for seven days straight without sleep. Because I wanted to learn—to listen—to understand what those tourists were doing and to figure out how I could make money from them.'

'How *did* you make money from them?'

'I flipped an abandoned house in the centre of the village, in the middle of everything—near the local shop, the café and the bar—and turned it into a rustic den of opulence. A two-floor haven. Using materials hidden in basements of the local community.'

'The community?'

'They…helped me.'

She heard it. The croak of distaste.

'I'm glad someone did,' she whispered. 'I'm glad someone helped you.'

'It was a long time ago,' he dismissed. 'I don't need help
any more. But if I learnt anything from living in the middle
of nowhere, I learned two things. If you climb up, you hold
your hand out for the next person. You protect your own. *I
protect my own.*'

His voice was fierce—animated—and she sat rooted, listening to every word. She didn't want to interrupt. She would
never have imagined this was how he'd made his money. His
billions.

'My first success was everyone's. Because money came
along with the tourists who wanted to stay in what I'd built.
Social media influencers wanted a taste of civilisation in
an uncivilised landscape…to take pretty pictures of sunsets
burning over windswept olive trees. I brought tourists into
the community that had once protected me. And I paid them
back tenfold before I sold that little hub of opulence. And then
I made it out. I got out of that village because of *me*. And
with a little luck guiding the way I did it all again. All over
Sicily. I took broken things and made them pretty. Sold them
for far more than they were worth. It took me to Italia. To
Roma. And there I built my business—Russo Renovations.
And now my rebuilds are coveted. Worldwide.'

'Who taught you how to fix things? To build?'

'Myself. Books…' He hooked a brow. 'The internet.'

'And the London hotel?' she asked. 'Is that yours too?'

His eyes flashed and her stomach tugged.

'Mine,' he confirmed.

She nodded. It all made sense. Why he'd been there—why
he'd been the one to find her. But it didn't sound as if luck
had been the catalyst for his success, and she told him so.

'I don't believe it was luck that guided you,' she said.

He shrugged. 'What did, then?'

'Tenacity.'

'The boy I once was would have liked to hear himself called tenacious.'

'And the billionaire?'

'He wouldn't care.'

He smiled, but still it didn't reach his eyes. And she wanted to ask why he didn't care. But he'd already revealed so much. Told her a story so honest that she had goose bumps on her skin beneath her jumper.

'You asked me how I made my money,' he reminded her, stepping backwards so that his black-sheathed body was framed by the view of the sea. The vastness of it. 'Now I have told you. Are you ready?'

'I'm ready,' she told him—because she was. She'd lock away her feelings. Use the logical part of her brain to do what she needed to do. As she had been taught to do. *As he had.* 'I'm ready to take the pregnancy test now.'

Flora unbuckled herself and stepped out of the helicopter with an ease she didn't really feel. Because it wasn't about either of them, was it? This was all about a potential child.

*Their child.*

He moved to her and whispered, 'Welcome home, Flora.'

'Home?' she echoed. 'You live *here*?'

'*Si,*' he said.

She looked at his home. A floating kingdom of slick black and white lines and blue angles on a still ocean. With nothing but more ocean at its back.

She gasped, unable to hold it back. 'It's a palace!'

'Three hundred feet of space,' he confirmed without ego. Without a smile. 'Multiple decks above and below sea level. Every toy at my disposal—every recreational device a billionaire could need. And twenty-plus staff to deliver every-thing on a silver platter.'

'A multi-billionaire,' she corrected, and smiled a smile she wasn't feeling. Because inside she was crying for the boy who had saved a village.

Because who had raised him?

His mother hadn't been able to look after him. His father had thrown him away, calling his illegitimacy shameful but doing nothing to fix it. Doing nothing to legitimise him. His father had hidden him away in a village where people relied on each other to survive.

The money…the opulence… None of it mattered, did it? But the story did. It was a story she'd like to tell her child. *If* she was pregnant. The story of how their father had lifted a village below the poverty line and turned himself into a billionaire.

The reality of it all caused her temples to throb.

The hand resting beside his thigh was so big, so strong. But all she could imagine was a smaller hand, a cold hand, attached to a hungry body…

She wanted to wrap her arms around his neck and pull him close to her, whisper words for the little boy she'd never met. She couldn't do that. But she could hold his hand.

She took it. Pushed her fingers through his and held the smile on her face in place as she said, 'Show me the way, Raffaele.'

'Flora…?'

Her eyes moved up the length of him. Over the muscular body of a man she'd never have guessed had once been hungry. Or cold.

'Raffaele…?'

'Why did you get off the chopper?' he asked.

'Because we want the same thing.'

His eyes narrowed. 'What's that?'

'For our baby—if I'm pregnant—to be protected. Safe.' She pulled in a deep breath and added, 'Loved.' And the last word caught her in the ribs.

Who was going to love her?

Who would love Raffaele?

*Could she?*

Raffaele didn't respond—because why would he damage the tentative connection they'd formed? The connection that had encouraged her to get her off the chopper? Why would he admit to her that he didn't love? That he didn't know how to love and didn't want to learn.

His mother had loved completely. With all of herself. *Selfishly.* She'd neglected everything around her because of that love. Until the promise—*the lie*—of its return to had driven her to death's door.

'What I told you has made you think that?' he asked.

He wouldn't have summarised his rise to wealth using those words. *Protected...safe... Loved.* He certainly hadn't been loved, protected, or kept safe.

'Yes,' she said. 'Your origin... Your beginning...' She shrugged. 'They're powerful.'

'They hold no power over me,' he dismissed. Because they didn't. He'd only told her because she'd asked. And the story he'd told her hadn't been his origin. It had been an ending. An end to the constant worry of watching over his mother. Because once he'd left that village he'd paid someone else to watch her for him.

Raffaele hardened himself against the woman holding his hand. The small wisp of a woman who'd broken his control, encouraged him with her whispers in the dark to throw that glass against the wall and let the shards fall where they might…

Step for step they moved along the deck. His hand absently pulled open the glass door and he led them inside. A sense of unease settled over him as he recognised the pull in his groin for what it was.

*Desire.*

His eyes raked over her. He wanted the softness of that hand holding his against his chest. He wanted to bury the memories she'd pulled out of his mouth in the warmth of her body. To find oblivion as he sheathed himself inside her and to drown out the part of the story he hadn't told her.

How could he tell her that the hand she held so softly, so carefully, hadn't been able to reach his mother? That he hadn't been able to protect her or make her feel safe?

His *mamma* had never grasped the hand he'd held out. Yes, she'd accepted his wealth. Accepted him turning that dilapidated house on the hill into a beacon of privilege. But she'd never accepted *him*.

So what did it matter that he hadn't been there? Would she have taken his hand that night when she'd seen no alternative?

He'd never know.

'Which way?'

Eyes bright, Flora turned to him.

'Raffaele?'

He swallowed down the lump in throat. 'Straight ahead.'

She smiled. A small, delicate pout of her lips. And, oh, how he wanted to lean down and sample their fullness. Taste her again. But this time with his name on her lips. He wanted to hear her panting it. Screaming every syllable into his mouth.

*Raffaele.*

He tightened his hold on her hand and guided her through

the main saloon into the corridor that broke off into multiple master suites. Led her towards his suite. His room. His bed.

*What was this woman doing to his control?*

He'd enjoyed being anonymous. He'd enjoyed her casual approach to his wealth. To him.

*Because you are weak around her and she sees what you are. A lonely boy with a dream of getting out.*

Had he ever really got out?

The fingers entwined in his flexed. He looked down at the small hand. The elegant fingertips pressing against his knuckles.

She didn't care, did she? About the wealth? She'd asked him to take her to his bed, make love to her, without even knowing his name. She'd followed him across the sea. And only when his yacht had been thrust in her face had she considered that he might be part of a world she wasn't.

He hardened. Every part of him throbbed with an absurd need to be inside her. To drown in her dismissal of his name and his wealth. Because all that had mattered the night she'd met him was what he was feeling right now.

An intoxicating need to be with her.

And he didn't understand it. This *need*. He didn't understand *her*. She'd cared about the *story*. The one he'd told no one. Her decision to get on his boat had come because of a story of weakness. Of *him* being weak.

He didn't even know why he'd told her.

*Lies.*

He knew. He'd wanted to make the innocent wonder in her eyes every time she looked at him vanish. To stop this hold she had over him. To stop this lack of control he felt near her.

But it hadn't stopped. It had intensified.

*If you told her about your mother...how you failed—*

He blocked the intrusive thoughts and focused on his next step. Their destination. Their fate.

He'd figure her out later. But first things first…

He pushed open the door to his suite and pulled her over the threshold without pause or hesitation. He was ready to confirm what he somehow already knew without rhyme or reason. She *was* pregnant. And in a few minutes he'd be bound to her for ever.

He wouldn't fail his own again.

That was his promise.

*His vow.*

He wouldn't look away this time.

# CHAPTER SIX

RAFFAELE HADN'T SAID a word.

Every inch of his body was relaxed as he lounged on the cream leather high-back chair as if it were his *throne*, one leg lazily over the other, his arms languid. Hands that didn't tremble rested on the tips of the arms as the pregnancy test sat on the table between them.

Flora was not relaxed.

But his eyes kept her rooted. Perched on the end of the cream leather sofa, knees together, fingers steepled. *Waiting.*

He watched her, and she watched the pregnancy test.

Flora cleared her throat. It was too tight. Too dry.

She reached for the glass of water on the edge of the table. Far away from the device in the middle.

Tentatively, she raised it to her lips, careful to think through the steps. *Open her mouth. Take a sip. Close her mouth. Swallow. Put the glass back.* Rational steps. Logical.

The suite was all crisp lines in creams and greys. All shiny. The low table between them gleamed. If she leaned over— inspected the plastic blue and white oval device—she'd see her reflection in it.

They were in the bedroom of the master suite. *His* suite. Which was really as big as any house, with a separate dining area, a lounge and bathroom.

An enormous bed dominated one section of the room,

with the crispest white sheets, the plumpest pillows and the deepest mattress she'd ever seen. Subtle lights surrounded it. Built into the walls themselves.

Only a soft glow, so as not to take away from the view, she assumed. Because the view of the ocean was vast, and it surrounded them. Never-ending. Water usually calmed her. Her trips to the beach were her escape. Her chance to be still. To let her mind wander.

She couldn't look at it now. But she couldn't stop looking at the bed.

She flicked her gaze back to the test. It wasn't the kind of test she'd pictured in her head. It was smart. It wouldn't show her any pink lines. She wouldn't have to apply her maths skills. She wouldn't have to add one line with another to make two. *If* she was pregnant it would flash with the word *pregnant* and show how many weeks life had been growing inside her. She would know in less than five minutes what she hadn't known for weeks.

Unable to bear it any longer, she leant forward, reached out her hand.

'It's not time.'

Her hand froze in mid-air. 'How much longer?'

'Thirty seconds.'

She dropped her hand. Returned to her perch.

She'd asked Raffaele to read the instructions to her twice. It wasn't rocket science, but she'd wanted to make sure she did it right.

And, calmly, he had. Each word level. Clear. Emotionless. She'd known he wasn't telling her a story any more, but a part of her had wanted to hear what he was feeling. How he felt about her. About the possibility of a baby they'd made together.

Raffaele had whisked her through doors made of glass, through corridors that smelt of newness and quality, but when he'd opened the door to this room he'd let go of her hand. She rubbed at it now. There were no visible marks. No evidence of his touch. But she tingled with it. The sensation of skin against skin. All thoughts of the boy vanished and replaced with thoughts of the man beside her.

Of this room he'd led her to.

The bed.

She cleared her throat. Swiped her tongue against her teeth. That wasn't logical. She *needed* to be logical. Those feelings, those impulses that had gripped her when she'd walked in, that had urged her to climb onto the bed, to surrender to her body's needs, needed to be buried.

'It's time, *piccolina*.'

Her gaze snapped to his. Before she could stop herself, she spoke. 'I'm scared.'

'It can't hurt you.'

'What if I hurt *it*?'

He blinked. Slowly. Fluttering shadows kissing his chiselled cheekbones. 'Why would you think that?'

'No…' She stumbled, realising what that had sounded like. 'I wouldn't hurt a baby. I wouldn't hurt anyone. Not physically. Not emotionally. Not on purpose.'

Because that was always her goal, wasn't it? Not to hurt those she loved with her behaviour. Not to make them worry. But unconsciously…

'What if I get it all wrong?' she asked, her throat tight. 'What if I'm a terrible mother?'

His gaze softened. 'That you worry about being bad means you will do everything you can to be good. That you will care. Deeply.'

She frowned. He'd told her his story… Didn't he deserve hers, too?

'Aren't you worried?' she asked. 'A little scared?'

'No.' His shoulders stiffened. 'I'm confident I'll know the things not to do.'

'How?'

'I wasn't always rich,' he reminded her, and she watched his Adam's apple drop and rise in the now open collar at his throat. The tie was gone. Laced over the arm of the chair. 'Our child will never have to worry about trading skills or finding the easiest route to a major city. I can provide all the things I never had.'

'Money doesn't equal happiness. Money doesn't mean love.' She shook her head, another long strand of hair breaking free of her loose bun. She reached up and pulled out the hair tie. Shook her head again until her hair fell about her shoulders. 'It's made of paper. *Things* don't raise a baby. People do.' She pushed the black band onto her wrist and turned her gaze to his. '*We* will.'

A pulse hammered in his cheek. 'Money will provide the foundations.' He unhooked his leg, planted his feet squarely on the cream rug beneath his feet. 'It will provide all the things we spoke about. Protection. Safety. Food. Central heating.'

'I was always warm…' An image of her mother and father flashed in her head, with their big smiles and open arms. 'Always safe.' She blinked away the unexpected tears obscuring her view. 'I never had to worry about the plumbing…the bills,' she continued, with a lump in her throat. 'If I was cold, my mum and my dad they turned up the heating. Hugged me. Wrapped me in a blanket. Tucked me into bed…' She whimpered and the dam broke.

He stood, but she held up an open palm.

'Please, don't touch me.'

He froze, eyes wide, and stared at her. 'Why not?'

'Because if you do—' she scrubbed the back of her hand across her eyes '—I'll cry.'

'You're already crying.'

She snorted. 'Oh, my God!' She pulled at the end of her jumper until it swallowed her hand and rubbed it across her offensive nose. How dared it make such a sound in front of—?

She looked up at the man watching her so intently. 'I don't usually make piggy sounds,' she promised, attempting a smile. But it felt too tight. Too pinched.

'It's not every day you take a pregnancy test.'

She looked at the test.

Her parents had claimed her. Wanted her. Always loved their adopted miracle baby.

No, they had always loved *her*, she realised. After London, after the file, there had only been one place she wanted to run to. Straight into the arms of her mum. Straight back home. Because that was where she'd always felt safe. Even though there were things her parents hadn't told her. Even though they'd sheltered her.

'Why are you so afraid when your childhood was a place of warmth?'

His question broke into the realisation it had taken her too long to understand. Her parents loved her.

'It's not just fear,' she admitted. She saw it then. The flicker of his shadowed jaw. The thud of apprehension. 'I'm not *just* afraid. I'm feeling a whole host of things I don't know what to do with.'

'You're allowed to feel everything,' he assured her. 'You can cry.' He winked. *'Snort.'*

This time, her smile was genuine.

'I burst into your life and turned it upside down. You will find your feet,' he promised, 'and I will help.'

'How can you guide me when you don't know the way, either? When you don't know me?'

'What do you think I need to know?'

'I…'

The room felt too small. Airless. He deserved the redacted parts of her story too, didn't he? The parts only she knew.

She dragged in a fortifying breath. 'How much of the report on me did you read?'

'The important bits.'

'Which were…?' she pressed. Because she needed to know what he already knew and the parts she'd have to tell him.

'Where to find you.'

'That's it?' She frowned. 'My address?'

He rolled his neck, as if the end of her tears had released his muscles. 'Can I sit?'

'What?' she asked, confused, and looked at the chair behind him. 'Of course. Sit down.'

'No.' He dipped his head to the space beside her. 'I want to sit next to you.'

'Oh…'

'Unless you don't want me to.'

She looked at the space between them. From his chair to where she was perched on the sofa. 'Okay…' A flush crawled up her throat. 'You *should* sit next to me,' she said—because he should. 'We should find out what the test says together, not while we're sitting six feet apart.'

He came to her. Soundless steps of solid muscle. Stalking towards her. He sat down. Mirrored her and perched at the end of the seat. He looked at the test, and she looked at him.

Her heart did a double beat. Now was the time, wasn't it? To give him all the facts. Before they looked at the test. Her story in exchange for his.

'Tell me what you know of my past,' she started, because it was the right thing to say. 'And I'll fill in the blanks.'

'I know that your birth name is Flora Campbell. You were born to a woman named Clara Campbell. Father unknown.

Your parents adopted you at fourteen weeks old and you became Flora Bick.'

'Is that it? My file didn't tell you that my biological mother
was an addict? That she was addicted to substances? Hard
ones?' She swallowed, but didn't allow herself to look away
from him. 'They were in my system when I was born. I was
born an addict…' Her chest hurt and she rubbed at it.

His fingers flexed on his knees and, absurdly, she wanted
to hold them. His hand. Not for him this time. But for herself.

He turned his body, his gaze, and she locked on to the
warmth of him. The reality.

'You can tell me.'

He needed the facts too, didn't he?

She pushed out a silent breath 'I have an addictive personality.'

'I know. You said so that night.'

*Had she?*

She felt as if she'd said so much and yet so little. She swallowed the urge to relive every moment of their time together.
Every word. Every caress of his fingers. Every kiss.

'I obsess. And I'm impulsive.'

'Your impulsivity brought you to me,' he countered. 'To
my bed.'

He didn't touch her, but his words shot straight to her stomach. They arrowed with piercing accuracy to the feminine
heart of her. She pulsed with the memory.

'What if I give the bad bits to the baby? The things inside
me? What if I can't—?' She struggled to find the words she
needed to explain.

'We might have made a baby, *piccolina*. How can a baby
be bad?'

'My parents have always encouraged me to stay in control
of my emotions. To be led by my head and not my heart—to

measure my impulses against what the consequences might be. I didn't do that in London. I just wanted—' she sucked in a lungful of air '—you.'

'Our attraction isn't something to be viewed as toxic. It's natural, Flora. It is human to desire. To want. You acted freely in London. You were driven by your feelings and you expressed them without remorse. Without restraint. How can it be a bad thing to be free?'

'Free?' she echoed.

Something strange was happening in her chest. It was getting lighter. The burden of expectation she'd carried around her whole life was being lifted.

'What if you do not let fear of what you can't control overtake this moment? What if you pick up the pregnancy test and see what it says? Be present in this moment and nowhere else?'

His eyes held hers and she clung to them. To the anchor of them that was holding her steady when she felt rudderless.

'I understand your fear—' he said.

'How?' she interrupted. 'How can you understand?'

'Because I understand the fear of the parts inside us that we can't control,' he said, his jaw determined. 'The things that live inside us that we cannot change. My mother was depressed. Deeply so. I didn't realise it was a condition until my teens. I didn't understand it was a mental illness. I only understood that she was very angry.' His nostrils flared. 'With me.'

He dismissed the platitude she was about to use.

'I'm sharing information that you think is important,' he said. 'Your biological mother was a drug addict. Mine was very sick. You think your mother's sickness might live in you, that it reveals itself in your impulsivity. If you believe that, then my mother's illness could live in me too. The difference between what came before and what comes after is the choice we make. The knowledge we use to guide us to make the right decisions.'

'Is that why you told me you would marry me before we even knew we needed options?' She swallowed, trying to organise everything that had happened in the last few hours. 'Because you—?'

'Because I need to know that what is mine is safe. I will keep you safe,' he promised. 'Both of you.'

Her breath hitched. She believed him. He was claiming her—*them*—even before they knew if the test was positive.

'I'm still scared, Raffaele.'

'No. You're not afraid of this.' His eyes flicked to the test. 'The baby does not scare you.'

'What do you mean?'

'You're scared of the night you let your guard down… leaned in to the woman *inside* you…'

He placed a hand on his chest, fingers splayed, and she wanted to touch them. Place her hand on top of his.

'Because the woman you let out,' he continued, 'upheaved your world. Shook it to its roots.'

'She upheaved your world too,' she added, reminding him that she wasn't the only casualty of her actions the night they'd met. 'Not just mine.'

'No. We did it together,' he corrected. 'We claimed that night, and now we must claim this moment too. Know who we must become to raise a child. *That* is what scares you, *piccolina*, isn't it?'

'What…?' she asked.

But he was so close to putting all the facts she'd given him together. So close to seeing the part of herself she hadn't revealed, had been too afraid to voice.

'Who you are with me.'

She felt…what? Relief? No, it was more than that. Her skin prickled. Her mind itched. She wanted to close the inches between them on the sofa and thank him. For seeing what she couldn't.

She closed her eyes. For just a moment she shut him out— and the test, the future—and looked inside at herself. Saw the fear of breaking the rules and hurting those around her, and the worry of who she might become if they didn't rein her in…control her impulsivity and her need to have what she wanted.

Her eyelids snapped open. She had wanted him, and together they might have made a baby. And he was right—how could that be bad?

'Be brave,' he said. 'Choose to be yourself. For you…for our baby.'

Her breath caught. 'You are so sure I am pregnant, Raffaele?'

The darkness of his pupils panned out. Spread to turn his eyes into a pulsing ring of colour. 'As sure as you know my name.'

'Have you always been so…*sure*? Of everything?'

'Always.' He swallowed thickly. 'I've always known what it is I must do. Who I must be.'

'And you just…do it?'

'Yes.'

Could it be so simple?

Flora wanted to be brave. She wanted to be herself *for* herself in every moment. In this one and the next. She liked the woman she'd been in London, and she liked the woman sitting next to him on the sofa now.

Raw and honest. That was what they'd been with each other since they'd met. Physically in London. Emotionally in the middle of the sea. And he hadn't flinched. Hadn't looked away from the person she had presented to him. He was *encouraging* her to be herself.

She leant forward, reached out and took the test in both hands. She glanced up at him. He wasn't smiling. Wasn't hurrying her to turn the test over. He was waiting. Because he knew what it would say and so did she.

She turned it over. 'I'm pregnant.'

It wasn't tears this time, as she'd expected. And it wasn't fear making every hair on her body stand to attention. There was a quiet joy in her chest. In her heart. She handed him the test but he didn't reach to take it. He looked at her as she looked at him.

They locked on to each other's eyes.

Looked at each other.

'*We're* pregnant,' she corrected, and couldn't help the smile.

'So we are,' he agreed. His voice was low. Deep.

The bomb had detonated and yet the shards weren't piercing her skin. She was not collateral damage. She felt determined. Empowered. Safe to explore what she was feeling. And she was feeling everything. And the man beside her was giving her time to feel. Explore those feelings. Define them.

His stillness was a weighted blanket. His confidence soothed her…and it all came to her in a flood. The need to protect her child. To raise it with love and hope. The way her parents had raised her.

The Bicks. It made sense now, their over-protectiveness. They'd done it all because they loved her. Because they'd claimed her as theirs and she *was* theirs. She was Flora Bick, the daughter of farmers. And she loved her parents. Did they get everything right? No. But they did it all from a place of love. For her. Their daughter. The kind of love she already felt so deeply—so quickly—for the baby in her belly.

*Her baby.*

'I need to call my mother.'

He nodded and reached into his inside pocket.

'Call your mother, *piccolina*.'

He handed her the phone, and with trembling fingers, she took it.

'What happens next?'

He shook his head. 'No.'

'No, what?' And then he did what she hadn't expected. What she hadn't seen coming. He touched her. With both his hands. He cupped her face, held it steady, and looked at her. *Really* looked. And she felt seen. With all her flaws on display. And still he held her.

Raffaele thrust his fingers deeper into her hair. 'Be present,' he told her. 'In *this* moment. Not the next. Talk to your family.' His fingers pressed into her neck. 'Then *we* will talk.'

And she wanted them to. Because they needed to figure out what came next. What they wanted to come next. What she wanted to come next.

Did she want to focus on the baby? The baby's needs for the future? Or did she want this moment to be about *them*? Future parents. Once lovers. They were bound now by the biggest secret of all. They were going to become an unexpected family...

Only one way to find out...

She leaned in until she felt the heat of his breath on her mouth. One more inch and her lips would meet his. A tremble raked through her. She closed her eyes...

He shifted, feathering his lips against her forehead. And then, before she could analyse what that type of kiss meant, he was standing.

She met his eyes. Tried to figure out what she saw there.

'Call your family. Tell them that you are safe, you are

warm, and you are pregnant with my child,' he said, and held her gaze for a moment too long. It steadied the hands that still trembled. 'But tell them you won't be coming home.'

She nodded. And he was gone. Striding out through the door and closing it behind him without a sound.

Flora kicked off her pumps, pulled her legs up beneath her and crossed them. She placed the pregnancy test beside her, in Raffaele's vacated seat. Then swiped up on his phone and punched in the numbers for home.

Flora talked to her mum. She asked her not to speak. She told her she loved her. Loved both her parents. And she told her she was about to become a mother herself. And that she hoped she'd be able to love her baby just as much as they loved her.

She told her that she was safe, but she wouldn't be home for a while, because she had to get ready for parenthood with the father of her child.

She was going to marry Raffaele Russo.

Flora Bick would be his wife.

Because she *was* Flora Bick—daughter of dairy farmers. She always had been.

Her mother sobbed. Said words of love mixed with a little fear and a lot of joy. And Flora ended the call with her mother's excited voice still in her ear.

It was time to stop ignoring her needs, wasn't it? Because they were natural, weren't they? Natural to her, anyway. Instinctive.

She pulled her jumper over her head and threw it onto the sofa, along with Raffaele's phone.

Flora was going to listen to her instincts. She was going to twist those fancy taps and fill that claw-footed bath with bubbles and climb inside it.

Because, right now, she wanted a bubble bath.

# CHAPTER SEVEN

RAFFAELE OUTSTRETCHED HIS arms and placed them flat on the veneered surface of the long, rectangular table. Two place settings and enough food to feed fourteen people, hidden beneath silver cloches, waited for them on a table that had never seen so much food.

Sitting in his glass cage of opulence, he'd never felt more exposed. Every wall looked out to the sea apart from the one leading from the bedroom. Where she was.

He scrubbed a hand over his chest. His chest was on fire. The idea of eating—

He swallowed down the thought.

She would eat and he'd watch.

He pinched his lips together. He hadn't needed the pregnancy test to confirm he'd been right to chase her.

His baby was growing inside her right now.

Picking up a glass, he swallowed down ice-cold water. Felt it travel down his throat. Into his gut. But it didn't ease the burn. The rawness of the last few hours was making his stomach twist and tug.

He'd exposed more of himself to Flora than he ever had to anyone. He'd dug deep into memories he'd buried beneath his billions and spoken of them as if they didn't matter and had little consequence to his life. He'd exposed his weakest self.

And instead of demanding she go with him—instead of

picking her up and throwing her over his shoulder to his bed-room to take the test, to get proof that their one night had had consequences—he'd told her his story. And she'd been seduced by the truth. Had given him her truth in exchange.

Why had he done it? Talked? Why had he given his story to her? The facts. Unvarnished.

Because he hadn't been able to stop himself.

But he hadn't expected to see himself mirrored in her words.

In her honest vulnerability.

The confession of her fears had given voice to words he'd never had before. He'd never spoken aloud of the things that lived inside him. He'd pushed them down deep. Ignored the possibility of them and their destruction. His mother's mental illness… His father's ability to destroy…reject…abandon. He was made from weakness too, and they'd formed a connection.

Connection? His face twisted in displeasure. It was chemistry, not a *connection*. And that part didn't matter. Only the baby. Only keeping Flora healthy.

*A host for your heir?*

He rolled his shoulders. A host for his heir sounded cold. Emotionless. She was not cold. She *felt* things. Made *him* feel things.

The burn in his chest was setting fire to his throat.

He must be sick…coming down with something. The flu?

He pressed an open palm to his forehead. He didn't have a fever.

*What was wrong with him?*

There was a rap at the door.

He sighed. Heavily. More food.

*'Entra!'* he called absently, and picked a piece of invis-ible lint off his cuff.

'Raffaele…'

His eyes shot to the door and there she stood. The slight wisp of a woman who'd infiltrated his life and turned it upside down. And she was wet. Her hair was dark, almost black, hanging limply over her shoulders.

'Flora…' He said her name and, oh, it tasted sweet to his tongue. Eased his indigestion…calmed the roughness of his throat.

A rush of yearning pulsed through him in waves. To get closer to their baby. To get closer to *her*. To inhale her clean scent and comb his fingers through her hair.

'Why did you knock?' he asked, focusing on anything but the scent of soap clinging to the air and seeping into his lungs.

'Because it's polite. I'll always knock if the door's closed. But if it's open…' Her eyes flashed with challenge. 'I'll come inside.'

She moved into the room. Her movement drew his gaze to her bare feet, to the knot of her ankle bone, where an angry line ran across her otherwise perfect skin. He wanted to kiss the imperfection. Bring it to his lips.

He concentrated on her legs. The taut, milky skin of her calves, leading upwards to where the hem of his white shirt kissed her thighs.

She stopped at his side. The delicate warmth of her body hit him. She raised her arm and held out his phone. His eyes shot to her fingers, to the elegant digits. He reached for it. His fingers brushed overs hers. Connection zapped through him. *Chemistry.*

She stepped back. Disengaging their hands.

She felt it too. *Still.*

He looked up at her, standing above him, looking down at him. Soap and warmth seeped through his nostrils. Delicate scents that he couldn't place, but that he recognised were only hers.

He would recognise her scent anywhere. The subtlety of it. It punched him in the gut, that sense of knowing. Of familiarity.

'Open doors are not always an invitation to enter, *piccolina*.'

The black of her pupils washed through the brown. 'But sometimes the temptation is too hard to resist…'

He felt it. The shift. The pulsing between them of the shared memory of that night six weeks ago when she'd entered his domain uninvited.

Her mouth parted. She exhaled. He wanted to taste her. Her mouth. Her lips.

He should have kissed her. Pushed his lips against hers when she'd invited him to do so. Should have celebrated the confirmation that she was pregnant in the same way all this had started. With his undiminished need to be inside her.

*Why didn't you?*

*It wasn't the time.*

*Lies. You're afraid of who you are with her.*

He was not afraid. He was in control. Of all things.

'You're to be the mother of my child. You do not need to knock,' he said throatily, and swallowed down the lust storming through him. Making his blood heavy. Hot. *'You,'* he said, reinforcing his words with unrelenting arousal thickening his voice, 'will enter whichever room you like, take any seat you want. You need no one's permission.'

'Not even yours?' she asked.

'Not even mine,' he answered. Too quickly. Too easily.

It roared through him then. The temptation to stand, to push his chair back and hold her by the hips. Place her on the veneered table. Step between her thighs, between the legs that he knew would fall apart for him on command. Push the plates covered with silver cloches onto the floor and sink inside her. Untether the leash of rigid control as he had six weeks ago. To pop every button on the shirt that she wore and reveal the nakedness beneath with his teeth.

And she *was* naked, wasn't she? Under his shirt? He could see the pink shadows around her puckered nipples pressing against the silk. The swell of her breasts…

He hardened, painfully, and tried to turn off the image in his head of a naked Flora in his arms. Beneath him. Moaning…

Now was not the time for kissing, either. Not when his control was hanging only by a thread.

Raffaele cleared his throat. Looked away and purposely broke the spell. He placed his phone on the table next to his empty plate. 'Would you like something to eat?' he asked, and lifted a cloche to reveal some chocolate-covered delights.

'I'd like something else to wear.'

He placed the cloche back over the food and trained his gaze on the next platter of food. He wouldn't think of his shirt next to her skin. He would not think of a naked Flora in his bath. Drying her body with his towels. Leaving her scent all over his bedroom, as she had in London. He'd still been able to smell her scent there only hours ago. Now here she was, in the flesh. Spreading her scent everywhere.

'You don't like my shirt?'

He lifted another cloche. *Porridge?*

She wrinkled her nose and lifted her arms. The sleeves hid her hands. 'It's a little big.'

He replaced the cloche. 'Clothes are arriving for you within the next thirty minutes.'

'You have clothes arriving?' She pointed a hidden finger at her chest. It looked like a handless arm. 'For me?'

'You are the one stealing my clothes in the absence of yours.'

'Borrowing,' she corrected.

'Sit. Eat.' He squared his shoulders. 'The clothes will come.'

Dear God, he hoped it would be soon, or his erection would never go down.

'A laptop and a mobile phone, too.'

'You didn't have to do that, but thank you.' She sat in the white leather seat next to him at the head of the table. Her eyes moved over it. 'Do you always eat so formally?'

'This can hardly be called a formal meal. You're wearing a shirt and nothing else.' His eyes moved over her—the open collar at her throat, the buttons undone just enough for him to see the subtle swell of her breasts.

'It's a *white* shirt.' A blush warmed her cheeks. 'They're always for best, aren't they?'

He cocked a brow. 'Sunday best?'

'It's Tuesday.'

She laughed. A gentle titter of breath. And there was the burn again in his chest.

'But something like that.' She reached for another lid and lifted it. 'Pancakes? Did you have someone cook the entire breakfast menu?'

*He had.*

'You didn't eat breakfast.' He looked at his watch. He should have ordered lunch. Even an early dinner. He frowned. 'Give me a list of the meals you would like and a menu will be prepared.'

Eyes wide, she interrupted. 'For my preference?'

'*Si*—who else's?'

'Yours *and* mine, maybe,' she answered, and used a pair of tongs to scoop several pancakes onto her plate. She lifted another lid and found fruit. She spilled a heaped ladle-full on to her plate. 'In our house it's eat it or starve.'

'Eat it or starve?' he repeated. 'I'm not familiar with the phrase.'

'What there is to eat, is what there is to eat—so you eat it.'

'But you live on a farm.'

'A dairy farm.' She rolled up the sleeves, revealing her delicate forearms. 'So there's always milk.' She picked up her cutlery and paused. 'Are you eating?'

'No.' He bowed his head towards her plate. 'But, please…'

Knife and fork in hand, she looked at her food. 'Aren't you going to ask me how it went?'

'I can see how it went,' he said. 'You've had a bath.'

'A long one,' she agreed. 'But that's not what I meant.'

'I have no desire to know what happened on the phone with your family,' he dismissed. 'The only family I care about is sitting at this table.'

That stung.

'*I* care,' she whispered.

His gaze narrowed. 'So I should?'

She heard the inflection of his words. The question.

Quietly, she put her cutlery down and gave him her full attention. 'They're my family. Of course they should matter.'

'To me?' he asked. 'Why would they matter to me?'

A boy with dark hair curling around his ears appeared in her mind without invitation. A boy dipping torn bread into cheese and handing it to the shadow of a woman she couldn't picture. Couldn't conjure anything but that shadow, which appeared as clear in her mind as a photograph.

'Don't you understand?' she asked.

But how *could* he understand? Her family wasn't perfect, but…

His gaze flicked to the left and then zeroed back on her within the flash of a millisecond. 'Understand what?'

Flora's heart stopped as she took in the deep frown lines

between the darkly shaped eyebrows, the focused intensity of his gaze.

'They're your family now, too.'

Slowly he nodded, and she let out a breath she hadn't realised she was holding.

His hands flexed where he'd placed them on the table. 'What do they need?'

'What do you mean?'

He splayed his fingers, palms forward. 'Is the farm in some sort of financial trouble?'

'Of course not,' she dismissed. 'The farm is doing well. The farm is fine. What does that have to do with anything?'

'Their livelihood—your family home—is safe?' He frowned. 'Then they don't need *me*.'

'Parents are not accepting dowries these days, Raffaele, and I'm pretty sure it used to be the other way around.'

'Dowries?' His frown deepened, before vanishing completely. Leaving his face a smooth mix of understanding and relief. 'How much would they like?'

She shook her head. 'No, that's not what I meant.'

'Then what *did* you mean?'

Flora shifted in her seat. Twisted her bottom and joined her knees until she faced him fully. 'No payment is required. No membership fees. We are having a baby together, so our families will...' she held her hands out in front of her and pulled them far apart '...merge.' She clapped her hands together.

The frown returned, and her urge was to stand up and place her thumb at the base of those lines. Swipe upwards and smooth them free. But she didn't. She sat and waited for him to join the dots. For him to understand what she meant.

They were all family now, whether or not he understood it.

'You will take *my* name,' he intoned.

'They'll still be my family. And my mother's birthday is in two weeks.'

'We will be in Sicily,' he interjected.

'Sicily?' she asked. 'I thought you lived here? On the boat?'

'We can't raise our baby on a super-yacht.'

'You want to raise the baby in Italy?'

'Sicily,' he corrected. 'I want to raise *our* baby in Sicily.'

'Where you grew up?'

'Yes.'

'Why? I thought you said it was out of the way? Won't we need a hospital?'

'The village is not what it once was.'

'Because you changed it?'

He nodded. 'We will have no trouble with transportation. Nor with access to a hospital. Most things will come to us. And they are already being organised.'

'Like what?'

'A doctor.'

'A *doctor*?'

'To make sure your pregnancy is going as expected.'

'Why wouldn't it?'

'You can ask the doctor. It is just a formality. Something to tick off the list.'

'You have a list?'

'Several.'

'Can I see them?'

'They are in my head.'

'Download them for me and we can compare notes.'

'Unfortunately my brain isn't connected to the internet.'

'Summarise the lists for me,' she said, 'and then we won't have to figure out how to connect you.'

'We will get you some clothes first. Then travel to Sicily, where we will be married—'

*'Married?'*

'By next week,' he answered, as if this was the most normal thing in the world. He looked out of the window at the greying clouds. 'If the weather holds, even sooner.'

'Why so fast?'

'Why not?' he asked nonchalantly. 'And after the wedding we'll prepare the house for the birth of our child.'

'The house you grew up in?'

'The very same.'

'I'd like to see where you grew up, and my parents would like to meet you.'

'Impossible,' he dismissed.

'Why impossible?' she asked, when no explanation was forthcoming.

'My pilot has taken the chopper to collect clothes from a boutique in Cornwall.' He named the shop.

Flora gasped. 'They dress celebrities!'

'Now they dress billionaires' fiancées too,' he added smoothly, and her heart hiccupped.

'I'm not your fiancée yet.'

'Semantics,' he dismissed. 'When my pilot returns,' Raffaele continued, 'we lift anchor,' he said. 'We will arrive in Sicily in three days—a week at worst.'

'Okay…' She placed her hands on her thighs, squared her shoulders and put on her most serious face. 'First, you need to *ask* if I'd like to marry you—rather than *tell* me I will. Second, *if* I agree to marry you, you need to ask if I'd *like* to take your name.'

'Would you like me to get down on one knee too?'

Her stomach flipped. He was good on his knees… A blush heated her all the way up from her chest, to turn her cheeks into a crimson beacon. She ignored it. And her wayward thoughts. And the memory of his kisses.

'The words will do just fine,' she said.

His chest puffed out. 'Flora?'

She swallowed thickly. 'Yes, Raffaele.'

'Will you marry me and take my name?'

'Is that one question or two?'

Thick eyebrows arched. 'Pardon?'

'Will I marry you is one question, right?'

He dipped his head. *'Si.'*

'If I say yes to marriage, but no to taking your name, does that instantly cancel out the first question, so the second doesn't really matter?'

He was trying to take control of her life, and she wasn't sure if she was grateful or overwhelmed. Both, she realised.

'Flora.'

The sound of command in her name stopped her mid-sentence.

'Why are you avoiding the question?'

She pointed her toes and rose on the balls of her feet. 'Which one?' she asked. Because maybe she wasn't ready to give her thoughts voice. To part the rational ones from the illogical. 'Marrying you or taking your name?'

'There's only one question—which you understand perfectly.'

'I do,' she admitted.

'But you're not ready to answer it?'

She already knew the answer, didn't she? Hadn't she already decided?

She had, but she'd only accepted the *idea* of marriage. Now he was actually asking. Now he was making the possibility a reality.

And she didn't want the answer to be decided for her. She wanted to be an active participant in her own life. Not just pulled along on someone else's schedule—someone else's plan for her.

'Do I really have a choice?' she said. 'Or did you ask simply because I requested that you did? If I hadn't brought it up, would you have simply lifted anchor and sailed away to Sicily?'

'Yes. I would have.'

She folded her hands across her midriff and looked at her untouched plate. *Honesty.* She appreciated that. But—

'If I don't give you an answer now,' she asked, and reached for her fork, moved it beside her knife, 'what will you do?'

'I will wait.'

Her eyes snapped to his. 'Until you get the answer you want?'

'Until you give me the answer that is yours and yours alone.'

Hers and hers alone? She sucked in a deep lungful of air and held it in her chest until it burned. 'What if you have to wait for ever?'

'For ever is a long time,' he said. 'But I'm asking for for ever.'

He shrugged in a gesture of indifference. Because he knew she'd give the answer he wanted and this was just a play for time?

'It only seems fair you ask for the same from me,' he finished, and her heart squeezed. 'But I do not understand your hesitation about marri—'

'My hesitation has everything to do with my life before *this*. Before *you*. Because then I didn't have choices. I just acted. I don't want to just act. Take the next inevitable step,' she corrected. 'I want to be an active participant in my life. In my decisions.'

'Explain it to me,' he urged. 'Tell me about how your life has been.'

'My parents always encouraged me to do the right thing. To be logical—rational. In control. To ignore my feelings and embrace structure. If I was ever in doubt, I followed the path of routine. Other people's plans for my life.'

'And you chose to do this why?'

'It was all I ever knew. And following someone else's plan was always easier because it made my parents happy. I was home-schooled…sheltered…'

'Sheltered?'

'From anything that might have…' Flora hesitated.

'Introduced you to something that could sway your tendencies towards addiction?'

'Exactly. But I didn't know that. So I did everything they requested of me. I ignored my tendencies to obsess. I tried to be the kind of daughter I thought they wanted—'

'And forgot what *you* wanted?'

Her shoulders sagged. 'Exactly.'

'What kind of daughter did they want you to be?'

'They wanted me to be safe. I understand that now. Since I found out about the adoption. My biological mother…'

'They wanted to keep you safe from yourself?'

She nodded.

'But if you weren't allowed to explore your natural personality, how could your parents—or you—know you were a risk to yourself?'

'They didn't. Couldn't. But they did it because they love me.'

His chiselled jaw hardened into angles of determination. 'If marriage wasn't an option, what would be your choice? Would you want to be a single mother? Raise our child alone? Put it up for adoption—?'

'Adoption?'

She thought of the lonely boy with a mother who didn't

care. She thought of her biological mother, who had given her up.

She hoped her birth mother had done it out of a kind of love, in the hope that she would find a family like the Bicks. That her daughter would be raised with love and hope as an anchor in this world. She had been lucky to have found her parents. Because the root of her childhood, and all her teenage years into adulthood, had been a constant love. Family.

No, they hadn't got it all right, but she would work through those feelings later, with her mum and dad. All that was important to her right now was their love. And she had that. In abundance. And she wanted that for her baby. Their unexpected family.

'Adoption would never be a choice for me,' she said.

'I am presenting you with what the other options would be if you chose not—'

'I don't want any of those options.'

'Then what *do* you want?'

'I…'

Raffaele thrust back his chair, closed the distance between them, and before she could fully dispel the breath in her lungs he was on his knees before her.

'I'm listening,' he told her. 'I'm not afraid of you, and you shouldn't be afraid of yourself. Afraid to give voice to the thoughts in your head.'

'What's happening in *your* head?' she asked, because she wanted to know. Wanted to know him better.

'I want to know the answer to a different question,' he asked.

'Ask it.'

'Why were you in London?'

'To collect my adoption file from the local authority. I'd found out six months before that my parents weren't biologically related to me. I fell—'

'And broke your ankle?'

'How do you know that? From your investigator?'

'The scar.'

His head dipped to her feet and he claimed her right foot with his palm. His thumb stroked against the ugly pink scar running the span of her right ankle above the knot of the bone.

'How did it happen?' he asked, keeping his head bent, continuing the rhythmic stroking of her scar, back and forth. Back and forth.

She trembled. 'I didn't listen to my head.'

'What did you listen to?'

'Instinct…' she breathed. 'There was a storm. It moved some slats on the barn roof. They just needed to be pushed over. Back into place.'

'And you wanted to fix it?'

'I wanted to fix it,' she agreed.

He placed her foot back onto the cold wooden floor and placed his hands on the armrests either side of her. She didn't feel trapped. She felt *cocooned*. Cushioned from the world and its expectations of her. In a bubble where she could be free, surrounded by the strength, the power, of his presence.

'I fell,' she confessed. 'My ankle…it was badly broken. And it was as if everything my mum and dad had feared happened in an instant. It only took one choice—one bad choice—to follow my urges and it ended badly. It ended *very* badly, Raffaele.'

He didn't push. He sat back on his heels and waited for her to tell her story, to give him her version of events in her own words.

'My parents had always known the circumstances of my birth—the drugs in my system. It was in my medical records, too. The doctor at the hospital explained that I should be careful with the strong painkillers that he wanted to prescribe to me because of my history with addiction. That's when my parents confessed that I was adopted. After that I did everything I could to find out how to locate my birth parents.'

'And you ended up in London?'

'Six months later,' she confirmed. 'To collect my adoption file from the local authority. And it said so much and yet so little.'

He frowned. 'Why were you wearing a ball gown?'

'I saw it and tried it on. I liked how it felt against my skin. I'd never had anything like that. And for once I didn't want to stop myself from doing something that I wanted to do.'

'And the hotel? Few farmer's daughters visit The Priato.'

'I wanted to step out of my life—just for a night—and experience things I never had. So I booked myself in and—'

'Found me just when your world was imploding?'

'Yes,' she said huskily.

'And now it is imploding again you want to take a minute? Work through your emotions before you make a rational decision?'

He understood her. He understood why she couldn't accept his proposal right now, even though she wanted to.

Raffaele leaned into her, his height meaning they were face to face, with her sitting down and him on his knees. Eye to eye.

'What are your instincts telling you to do?'

'To marry you,' she answered honestly—because she'd already decided. But she had to understand *why* she'd made that decision. Was it impulse? Or was it logical? Did it have to be either?

'Trust them,' he said. 'Your instincts.'

'What if it's the wrong decision?'

'What if it isn't?' he countered.

Her heart thumped in her chest, because her real fear was that she was going to fall so completely into this man's eyes she wouldn't be able to see a way out. And how would he guide her when he didn't know she was falling?

A question hit her. Announced itself loudly in her brain. So she asked it. 'Why were *you* in London?'

His mouth compressed and his hands slid away from the armrests. He stood. 'You know why.'

'Because you were grieving.'

His eyes hardened, but she pushed because she wanted to know. To understand him. *His* choices.

'But why London? Why that—?'

There was a knock at the door.

Flora jumped to her feet like a startled teenager and crashed straight into his chest. She looked up into his face, her palms resting on hard muscle. She could feel his heart beneath her fingers. A heavy thud which matched her own.

Simultaneously, they both looked at the door, and before she could ask him not to answer it, but to answer her question instead, he strode towards the door and yanked it open.

After a few minutes of whispered murmurs in Italian with whoever was on the other side of the door, he turned to her.

'They're lifting the anchor in fifteen minutes,' he informed her, and his eyes told her this was it.

She must decide.

Was she in or out?

Flora stared back at him, at this beautiful man she'd made a baby with, and squared her shoulders.

She'd thrown her doubts and her needs into the world and someone had listened—*he'd* listened. He had got down on his knees and talked her through her feelings. Without judgement. Without pressure.

However flighty she'd been, he'd listened to her needs—

not told her to ignore her emotions, but to work through the choices that were available and come to a logical conclusion. She hadn't had to choose her feelings over rationality. She'd combined the two. They'd worked through her feelings. Her thoughts. *Together.*

She was in, wasn't she? *All in.*

The thoughts and the lists in his head that she wasn't privy to pushed at the corners of her mind, but she held them back and focused on him, on this moment, and staked her claim.

'I'm ready,' she declared—because she was.

She stepped towards him. Put one foot in front of the other and felt her stomach fizz with an unknown feeling.

Anticipation?

No. It was excitement.

His bulk covered the entrance to the door, but as she approached he stepped aside and there was a woman. Smiling at her.

'Grace will show you to your room,' he said, nodding towards the smiling stranger.

Flora didn't smile back. Her eyes snapped to Raffaele's and her excitement fizzled out into a frown. 'My room?' she echoed.

'The VIP suite,' he answered, without a flicker of hesitation.

'And where will you sleep?'

'In my bed.'

*Without me?*

The words hugged the inside of her vocal cords. They were going to have different rooms. Separate beds. New rules for their life.

Realisation dawned over why he'd refused her mouth— *her kiss*—earlier.

He didn't want her.

Raffaele just wanted the baby.

# CHAPTER EIGHT

CONTROL.

For the last four days he'd been trying to cling on to it, and every day it miraculously came to him. Because it had to. Because she was here, and she was carrying his baby. She was safe in his palace on the sea. He would feed her, dress her, listen to her. But he would not take her to his bed.

He wouldn't lose control again in the delicate contours of her skin. Would not kiss the freckles on the bridge of her nose as he counted eyelashes so long he didn't understand their growth.

He couldn't keep her safe if he did that, could he? If he allowed himself to get too deep, to feel too much?

But every day her eyes begged. Moved over him at breakfast, at lunch, at dinner. With agonising *want* in her eyes.

And by God, he wanted too. Pulsed with it as he answered questions about his hotels, his renovations, his ability to strip things apart and put them back together. About how the deconstruction of something whole could reveal its secrets.

The Priato—his hotel in London—had many such secrets. Not only the secret door she'd found, but tunnels and concealed rooms. She'd asked if he would take her back there, to the place they'd met, and reveal them to her. Expose the secrets the previous owner had concealed from all but a select few.

She'd asked for more details about his business, about Russo Renovations' global allure. And he'd answered. He'd nodded or shaken his head when she'd asked about his family. No, she couldn't meet them. He had none. No cousins, no aunts—just him.

It had always just been him. On the outside looking in. The generosity of the community had given him a bowl or two of freshly made pasta covered in home-made passata to take home, but no one had ever invited him to sit at their table.

She'd told him stories of her life as she sat beside him on the sofa, a blanket pulled up to her chin. She'd left her feet exposed, dangling her toes over the edge, wiggling them. Cute little digits he'd longed to reach for. To apply pressure to the ball of her foot. Massage the flesh.

He hadn't touched her feet. He had not touched *her*. But he had listened. And that was new to him. Because he never listened. Not to the women he took to bed. Not to the women who hung on his arm, adorned in the glittering diamonds and jewels he presented them with before he shooed them away. Bored when his sexual appetite had diminished.

It was not diminished for her.

His hunger for her had intensified.

But he'd made himself pay attention to Flora's words and not her body. Because he'd wanted to hear them. Her words. Her voice. And she liked to talk…to ask questions.

She'd told him of her life on the farm. Of cousins. Of aunts and uncles. Growing up with a family. Birthdays, Christmases, holidays together as a family.

*His* family now. Supposedly. Because of the child growing inside her.

The sky rumbled. His already white knuckles clenched harder around the metal rail. He looked up and let the rain, which had only been a drizzle moments ago, beat down on his face and closed his eyes.

He prayed for control now.

'Sir?'

The boat rocked, but he did not loosen his grip. He turned to his captain, his jaw set, and readied himself.

His captain's eyes were wide and unblinking, and he said, 'We still can't find her, sir.'

A roar bloomed inside him. Puffing out his chest. 'Three hundred feet of space and you can't find her? You navigate across the sea,' he said, his chest burning, his voice hoarse. 'Multiple decks above and below sea level are under your control. Every technological device is at your disposal to locate land, some off the map. You have twenty staff below you in rank to support you. And yet—' he swallowed down the fury in his throat '—you cannot locate one woman?'

The captain held out his umbrella for Raffaele. He pushed it away, let the elements which were accelerating in speed punish his body.

Because he deserved to be punished, didn't he?

He'd lost her.

Misplaced a whole woman.

'She's still aboard the ship.'

'You know this?' he countered. The wind carried his voice to create a formidable growl. 'You can report this as a fact?'

'Anchor dropped less than an hour ago.'

'And not everyone is accounted for,' he interjected cuttingly.

He ran tense fingers through his hair. Sliding the wet strands backwards.

'The storm will pass,' his captain assured him. 'Everything is in place to ride it out. A boat of this size is more than equipped to deal with any storm, sir.'

Raffaele gritted his teeth. He understood his captain's intentions, and he knew what his boat was capable of. It would withstand extreme weather. This was his home, and he spent half his life at sea. His boat was safe.

But he knew the backlash of storms. The tragedy. The last one—

He slammed the door on that memory.

It was a different kind of storm today.

His boat was a cut above all other super-yachts, with its cables creating a lightning shield from masthead to bow. The glass bridge held various devices and instruments worth hundreds of thousands of dollars to warn them of incoming weather via satellite. There were radars to see through a storm. Closed circuit television triggered by radio announcements and alarms recorded strategic points on the boat.

'Have you checked the CCTV footage?' Raffaele asked, and clenched his fists to try and stunt the urge to grab this man by his shirt and rattle him until he gave the answer he wanted. *Needed.*

'Of course.' His captain shook his head. 'Nothing. No sign of her. But there's so many places to hide. So many rooms to explore.' He dragged in a stuttering breath, and promised, 'We will find her.'

Drops of water ran over Raffaele's forehead, down his haughty nose, and dripped onto the soaked decking. Absently, he dashed them away.

'She will be found,' he agreed stonily. 'But not by you.' He moved unseeingly past him and called over his shoulder, 'Go back to your bridge, *Captain*,' he sneered. 'And keep your staff indoors. Look after your responsibilities.' He tugged open the door to the lounge. 'I will take care of mine.'

His heart clenched. Refusing to beat. Refusing to let him move until he acknowledged the words he'd refused to hear.

To consider in his conscious thinking because of it what they meant.

*He'd failed. Again.*

Because they were *all* his responsibility. The staff. The crew.

It wasn't his captain's fault that a freak tropical storm had headed straight for them as they sat idle in the middle of the Mediterranean Sea—a storm expected to peak in two days' time.

It wasn't his fault that the storm had dragged all the staff and occupants of the super-yacht from their beds before the sun had graced them with its unsuccessful efforts to clear the sky.

Raffaele looked at the waves. They were like a foaming, galloping herd of angry stallions.

He shoved back the sleeve of his sodden jumper.

It was nearly six.

But what was time when it seemed his had run out?

Another rumble shook the boat. Shook him from the outside in with a startling clarity.

It was Raffaele's responsibility to make sure every member of his staff was safe. Protected.

It was Raffaele's job to account for every unforeseen danger. To guard against it. To protect his own.

It wasn't the captain's fault Flora had not been in her bed when a head-count had been made. She should have been in *his* bed. Next to him…under him. He didn't care what position.

Only that she was *safe*.

And she wasn't.

Lightning flashed and every glass window, every polished surface, reflected the ferocity of the storm that had headed their way. He moved inside through the double doors, felt the wind pushing them closed behind him.

Raffaele just stood there. Taking in the reinforced double port windows. His boat was a 'go anywhere' explorer superyacht. The biggest of its kind. The safest.

She had to be here.

He'd found her once. He would find her again.


Toes. Ten of them. Perfectly formed and unadorned. They peeped out from beneath a heavy red blanket with golden edges—the perfect camouflage. The sofa she was sprawled out on was an exact match. Of all the nooks and crannies, the multiple rooms, the suites, she'd chosen to come here.

The Sky Lounge.

The rain beat down on the glass roof. *Pitter-patter. Pitter-patter.* His ears whooshed. His skin tingled.

He didn't know if he'd been standing there for minutes or hours—only that he'd found her.

He'd ascended the spiralling stairs and there she'd been. His legs wooden, he'd moved soundlessly across the carpeted floor. No lights were lit. There was only the low light from the darkened sky above them. The chandeliers glinted in the shadows like strands of suspended diamonds.

He stood in front of her sleeping figure. She was huddled deeply beneath the heavy blanket in the furthest corner. Hidden out of sight. All but her feet, which were dangling over the edge of a gold-leaf-decorated sofa with mahogany trim. Oblivious to the storm. Oblivious to him.

He closed his eyes. Let it sink in. The subtle scent of her. The presence of her crawled over his skin. His body. Was it relief her felt? It didn't feel like relief. He couldn't breathe. His lungs wouldn't inflate. His mind wouldn't stop—

'Raffaele…?' Flora spoke his name in a soft caress.

His eyes snapped open. Zeroed in on her sleep-flushed face. His heart crashed against his ribcage.

Her warm brown eyes shone with surprise. The blanket slid down her bare shoulder as she sat up and brought her legs in front of her. She wore nothing but a blue silk vest and matching shorts.

Every emotion he'd been holding in check, every feeling he hadn't given a name, pulsed to the surface of his skin. His face contorted. Rage burnt through him. And he homed in on that anger, the swell of it inside him, and spat its heat into existence.

'Don't you *ever* do that to me again.'

'Do what?' Flora asked huskily, the grogginess of sleep lifting as though she'd never closed her eyes.

She stood, the blanket pooling around her feet. She stepped out of it. Inched towards him. Never had she seen his features so drawn. So tight.

Her eyes moved over him. The body-fitting black jumper clung to every muscle of his chest, revealing hardened abs. His dark blue jeans—

She inhaled deeply, and trembled.

He was soaked through. He looked like a man who had battled the kraken and won, but somehow, she realised as her gaze moved over his face, had also lost. There were no visible bruises, no wounds, but haunted eyes met hers.

Her hand moved of its own volition to his cheek. 'What's happened?'

He shrugged her off and she felt it like a physical blow to her sternum. The veins in his neck bulged.

'Raffaele?'

The heavens opened above them. Rain hammered down on the glass roof. A rumbling roar of thunder filled the electric silence.

His nostrils flared.

'The storm?' she asked, eyebrows high on her forehead.

'I couldn't find you,' he said, his jaw tight, his mouth barely parted.

'I couldn't sleep…' she replied, her brain buzzing.

'So you climbed to the highest room?' he asked, his voice low. Grim. 'Went to the darkest corner and hid beneath a blanket?'

She half turned to the sofa and splayed out her hands at her temporary bed. 'I wasn't hiding.'

She turned back to him, her chest heaving, her feet planted firmly to the floor, and readied herself for a fight she did not know how to win because she didn't understand the stakes.

'I fell asleep listening to the rain,' she explained, and made herself breathe. Slowly. Deeply through her nose. 'Why are you so angry?'

'I am not angry.' He moved to her, a half-step which brought her face directly in line with his chest. 'I am *furious*,' he hissed between gritted teeth.

She lifted her chin defiantly. 'You said I could go through any door—take any seat—'

'Not in the middle of a storm!'

She stilled. Eyes turning wide. Those tight muscles… The rasp of his breath… Her eyes ran over him again.

'You're…' she pressed her open palms to his chest '… you're trembling.' Instantly she pulled her hands away and looked down at the wetness coating her fingers. 'You need to take this off.'

Her hands travelled to find the hem of his jumper and—

His fingers, a steel band around her wrist, halted her attempt to lift the wet wool away from his skin.

'What happened?' she repeated her earlier question.

'*You* happened, *piccolina*.'

'What do you mean?' she asked, her brain doing somersaults to try and make it make sense. 'Have I done something wrong?'

Quick as the lightning flashing above them, he released his hold on her. Stepped back.

'Why are you so afraid?' she whispered, her heart pounding.

'I'm not afraid.'

She heard it. The lie. He was terrified.

'You have no reason to be angry with me, Raffaele. Or furious,' she whispered. Quietly. As if trying not to poke at whatever beast he was containing inside the hunch of his powerful shoulders.

'What is it?' she asked again. 'What's turned you into such...'

'A mess?' he finished for her roughly. His Adam's apple was moving heavily up and down the length of his taut throat.

'I wouldn't choose those words,' she rejected. 'You don't look a *mess*. You're...' She reached up and stroked her hands along the rigid lines of his shoulders. 'You're a barely contained mass of energy.'

But she wasn't scared of his power...of his barely contained emotion. She dropped her hands to her sides. This wasn't anger. She could sense it in the heavy air surrounding them.

Her brows knitted. 'It's not the storm you're afraid of, is it, Raffaele?' Her insides twisted. Her brain flashed with every conversation they'd had since leaving the farm. 'Were you afraid for me?'

Her mouth ran dry. Goosebumps rose all over her skin. She felt exposed. Naked. She ran her fingers over her arms and folded them across her chest. *She* had scared him.

Flora retreated into her head. Into her body. Back to the place she always went when she got it wrong...hurt those she loved.

*Loved?*

She swallowed down the pain in her throat. Looked at the man watching her every movement with such intensity she felt it. *Inside.*

How could she even consider that what she felt might be love when he didn't want her?

He wanted the baby.

He didn't even want to take her to bed.

She pressed her fingers into her arms to centre herself. She'd thought they had a connection. Talking over breakfast, dinner, lunch…

'Why? I thought—' She'd thought she understood the rules, but this wasn't the game she'd thought she was playing. Not this game of…of *fear.* 'I thought we were becoming friends. Finding some sort of common ground—a companionship. Of sorts…' She sniffed. 'Some kind of a foundation for marriage as we won't be having sex—'

A growl interrupted her. A deep, wordless roar of denial. She ignored it. Ignored him.

'You couldn't find me,' she continued. 'And you were afraid of where I might be—what choices I'd made during the storm. You were *concerned*,' she sneered, but it bit at her, the hotness of tears.

Flora refused to let them turn her into an emotional wreck. She wouldn't revert to doing the right thing. *Saying* the right thing.

'You thought I was going to do what? Stand outside with a metal stick and wait for lightning to strike? You thought I might compromise my safety—the baby's?'

He reached for her. 'Flora—'

'Don't you dare tell me I'm wrong.' She stepped back until the backs of her legs touched the sofa.

'You *are* wrong.'

She pointed a trembling finger at the centre of his chest. 'Don't you dare contradict yourself. Your boat is an explorer—you told me—and it's built for extreme weather. Because this is your home—where you come back to after every renovation…every job. It's safe because you made it to be safe. Built it—designed it,' she corrected breathlessly.

'Nothing is completely storm-proof,' he explained, but she shook her head.

'You feared for me, Raffaele,' she said.

Old hurts bloomed fast. The barn—the fall—her night in London. Was everybody right not to trust her?

'How can we get married?' she asked.

'You're pregnant—'

'Yes. I'm pregnant. But how can I marry you when you don't trust me?'

# CHAPTER NINE

'IT'S NOT YOU,' he confessed. 'It's the—'

Every instinct told Raffaele to hold his tongue. Not to speak out loud. Not to bring back to life the memory he'd buried deep, so very long ago.

He knew why he was overreacting. Knew why he'd put all his regressed pain into her and turned it into something ugly. *Angry.*

And then she'd pushed against his rage. It had replaced his rage with guilt. Regret. He'd hurt her. And the only way he could fix this…

He didn't want to remember—didn't want to share it with Flora. But it pushed at the edges of his mind…pushed itself inside. Uninvited. The memory of being lost—misplaced in plain sight.

No one had noticed for three days. No one had reported him missing. Raised the alarm. No one had checked in on his mother…

Words wouldn't come.

He couldn't speak.

'How could you think I'd put myself in danger?' she asked.

'No, I didn't.' He rejected her assertion and curled his fingers into his palms to resist pulling her into him. Holding her shivering body against him to infuse her with any warmth he had left in his skin…give it to her.

*His friend? His companion? His lover?*

He squashed the thoughts down. He didn't need friends. He couldn't allow her to be his lover. And he didn't deserve companionship. But she'd offered all of them freely since her arrival. Talking about the future. About the past. *Her* past. Full of love and devotion for her family.

Now *his* family.

People he hadn't met—didn't want to meet.

So what had he done? He'd squashed all those hopeful words from Flora's mouth under his big foot because of his past. His neglectful family. His mother.

*No. This isn't about your mother. It's about you.*

A gush of air escaped his mouth.

It *was* about him. His overreaction was rooted in the roots of his existence. Because he had been born from neglect. To a mother who should have been keeping an eye on him. But who never looked his way. Never looked at him when it mattered. And then he'd done the same. Looked away at the wrong moment. Neglected his responsibilities.

'I thought *I* had put you in danger,' he confessed. His chest heaved. 'Do you understand? I couldn't find you…'

Her arms flew back around her midriff and he wanted to prise them open and climb inside her embrace. Press their bodies together in an intimate, unbreakable lock.

*What was wrong with him?*

He was a mess.

A frantic mess.

'But I wasn't lost, Raffaele.'

'You were lost to *me*,' he growled. 'It's protocol, in any extreme weather, to do a head-count of all the staff and residents on the boat—'

'I didn't know that,' she interrupted. 'I didn't know a little bit of heavy rain would be of concern to a boat of this magnitude. I wanted a different space—a different view.' She looked up at the glass roof.

'This is only the beginning,' he told her. 'A storm like this will only get worse. Reach a peak we won't fully understand until it arrives. I've seen—'

'I didn't know that either.'

'It was my responsibility to tell you, *piccolina*.'

'I'm not your responsibility, Raffaele.'

'You are carrying my child,' he reminded her. 'I should be protecting you. You should be in my bed, where I can see you, keep you safe.'

'*You* chose separate bedrooms. *You* chose—'

'To stay in control.'

'You chose not to be with me in a physical sense even when you said it was natural.'

'It *is* natural.'

'Then why—?'

He couldn't help it. Raffaele reached for her. Held her elbows in his big palms as if she were the last point of safety. The only lifeboat when he was sinking deep into uncharted territory.

'Have you not enjoyed my company? Have I not been enough to keep you entertained without sex?'

He had to know. Had to know if, despite what they'd shared, all she wanted was the billionaire. The façade. The man who offered women nothing but sex.

'Of course I've enjoyed it. The last four days have been heady. Real. Honest.'

*Real? Honest?* Those two words punched him in his temples. Rocked his stance. Weakened his knees.

They had been real. He'd never spent so much time with a woman. Never eaten three square meals with another human being every day. Meals without the due ceremony of a restaurant, a chef, a menu.

Never had he eaten a meal on his lap with some flickering film in the background as a woman showed him how clever her new laptop was.

Never had he refused to take a willing woman to bed.

Never had he listened to a woman speak.

Of course he'd heard the phonetic hum of her words, but he'd never wanted to understand what they meant. How words spoken revealed truths about the speaker. *About Flora*. He'd wanted all her words. To stay in an idle stupor and pay attention to her chorus.

Had he been a fool for wanting that?

'Couples do more than share the same bed. Couples have disagreements, they worry, they fight,' he said, before he could pull the words back.

He smoothed a hand across his forehead, but knew the deep frown lines grew deeper.

She didn't blink at his choice of word. She counter-attacked without hesitation. 'Couples trust each other,' she corrected. 'My mother and father—'

'This has nothing to do with your parents. It is about us navigating our way to a wedding. Marriage. The birth of our child.'

'You say you haven't had a long-term relationship. Neither have I. But my parents… Of course they quarrel about the small things—and the big things. But they trust each other. Support each other. They don't chase each other across one hundred acres of field just because one gets up early and goes off somewhere on the farm. They don't think the other one is in danger because it rains and they can't see them.'

Her freckled nose wrinkled.

'Because at the end of the day,' she continued, 'my parents sleep in the same bed.'

He heard the tremble in her words. He wanted to press his mouth to her, steady that tremble. Swallow the pain he'd inflicted and put it back where it belonged. Inside him. *Contained.*

'That's a couple,' she said. 'They're a couple. I don't know what we are—what we can be when you've let everything I told you about my past turn you into a wild man searching for a person who wasn't lost just because it was raining.'

'It's a storm.'

He tugged her closer until she was pushed against his chest. The warmth rocked him to the core. The instant flare of need.

*Mine.*

The word roared through every vein. Every brain synapse. *Safe.*

That word hummed in its wake.

He dipped his head lower. 'Not once did your past cross my mind when I couldn't find you,' he said, his voice gruff. 'Not once did I think of the stories you've shared with me since I came into your life on the farm. Not once did I worry about what your parents fear—what *you* fear—about your past.'

And he hadn't. His worry had been purely selfish. Driven by his need to know that she was safe, that she was protected.

She arched her neck defiantly to meet his gaze dead-on. *'Liar...'*

The whisper of her breath teased at his lips. Hardening him. *Everywhere.*

'Why would I lie?' he growled.

'Why *wouldn't* you?' She flicked the pink tip of her tongue over her lips. 'You want this marriage because of the baby. And you need me to gain both. But you don't *want* me.'

He knew he had made her believe that. It had helped him stay in control. But now he had to be honest. With himself... with her.

'I want marriage,' he agreed. 'I want our baby, too.'

Their gazes clashed. Locked. Hers was a sad glare of triumph. His pulsed with a need to tell the truth. So he did.

'But I have never stopped wanting you.'

His confession was a low growl of truth. Of honesty. They'd spent the last four days connecting like normal people. Acting like a couple.

'You want me?' she repeated, slicing through his internal justification of what was happening to him. To *them*.

'And what do *you* want, *piccolina*?'

'Does it matter?' Her eyes flashed fire. 'You don't trust me.'

Attraction. *Desire*. It simmered beneath the surface. His unwavering need to be inside her. But she deserved the truth. A truth he could no longer deny. A truth he would not deny her any longer—because she was right.

'I don't trust *myself*.'

He thrust the truth into the air pulsing between them, and she caught it.

Her eyes widened. 'Tell me why?' she urged, and his heart thudded with his mistakes.

It all came out in a flood. 'I was trapped in a storm once— by a fallen tree. I couldn't get home for three days. I was stuck. Too far from the house, too far from the village to call for help.'

'What about your mother? Didn't she come looking for you?'

He shook his head.

Brown eyes narrowed below arched brows. 'How old were you?'

'Eleven...twelve...' he answered absently, his chest heavy

with the memory. 'I'd had to walk through a pathless tree line to get to the next village. We needed things, and no one in my village had any odd jobs for me. It started with drizzle. Then came the thunder. The winds...'

'What happened?'

'I fell, and so did a tree.'

'And it trapped you? The tree?'

'For three days.'

'Were you hurt?'

'It wasn't broken bones I was worried about. And it wasn't the hunger. Not even the rain.'

'What was it?' she asked huskily.

'I couldn't get back to—'

'To your mum?' she asked.

'I was found three days later. By Matteo the village bar-owner. There was devastation *everywhere*. The tree...it saved me. Sheltered me when no one knew I was missing. I had no broken bones...was only suffering from exposure. Shock. Bruises. But my mother—'

He tried to hold it at bay. The visceral memory that was flooding his every sense.

'When I was carried back to my mother she was in a stupor. She hadn't eaten. We both went to the hospital that day. Airlifted. I will never forgive myself for many things, but not making it home in that storm—I couldn't look after her.'

Horror filled her eyes. 'You could have *died*, Raffaele.'

'And so could my mother. One day later—even an hour later...'

'No, *you* could be dead.'

'I am alive,' he corrected.

And the biggest punch in the gut was the memory that came next. A memory he wasn't ready to share. *Couldn't* share. Because then she would know that the storm hadn't been the only time he'd failed his mother. Failed to be there for her when she needed him.

And the next time had been fatal.

A tear rolled down her cheek and he closed his eyes. Shut out the pity he did not deserve.

Her fingers feathered his jaw. Gentle. Soft. He released her elbows. Pushed away her tenderness.

'Look at me, Raffaele…' she breathed. 'Open your eyes.'

He did, and met the innocence of hers. The pity.

'You can't control the weather. You're not responsible for storms. You weren't then and you're not now. Do you understand?'

He couldn't speak. Wouldn't lie. It *had* been his fault. Then. And after…

She grabbed his hand and placed it on her chest. The thud of her heart pulsed against his palm.

'I'm safe,' she said, and then she pulled his hand down between the centre of her breasts and pushed the flat of his palm firmly but gently against her stomach. 'And so is the baby.'

*'Piccolina…'*

'I'm listening,' she said.

She was smiling at the endearment he'd used on this night when her size had been small against the mass of him, but her presence had been mighty and all-consuming. And now she stood before him again, touching him. And hers was the biggest presence he'd ever felt.

She was bigger than the storm.

Louder than his desire.

She deserved the truth, didn't she? The truth of why he hadn't taken her to his bed? Hadn't been there to weather the storm with her?

'These last four days…' he started, refusing to let himself hold back. She deserved this much. She was to be the mother of his baby. She was to be his wife. 'I've held you at bay. Said goodnight and watched you close the door with me on the other side. Because—'

'Because?' she prompted gently, and her small hand was still on top of his, both sheltering the baby inside her.

*Their baby.*

'The night we met I was out of control. I allowed myself to lose control. And when you disappeared in London, with the possibility of my baby growing inside you, I promised myself I'd never let myself feel that way again. But you make me feel—'

'Out of control?' she finished for him.

He swallowed thickly. 'Completely.'

'You're afraid of who you are with me?'

'I'm frightened of the man I could become in your arms. That I will forget my duty—my responsibilities—that I won't be able to protect you.'

'Then we will protect each other.' She moved, gripping his face and standing on tiptoe. 'We can keep each other safe in the storm, Raffaele,' she said. 'And we can control *this*.' She leaned in and feathered her lips against his unmoving ones. 'This is natural. This desire. You told me so. So show me you're not afraid of me—because I'm not afraid of you. And you shouldn't be afraid of yourself. Be with me the way I want to be with you. Let's choose to be the people we are with each other and let's make this work. Prove our marriage can work because we *choose* it. We choose *us*.'

It snapped. The leash on his control. And he thrust his mouth on hers. Pushed his fingers into her hair.

Raffaele had claimed his choice.

He pushed his tongue into her mouth. She gripped onto his shoulders, thrust her hips against the hardness of him.

'I want you so badly,' he confessed into her mouth. 'I des-

perately need to be inside you, *piccolina*. I hurt. The want…
It hurts.'

She broke free from his embrace, just enough to reach
down to the hem of his jumper. He lifted his arms instinctively and let her pull it off.

He trembled.

Desire flared in her eyes. She looked from his mouth to
his chest and discarded the jumper at their feet. She placed
her hand on his chest. 'Trust me to make it better,' she said,
and he thickened—his blood, his erection. 'Trust your body
to tell you what it needs…because I need you.'

She reached for the hem of her silk vest. The blue silk had
darkened from the wetness he'd transferred from himself to
her. The fabric stuck to the outline of her breasts, her peaked
nipples. She pulled the vest over her head.

'I want you,' she said. 'And I trust this is the right choice.
So trust me to navigate the next steps.'

He growled, gripping her wrists and pulling her bare
chest to his. He'd asked for her trust using exactly the same
words…could he do it?

He wanted her. Her words. Her softness.

He chose this. Chose to trust in the moment's truth. In
the realness of it.

Even if it was just for now.

Until the storm passed.


His kiss was urgent, demanding. And she gave herself up to
his possession. Surrendered to the passion, they'd been denying themselves for four whole days and four long nights.

Flora was breathless. An urgency pulsed through her to
feel more than his hard chest against the heavy swell of her
breasts, or the push of his muscles against her peaked nipples,
or the swell of his shoulders under the bite of her fingertips.

She wanted it all.

Trembling fingers reached for his belt. He stilled against her, but she wouldn't deny herself what they both clearly wanted. She wouldn't let doubt about who she was make her refuse to voice her needs. Because she trusted them. Her needs. And he trusted them. And now he needed to trust her. Trust himself to be the man he was with her.

Because she wanted this—the person he'd been for the past four days and the man who was shuddering against her.

She wanted this moment.

For ever.

She'd fallen straight into his eyes, hadn't she? But she didn't want to find the way out. She wanted to fall deeper. She'd fallen in love with this gentle giant who wanted to keep her safe. Protect her. Marry her.

She was in love, and love guided her hand to unbuckle him. And with her whole heart, with all that she was, all she was allowing herself to be at this moment, she knew fear would not beat her away from life again in case she hurt those she loved.

She was a woman who would claim the wants of her body and the needs of her heart from this day forth.

Because what was life without risk? Without choice?

It was a tick list. Safe. Predictable. All the things she no longer wanted. She wanted choice, and she wanted risk. Because she felt safe to explore the boundaries with this man now beside her...didn't she?

'I need you inside me, Raffaele,' she pleaded breathlessly. Euphorically.

She demanded what she wanted. What she needed. And he didn't deny her.

His hand beneath her bottom, he picked her up. He didn't speak. He backed her up, step by step, as he deepened his kiss, until her back met the wall.

The storm howled above them. Mirroring the howl of her body. 'Love me, Raffaele. Trust yourself to love me. *Now*,' she demanded.

And he moaned into her mouth and she swallowed the sound. The *power* he was giving to her.

With one hand still holding her bottom, he reached for his jeans, dragged them down over his backside until his erection pressed against the heart of her.

She moaned, and he broke free from her mouth, both of them panting.

'Say it again, *piccolina*. Tell me you need me inside you,' he rasped, his chest heaving. 'Tell me,' he urged, his eyes intense, looking at nothing but *her*. 'Tell me you need me.'

'I need you inside me, Raffaele...' She sucked in a shallow gasp of air as she said the words she wanted to say and the words he needed to hear. 'I need you.'

He reached down to the barrier between them and with a roar ripped her underwear from her body. He claimed her mouth. Closed his eyes and thrust inside her.

She tore her mouth from his and screamed his name. *'Raffaele!'*

She clung to him, panted her ecstasy into existence as he loved her body with a ferocious intensity.

This was living.

This was life.

This was love.

Flora grabbed his face. 'Look at me,' she demanded. 'Open your eyes and see me.'

Still moving inside her, he opened his eyes. Saw her.

And she saw him.

'I trust you,' she declared. 'Let go.'

His jaw tensed.

'Trust yourself.'

The pulse in his cheek throbbed frantically. 'I...'

She felt him holding back. Holding on to the fear. So by instinct she tilted her hips, taking him deeper into the pulsing, clenching heart of her.

'Come for me now, Raffaele,' she demanded. 'Let go.'

He thrust harder, deeper inside her.

'Yes,' she whispered. *'Yes!'*

Harder, deeper, faster, he thrust. His eyes never leaving hers until the moment had nowhere to ascend to. Only the greater pleasure of climax.

*'Flora!'* He gripped her hips, roared his release into the world, into her, and let go.

And so did she. Clinging to the man she was in love with. The father of her baby. The man she was going to marry.

Raffaele buried his mouth in the crook of her neck. She smoothed her fingers through his damp hair and panted in sync with his every breath. Their booming hearts pressed against each other in a crushing caress.

Flora placed her lips to his forehead, inhaled the heat of him, the vulnerability of this moment. But she wasn't ready to tell him. Confess her love. Not in the throes of ecstasy. Not in the storm that had set his mind and body on edge.

He raised his head, his breathing shallow and deep. He rasped, 'That shouldn't have happened.'

'You're still inside me,' she whispered.

And she couldn't help it. Her muscles contracted around him as if to prove her point.

He groaned deep in his throat, the skin pulling tight across his cheekbones. 'It shouldn't have been like this.'

'What should it have been like?' she asked, her voice just as low as his. But she didn't let the rejection in his words penetrate her mind. Because she recognised it for what it was.

Fear.

She'd lived with it her entire life—had felt it when he'd confronted her and thought she was missing.

He feathered his fingers over her hips. 'I came to you in anger...a *misplaced* anger,' he corrected. 'I never should have put my reactions because of the past on you. I see that now.'

'But I did the same thing,' she said—because she had, hadn't she? 'Your fears smashed against mine and exploded into—'

'Sex.'

The hands at her hips pressed into her hipbones and lifted her, breaking their intimate seal and bringing her to her feet. He tugged up his jeans and then reached for the blanket on the floor.

He wrapped it around her shoulders, cocooning her nakedness. Concealing it. But the rawness remained and she wanted to explore it. To explore her feelings. To make him explore his.

But he'd retreated. Physically. He'd stepped back until the distance between them was a palpable length. And emotionally she felt it too. As if the words they'd whispered between kisses had never been spoken. As if he hadn't released whatever power the storm had over him into her body.

'And wasn't that reaction normal?' she asked. 'The sex?'

'It shouldn't have been so desperate. So animalistic.'

'But it was. Because that's how we were feeling.'

'It shouldn't have been like that for *you*.'

'Why not for me?' She swallowed thickly. 'I wanted this. I wanted you. And you wanted me too.'

'You are *pregnant*,' he interjected fiercely. 'And I...' He exhaled a shaky breath. 'I took you against a wall...without softness, without care. I could have hurt you...the baby—'

'You didn't hurt me. Pregnancy doesn't make me breakable.'

'How do you know that?'

'I was raised on a farm.'

'We are not animals, Flora.' He scrubbed a hand over his face. 'We are human beings.'

She let her breath calm and tried to clear her mind. It wasn't the pleasure he'd given her that had pushed words of love into her head, was it? It was him, filling her mind, her body, her heart...

He kept on ripping apart the doubts she presented to him... the fear that who she was wouldn't be wanted. Because he wanted her. Despite his best intentions to stem the urgency in him to—

*Love her?*

She searched his face. Ran her gaze over every tight muscle. Heard the shallow rasps of his breath. Even if he was feeling things for her he wasn't ready.

*And you are?*

She was ready because she refused to be anything else. Refused to hide from her feelings any more. But him? He was a man who had loved her body in his grief six weeks ago—a man now vulnerable and raw from the memory of a storm that should have killed him who had loved her body today.

If she could persuade him to explore this side of their relationship, maybe he'd...

'We're going to be stuck on this boat for a few more days, aren't we?' she said.

'Yes.'

'Until we leave, I want to do everything we've been doing. Sharing breakfast...all our meals. And at night I want to explore this chemistry between us.'

'Burn it out?'

'Understand it,' she corrected. 'Give it a place in our lives before we get married. Before we have a baby. So you don't fear it.'

'I am not scared of sex.'

'But you *are* afraid of having sex with me. Why?' she asked, eyes narrowed. 'Because of the intensity of it?'

His eyes darkened. 'Because I can't protect you when I'm buried deep inside you.'

'I don't need protection.' She clutched the blanket closer around her midriff. 'I need—'

'Not this,' he said roughly. 'You need—'

'I need you to stop sweeping our attraction for each other under the carpet. I'm tired of hiding from the elephant in the room,' she interrupted honestly. 'But if your goal in our relationship is to keep me safe…what better way to protect me than keeping me close? Isn't that what you said? That if I'd been in your bed then you could have protected me from the storm?'

'Flora…' he growled.

'Let's go to bed, Raffaele. Give this side of our relationship enough time to either run its course or…'

'Or?'

'Or we accept our chemistry as part of our lives.'

His eyes intense, he prowled towards her. 'The things I could teach you, *piccolina*…'

Her eyes travelled down from his thick throat to his broad muscular shoulders, then to the fine black hair over his washboard abs, and lingered on the V leading down beneath his jeans.

His muscles rippled with tension. Her insides clenched with instant desire. To be with him. *Again*.

'Then teach me, Raffaele,' she said, and her heart hammered.

Because she knew—could feel it in the heart of her soul—that the boy who'd become a man, whose mother hadn't loved him enough, whose father had rejected him, didn't understand family and didn't know love.

But she did.

'You want me to teach you the pleasures of the body?' he asked.

'Yes.'

He reached for her, put his thumb and forefinger beneath her chin. He gripped it, looked into her eyes. Searched them. Deeply. And she let him seek out her secrets, let him understand what she wanted, with her unflinching stare.

His voice ragged, he said, 'Until it burns out?'

'*If* it burns out,' she insisted.

'It will,' he assured her.

'And you want that?'

He moved his hand down her chin to grip her throat with light fingers. 'I want the self-control not to touch you.'

'Love me until you can control yourself, then.' Her mouth parted and she lifted her chin and pushed it into his palm. 'Until you can touch me without feeling the way I feel when you touch me.'

'*How* do you feel when I touch you?'

'I want you,' she admitted. 'Inside me. Again and again.'

He swiped his thumb against the hammering pulse in her throat. 'And now?'

'I want to make love all over again,' she said.

'The temptation to do it again doesn't frighten you any more?' he asked. 'That feeling made you run from my bed once...'

'That was six weeks ago. I'm not that woman now. I'm not afraid.'

'You should be.'

'Not of you,' she replied without hesitation. 'And not of myself,' she said.

And those words felt powerful. *She* felt powerful. Fearless.

She let the blanket slip from her shoulders. 'Not of this...'

He moved his hands to grip her hips and drag her body into his. 'Just until we leave the boat,' he said, his mouth hovering over hers.

'Or not,' she replied, and moved forward to catch his mouth.

But he leaned away. 'It will end,' he promised, and then he slammed his mouth against hers. Making his words the last.

Flora thrust her hands into his hair and pushed her tongue into his mouth. She was going to make sure his promise was one he couldn't keep. He might teach her the pleasures of the body. But she would teach him love.

Teach him to trust it.

To trust her the way she trusted him…

# CHAPTER TEN

THE STORM HAD PASSED.

Raffaele slipped the grey button through the hole that housed it. Then the next. Methodically. Without emotion. He reached his throat and pushed the last button through the loop. He picked up his tie from beside the basin. Threaded the charcoal silk through the collar of his matching shirt. Flipped and twisted it between his fingers and pulled, forming a knot against his neck.

He reached for his suit jacket, pushed his arms through, and only then did he meet his reflection. Stare at the man who had stepped on this boat seven days ago and, regardless of what had happened in between, would be leaving as him too.

The man in the suit.

The billionaire.

*In control.*

Resolute in his decision, he turned. His leather shoes slapped against the marble floor. The burn in his chest set fire to his throat. He knew it wasn't indigestion. It was the burn of the man he'd been for the last three days, disgusted at what he was about to do.

He was going to take back control of himself. Of all their lives. His. Flora's. The baby's.

This piece of paper with its numbered lines would end

whatever step out of time he'd allowed himself these past three days.

He picked it up from the gilded table, opened the bathroom door and stepped into the master suite. The bedroom.

And stood there.

Looking at the evidence of how the last few days had overturned his life.

*Flora.*

She was everywhere.

The white towelling robe he'd draped around her after their swim, only to discard it as soon as they'd closed the door to their rooms, flung on the back of a chair.

Her black panties lay on the floor. Panties he'd slowly taken down her thighs on the sofa last night. Gently teasing them down her legs and over her ankles to present himself between her legs on his knees and taste her.

The taste had lingered in his mouth and drugged him into a stupor of desire. He hadn't been able to sate it. That desire. That need to grip her hips, lower her onto any available surface and thrust himself inside her. Again and again.

In the pool.

On the floor.

The sofa.

The bed.

Slowly, he let his gaze fall on every piece of evidence of her until his gaze came to Flora herself. Asleep. Oblivious. A white sheet drawn up to her hips, her bare back exposed, her brown hair spread out over the pillow as her hand rested on his side of the bed. His vacated spot.

He'd left.

And he wasn't going back.

He couldn't. Not the man who had draped his arms around

her, pulled her to his chest in the Sky Lounge with a blanket shared between them as they watched the storm.

Because she'd been right. He had needed to give this part of their relationship a place in their lives. And now he had. And it would remain on his boat. The intensity. The chaos.

In the real world, he wasn't the man who had claimed her softness with his unrelenting urgency. Nor the man who had accepted her tenderness, her cuddles, her laughter.

His heart hiccupped painfully in his chest.

He couldn't let himself be weak. He couldn't let emotion in. On the boat, it had been simple. Keep her close—keep her safe. But in the eastern hills of Scarlata, in the house on the hill, he would need all his senses. A rational mind.

Raffaele squared his shoulders. It couldn't be helped. She'd refused to talk about what would happen next. When they got to Sicily. To the house that had never been a home. A house they would turn into a home now. To wipe away the past.

*Why? For redemption?*

Stepping further into the room, Raffaele shook the question off. The decision to go back had nothing to do with redemption and everything about giving his child roots, didn't it?

He sat down on the edge of the bed and feathered his fingers down her bare spine. He'd kissed each dip. Memorised it with his tongue. Tasted it with his mouth. She tasted of rain and sunshine. And the taste made his guts twist like a never-ending storm inside him.

That morning in the Sky Lounge he'd allowed the instant rush of desire flowing through his veins to gather in his loins. He'd lost his head. Given in to the temptation of finding oblivion in her body again. And he'd done it every day since. Three days…

And still he burned.

His lust undiminished.

She stirred beneath his fingers. Her eyes obscured by her hair, she smiled into the pillow. 'Did you have a nice shower?' she asked.

He removed his hand from her skin. 'I did.'

Pushing the hair from her eyes, she peeped up at him from beneath lowered lashes.

'You've shaved,' she declared.

Reaching out, she placed her fingertips to his cheek, swiped them down to meet his jaw. He caught her wrist gently, so as not to expose how her touch affected him. Hardened him. Mocked him for his lack of control. He pulled her fingers away and brought her knuckles to his mouth, brushed them against his lips.

Briefly, he closed his eyes.

Regained control of himself.

But the loss of his sight increased the scent of their shared arousal, coating the sheets, her skin...

His eyes opened and there were hers. Bright. Trusting. He placed her hand on the bed and handed her his neatly prepared list.

She had been so sure that their passion wouldn't burn itself out—and she'd been right. He'd known she would be. But he'd also known that it had to end once they reach Sicily. Once they reached their new home.

His chest was heavy, tight, and he kept his eyes on the piece of paper between them.

The storm outside was over, and now he'd contain the one inside him—whatever it took.

'It's time to leave, *piccolina*.'


'We're leaving?' Flora asked as she reached for the paper he was holding out to her.

'As soon as you are ready,' he confirmed.

Gripping the sheet between her fingers, she sat up, pulling it to cover her breasts, and took the paper from him.

'Lovely penmanship!' She flashed her teeth. 'I write like a toddler,' she confessed. 'Is it a letter? Numbered to count the ways you—?'

'No,' he interrupted, before the word *love* teased through her lips and presented itself, and he pushed the paper closer towards her.

'Okay. Someone needs some coffee…'

'I've had several.'

'Over-caffeinated?' she murmured under her breath, and focused on the flicks and twirls of his handwritten note.

She tucked her hair behind her ears. 'It's a list.' She frowned at him. 'What do we need this for?'

'Read it.'

Her eyes swept over the numbered bullet points on the list dated today: *dress-fitting, hairstylist, photographer, wedding—*

'You want to get married *today*?'

'It's all arranged. We will arrive in Scarlata in three hours. Everything will be at the house waiting for us. Hairstylists. Flowers…' He shrugged. 'Tonight we will be married, and tomorrow—' He dipped his head to the list in her clenched fingers.

She followed his gaze. Ran through the next bullet points, the following week mapped out for her, marking each day's events. A nicely scripted list of what he expected her to do with her life.

'The doctor?' she asked, her eyes searching for the man he'd been last night.

But his face was a mask of shadows she didn't understand. Cloaked in an air of finality…

Raffaele nodded. 'That list comprises all the things that must be done before our new life can begin.'

'But…' She swallowed down on the anxiety bubbling in her chest. 'I haven't even chosen a dress.'

'A dress is a dress,' he dismissed evenly.

'My mum would like to see it,' she said. '*I* would like to see it. To choose—'

'Choices will be available for you. Your mother will see photographs,' he said, and her eyes widened.

After everything she'd told him of her family, the importance of her parents to her—had he forgotten? It was as if she'd never said it. Hadn't told him about her lack of choices growing up.

'The photographer—' he pointed to the list '—number three,' he said, redirecting her gaze, 'will be there when the team gets you ready for the church.'

'Church?' she echoed.

For a week there had been no routines, no carefully executed plans, and yet here he was, presenting one to her with a documented list of how she was to spend her life. Without her input…

'The church in Scarlata,' he said. 'It's small. The building has been an ongoing restoration project for many years.' He looked at the list, and she looked at him. 'Our nuptials,' he continued, 'will be documented. For our child. But you can present the pictures to your family as well. It will be as if they were there with us.'

'And who *will* be there?'

'Only you and me,' he answered.

'Because we're the only ones that matter?'

'It is a legal binding. To give our child protection. *My* protection. Nothing else matters,' he dismissed.

'Then why a church?' she asked. 'Why not some office?'

'When our child is grown—'

She halted him with a raised hand. 'The church, the dress, the photographer...' She pulled the sheet tighter around her. 'Is all this for a baby who doesn't have a name yet?'

'It will have *my* name,' he corrected. 'And so will you. By the end of today you will be my wife,' he said. 'Signora Flora Russo.'

'And we'll spend the first day of our marriage in a doctor's surgery?'

'We have spent the last three days in bed—'

'Not all the time,' she rejected—because they hadn't. He had shown her the heights her body could reach in his arms. But he'd also held her in the dark, close to his body, folded her into the curve of his hips, and listened to her whisper stories of her life.

'These last three days—'

'Were what?' she asked, before she could stop herself. The words vibrated in the air between them.

'A step out of time,' he clarified. 'The honeymoon is over, Flora. It's time to focus on what matters.'

'And what's that?'

'The baby.'

They'd spent three days together without rules, without lists. They'd explored one another without restraint. But now it seemed that it was time to learn new rules. New routines. As Raffaele's wife. As Signora Flora Russo.

And she didn't know how she felt about it. The list...

His restraint laced through his cleanly shaved jaw. He'd downloaded the list that he'd written in his head seven days ago and nothing had changed. Not for him. While for her...

He hadn't learnt a thing. She was a bad teacher. She should have been able to share with him that she loved him. And he should have told her he loved her. Should have asked her to prepare this list with him—do it *together*. But he'd done it without her. Without any consideration of her feelings. The last three days hadn't diminished their desire, but she hadn't been able to show him that he could let it control him beyond that.

These things on this list were all about him getting control back.

*That* wasn't love.

Flora swept her gaze over the man on the edge of the bed. So close and yet so far. He was a shadow of that vulnerable man in the storm—the fierce lover he'd been since...

Had their time together meant nothing?

Was he still searching for the control he hadn't had trapped beneath that tree? Did he feel trapped with her? Was this list his escape? By leaving the boat and heading back to reality he could regain control without the chaotic input of emotion, of passion?

Flora would let him have it. The control. For now. Because she was too overwhelmed to do anything else or consider what this shift in mood meant. What his list meant for their future.

Flora did what she always did when she was doubting her feelings—her choices—and the chaotic emotions in her chest. She ignored them and followed the script.

'Okay,' she said, and laid the list on her lap. 'Number one: pack!'

The following hours moved at breakneck speed. Flora showered, dried, and dressed in an ankle-length coral skirt and matching full-sleeve top, with the daintiest buttons down the front. Her newly gained wardrobe was packed and presented to her in new leather suitcases. Three of them and a laptop case. A new tan leather shoulder bag. Her new phone.

And now they were all settled into the helicopter.

To take her towards her new life.

But she'd kept the list in her pocket. Folded into a perfect square beside her thigh.

The thigh that was millimetres from Raffaele's.

The thigh that did not move as they flew towards land.

*Sicily.*

They flew over peaked mountain hillsides full of olive groves and windswept trees. Above coastal towns, gleaming white, beside the sea. And as they moved deeper inland they were silent, both of them. Not speaking a word as reality got closer and closer.

The reality of marriage. Of suits and dresses. Of weddings and lists. Of a script penned by Raffaele for her, and for a baby that wasn't here yet.

But *they* were here.

He hadn't reached for her hand. Even though today he wasn't flying. He sat beside her, frozen as a statue. Untouchable.

The pilot's voice infiltrated the cabin. There was the village of Scarlata.

She looked down with bated breath and saw a village sandwiched between soaring mountains. Red-roofed houses, shops, cafés with tables dotted outside and fairy lights on every door, every window. It was a hub of activity. Of beauty.

She broke the silence. 'How long has it been since you've been back?' she asked.

He gave a cursory glance at the view. 'Never.'

'What do you mean, *never*?'

'After I sold the retreat…' he pointed down to a house in the middle of the square '… I never had any reason to go back to the village. I pumped money in when I could, and had people do what needed to be done to create the vision that I had for Scarlata, for its people. It's now a sought-after tourist destination. They didn't need me to oversee them fulfilling their destiny.'

'And your mother?'

'I paid people to do what needed to be done for her,' he said stonily. 'I came back to her when my father died, broke the news to her, and paid someone else to deal with the aftermath.'

'The aftermath?' she asked, but he didn't answer.

Flora's stomach flipped as they flew up the hillside to the land above it…as she saw what was built there.

'Is that your house?'

His eyes unreadable, he replied, 'It will be.'

'It's beautiful!' she gasped, extending her neck so she could admire its architecture. Tall white walls, intricately patterned columns, verandas, balconies on each floor with stone table and chair sets, climbing trellises of green foliage that ascended to a steepled roof…

And behind it the background was stunning. A forest of trees in greens and browns, and more mountains.

'This is where you grew up?' she asked, turning to him as the helicopter landed in a clearing marked with a big H.

'The only thing that remains of the house I grew up in are the foundations. Everything else—' he dipped his broad shoulders in a shrug '—is brand-new.'

'But you lived *here*?'

'With my mother.'

'Did she like it?' she asked.

'Like what?'

'How you transformed it?' Flora said, trying to imagine growing up here. What it had been like before he'd rebuilt it. 'The house? This isn't the home of a boy struggling to find food.'

'No,' he agreed. 'It is the house of the billionaire who re-built it. It was never my home, but it will be now.'

He unbuckled his belt and reached for hers.

Palms forward, she halted his touch. 'I can do it,' she said, and she did. Popped the buckle and untangled herself from the harness.

The proximity of their bodies belied the distance she could feel between them. He'd retreated somewhere inside himself, to a place she couldn't follow. Even his touch felt different. The hand at the base of her spine as he'd reached to help her had been incidental, courteous.

*He* felt different. Restrained. When the last three days he had been anything but.

'So did she?' she asked, focusing on him rather than try-ing to organise her feelings. Admit what was happening.

His gaze narrowed. 'Did she what?'

'Did she like it? The house you built for her?'

'She didn't care.'

'Did you?'

'Did I what?'

'Care?' she pushed.

'About my mother?' he asked. 'Of course. I cared that the house she wanted to remain in was safe. That it had every-thing she could need and more. I built extra rooms, extended the floors to accommodate staff to cook, clean, watch her.'

'What do you think she would have thought about us com-ing here? Making it our home?'

'She probably wouldn't have noticed.'

'Your mother wouldn't have noticed that her son had brought home the woman he was going to marry?'

He shifted in his seat. 'They are waiting for us, *piccolina*.' He nodded towards the double oak doors.

Staff stood there. *Security guards?* Men in black suits and sunglasses.

'You need security?' she asked. 'Here?'

'I'm a billionaire, Flora. I need security everywhere, and so will you,' he said tightly.

'You didn't have any at the hotel.'

'And look what happened.'

'You didn't have any on the boat.'

'We were in the middle of the sea.' He exhaled deeply. 'You are stalling,' he declared. 'Why?'

'Because once I step off this helicopter I won't see you again until we make our vows—promises.'

He frowned. 'And you've changed your mind?'

'Of course not. But...'

'But what?'

'Tell me something...' she started, and tried to swallow down the emerging reality of her future. Her shared future with this man. The personification of wealth and privilege. Cold self-control. 'Of all the places we could get married and build a home,' she continued, and placed her open palm on his thigh, 'why here, Raffaele?'

She felt the muscles tense beneath her hand. Her insides churned as she prodded to find the man beneath the suit. The man she'd slept with. Talked to. Eaten with. The man who had disappeared into the bathroom to have a shower and not come out.

'Why come back when your mum isn't here? Not once have I heard you call this house your home. Not once have I heard—'

His eyes blazed. 'Enough, *piccolina*,' he said between un-moving lips.

There he was. Simmering beneath the surface. The man

she'd fallen in love with. With that all-consuming energy pressing against his skin.

'Enough of what, Raffaele? Acknowledging the elephant in the room?'

Unflinching, she held his gaze steady, although she wasn't sure it was the right move. Her rational brain told her to get out of the helicopter and fall into the hands of the people Raffaele had arranged to get her ready for a wedding.

To follow the plan.

The script for her wedding.

When she hadn't even seen the dress.

Hadn't even seen the church where the ceremony would take place.

And she wasn't sure if she was marrying the man who'd shared a bed with her last night or this man beside her who was fighting her. Fighting the status quo they'd created of touching freely, expressing themselves with words, kisses, intimacy.

'If it's so hard to be back here—' she said.

'It's not *hard*.'

'You're lying.'

'And you know this because you know me so well?'

'Maybe I don't know you at all,' she replied. 'I don't know the person you're trying to be right now.'

'Who am I trying to be?'

'Cold. Indifferent.'

'Maybe I *am* cold.' He looked straight through her. 'Indifferent.'

'You're neither of those things.'

He crossed his leg and flicked at a piece of invisible lint. 'Am I not?'

'You're pretending you are,' she said, slowly joining the

dots in her mind. 'Only with me you haven't been like that. Not in London. Not on your boat. Only here.'

'How do you know I haven't been pretending all this time just to get you here?'

'Because I know,' she said without hesitation.

The man beside her was a lie, and the truth she'd experienced with him had been too honest, too raw, for it to come from anyone other than the man he hid beneath his suit.

'I was there with you. Making promises in the storm. And now that we're not there you're pretending you've forgotten that we promised each other to give the chaotic chemistry between us a home if we couldn't burn it out.'

He picked up the hand on his thigh and placed in on hers. 'But it *has* burnt out—like a pinched flame, *piccolina*.'

'No, I can feel it still simmering between us. This charge…' She swallowed down the hurt of his unexpected rejection. 'You're running from it,' she declared. 'Hiding from me…from yourself. And I'm done with running from the elephant in the room.' She sat straighter, taller. 'Stop lying,' she demanded. 'To me. To yourself. Because I'm not going in there until I understand what's happening between us. What's changed. Why we're here.'

'You can't refuse to get out of a helicopter every time we travel in one,' he hissed.

'I can do what I want,' she countered, heat flushing all the way up from her chest to heat her face. 'It's called being a grown-up. Facing the situation presented to you and gathering all the facts, whether or not you want to learn them. Don't redact the truth with me—I never want to be in the dark again. That list…it overwhelmed me. But I've got myself together now. I've remembered who I am. The woman I want to be. I want to face the facts—all of them—right here and now. Don't you?'

He didn't speak for the longest time. Didn't move.

'*Tell* me,' she said, her throat dry. Her brain was twisting itself to understand the information he was hiding from her. Find the facts. 'Explain why we're here? Why is it so important to you to have your new family—*me*—in a home where you never knew any genuine sense of family...where you were never shown love, only rejection?'

With a slight shake of his head, Raffaele closed his eyes briefly. 'We have spoken about origins, Flora. Knowing our roots.' He shrugged. 'These are mine. This house was once a place to be avoided. The people inside unimportant. Insignificant. Now it is a beacon of privilege. It is because of *this* house that Scarlata pulses with life. When our baby grows,' he said, keeping his eyes on the house, 'the strength of what its father has become will outweigh the whispers I once endured. Our child will be strong because of these roots. *My* roots. This house that was once nothing more than a shell will be a family home.'

He turned to her then.

'*Our* home, *piccolina*. I don't want this love you talk of. I wouldn't thrust it upon anyone—especially our child. I've seen first-hand how love manipulates. Breaks those it claims to care for irreparably.'

'Your mum?'

'Love broke my mother. The lie of it. The illusion. She waited all her adult life for love to return to her, and when it didn't—when her love died—she chose to end her life.'

Horrified, she let her hand fly to her mouth. 'Love ended her life?'

'No. Love doesn't exist. It was the illusion of love that killed her,' he confirmed, his tone flat. Emotionless.

'What about her love for you?'

'She didn't love me. She provided a bed. A roof.'

'The same things you're offering me?'

'No, I am offering you what I have offered from the very beginning,' he answered. 'Nothing has changed.'

'*I've* changed.' She placed a hand on her chest. 'Inside.'

'We did as you suggested. We burnt out the fire. We know one another. Know why we're entering this marriage.'

'I don't understand what's happened…'

He tilted her chin between his thumb and forefinger, bringing their gazes in line with one another. 'I can touch you with control.'

But he couldn't. He might be desperate to believe that he could, but he hadn't been quick enough to conceal the flash of heat in his eyes.

'Lying again, Raffaele?' she challenged him, feeling her body instantly responding to *this* man. The truth in his eyes. The heat in them. The longing she recognised in him because it weighed down in her own stomach, pushing the heat lower.

'And what if I can't touch you the same way?' she asked.

'You must,' he insisted.

'Why?' she asked. 'Because you don't want me? Don't want the woman you told me I could be—*should* be?' she corrected.

She saw his eyes glued to her lips, to the words spilling out of her because she couldn't stop them. Didn't want to stop them.

'I *feel*, Raffaele. I *want*. I'm a woman who needs *you*. Needs the man who collected me from the farm. The man I met in London. The man on the yacht.'

The grip on her chin tightened. 'This last week,' he said quietly—*roughly*. 'The storm…the explosions of emotion from you.' His nostrils flared. 'And from me,' he admitted. 'The turbulence of it—of us—has made me want…'

She saw that the admission had cost him. It was written on every granite line etched into his beautiful face.

'You want the exact opposite of what we could be?'

'And what do you *think* we could be, Flora?'

'Happy.'

'What happened on the boat wasn't happiness,' he snarled. 'It was sex.'

'And you've gone full circle back to being afraid of having sex with me?'

'It's not about fear. It's not about sex.'

'What *is* it about?' But just like that the penny dropped, and she answered for him, without pause. 'The baby.'

'It was only ever about the baby.' He released her chin. 'Our time on the yacht was a mistake. Now we move past it.'

'How?' she asked huskily.

'We go inside,' he said. 'We follow the list. We do the right thing for our child, the way our parents did not do it for us.'

She reached into her pocket. Let the crisp lines of the folded square of paper slip and slide in her grasp. She pulled it out and handed it to him. 'I don't need this,' she said. 'I don't want it. You don't need to pay people to look after me, Raffaele. I can look after myself.'

A pulse hammered in his naked jaw. Realisation punched her in the sternum. Trapping her breath into her lungs. Filling every sense with a feeling she recognised. Had lived with her entire life.

Fear.

She sucked in a breath and allowed herself to process her own wants, her own needs, and saw his. The needs he was trying to hide so desperately behind his suit. His billions. Behind the group of people he paid to take care of the things he didn't want to face in case he got it wrong.

But that was life. Getting it wrong and still choosing to live.

Now Flora saw this moment for what it was. What it meant to him. A man who hadn't been home since he was a boy to a house without his mother. He had left behind a village that he had lifted up. He had become vulnerable in the beginning of a storm because of his memories.

She dropped the list on the floor. His gaze lingered it on it. Her hand rose and she gripped his chin between her thumb and forefinger, as he'd done to her.

'I want us to leave this helicopter without fear,' she said.

'I am not—'

'Shh…' she said gently, and watched his lips stretch and thin. 'I want you to choose to be the man you are with me, because I'm not going anywhere without him. We are going to go into that house and make it a home. Fill it full of feelings. *Our* feelings. We can write our own history, starting now, if you trust your instincts the way you showed me to trust mine. It frightened me in the storm. Frightened me that I'd made all the wrong choices and that the woman I was becoming was the wrong woman for me to be. It was the feeling of fear I've had since you came back to me.'

'And now the fear is gone?'

'Because of you.' She leaned in, bringing her mouth millimetres from his. 'You let me talk, feel, touch. Explore myself without judgement. However chaotic—however illogical my feelings were…'

She flicked her tongue over her trembling lips.

'You showed me the man you are.' She stroked a hand across the tightness of his left shoulder. 'The man beneath this suit. I need to be claimed by *that* man. The man desperate to be inside me. Because he has wants—needs—just like me. He isn't cold or indifferent. Choose to be *him*. If you want to be with me, choose instinct, Raffaele. Let go of the list.'

She feathered her lips against his and he trembled against her.

'Let go of this façade the way you did in the storm. Because I see you, Raffaele,' she said. 'And you see me. So let's not stop looking at each other *now*, when everything is about to change.'

She pulled away, dropping her hands from his body, and met the blazing ethereal blue of his.

'What do you want, Raffaele?'

For a long heartbeat he didn't move. Then he did. He bent down and picked up his handwritten list. He opened each fold with careful precision.

'I want to let go,' he rasped, and tore the list in two and let the pieces flutter to the floor. 'I want to let go of everything but *this*. But *you*.' He grasped her hand, threaded his fingers between hers. 'I want to marry you. I want this day to end with the woman you are being bound to the man you make me want to be.'

'For us?'

His Adam's apple bobbed above the knot of his tie. 'For *me*,' he said. 'Marry me because...'

Her breath hitched. 'Because...?'

'Because I can't imagine starting tomorrow without you in my bed. In my arms. I need you there. Beside me. *With* me.' He reached up, brushed his thumb along her cheekbone. 'Looking at me with those all-seeing brown eyes.' He gripped her face, pulled her into him, and asked, 'Will you marry me, Flora Bick?'

She closed her eyes and pressed her forehead to his. She pushed down her need for the words—for Raffaele to choose this moment to confess that this, what they were feeling, was love. He still wasn't ready. She was, but she would wait until he could hear the words. Understand that she wasn't an illusion. That her love wasn't a lie. They had fallen in love.

*What if he can't hear it? Understand? What if he doesn't want to learn what this means?*

She slammed the door on those questions because they came from a place of fear, and she wouldn't let fear chase her away from what she wanted ever again. Because the first time she had put fear aside she'd met him. And now they were going to be a family. *Her* family.

How could it be a bad thing to set aside all those raging doubts when they'd given her *him*?

Flora met his gaze. Both of them were searching, both looking. And she said, 'Okay.'

She swallowed the exhalation against her lips. The relief mirrored in her smile shook, but she smiled through it. Through any lingering doubt. This was the right decision.

'I'll marry you, Raffaele Russo.'

# CHAPTER ELEVEN

'I HAVE COME HOME.'

Raffaele stared at the grave, yet to be marked with a tomb-stone. There was only a white cross, etched with her name.

*Maria Russo*

Flowers were delivered from the gardens surrounding the house every week, cut and collected by the hands of the people he paid to keep her company even in death.

He delivered them today. Placed the white-headed blooms on the deep rich soil.

At his request, she'd been brought home after the inquest into her death in Italy. Had been buried as she had lived and died—without him.

His guilt was heavy. Still. It sat on his shoulders and refused to loosen its grip, even on his wedding day.

He'd left the house unseen, his departure unnoticed, and walked through the knotted trees in his wedding suit with one of the white blooms in his buttonhole. He'd made his way down the hill on the outskirts of the village and walked to the church. Arriving at the back gate to the small graveyard.

To see his mother.

'I am getting married, Mamma,' he said now, to the winds, to the soil, to the earth that protected her.

To his mother.

'She is fierce,' he continued. 'This Flora Bick. She was

hiding when I found her on the English coast. All jeans and pumps and cows. And still I saw her. *Shining.* But now she will wear ball gowns. Because she was born to do so, Mamma. She was born to walk into a room and shine the way you deserved to shine. In jewels, in dresses of silk, protected by a name of privilege. Protected and adored with my father's wealth. I'm sorry my wealth wasn't enough. I'm sorry I didn't give you the choice to grieve in your own home when the man you loved died and with him your dreams of reconnecting with him. I'm sorry I was the one to tell you he was dead, and I'm sorry that I didn't let you scream, cry, break things... I should have stayed with you. I never should have sent you to that private clinic, however esteemed it was. Because it was not where you wanted to be. But you found a way out, didn't you? A way to be with *him.*'

He shoved down the childish urge to ask her why *he* hadn't been enough to make her choose a different path out of that facility. Why she hadn't talked to the therapists provided there. Talked to *him.*

It didn't matter. This was idiotic. But he needed her to know that he had not forgotten her. And to tell her what would happen next.

'She wants me to do something—give her something I cannot. Because the rage—' he swallowed down the lump in his throat '—the regret... It's mine, isn't it? It belongs to me. And forgiveness is yours to give. But still you do not speak to me.'

Raffaele closed his eyes, listened to the rustle of the trees and the call of the crows high in their towers.

Otherwise there was silence.

Had he expected anything else?

'For years you told me you didn't want me. Didn't need

me to bring home food. You didn't need me to brush your hair. Help you slide into the bath…'

His voice trailed off as he remembered her frailty. Her refusal to fight. And in the end he hadn't been strong enough to fight for them both.

'I didn't listen to you. I just kept brushing your hair. Kept trying to—'

He sucked it in. The frustration. The hotness of it. The visceral kick to his guts, as strong as it had ever been, that he hadn't been able to save her from herself.

'I'm sorry I didn't listen to you. That I let your words get into my head and in the way of the duty I was bound to. And then I stopped brushing your hair.'

Every word he'd wanted to say for three months he said now. To whom, he didn't know. She was gone. This white cross… This soft overturned earth… They were nothing more than a shrine for mourners. This graveyard was for the living, not the dead. But he carried on talking because he couldn't stop.

'I will get married today, Mamma, and I promise you this: I will protect my family. I will never pay for someone to care for them for me. She will get my name. My wealth will protect her. But I will never give her this disease—this promise of love that destroyed you. I cannot love her. But I will turn your house into the home you were never given, the home you were denied. Know from this day that everything my father denied to you I will give to her. To my wife. I cannot claim your forgiveness, but my promise is my redemption. *She* is my redemption.'

He turned his back on the grave, his breathing fast and shallow, and stopped. Everything blurred into one image. One person. One woman.

Her brown hair was in an elegant chignon. A pearl-tipped

tiara sat in her hair. She wore a wedding dress with long lace sleeves with an intricately sewn pearl pattern down the length of the arms…around her throat.

'How did you find me?'

*She* was his redemption?

Confirmed by a loveless vow promised to a dead woman?

Flora's heart thumped wildly against the pearl buttons of the boned bodice of her dress.

*Her wedding dress.*

Here she stood, outside the church she was going to get married in, a bouquet in her hands of every colour, listening to a man who was promising never to love her.

And it hurt. It was palpable. His rejection of a love she hadn't voiced. Already it was unwanted.

*Her love.*

And by God, she wanted to touch him. Grab him by the shoulders and tell him to open his ears, his heart. Tell him he was wrong, and that all the things he'd promised to his mother—to provide for his wife—she didn't want them. Any of them. She didn't care about his money. His name. His protection. She wanted the unconditional love her parents had raised her with. She wanted to love him unconditionally and wanted it in return. Wanted to fill their house with love, not…*things.*

Instead, she swallowed her words down deep, until they lodged themselves in her chest to remain unspoken. Because they wouldn't matter. She knew that because he was not ready to let go of the woman whose grave lay behind him. Because he had not forgiven himself for her death.

She had no clue what the right words to say were. But she knew they shouldn't be about her. Because this was firmly about him.

So she trusted her instinct, lifted one flat white pump and trod onto the mossy grass, brought herself closer to him. To the man now frozen in the graveyard, looking at her as though he'd conjured a ghost.

She reached him, stood before him. His breathing was audible, the heavy rise and fall of his chest rapid. Flora placed her hand on his chest and looked up into his eyes. His face was the sculpted face of a mystic. Dark. Tortured.

'I followed you, of course.' She smiled tightly. 'We're getting married, aren't we?'

Reaching down, she caught his hand and gave his tight fingers a quick squeeze. Then she nodded and stepped beside him, knelt down. The hem of her dress disappeared into the grass.

She spoke to Raffaele's mum.

'Signora Russo,' she started, 'I promise to always follow my instinct and guide your son to make the best choice for *him*. I hope this brings you peace.'

She took her bouquet in both her hands and pulled it apart, separating it into two parts. Then she laid half of the dainty rainbow-coloured flowers beside the white ones already there.

She stood, turning her back on the grave. 'Ready?' she asked.

'For what?' he asked huskily.

'You wrote the list.' She tapped her wrist and pointed to an invisible watch. 'It's time.'

'Why did you follow me?'

'I saw you leave. And I saw an opportunity to escape the photographer taking endless pictures of me being plucked and pruned and I broke free.'

He flinched. 'In your wedding dress?' he asked, his voice a broken husk of accusation. 'You could have hurt yourself.'

'*You're* in your wedding suit.'

It was a suit lighter in tone than the grey one he'd worn to travel in that morning. A thick Windsor knot was tied at his throat. There was a flower in his buttonhole. And he was beautiful.

But he was not ready, was he? To claim a wife. To love a family.

'I still can't wear heels.' She lifted the hem of her dress and gave him a glimpse of her white-stockinged calves. 'The walk was easy enough.'

'You didn't call out? Didn't tell me you were there?'

'I assumed you'd be making your way here, to the church, and I wanted to be with you—not in a fancy car with strangers. I thought, *If we're doing this, we should do it together. Go inside together and get married.*'

'That is not the way this works.' His eyes narrowed. 'I'm supposed to be inside. Waiting for you.'

'I thought this could be *our* way.' She held out her hand, palm forward. 'Shall we…?'

'But the photographer…' he said.

'He doesn't matter,' she dismissed.

'The pictures?' he said. 'For your mother?'

'We'll have photos taken later,' she said.

His eyes darted to the hem of her dress, her scuffed white pumps. 'Your dress…'

'It doesn't matter.'

'Then what *does* matter?' he asked.

And this time her smile faltered. Flashed with the uncertainty on the edge of her thoughts. She wanted to say it was love that mattered. But she needed him to see, to understand that *he* mattered too. So very much to her. That she would take care of him when he was putting everything but himself on the list.

'Trusting yourself to write new rules,' she said, her chest tight. 'With me standing right beside you.'

Her hand, unclaimed, trembled in the air.

'Trusting myself?' he echoed.

'Let's write a brand-new script. Walk into that church by ourselves, *for* ourselves, together. Just you and me. I'll give myself away because you'll be there, claiming me, just the way I'll claim you.'

His hand rose from his side, reached out, and there in the graveyard their fingertips met. He pulled her in and she reached out for his shoulders. He gripped her waist and looked down into her face as she looked up into his.

'Together?'

She nodded. Did he get it now? Did he understand?

'Side by side, Raffaele. Through those doors, up the aisle, to say the words, vows, and promises to the only people that matter. The people getting married. *Us.*'

His chest heaved against hers. He dipped his head. But she didn't look at his lips. Didn't let herself feel the warmth of his breath on her lips. Because it wasn't a time for kisses. It was a time for words.

'Let go, Raffaele, and put all that rage and regret inside you into something new. You can't build on rotten foundations—so let's rip them out. Start again. Start again with me. Right now. Start something that's ours. Nothing to do with the past and everything to do with the future.'

His fingertips pressed into her hips and she felt the fight in his body. The battle between duty and the temptation of what she was offering. A life where they mattered to each other. Made choices *together*.

This time she didn't resist. She inched in at the same time he did. Their lips met. Held. Pressed to each other. A promise? A vow?

He grasped her hand tightly and pulled away. 'Let's get married, *piccolina*.'

Step by step they walked up the path leading to the front of the church. Hand in hand they turned the corner. And then—

*Applause.*

It burst the silence with a thrum of a hundred clapping hands and smiling eyes.

A man in an ill-fitting suit stepped forward. The gasp she heard from Raffaele's lips pushed every hair on her body into an upright position.

'Matteo…' Raffaele's said.

And the man pulled him into a tight embrace and held him against him for longer than was customary in any tradition, whispering words she couldn't hear into his ear.

Raffaele closed his eyes, and she felt the surge of emotion in the hand clasping hers. The man stepped back, stood eye to eye with Raffaele, and both men nodded.

The man Matteo turned his attention and his smile to her. Kissed her heartily on both cheeks and squeezed her hand. And so it went on. Embraces and kisses. But not once did Raffaele let go of her hand, as side by side they moved through the crowd.

The community.

The community who had saved the boy who'd pulled them up in the world.

Who loved the man the boy had become.

And Flora felt it in every hug. Every handshake. Each heavy tap on the shoulder.

He'd always been loved.

He'd just never understood it.

Pulled along by grasping hands, they stood at the entrance of the church. An arch of green foliage with red, violet and white flowers surrounded the double oak doors.

The doors opened.

Hand in hand, they stepped inside.

'Raffaele…' she whispered, frozen in the face of such awe-inspiring beauty.

White silk and huge bouquets dressed every pew. There were long-stemmed flowers between candles that flickered throughout the space, and she felt as if she had stepped out of one time and into another.

On cue, the sun streamed through the high arched stained-glass windows on either side of them. Reflecting on every stone surface in a canvas of colour.

Tears filled her eyes. 'It's beautiful…'

The long, slow melodic swipe of a bow against a violin string whispered across the stillness of the church.

'Look up,' he said, his voice a throaty whisper.

Flora looked up at the stone-columned balcony above them. 'A string quartet?'

As if on cue, a vocalist with pink flowers in her hair stepped forward, began to sing 'Ave Maria'.

'It's time,' he said.

She looked at him. At the man who had given her a night of freedom in London, chased her—hunted her—to the farm and made her not only confront the confirmation of her pregnancy but the woman she wanted to be. With him. She trembled. She had never felt freer than she did right now. She was trusting in her instincts. Was trusting herself to be herself. Because of him.

She stood taller, squared her shoulders. 'Are you ready?' she asked.

'I am ready, Flora Bick,' he said, a pulse flickering in his jaw, 'to end this day with you as my wife.'

'And you as my husband,' she replied.

Their threaded fingers clasped tighter and they stepped onto the red carpet leading to the altar.

*Together.*

And behind them the villagers took their pews as, hand in hand, Raffaele and Flora took centre stage and presented themselves to the priest who would bind them.

Flora feathered her fingers against Raffaele's cheek and held back the tears misting her view as she spoke the words of her heart. The words he needed to hear.

'I know there wasn't time for my family to be here,' she said. 'But I'm so glad yours could be.'

Her heart stuttered for the boy under the tree. Cold and alone. For the boy caring for his mother when she should have been caring for him. For the boy standing at those iron gates, refused entry to a heritage that was his by birth.

Her grip tightened on the hand in hers. They were joined in front of his people. His family. Because sometimes family was the love of strangers. Sometimes it was a village.

'Look at them,' she ordered, and his eyes left hers to move over their audience.

The huge stained-glass windows threw rainbow patterns on their unexpected guests.

'They're all here for you.'

Slowly, his eyes moved back to hers.

'And so am I,' she promised, and that was her vow. Her promise.

She hoped he heard it, and that in time he would understand it. Embrace it as fully as he'd made her embrace herself.

*Family.*

*Love.*

# CHAPTER TWELVE

RAFFAELE COULD NOT release his hold on his wife and she had not let go of him. She'd stayed by his side since they'd left the church to thunderous applause.

The photographer had caught up with them at the ceremony, as had his security team, who had managed to lose two whole human beings.

The day had been...surreal.

The ghosts who had haunted him every day since his departure from the village were alive, and present on his wedding day.

His gut clenched. It was too perfect. This life was not meant for him. And yet here it was. A village cheering for him and his new bride, sending them back to their house. To a house that was to become a home.

*His* home.

He couldn't breathe.

He tugged the knot free at his throat.

'Are you okay?'

The voice was velvet against his prickling eardrums.

'I will be,' he assured her roughly, and shrugged off his suit jacket.

Raffaele wanted out. Out of the car. Out of his suit. He wanted to present himself, on his knees, as the man she wanted. *Him.* Bound by the gold band on his finger by choice. *His* choice.

He was married. And he was taking her home. In a dirt-rimmed wedding dress and mud-caked leather shoes. He wanted her out of the dress, too. He wanted to strip it from her body and reveal the softness he yearned for. Craved so desperately it hurt in his bones. He wanted to sink inside her and lose himself . Ignore the conflict in his chest. These warring emotions he couldn't name. Didn't want to.

Because if he did everything would disappear. She would vanish.

Breathless, they sat beside each other in the back of the luxury car. Breathing ragged. *Tight.* Staring at each other.

'Kiss me,' she demanded, and her eyes begged for him to do exactly what he wanted to do. Climb between her thighs and possess her.

He hooked his jacket onto the clip. 'I will not consummate our marriage in a car, Signora Russo.' His voice was tight. Not his own.

'Why not, Signor Russo?'

Her brown eyes flashed, molten, and he was melting under the onslaught. Caught in her challenging gaze.

'No one can see us,' she said. 'The windows are tinted. No one will hear us behind the privacy glass.'

'We'll be back at the house in—'

'I want you here,' she interrupted. 'I want you *now*. The only reason you could have for not doing what we both want is because you're scared.'

*'Scared?'* he growled. 'Never.'

But the lie tasted foul in his mouth. His body instantly rejecting his confident conformation. It didn't feel real. Any of it. This illusion she'd created of his life that he was wanted. Needed. By a community he'd thought had forgotten him.

She had challenged him every step of the way to confront the demons inside him. To tell them, as she had told his mother, that he should focus on his needs. His wants. What was good for him and no one else. Should bury his skeletons and rebuild a brighter future without fear. Let go of everything he'd held on to for thirty years…

And she'd be there when he did. Standing beside him. Holding his hand. He was not a child—he did not need a guide. But he needed *her*. What did that mean? Could they make this marriage work? Was it possible to have passion and commitment and family even if he couldn't offer her everything she wanted? Would Flora accept that?

He didn't know if this woman—*his wife*—was good for him. Or if he was bad for her.

'Show me,' she dared him. 'Make love to your wife.'

She reached for the small rounded pearl buttons and popped one free. Then another. Another… Revealing the swell of her white lace-covered breasts. She reached down to the hem of her skirt and folded it up, inch by inch, revealing her legs, then the bare flesh above her stockings, until the skirt sat on her hips.

He couldn't tear his gaze away. Her actions penetrated the heart of him. She *knew*. Recognised the chaotic *want* in him that wouldn't diminish. His undisguised need to be inside his wife. The chemistry he'd failed to deny between them. And here it was, demanding a place, a home, in their marriage.

'Love me, Raffaele.'

In that moment, he let go.

Her head fell back against the leather headrest and he devoured her neck. Licked the crevices behind her ear and worked down. Sucking, biting, until he got to her half-open bodice, found the tops of her breasts.

'You're beautiful…' His eyes caught and held the blazing brown of hers.

'I need you, Raffaele,' she said huskily, her mouth parted,

gasping for him with a rawness he felt in the hardening swell of his body.

And she was calling for him to answer it. Their shared hunger. To release the emotions, the feelings, burning in his chest and let her taste them. Swallow them.

He roared and claimed her lips urgently, thrusting his tongue inside her mouth and ripping the dress from her body. His hands sought out her lace-covered breasts, pulled the lace down until his palms found her hardened peaked nipples and squeezed. He tilted his hips and pushed his throbbing length to her core.

Her small hands were on his belt, unbuckling him with swift fingers. She reached for the zip, pulled it down and reached inside.

'Flora!' He moaned her name fiercely as she took the velvet length of him in her hand and stroked him.

She placed a hand on his chest and pushed him away from her mouth. 'Sit down,' she ordered, and he grappled with his own tongue.

She pushed her breasts against his still-clothed chest, pushing harder until their positions were reversed and she sat between his thighs, his erection hard and pulsing between them.

She moved and straddled him. He gripped her thighs as she lowered herself onto him. He stared into her eyes because he couldn't look away. He didn't want to. Because this familiarity between them—this *knowing*—had always belonged to them, hadn't it? From the very first night they'd met…

She sank down, filling herself with the thickness of him deep inside her. 'Now…' she breathed, and her hips rose, teasing his length at her entrance, and then pushed back down.

'Flora…' he said huskily, because the pressure was building inside him with every lift of her hips and…

He thrust up his hips and she braced herself with a hand on the car's ceiling as she screamed his name. 'Raffaele!'

She pushed down, and he thrust again, until their synchronised rhythm was frantic. Chaotic.

'Harder!' she gasped, panting her need into existence. The need that mirrored his own.

He gripped her hips. Thrust harder.

Her hand on his jaw tightened, refusing to let him look away. And he looked at her—saw her for what she was—and stared at her in awe. In amazement. Mesmerised by her wide eyes. Her gasping mouth. Her innocence. And he matched her thrust for thrust, arching his hips to allow her to take him deeper in a reverse image of the night they'd met.

A deep blush bloomed on her neck...her cheeks. He could feel the heat radiating from her. The hotness filling the air between them with humidity—trapping them both inside it. Inside the bubble of desire they hadn't been able to deny the night they'd met in the shadows. And neither could they deny it now, in marriage and in the day's light. In the real world where they would live. Together.

'It's your turn to come for me, *piccolina*.' He pushed his hand between their joined bodies and applied pressure to her swollen nub. 'Let go,' he commanded, as she had him.

She clenched around him, squeezed, until they both roared their release into the air between them and let go together...

Breathing hard, she collapsed on top of him, her face buried in the crook of his neck. He cupped the back of her head and held her against him. The realness of her. This mystical woman who'd appeared in his life and filled every moment with...*magic*. Opened the door to a world he'd never thought possible. Not possible for him. She wanted to drag him inside to a place where family lived.

'I love you, Raffaele.'

His fingers loosened their grip on her.

The bubble popped.

Just as he had known it would.

Because this life was not his to claim. And neither was she.

He could lie. Whisper words of love. Convince her of the illusion of it the way his father had convinced his mother. He could keep her prisoner with his love. A love that would never come.

Or he could set her free.

She rose on his lap, held his gaze, and waited for him to repeat her words. Her lie.

So he made his choice. The only choice he could.

'I cannot love you back.'

Flora had expected it. His denial. And she smiled through the rejection because she knew the truth.

She loved him and he loved her.

She climbed off his lap and sat beside him, this man who had turned from fire to ice with those three little words. She fixed her bra, pulled the ripped seams of her dress together, and waited.

She was ready. Ready to teach a man who'd never known love how to accept it.

Raffaele tucked himself away and straightened his clothes, then turned to her, a pulse pounding in his bristled cheek.

'I can never love you,' he said, his face unreadable.

'What makes you think you don't already love me?' she asked gently.

'Because love doesn't exist. This is sex, Flora. A chemical connection in order to procreate.'

'But I'm already pregnant, so why do we keep making love?' she asked. 'Because you love—?'

'Because I enjoy sex, and I enjoy having it with you. Desire is natural.'

'And love isn't?'

'Love is a myth used to manipulate the weak.'

'I'm not weak, and neither are you.'

She placed her hand on his thigh and gave the tight muscles a squeeze. She watched him looking at the hand on his grey-covered thigh. Saw the debate flickering across his taut features. His hand moved. Reached for hers and hesitated. A palpable pause. Then he picked up her hand and placed it on her lap and turned his unwavering gaze to hers.

Flora held up her hand and pre-empted his rebuttal with a shake of her head. 'I'm aware that eavesdropping is a sin, but I will pay the price—because everything I heard you say to your mother I already knew. You only confirmed it.'

'Confirmed what?'

'That you don't know what love is.'

'I know exactly what it is,' he rejected. 'It is a myth. A lie.'

She shook her head. 'All your life you've been told stories of the man who promised to love your mother, promised to come back to her, and rejected her in the most callous way. He hid you both in a village that was nowhere in anyone's consciousness. He left you both to survive on the lie that he'd come back. That isn't love.'

'I never said it was.'

She ignored him. Because she understood him now. Understood his avoidance of anything other than providing the essentials. Food. Warmth. Shelter. But never love. Because he'd only ever experienced a kind of love that would have broken the strongest of men.

'Your father tricked your mother into thinking his seduction was love,' she continued, trying her hardest to keep her voice level. 'He lied to her and she believed him. And she made you believe too, in some distorted view of love.'

He was looking at her, but she knew he was somewhere far away. His eyes were…haunted.

'Why was she in so much pain if it wasn't love?' he asked between gritted teeth.

'Love isn't pain.'

She wanted to reach for him. Hold his hand and ask him her next question.

She resisted, and continued, 'Was that when the doctors diagnosed her with depression?'

'Yes,' he hissed heavily. 'And medicated her.'

She nodded. 'She wasn't well, Raffaele. She was sick and she was relying on a little boy to carry her pain for her. She focused all her energy on the wrong place. The wrong person. Because her attention should have been on you. She pretended she'd had a great romance with an Italian noble—but her romance was a tragedy. It wasn't love. Her happily-ever-after was never coming—but ours can. If we trust in what we're feeling.'

That pulse pounded in his cheek. He was coming back to her from wherever he'd gone. Into the past? But would he hear her? Understand?

She pushed on. 'That storm took you both to hospital—it saved her and broke you when it should have given you every urge to live life without restraint. It should have told you she wasn't accountable for her lack of love. Her lack of care for you when she couldn't care for herself. Love doesn't hurt. I won't hurt you,' she promised. 'So let me love you. And admit,' she said, 'that you love me too.'

'I don't,' he said roughly. 'I don't love you.'

'Wanting to take care of someone *is* love, Raffaele,' she insisted. 'Keeping them safe. Feeding them breakfast in the afternoon because they skipped it that morning. It's looking for someone in a storm because you need to know they're safe. It's Matteo,' she said, as the memory of the man's name jolted a memory of what he'd told her about the storm.

Matteo had rescued him.

'Matteo the bar-owner,' she continued, 'showed up at your wedding, with all the villagers at his back, to see the boy he rescued from a storm living his life. They *all* came to see you get married.'

'It was just respect for what I did for them—'

'No,' she rejected, her voice a harsh rasp. 'It was for *you*. Love is lots of things, but most of all it's actions.'

She steeled herself for the next part. For the bit that would hurt him the most. She was going to rip off the plaster and make him hear it.

'Love is a little boy brushing his mother's hair when all she wants to do is sleep.'

'How could I have loved her, Flora?' he whispered. 'As soon as I could, I left her. I only came back when I learned of my father's death. I didn't want her to be alone when she found out.'

'Because of what might happen?' she asked quietly.

'It happened anyway,' he said. 'I came back. I told her. And she died. Because as soon as I'd told her I left again and paid other people to look after her. To hear her cries. Her screaming that this was not how it was supposed to be. He promised he'd return, but now he was dead. I left her alone in her grief and she ended her life. If love was all the things—the *actions*—you say it is, I would have stayed and watched her with my own eyes. Not paid for doctors to care for a woman they couldn't protect.'

'It was never your job to protect her from herself,' she told him. 'Your mother made her own choices. Choices you'll never understand. Just like I will never understand why my mother gave me up for adoption.'

'They are not the same thing,' he snarled, teeth bared.

'You're right. They're not. Because I grew up with a family that loved me. I understand all the choices they made now. Because love *is* wanting to protect your own. Your family. Did they always get it right? No. But I understand it now. I understand it was love that pushed them to decide what they did.'

'I failed my mother because of *my* decisions and now she is dead,' he said. 'Because of me. Because I looked away. *That* is not love.'

He closed his eyes. Shut her out. And she let him.

He laid his head back against the headrest. 'What is your compulsion to have life-changing conversations in moving transport?'

'Instinct,' she replied. 'Because every time we've been in the helicopter, a car, I know that when we get out things will happen. And I want to decide with you—*together*—what happens next.'

He didn't open his eyes, but the fingers splayed on his spread thigh flexed.

'We could be in bed. We could be anywhere but here,' he said, his voice gruff, coming from somewhere deep in his chest.

'Still hiding from the elephant in the room?'

His eyes flew open. 'I am not hiding. I am answering your questions—your statements of love—truthfully, however much you might dislike my replies.'

'And then what will you be doing?'

'Everything I said I would,' he clipped.

She slapped straight back. 'In the storm on the boat you said you should never have put your reaction to the past on me. But you still are, Raffaele. I'm not your mother, and you're not your father. I don't know how to make you understand that this is love—'

'"This" is simple, Flora.'

'It is?'

'We will be lovers. Companions. Maybe even friends. And we will raise a baby together. But understand this…'

He shuffled closer to her. She could smell herself on his skin. Their shared arousal. The desire still simmering between them to be closer. To entwine their hands and touch each other. But he didn't touch her, so she wouldn't touch him either. She wouldn't hide in his kisses and she wouldn't let him hide in hers.

'Love will never find you in *that* house.'

He pointed out of the window to the house the car was now pulling up to. The house that would be her new home. He should be carrying her over the threshold to start her new life as Signora Russo.

'Because it never found you?' she asked quietly. 'I'm not your redemption for whatever guilt you feel about the past. I'm your wife, and I'm asking you to let me love you, to love me in return. Because that little boy deserved more than the kindness of strangers. He deserved to be loved and so do you.'

She placed her hand to his chest and everything in her told her to climb back onto his lap and hold him. Hold him until he understood that the love she gave him with her body came from her heart. Her soul.

'Love me, Raffaele,' she said. 'Trust yourself to love me. Now.'

She was asking him just as she had in the storm, but now she needed all his love. Not only his body. But his heart.

'I can't.'

She held the breath in her lungs. Let it burn. Let it stem the tears threatening to spill all over her cheeks.

She wasn't a very good teacher, it would seem.

*One more lesson.* Her heart roared. *The hardest.*

And if it didn't work this love affair would be over and she'd raise her baby by herself. Surrounded with love that was unconditional. But she would give him one more chance to choose love. To choose family. To love her.

And he would choose her, wouldn't he?

She blew out the air between her lips and put the last lesson she had to teach into motion.

Pulling her hand from his body, she turned her eyes straight ahead. She said, 'Get out of the car, Raffaele.'

'What?' he growled.

She did not turn. She would not look at him.

'Why?'

'You said love won't find me in that house, so I'm not going in.'

'It's our wedding day, Flora.'

'And you have vowed never to love me. I won't raise my baby in a house without love.'

'Flora—'

'Get out.'

The silence rippled with tension, charged with everything she held back. This time on purpose—not because she was being illogical or chaotic. Because even if she said all those words, expressed all the thoughts in her head, she knew he wouldn't hear them.

She needed to show him.

'Where will you go?' he asked.

Forcing herself not to react, not to turn and ask him if it was really that easy to get out of the car and let her drive away, she kept her eyes forward and replied as neutrally as her raging heart would allow.

'To a place where love has always found me.'

She reached over him, eyes downcast, and refused to recognise the scent of him. She opened the door for him.

'I'm going home. The adventure is over.'

'You're pregnant—'

'Yes, and we will figure that out as we need to.'

She looked at him then. Watched his world ripple in confusion. But this was the only way she could help him. Make him understand that nothing else mattered but what he was willing to close the door on. What he was willing to sacrifice because of the little boy he once was, who wouldn't let the man he had become accept love because he didn't think he deserved it.

Eyes wide, he got out and stared back at her.

She knew he'd have to figure out how to fix this—if he wanted to—all on his own. Trust himself.

She made herself turn. Made herself look away. She was doing the right thing.

She rapped on the privacy glass until the driver opened it. 'To the airport, please, driver.'

The driver nodded, and the glass once again ascended.

'Flora, your dress…'

He was reminding her of the passion that only moments ago had torn through them both. She reached for his suit jacket, still on the hook, and put it on. Slid her arms into the silk-lined sleeves, pulled them over the intricate lace covering her arms. The jacket was still warm from his body.

She ignored it. She squared her shoulders. 'Goodbye, Raffaele.'

Only when she heard the click of the door did she let her shoulders sag. Let herself pant, sucking in the air she'd been denying herself. She twisted on the seat to sit up on her knees, looking out of the rear window. And there was her husband, standing on the gravel drive, letting his wife drive away.

He was letting her go.

She crumpled into a tearful mess on the back seat where she'd made love to her husband.

Because she was leaving him and she didn't want to.

# CHAPTER THIRTEEN

THERE WAS MONEY in the pocket of the suit jacket that Flora has taken. Lots of it. Enough to buy her a first-class round-the-world ticket. She would find it. She'd be fine.

*But will you?*

It had paralysed him. Watching her, everything he'd chased after—*hunted*—driving away with his baby in her belly. His family.

Something had torn inside Raffaele with every crunch of the tyres driving over the gravel.

She'd asked him repeatedly to let go, and with his body he had. But she wanted him to let go with his heart. To *love*. And he couldn't let go with his heart because love had never been inside it. There was nothing inside it for her. For his baby.

Maybe this was the best choice. He would provide them with the protection of his name. Financially he'd give them anything, everything, and he would never deny his child its roots…its story.

*Is this how your story ends? Stuck in this house? Prisoner of the past? With your future driving away?*

He couldn't move. Not towards the house behind him, and not towards the car. He was stuck. Breaking inside. Was this his choice? To hold on to fear when Flora—?

She wasn't afraid, was she? Not of his failings—not even when he'd thrust the truth of his neglect at her. Her innocent eyes had still looked at him with hunger. With warmth. There had been softness in even her most hungry caress. She'd touched him with love.

*Pain.* It sliced through him. Acute. *Searing.*

The car had reached the end of the drive. Soon it was going to vanish out of sight, move down the hill on the road he'd had built into the mountain and drive out of his sight, out of his life.

He didn't think—he just ran. *Fast.*

His legs pumped along with the thud of his leather-sheathed feet on the uneven ground.

But the car didn't stop.

He wanted to roar. Demand her presence. So why didn't he? He knew her name. She was no longer anonymous. She was his wife. She had given him all of herself. All of her trust. All of her...

*Love?*

His chest heaving, he stood at the end of the drive and let go. Let go of the fear, of the past, and trusted his instincts. He roared his needs, his wants into the air and called out loud, fierce. He was a man calling for his mate. His love.

*'Flora!'*

Just as he was preparing to sprint down the hill the car stopped—and so did his heart. The car door opened. With bated breath he watched her climb out and stand there, looking at him at the top of the hill.

Then they both ran.

He ran so fast he felt as if he was flying. Running free towards the future. Towards love. *His destiny.* And he wouldn't look away.

He loved her. Loved her chaotic fierceness. Her innocence. He wanted every word he'd whispered to her about trusting herself to apply to him. He wanted to trust her. To believe that this was love and he deserved it. He wanted to be the man she'd made him. The man he was beneath the suit. The man he'd always been.

Because he wasn't trapped under a tree.

He wasn't lost any more.

He was *found*.

Their bodies slammed together. His fingers thrust into her hair and pulled her mouth to hers. And he kissed her with everything he was.

He kissed her for every year he hadn't felt loved. For every time he'd chosen control instead of his feelings. Put on his suit and written a list, pretending his feelings weren't involved.

She would make him feel. She would teach him to love openly, without fear. Just the way he was loving her now. In the open. In the gentle light of the late-afternoon sun.

Gripping her arms, he pushed her away from him and panted, 'Flora—'

'I know,' she soothed—and he knew she did. 'It's hard to trust it, isn't it?'

'Yes.'

'You'll get better at it,' she promised.

He swallowed heavily, still holding her tightly in place in front of him.

'I have never known family. I have never known love. But I want to learn. I want to love you. Be a family. Be in a marriage and be parents to our child. I want you for me—but I want this marriage for *us*. I want us to be a team. Do things for each other and with each other. I want to turn that house into a home with you. Not in redemption. I see that now. I understand that whatever choices I made, I couldn't choose for my mother. Her choices were her own, as mine are my own. I want to trust in my own decisions. Because how could I not when they have brought me to you? Will you let me love you, Flora? Will you let me practise my love on you every day?'

He fell to his knees.

'Will you be my wife?'

'I already am.'

She fell to her knees beside him and cradled his face, looked into his eyes, claiming his world as her own. Driving the flag in.

'I love you, Raffaele Russo.'

'It was always you,' he said. 'From the first night you broke open my chest and brought my soul, my heart, back to life. And that was love, wasn't it? Even then. Because you are my destiny.'

She stroked his face. 'Destiny,' she agreed.

'I love you,' he said, and he heard the tremble in his own voice. The release.

And then he gave in to what his body wanted, his heart wanted, and kissed her thoroughly there on the gravel driveway, until the only thing left to do was to pick her up and carry her over the threshold.

'I promise to turn this house into a home and fill it with love, Flora. *My* love.'

He looked down into her face and she looked back up into his. And there was the world. *His* world.

'I love you. I always did. I always will.'

# EPILOGUE

'YOU'RE SO STRONG, Flora,' Raffaele said huskily, anticipation humming in his every muscle.

'I'm not…'

'You are.'

She closed her eyes and squeezed his fingers. He let her squeeze, let himself be the unbreakable strength she needed to beat against in order to bring new life into the world. A life *they* had made.

Flora had refused a private suite at the hospital. Refused to leave her home. *Their* home.

Why would she leave it to be surrounded by strangers when all she could ever want was right here? she'd said. Her family.

She wanted their baby to be born in their home. Here. In a room that sang with life. With love. A love she had injected into every surface, every wall, until the house he'd never considered a home had become his home because of her. Because she was in it.

He'd fought hard to trust her choice to bring their baby into the world with only a midwife. He hadn't put every doctor in Sicily on standby. The air ambulance was not waiting in the gardens and the suite at the hospital was not prepared.

He was still learning to trust that love was actions, but he was practising and developing his skills every day. She was patient, but stern, and sometimes hot words turned to hotter kisses.

He *was* Sicilian after all.

And sometimes no words were needed at all. Because couples fought, he had learnt, but then they made love and made up. And they were a couple. They were a family. Every night he climbed into bed beside his wife and knew that this was where he belonged. By her side.

But right now he felt absolutely helpless. He wanted to take all the pain from her. But he couldn't. So he stood strong and rubbed her back. Kissed her forehead and placed water to her lips. He would love her in all the silent ways she'd taught him to love. Take care of her not only in the big ways, but the small ways too. Be present for her.

*'Raffaele...!'*

His gut clenched.

In thirty-six hours, every minute—every *second*—had been for this.

The last shout of his name.

The final push.

A wail erupted from a bundle of wrinkled skin topped with the darkest curly hair.

Raffaele looked at his wife—at her flushed cheeks, her damp brow. Her gasping mouth. His wife. His heart.

He turned back to the baby. His baby. His family. A miracle...

'Congratulations, Signor and Signora Russo. She's perfect.'

'A girl?' he croaked, feeling the lump in his throat growing.

The midwife smiled. 'With ten fingers and ten toes,' she clarified.

'She's really here...?' Flora's voice was a throaty expression of awe.

He nodded. Entwined their hands tightly. 'She's here,' he echoed.

Because she was. His daughter.

'Help me, Raffaele.'

'Of course!'

He turned to Flora, silently reprimanding himself for not anticipating her needs. She looked up at him, the smile on her lips tight but true.

'What do you need?' he asked.

'I need you to help me undo this…' She pulled at the fabric covering her. 'I want my baby on my chest.'

He placed his trembling hands on Flora's, also trembling, clumsily trying to undo the buttons of her nightdress.

'I'm so proud of you, *piccolina*,' he said, slipping each button through the hole which housed it.

His chest was full and bursting with so many feelings. Joy. Happiness. *Love.*

His task complete, he saw his wife reach for the hem of Raffaele's black tee.

'Take it off.'

Brows drawn together, he asked, 'Take what off?'

'Your T-shirt.' She tugged at it. 'Then get in bed and let's hold our baby for the first time together.'

He did as she requested. Slipped his T-shirt over his head. He didn't care if this was how things should be done. It was *their* way.

He climbed into bed beside his wife. Flora held out her hands, arms outstretched. 'We're ready.'

Their naked baby was placed on Flora's bare chest by the steady hands of the midwife. Instant and unconditional love bloomed in him fast and hard. For her. His daughter. Perfect in every way.

Flora feathered her lips over her daughter's head. 'I've ached for you for ever,' she whispered.

'And I have ached for you both,' he breathed, unable to stop his confession.

Because he *had* ached for this all his life. Unconditional love. To receive it. To give it. To be a family.

With a smile and a nod, all the necessities of the miracle of birth complete, the midwife slipped out of the room unseen by either Raffaele or Flora, leaving the new parents with awe and wonderment brimming in their tear-glazed eyes to introduce themselves to their daughter.

'I'm so very thankful you chose me to love, Flora,' he said.

'We chose each other,' she corrected.

'It was fate.'

'Destiny,' she said huskily.

Their worlds had collided one fateful night in London and since then they had been bound together for ever. Not because of their baby, but because of love. And their baby was proof of that love. A love he could taste in the air.

He let it fill his lungs, feed his life's essence.

'I love you, Flora,' he said, wrapping his arms around his family.

She smoothed her fingers down their daughter's cheek. 'I love you too, Raffaele.'

Raffaele held his family to his chest—to his heart. Skin to skin. He embraced them with his love and vowed that he would never stop loving them…

\* \* \* \* \*

# COMING SOON!

We really hope you enjoyed reading this book. If you're looking for more romance be sure to head to the shops when new books are available on

## Thursday 11<sup>th</sup> May

To see which titles are coming soon, please visit

**millsandboon.co.uk/nextmonth**

MILLS & BOON

# MILLS & BOON®

## Coming next month

### WHAT HER SICILIAN HUSBAND DESIRES
### Caitlin Crews

"Truly," he said, in that low voice of his that wound around and around inside her, "you are a thing of beauty, Chloe."

"So are you, Lao," she said softly, then found herself smiling when he looked surprised she should compliment him in return.

It made her wonder if he was so overwhelming, so wildly intense, and so astronomically remote in every way that mattered, that no one bothered to offer him compliments. But any such thoughts splintered, because he carried her hand to his lips and pressed a courtly sort of kiss to her knuckles.

It should have felt silly and old-fashioned, but it didn't. Not in an ancient castle, perched here above an island so steeped in history.

And not when the faint brush of his lips across the back of her hand made everything inside her seem to curl up tight, then begin to boil.

"Welcome, little one," he murmured, the heat in his gaze making everything inside her take notice, especially the tender flesh between her legs. And that heart of hers that would not stop its wild thundering. "To our wedding night. At last."

*Continue reading*
### WHAT HER SICILIAN HUSBAND DESIRES
### Caitlin Crews

*Available next month*
www.millsandboon.co.uk

Copyright ©2023 by Caitlin Crews

# LET'S TALK

# Romance

For exclusive extracts, competitions
and special offers, find us online:

- **f** facebook.com/millsandboon
- **𝕏** @MillsandBoon
- **◉** @MillsandBoonUK
- **♪** @MillsandBoonUK

Get in touch on 01413 063 232

For all the latest titles coming soon, visit
**millsandboon.co.uk/nextmonth**

# OUT NOW!

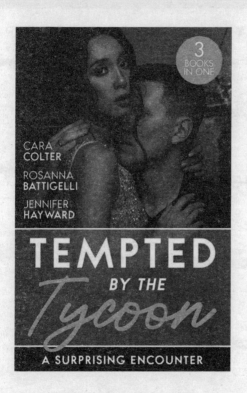

3 BOOKS IN ONE

CARA COLTER

ROSANNA BATTIGELLI

JENNIFER HAYWARD

## TEMPTED
### BY THE
### *Tycoon*

A SURPRISING ENCOUNTER

## Available at
## millsandboon.co.uk

MILLS & BOON

# MILLS & BOON

## THE HEART OF ROMANCE

---

**A ROMANCE FOR EVERY READER**

---

### MODERN

Prepare to be swept off your feet by sophisticated, sexy and seductive heroes, in some of the world's most glamourous and romantic locations, where power and passion collide.

### HISTORICAL

Escape with historical heroes from time gone by. Whether your passion is for wicked Regency Rakes, muscled Vikings or rugged Highlanders, awaken the romance of the past.

### MEDICAL

Set your pulse racing with dedicated, delectable doctors in the high-pressure world of medicine, where emotions run high and passion, comfort and love are the best medicine.

### *True Love*

Celebrate true love with tender stories of heartfelt romance from the rush of falling in love to the joy a new baby can bring, and a focus on the emotional heart of a relationship

### *Desire*

Indulge in secrets and scandal, intense drama and sizzling hot action with heroes who have it all: wealth, status, good looks...everything but the right woman.

### HEROES

The excitement of a gripping thriller, with intense romance at its heart. Resourceful, true-to-life women and strong, fearless men face danger and desire - a killer combination

---

To see which titles are coming soon, please visit

**millsandboon.co.uk/nextmonth**

# JOIN US ON SOCIAL MEDIA!

Stay up to date with our latest releases, author news and gossip, special offers and discounts, and all the behind-the-scenes action from Mills & Boon...

 @millsandboon

 @millsandboonuk

 facebook.com/millsandboon

 @millsandboonuk

*It might just be true love...*

# MILLS & BOON
## A ROMANCE FOR EVERY READER

- **FREE** delivery direct to your door

- **EXCLUSIVE** offers every month

- **SAVE** up to 30% on pre-paid subscriptions

# SUBSCRIBE AND SAVE

## millsandboon.co.uk/Subscribe

# GET YOUR ROMANCE FIX!

Get the latest romance news, exclusive author interviews, story extracts and much more!

blog.millsandboon.co.uk

# MILLS & BOON
## *True Love*
## Romance from the Heart

Celebrate true love with tender stories of
heartfelt romance, from the rush of falling in love
to the joy a new baby can bring, and a focus on the
emotional heart of a relationship.

Four True Love stories published every month, find them al

## millsandboon.co.uk/TrueLove